Forever PUCKED

New York Times Bestselling Author
HELENA HUNTING

super mc
+Beaver
forever

Being engaged to Alex Waters, team captain and the highest paid NHL player in the league, is awesome. How could it not be?

In addition to being an amazing hockey player, he's an incurable romantic with an XL heart, and an XXL hockey stick in his pants. And he knows how to use it. Incredibly, orgasmically well. Alex is the whole package and more. Literally. Like his package is insane. Total world record holder material.

So it makes complete sense that Violet Hall can't wait to nail him down to the matrimonial mattress and become Mrs. Violet Waters.

It's so romantic.

Violet is totally stoked to set a date.

Eventually. At some point. Likely before the next millennium. Or when Violet stops getting hives every time someone brings up the wedding, and their mothers stop colluding on stadium sized venues. Whichever comes first.

ACKNOWLEDGMENTS

Husband of mine; you make this possible. Thank you for being my sidekick, my best friend and my assistant when I need you. You wear all the hats. You're amazing and I love you for every sacrifice you make and every opportunity you give me to thrive.

Mom, Dad, Mel and Chris, I love you so much, thanks for being my family.

Debra, pepper is the best. Thank the lord I have you, because no one else could manage me. I love you.

Kimberly and the crew at RF Literary and Meire and Flavia at Bookcase; let's keep making magic happen.

Nina; you always have my back, and my front, and all the sides.

Jessica, let's sleep for after this. Thank you for keeping me on the level, particularly when plastic beavers are involved.

Shannon, insert smiling poop emoticon here. Thanks for managing the stressful parts! I love you.

Ellie, you are seriously amazing. Thank you for taking care of me. We make an amazing team.

Teeny, you are unbelievable. Like totally. Thank you for being there to walk me through all the things and then just take over, because you're made of magic.

Erika, one day, we'll appreciate the stamina together. You're what fabulous is made for. Thank you for being real.

Susi, muffin, I want to snuggle you like Miller.

Sarah, honestly, I'm not sure how I functioned before without you. Thanks for making sure I don't forget to breathe.

Hustlers; Alecia, Amanda, Ciara, Deb, Melissa, Jennie, Stephanie, Serena, Elaine, Sarah, Lauren, Christina, Elizabeth, Angy and Cherie you're part of my family. I love you ladies. Thank you for making releases so much fun and for being such an important part of my world!

Deb, Sarah & Jen, thank you for calming me down, because seriously, this one was a little whackadoodle.

Heather, you're the best stalker, I can't wait to see you and your hair again.

Kandace, you're the most amazing kind of human being. I'm so glad we had time in Vegas together.

Beaver Babes, you ladies are incredible! I love hanging out with you and chatting books, and getting excited for new projects! Thank you for being with me on this journey, you make my day brighter just for existing.

To my Backdoor Babes; Tara, Meghan, Deb and Katherine, I love that we can all just be weird together and it's okay.

My Smut Saloon ladies; Melanie, Jessica and Geneva, the gifs are the best way to communicate!

To my Pams, the Filets, my Nap girls; 101'ers, and Indies Tijan, Vi, Penelope, Susi, Deb, Erika, Katherine, Alice, Shalu, Amanda, Leisa, Kellie, Vicki, you are fabulous in ways I can't explain. Thank you for being my friends, my colleagues, my supporters, my teachers, my cheerleaders and my soft places to land.

My WC crew; thank you for celebrating this journey with me and for being my friends even though I don't get to see you every day anymore.

Colleen, thank you for The Bookworm, for being an inherently good person, and for being such an inspiration.

To all my author friends and colleagues; thank you for all the amazing things you do and share, for celebrating each other's successes, for sharing the platform and for making this such an amazing community to be part of.

To all the amazing bloggers and readers out there who have supported me from the beginning of my angst, to the ridiculous of my humour; thank you for loving these stories, for giving them a voice, for sharing your thoughts and for being such amazing women. I'm honoured and humbled and constantly amazed by what a generous community you are.

To my Originals; my fandom friends who started on this crazy journey back in 2008, I can't believe how far we've all come. Thank you for sticking with me, and for being the reason I'm here, doing this thing, and loving it.

I wouldn't have found my lady balls without you, Pepper.

ANNIVERSARIES SUCK CHEESY BALLS

VIOLET

Today is mine and Alex's one-year anniversary, and it sucks donkey dick. Well, it's one of our "anniversaries." Alex likes to celebrate every single milestone in our relationship because he's sappy and romantic like that. He also likes to have an excuse to buy me gifts. Lots of them. Extravagant ones. For my birthday he bought me a car. A nice car. With heated seats and automatic everything. New cars are scary because they don't have dings and dents, and they need to be maintained.

Anyway, I digress. Anniversaries. This month we're celebrating our "First Official Date" Anniversary. Alex likes to consider the first time we had sex our "real" anniversary, but since we hardly knew each other then, apart from how our genitalia fit together, I prefer to fast-forward a month to when I wasn't thinking with my beaver. Not totally, anyway.

It's still up for debate as to whether the day he locked me in the conference room at my work and forced me to have coffee with him later was our official first date. I'm inclined to go with the night he took me out for dinner and we ended up back at his place, banging on his couch, which is what we're celebrating tonight. It's marked on our calendar. There's even a sticker with a smiley face. I'm dubbing this one our *second sexiversary* because it's the second occasion when we had sex, and because it annoys Alex.

Sadly, we might not get the opportunity to fuck like it's our third time—we did it twice that first time, for those of you keeping score at home—again tonight. Alex is currently on a bus back to Chicago with the team after a series of four away games. He's been gone for more than a week. A snowstorm is blowing north through the Midwest, and last I heard from him, they were stuck at some rest stop—still more than two hours from home, and that's without the snow slowing them down.

It's already three in the afternoon. If they can't make it back before it gets dark and the storm picks up, he'll be stuck at a hotel for the night. We might be able to have phone sex, but that's not the same as hugging his wood with my beaver. So that's why this anniversary sucks.

And even *if* he makes it home tonight, he's bound to be bagged, which may put a damper on the sexiversary lovin'. Not that he won't perform. He will. He always does. But it won't be with the level of exuberance I've grown accustomed to over the past year. I might only get two orgasms out of him instead of the requisite three or four he usually strives for.

Charlene, my best friend and colleague at Stroker and Cobb Financial Management, peeks her head into my cubicle. She looks disembodied with the way the rest of her is out of sight. She's also smiling like she belongs in some kind of asylum.

"What's up?" I ask.

"You have a delivery."

"What kind of delivery?"

Alex likes to send me gifts at work. Once he had some guy dressed as a beaver sing a love song to me. It was mortifying. Jimmy, one of the other junior accountants, recorded it and posted it on YouTube. Obviously I made him take it down, but it had already gone viral.

"An Alex delivery."

I brace myself for humiliation as she grunts, moving my gift into view.

I don't say anything for a few long seconds. Alex is over the top with everything. But then, when you're the highest-paid NHL player in the league, you can afford to be extravagant and highly ridiculous.

"Not what you expected?" Charlene asks, biting her lip to keep from busting out laughing.

"What am I supposed to do with this?" I gesture to the four-foot stuffed beaver wearing a hockey jersey. It's almost as wide as it is tall. "I don't even know if it'll fit in my car."

I also don't want to carry it through the building.

"I'm sure we can make it fit." I ignore Charlene's eyebrow waggle. She's referencing my fiancé's monster cock. I'm not talking about a pet rooster, either. His dick is massive. I love it so much, even though putting it in my mouth is a workout all on its own.

I grab the beaver by its ears, hefting it into my cubicle so it's no longer blocking all the walking space between my office and the one across from me. Thank the lord Jimmy isn't in there or he'd be all over this. I need to hide the beaver. I don't have to see the back of the jersey to know it's got Alex's last name and number on it. This is a giant version of the small beaver Alex sent me back when he was first stalking me. Because I'm so awesome in bed. And he loves my boobs. And I told him I loved his cock. It was quite the first encounter.

My relationship with Alex Waters, center and team captain

for Chicago, started as a one-night stand. A poorly thought-out one. I would've run into him after our night of passion since my stepbrother, Buck, is on his team, but I hadn't thought that far ahead when I was sticking my hands down his pants a year ago.

The beaver is holding a heart-shaped box. I pluck it from his paws while Charlene puts her arm around it and takes a selfie. I open the card; of course, it's beaver-themed—a pair of cartoon beavers with little hearts above their heads. They're in love, just like Alex and me.

I flip it open, expecting Alex's usual hilarity, which is how it starts, but by the end I'm about to cry. He really is that damn sweet:

Violet,

A year ago you agreed to go for coffee with me, and then your boobs agreed to go on a real date. You came into my life and turned it upside down in the best way. I'll never look at Spiderman pajamas the same way, or Marvel Comic boxer briefs.

I love every inch of you, all your funny quirky ways, all the ridiculous things you say in your sleep—and when you're awake. Your unending praise for the MC also doesn't hurt.

I know you don't buy the whole love at first sight thing, but I believe some people are destined to be together.

Maybe we came together because of lust and Fielding, but we stayed together because of love.

You're my forever,

Alex

I love You!

I sigh and hold the card to my chest, absorbing his words into my heart. Not really. I'm actually considering checking Google to see if he copied this from some sappy love poem site and made a few modifications to fit us better. However, Alex was an English major in college, so it's possible he came up with this all on his own.

I save the Google search for later and open the heart-shaped box. I expect to find chocolate inside, but I'm pleasantly surprised to discover it's filled with those heavenly maple sugar candies I love so much. There's also a bag of Swedish Fish.

"You two are the weirdest couple on the face of the earth. You know that, right?"

"I prefer the term *quirky*, but yeah, I know."

Charlene nabs a maple candy before I can close the box. Granted, there are a lot of them. If I had to hazard a guess, I'd say there's a good hundred candies in there. I'll be in a maple sugar coma by the end of the day for sure. I can't stop once I've started.

I grab my phone from the top drawer of my desk, but before I can pull up Alex's contact, Charlene snatches it out of my hand.

"What're you doing?"

"You need to pose with the beaver so we can send Alex a picture," she says, as if this should be obvious. Which really, it should be. I'm from the generation where everything we do gets posted online for bored people to see. Welcome to the wonderful world of well-documented bad decisions.

I shuffle the beaver around. It's not easy since he's huge, and my cubicle is small. I back my chair into a corner and move the beaver between my legs. I shove the beaver down so his head is at waist level, and Charlene snaps a few pics. Then we turn it over, giggling like idiots as I arrange my skirt over the top of its head so it looks like the beaver's going to town on my beaver.

I strike several different poses, including a fake orgasm face, which is the exact moment my boss walks in on our little party.

"Mr. Stroker! Hey, hi!" I push the beaver away from my crotch, but it's too late. He's already seen me molesting it.

"Miss Hoar." He glances at Charlene, then to me. "Miss Hall." His arms are crossed over his chest, and his face remote. He's giving away nothing. "You two look like you're hard at work."

We're in so much trouble.

"I'm so sorry, Mr. Stroker. Alex sent me this for our anniversary—" I gesture to the gigantic beaver. "—and Charlene and I thought we'd send a picture so he knows I got it. We're not sure if the team's going to make it back tonight, because of the storm." I wave my hand toward the windows. It's snowing like crazy.

Not that it's going to stop him from firing me.

"He sent you a stuffed woodchuck for your anniversary?"

"It's not a woodchuck; it's a beaver," Charlene says.

He raises an eyebrow. "I'm not sure I want an explanation. Violet, I'd like to see you in my office."

"Now?"

"Yes, now."

My stomach does a flip, but I stand and smooth out my wrinkled skirt, shooting Charlene a look of terror. She mouths *sorry* at me, but it's not her fault. I would've done something equally as stupid with or without her help.

I follow Mr. Stroker down the hall to his office. He closes the door behind me and gestures to the chair opposite his desk. I'm totally about to get canned. This is the shittiest sexiversary ever.

"I really am sorry about that, Mr. Stroker. We were being silly. I know it wasn't work-appropriate behavior."

He puts up a hand to stop me. "Violet, have you seen some of the clips Jimmy and Dean slip into their presentations? You doing whatever you were doing with that beaver has nothing on those two."

I know exactly what he's talking about. Jimmy and Dean are the other junior accountants at our firm. They're even more ridiculous than Char and me. Last week they threw a slide into their presentation with two hockey players mashed up against the plexiglas with the caption "Happy Hump Day!" It looked like there was a whole lot more than humping going on in the picture. And that's one of their tamer ones.

"Still, it won't happen again." I sag in the chair, unable to mask my relief. I honestly thought he was going to tell me to pack up my office. Then I'd be a famous hockey player's unemployed fiancée rather than a modest financial contributor to our partnership.

"Sounds good."

Mr. Stroker shuffles account files around on his desk. I recognize the one on top as one I prepared, because it's in a violet-colored folder. Alex bought them for me. He thinks they're cute.

"I've reviewed your file for the Darcy account. I think you've made some very wise choices in terms of the funds you've selected. The returns have been high in the past eighteen months, and you've balanced their portfolio well."

"Oh. Well, thanks." This isn't at all what I thought I was coming here for. His praise is unexpected. He's a numbers guy, like so many of us in this department. It's always about the bottom line: whether or not we're making money for our clients or saving their asses from potential bankruptcy.

Mitch Darcy plays defense for Chicago. I met him through Alex. One night after the game his wife was there, and we started talking. She asked what I did for a living, so I told her. She seemed surprised that I worked a job other than servicing Alex's amazing dick.

Two weeks later, Mrs. Darcy made an appointment and specifically asked for me. Mr. Stroker took a risk by letting me draw up a proposal for the account. Of course he has to review it before anything can be implemented, but it's an opportunity I wouldn't have without all my connections. Those sometimes make me unpopular at work.

"This is a big deal, Violet." Mr. Stroker says, tapping his pen against the folder.

"Yes, sir."

"You're aware that Darcy renewed his contract for five more years at four million a year."

"Yes, sir. He also has endorsements with Power Juice and

Sports Mind totaling another two million annually for the next three years."

"Do you think you'll be ready to present this to the Darcys next week?"

I sit up straighter. "You want me to present?"

"His wife is rather insistent it be you."

"But I've never presented to a client this big before."

"You've been managing Miller's account for the past year without an issue," he argues.

Stroker is referring to my stepbrother, Buck, whose real name is Miller. Everyone has recently started calling him by his given name, but it's an adjustment for me. I'm not quite there yet.

Usually the accounts I handle are half a million or less. The Darcys' portfolio is far more significant. Way bigger than anything I've touched, apart from Buck's accounts, and I've always had Mr. Stroker look at those before I make any kind of change. I don't want to be responsible for screwing up Buck's fortune.

"You've got a handle on it. Why don't you call them and set up a meeting for next week. I'm open most mornings."

"Okay, great. I'll consult their game schedule and see what works best."

"Perfect. You arrange it, check the notes I've made on the PowerPoint, and at the end of the week—say, Friday afternoon—I'll set aside an hour and you can do a dry run for me so you feel prepared. How does that sound?"

"That sounds amazing, Mr. Stroker."

"It's just William, Violet. You can drop the formality now."

He's told me this before, but I find his last name entertaining. "Of course. Right, William."

He gives Randy Balls, another one of Alex's teammates, a run for his money with the dirty names.

"Great. Three o'clock Friday afternoon is open for me. Book the conference room with Edna on your way out." He passes over the folder and picks up the phone, which means I'm dismissed.

I thank him and stop to set things up with his assistant on the way back to my cubicle.

Charlene is sitting at her desk, chewing her nails and pretending to do some kind of research. When she sees me she grabs my arm and yanks me into her cubicle. "Why aren't you crying? Didn't you get fired?"

"No. Stroker didn't can my ass."

Charlene sighs with relief. "I'm so sorry. He rarely comes down this way." It's true. Junior accountants usually only see the boss-man in the conference room on meeting Monday, which was this morning. "Let's never take pictures like that again while we're at work."

"Agreed. We should have waited until I got home. Then we could've posed the beaver on the bed so it looks like he's taking me from behind, or holding my boobs."

"Such good ideas. So what did Stroker say?"

"I'm presenting to Mitch Darcy and his wife next week."

"You're what?" she practically screeches this, so anyone within earshot, which is most of the office, peeks their head over the edge of their cube wall.

"It's okay, everyone. I told Charlene I'm thinking about going vegan."

Jimmy seems to have returned from his coffee break. He looks suspicious, and rightfully so—I'm the first one to order a Philly cheesesteak when he gets takeout—but he's on the phone, so he goes back to his call. The rest of the office is used to our ridiculousness, so they resume whatever they were doing, too.

I lower my voice to a whisper. "I get to present."

"That's a big account," Charlene whispers back.

"I know."

"That's amazing."

I know she means it, but I recognize the wistful look in her eyes. We're close, but we're still competing with each other, and with Jimmy and Dean, for a senior accountant position when it comes open. Being allowed to present to one of the bigger clients gives me an advantage over everyone else.

The people who don't like me at the office are really going to hate me now.

2

CARDBOARD CUTOUTS ARE TERRIFYING

VIOLET

I get a text from Alex at the end of the day telling me they're still hours from home. I'm super disappointed. And I swear not just because I won't get to have awesome sex after a week with only Buddy the Beaver—my super-special vibrator that actually looks like a beaver—to take care of my orgasm needs. As cute as it is, it's a poor replacement for Alex's dick. And the rest of Alex, too. I miss him.

Charlene checks her phone, smiling secretly. I imagine she has messages from her boyfriend, who happens to be Alex's best friend and teammate, Darren Westinghouse.

"How's Darren feel about bromancing it for another night with Alex?"

Charlene glances up. "Oh, uh, you know—disappointed he doesn't get to spoon with me tonight."

"My beaver needs something to hug, other than synthetic dick," I grumble.

Charlene pats me on the shoulder. "You've waited a week. What's another day?"

"I have MC separation anxiety."

I don't get how she can be so unaffected by the delay, but then Charlene and Darren's relationship is a little weird—and not like Alex and me weird. Darren's a quiet guy, and private, so the media attention their relationship has garnered, and all the odd speculation about it, means they've had a few rough patches along the way.

Plus, Charlene can be flighty. She falls out of love as fast as she falls into it. That they've been dating consistently, or mostly consistently, for well over half a year is actually amazing.

"Why don't we go out for dinner somewhere? We can celebrate you getting to present the Darcy account."

"I don't know if I feel like it…"

"We can leave your car here. I'll drive so you can have a drink, and I'll drop you off at home."

"What about tomorrow morning?"

"I'll pick you up."

"Really?" Charlene can barely make it to work on time as it is.

"It's supposed to snow like this all night. If we're late tomorrow, we can blame it on the plows," she suggests.

I glance out the window and look down at the streets below. They're blanketed in white, and traffic is stupid: people honking, sliding, and braking. I don't like winter driving all that much, and definitely not with this kind of traffic. Charlene is a much better driver than me, not that I'll ever admit that to her. Now that I don't have anyone to go home to, I guess dinner out sounds like a decent option.

"Yeah. Okay. Maybe I should call Sunny and Lily to see if

they want to join us. We can all be dickless together." Sunny is Alex's younger sister. She's dating Buck. In January she moved from Guelph to Chicago, which is a cute little city in Ontario, Canada. That's where she and Alex grew up.

Her house in Chicago was purchased by Alex. She pays rent, but instead of putting it toward the mortgage, he puts the money into an investment portfolio for her. That's all I know about it because Stroker deals with Alex's account directly. Which is fine. Sometimes I feel like Alex wants me to do it, but I'm not comfortable with the insane amount of money he makes. Not yet.

Seeing how well he takes care of his family tells me what I'll be in for when we get married, and sometimes that makes me nervous. I don't want to be responsible for investing it as well as enjoying it. Like I said, at least not yet. I mean, my yearly salary is less than the cost of the car Alex recently bought me. With cash.

Lily is Sunny's childhood best friend who also moved to Chicago recently. She lives with Sunny, and she's dating Randy "Balls" Ballistic, Buck's childhood best friend and another Chicago hockey player. I call him Horny Nut Sac—sometimes to his face, sometimes behind his back. It's super convenient that we're all hockey hookers. We hang out a lot when the boys are traveling for away games.

I pull out my phone, ready to send Sunny a message, but Charlene puts a hand up. "I'm on it. You pack up."

I shrug and shut down my computer, throw a few files into my laptop bag, and grab my coat. Charlene reappears at my cubicle, ready to go. "Sunny suggested we find a restaurant close to their place since they're both already at home."

I make a face. "It doesn't have to be vegan, does it?" Sunny doesn't eat animals or animal products. I don't have a problem with this, but if I'm not getting Alex's meat stick tonight, I might as well indulge in a burger or something equally disgusting and bloat-worthy.

"Lily says the restaurant has a wide selection. Plus, she doesn't think it's a good idea for Sunny to drive in this weather."

I sigh. "Fine." It makes sense to go that way, and not just because getting downtown would take forever in this weather for Sunny and Lily. Going to them will put us halfway to Alex's. And Sunny is a worse driver than me, which says a lot.

Charlene and I lug my stuffed beaver to the elevator. We get a few strange looks, but most of the people in our department are unfazed by us now. Charlene takes the tail, and I hold the head as we slip and slide down the slick sidewalk to the parking lot across from our building. Charlene and I should've parked our cars in the underground lot this morning, but there were no spots left. With Alex and Darren away, we sometimes have sleepovers and stay up too late. Then we have a hard time getting out of bed in the morning. Last night was one of those times.

Getting the beaver into the trunk of Charlene's car is a feat, but after some shoving and punching, we squeeze him in.

It takes three times as long as usual to get to Sunny's neighborhood. The traffic is terrible. I'm definitely glad I didn't drive or we'd be in a ditch.

We end up at a cute little place that isn't just for people who don't eat meat. They do, however, have a nice selection of food without faces for Sunny. I browse the menu. Even with the heat on full blast in Charlene's car, and our cozy spot in the back of the restaurant, I'm still frozen.

"Maybe I should get the French onion soup and the mozzarella sticks."

Charlene frowns. "Is that really a good idea, Vi? Onions and cheese? Those are, like, the worst combination in the world for you."

I'm moping because I won't get to see Alex tonight. Eating dairy is how I cope with stress and disappointment. However, it will also cause me to moop later. Dairy is hard enough on my system; add onions to the mix and I become lethal to anyone

14

within a ten-foot radius. "Alex won't be home to witness the aftermath."

Lily and Sunny exchange a look.

"Yeah, but what if the aftermath runs into tomorrow like it usually does?" Charlene says.

I ponder that for a moment, before reluctantly agreeing. "Good point."

I decide on a burger and fries, hold the onions, but I add a glass of wine. I don't need beer bloats to go with the burger bloats.

Sunny keeps checking her phone all through dinner, which isn't unusual. She and Buck spend a lot of time messaging each other when he's away—and when he's not. They're so in love. It's as sweet as it is surprising. Buck used to be a huge manwhore. Like, epically slutty.

Sunny has done a great job of taming him. He's like a big, well-groomed, fun-loving yeti when it comes to her.

After we order, we settle in with our drinks. Only Lily and I have fun ones, since Charlene is driving and Sunny isn't much for booze.

"How's the new job, Lily?" I ask.

Alex helped get Lily a job teaching skating to kids who are looking to go pro for hockey when she decided to move to Chicago. She's an incredible figure skater. She should have been an Olympic contender, but money got in the way of her dream when she was a teenager. She doesn't seem to let that hold her back, though.

"Amazing! I wasn't sure how I was going to feel about the change, but I love it. I really appreciate Alex recommending me."

"Alex is just glad he could help." My fiancé is amazingly generous, especially when it comes to family. While Lily isn't technically related, she grew up with the Waters family, so she's like a second sister to him. "I guess having unlimited access to Balls' balls doesn't hurt either, right?"

"Oh my God, she stays there almost every night they're home," Sunny supplies.

Lily blushes and looks down. "He's great. I'm meeting his mom this weekend."

"Really? Already? That's crazy!" Charlene says.

Lily tucks her dark hair behind her ear and looks around the table, suddenly uncertain. "You think so?"

I kick Charlene, at least I think I do, but Sunny is the one who flinches, so I flick Charlene in the side of the boob. "It's not crazy at all. Not everyone has to wait a year before family intros."

"A year?" Lily's eyes go wide.

Lily looks like a porcelain doll. Except not creepy. Which is a very important distinction. She's gorgeous and model thin, with almond-shaped eyes the color of dark chocolate and an Uma Thurman haircut circa *Pulp Fiction*. She and Randy have been officially dating for less than two months. But they've been banging each other since last summer, so it's not that unreasonable that she's meeting his mom.

Charlene cups her breast and shoots me an annoyed look. "We haven't been dating a year. And my mom lives in New York, and Darren's parents live in South Carolina. It's not like we can drop by for dinner."

I'd point out that Darren's parents have been in town on more than one occasion and she still hasn't taken the opportunity to meet them, but it's not my relationship, so I keep my mouth shut. For now.

"I think it's great that you're meeting Randy's mom. She'll love you!" Sunny says, redirecting the conversation. She embodies her name, radiating positivity and warmth all the time. She's also blond and blue-eyed with endless legs and a stunning, innocent face.

Lily gulps her mojito. "I sure hope so."

"I introduced Miller to my parents the day after we met, and they loved him right away. Well, mostly, until Alex told them why he was traded to Chicago."

He was traded last year around this time after getting caught in a public bathroom stall with his coach's niece. The door was open.

Sunny waves her hand in the air, then twirls a blond lock around her finger. "But they love him again now, so that's all that matters."

Our dinner arrives, and I demo my burger and fries. I order another drink to celebrate both my unfulfilled sexiversary with Alex and the presentation I'll be making next week. I'm the only one drinking like it's Friday night, but then Lily probably remembers her terrible hangover from the last time we tied one on. And we all have to work tomorrow.

I'm in no rush to go home, but everyone else's phone keeps going off. I send Alex a text, but I don't get a reply. It's disappointing on such a special day. Or a day that Alex has built up to be interpreted as such. I assumed there was going to be some seriously epic loving based on the ostentatiousness of this afternoon's gift alone. Unfortunately, his last message was sent several hours ago saying they were still stuck, his phone was dying, and he didn't think he was going to make it home tonight.

Me and my beaver are sad.

Charlene suggests we go, and Sunny and Lily agree with more enthusiasm than necessary, which I find odd. It's still snowing when we leave the restaurant, so I can see Charlene's point about getting home. Even though Sunny and Lily live two blocks away, they pile into the back of her car so we can drive them, too. It probably takes as long as it would to walk, but at least they don't have to deal with the freezing cold and blustery snow.

Both of them are huddled into their jackets, texting away on their phones and giving each other sly looks while I scan Alex's Facebook profile for signs of life. He hasn't posted anything since this morning, and that was a cheesy update about how much he loves me. It's sweet, but it leaves me even more disappointed.

Charlene pulls up to the house, staying a safe distance from the curb so there's enough room for the girls to open the door and not fall face first into the two-foot snow bank.

"Isn't that Randy's truck?" I ask.

"Oh, uh, um, he left it here for the week so I could drive it instead of my car. The tires are way better," Lily replies.

"Wow. He lets you drive his truck already?" It took forever before Alex let me drive his sports car. And then I dinged it and he took away my privileges. Not even blow jobs seem to be able to bring them back.

Lily shrugs. "Is that weird?"

"Thanks for the ride, Charlene! See you girls soon!" Sunny gets out of the car and pulls Lily along with her.

"Bye, guys. Thanks, Char! See you soon." Lily waves and hurries across the street, hand in hand with Sunny.

I figure Charlene and I will go back to her house and hang out some more since it's close. On occasion, I've been known to stay at her place when Alex and Darren are away, because I don't always like to be in his big, huge house by myself. I get all freaked out even though there's an insane alarm system. But instead of taking a right, she goes left, toward Alex's.

"We can go to your place. I'm sure I have a change of clothes," I suggest.

"I'm kind of tired. I won't be much fun." Charlene yawns, as if to prove her point.

I don't get why everyone is acting so weird tonight. Usually that's my job.

Charlene's phone buzzes, and then buzzes a few more times. She waits until we're at a stoplight before she checks it. I do the same with mine, but Alex hasn't messaged at all. It's really not like him. He's always in contact. Maybe he can't find a charger for his phone.

I don't say much on the drive. When Charlene pulls in Alex's driveway, the porchlight illuminates the door and the holiday wreath I have yet to take down. The driveway's been cleared of snow, as well as the steps. If it keeps snowing like this, the maintenance guys will have to circle back and do it again.

"Are you sure you don't want to come in for a bit? We can watch TV or something? Have a drink?" I'm already slightly buzzed; one more will help put me to sleep, and possibly take my mind off my disappointment.

I may pretend not to like all the gifts and the excessive sexiversary celebrations, but I've gotten used to them, just like I'm getting used to money going into my account all the time.

"I shouldn't drink with the roads the way they are." Charlene gestures to the white fluff skimming the windshield.

"You could stay over."

"I don't have a change of clothes, and all your stuff is too small. Except in the chest." She puts her car in park. "Want some help with your beaver?"

"What?" At first I think she means my actual beaver, but then I realize she's not propositioning me. "Oh. Right. No, I can get it."

"Okay." She gives me a bright smile, followed by a big yawn. "See you in the morning!"

I get that no one else is celebrating their sexiversary, but I feel like I'm the only one who's really bummed the boys aren't going to be home tonight.

Getting the beaver out of the trunk is harder than I expect. He's crammed in there pretty good, and Charlene's trunk is small and tight—almost exactly how Alex would describe my real beaver.

I tug until he comes free, close Char's trunk, and wave at her through the rear window. She honks and takes off as I shift the beaver around so I can see the stairs.

Coming home to an empty house is like spraining a wrist while watching porn: frustrating and unsatisfying. Stupid fucking snowstorm.

Getting up the stairs to the front door also isn't as easy as it should be. I trip on the last step and fall, but thankfully the beaver acts as a cushion, preventing me from hurting myself. I slap the snow off his beaver face and drag him to the door. Punching in the code, I shoulder my way inside. The front entry is dark, which is unusual. The lights are timed at night, unless the system's malfunctioned. Maybe it has. Alex will have to call the guy who fixes his ridiculous security system. I heave the beaver into the foyer and hit something. I have no idea what, as I can't see much.

Smacking the wall beside me, I shut the door, blocking out the frigid wind. I finally find the light switch and flick it on. Which is the exact moment I scream like a man with his nuts caught in a vice.

The foyer is filled with cardboard cutouts of Alex. His life-size condom advertisement is front and center, followed by his sports drink promo, the one for hockey sticks, the body wash advertisement, and even the one for the gel that soothes muscle aches. All of my Alex cutouts are welcoming me home, which would be cool, except it means someone has been inside the house, rearranging my shit. That's freaking terrifying.

"I have a gun!" I yell. This is a total lie. I've never even held a damn gun. Alex, who's from Canada where they don't even believe in guns, has held a gun, but I have not. I'm petrified that I'll accidentally shoot someone, or myself, so I can't bring myself to go near one. Alex thinks it's sweet.

Right now I wish I'd had the balls to hit the shooting range at least once when Sidney, my stepdad, offered to take me this fall because this feels like the beginning of a really bad horror movie. I move the giant beaver in front of me, as if it's going to protect me from the goddamn serial killer with an Alex cutout fetish.

A figure steps out from behind one of the cutouts, and I scream again. This time it's blood-curdling. I shove the beaver away from me, knocking over the first cardboard-cutout Alex. A domino effect follows, the two-dimensional versions of my man dropping to the floor with a whoosh and a series of low thuds. I turn around and start reefing on the door, trying to get out, but I've locked it, so it's not opening. And I'm freaking.

"Violet, baby, it's me." Alex's voice penetrates the haze of my terror. I stop trying to escape and turn to face him. There he is in 3D, standing in the middle of the fallen versions of himself.

"You scared the shit out of me!" I throw my purse at him.

He lunges to catch it before it can hit the floor. It was about three feet shy of hitting him.

"I'm sorry. I wanted to surprise you." He's smiling through his apology, which irks me.

I point at him. "It's not funny. You almost gave me a heart attack! I thought some psycho had broken into the house."

"I didn't mean to do that." His hands are raised, probably to reassure me that he's not a hologram, but in fact my real fiancé, and that he really is sorry. I'm not sure I buy it; he's still got a dimple popping. He takes tentative steps toward me, just in case I decide to kung fu him in the balls or something, I guess.

"Well, consider me surprised." It's a good thing I didn't have the dairy or I would've shit my damn pants. "Why didn't you call me to let me know you were going to be home?"

"It wouldn't have been much of a surprise then, would it?"

I replay dinner in my head: all the texts the girls were getting, their excitement at going home to dick-free beds.

"How long have you been planning this?" I cross my arms over my chest.

Alex's gaze darts down and stays there, despite the fact that I'm wearing a huge winter jacket and my boobs are hidden. "Only since we got stuck at the rest stop earlier today. I really wasn't sure if we were going to make it home. Then we got back on the road, and I decided I'd surprise you. I got here about half an hour ago. I had just enough time to set this up." He gestures to the fallen Alexes, and then to the beaver lying face down on the floor. "I see you got my present."

I give him my bitch brow. I spent the last three hours

21

thinking my beaver was sleeping alone tonight. I'm still getting over that, so I'm not as nice as I should be. "Thanks for sending it to my work."

"You don't like it? The pictures you sent me seem to indicate otherwise."

I roll my eyes. "It's ridiculous."

"Which is why you love it." He tucks my damp hair behind my ear, skimming my cheek with warm fingers.

I try to remain annoyed. "Where are we going to put it?"

"I was thinking we could bring it to the Chicago cottage. It can be our mascot."

Alex has two cottages. He likes to buy property. The Chicago cottage is just as nice as his Ontario cottage and only two hours away, on Lake Geneva, instead of a plane ride followed by two hours in the car. The beaver would be appropriate at the Ontario cottage, since it's in Canada, but I don't think they'd let it on the plane. The Chicago cottage isn't a bad second choice. Not that this is relevant to anything.

I haven't seen Alex in eight days. It's our First Real Date Sexiversary, and I totally didn't expect him to be here tonight. Although my heart still feels like it's going to explode out of my chest for a multitude of reasons, all I want is to rub up on him like a bear on a tree, or a beaver on some wood. Either way, there needs to be rubbing. Preferably leading to an orgasm.

He pulls me close, wrapping me in his arms, and I sink into him. He's so warm and solid and perfect. "I'm glad you're home, even if you almost gave me a heart attack."

"Me, too. I missed you." His hands move to my ass, and he squeezes softly. He bends to kiss me, which is when I get a whiff of stale, oniony yuck.

I purse my lips and wrinkle my nose. "Smells like you made out with a Big Mac."

He grimaces. "That bad, eh?"

He's close talking, so even though I try not to breathe, I still get hit with another shot of grossness. He smells like diesel exhaust, sweat masked with deodorant, and fast food.

"What'd you eat? A plate of raw onions?"

"We stopped at a diner. I had a burger." He sounds apologetic. Our dinners matched.

As much as I've missed him, I'm not having sex with him like this. I might have a year ago, but now I can wait until he showers and brushes his teeth. I should probably do the same.

"Let's go get cleaned up," I suggest.

Alex picks me up in a frontwards piggyback—a piggyfront—and carries me up the stairs. I don't bother trying to make conversation; I'm too busy kissing his neck, which tastes salty, but otherwise fine. Alex adjusts his grip when we get to the bedroom and pushes the door open. Candles cast a dim glow around the room, and rose petals—real, not fake based on the smell—litter the comforter. No wonder he hasn't had time to shower. He's been setting up a romantic reunion—apart from freaking me out with the cardboard-cutout army, anyway.

Little does he know I have plans of my own for us, and all the important stuff is downstairs in the living room by the fireplace. The rest is in the fridge. It's okay, though. If we don't make it down there tonight, there's always tomorrow, or the day after that.

He sets me on the bed and leans down, resting his head on my boobs so he can nuzzle in. When he pulls away after what I feel is too short a time, I clamp my legs around his waist.

He shifts so his chin rests in the valley of my boobs. His expression is serious, but his eyes reveal his amusement. "I can't get clean if you won't let me go."

He runs a gentle hand down the outside of my thigh, stopping at the back of my knee, urging me to disengage. I can feel the monster cock. He's already excited about being close to my beaver, so I'm reluctant to let go. Alex has a point, though.

My skirt is pooled around my waist, but I'm wearing opaque tights, so he can't see anything important. Like my undies. I can't remember which ones I put on this morning, having been in a bit of a rush.

Alex straightens with his palms still hooked under my knees. His hands are rough; I can hear the nylon fabric catching as he kneads the backs of my calves. I don't care though, he's touching me, and it's been more than a week, so I'm good with having to buy new tights. I can afford it.

His eyes move up my body, like he's studying a familiar map. He rubs his scruffy beard. "You want me to shave?"

"Please." My skin is extra sensitive in the winter. I don't want it to get all chafed, otherwise it will put a damper on sexy times this week. Whenever Alex comes home from being away, we have a lot of make-up-for-missed-occasions sex.

Alex lifts his shirt over his head and drops it on the floor. I'll never get tired of looking at his hard, hot body. I don't dare look away as he pops the button on his jeans and lowers the zipper. He pushes them to his ankles and steps out of them. Then the socks come off. I press my knees together as he slips his thumbs into the waistband of his boxer briefs and drags them down. It's like a striptease with no music, except for the rapid beating of my heart and the moan I accidentally set free.

He's gloriously naked and already hard. His erection juts straight out, the one eye staring right at me. Maybe the shower isn't all that important after all. I can deal with the onion breath and exhaust-fumes smell. I sit up and reach for him, but he takes a step back.

A small smirk tugs at the corner of his plush lips. "I thought you wanted me to get clean first."

"I changed my mind."

"What about shaving?"

"Shaving's for pussies. Bring it here." I motion him forward, but he doesn't move, so I pull my shirt over my head.

Which is when I realize I'm wearing a really ugly bra. It's old, and while it was once white, it's now all discolored and greying on the straps. There's even a snag in the satiny fabric over my left boob.

Alex lifts an eyebrow as his focus shifts from my face to my chest. "Nice."

"I was going to change after work!" My initial plan was to get suited up in new lingerie—which I purchased earlier in the week when Alex talked about celebrating the next sexiversary—before I was under the wrongful impression that he wouldn't be home tonight. I hurry to unclasp it, but of course, even that isn't in the best shape, so it's more difficult than usual. I'm writhing around on the bed like a tasered eel.

Alex chuckles and heads for the bathroom, calling over his shoulder, "Get naked and get in the shower with me."

He reaches in and turns on the tap, adjusting the temperature. He's half bent over, giving me a fabulous view of his perfect, tight ass. His ass really is fantastic—so muscular, so awesome for holding onto when he's pounding the orgasms out of me.

Alex opens the vanity and retrieves his shaving kit. He could totally forgo that part, and he knows I won't complain, but he's torturing me now. Whatever. Two can play at this game.

I kneel on the bed and pretend I'm watching him, which of course I am. I can also see my reflection in the mirror, which means so can he. Now that the hideous bra is gone, I take my time stripping out of the rest of my clothes while he uses the trimmer. It'll take his beard down enough to make shaving with a razor possible.

Alex glances at me as I drag the zipper down on my skirt and let it fall to the bed. Before I do the same with my tights I pull out the waistband and take a peek at my panties. They're also ugly and in horrible condition, so I speed up my impromptu striptease and push them over my hips together with the tights.

Thankfully, I had the foresight to take care of my beaver bush before Alex came home. I saunter into the bathroom. He isn't even paying attention to what he's doing to his face anymore. He keeps going over the same spot repeatedly while he watches my approach.

The room is already filling with steam. When I'm close enough, I press my boobs against his back and hug him from behind.

I run my hands over his abs, then lower, past his navel. I stop short of his massive erection, which incidentally is resting on top of the vanity with beard clippings sprinkled over it. Instead of grabbing his dick, I reach for my toothbrush and the toothpaste. If he's going to the trouble to freshen up, I should, too.

He's eyeing me with something close to contempt, or maybe it's sheer animal lust. Either way, it's reminiscent of the look he wears when he's in the penalty box. Sex after games when Alex has gotten a penalty is always the best. He gets so riled up. I take my toothbrush into the shower with me, wiping away the fog on the inside so I can watch Alex through the glass.

He's in a funny mood tonight. I can't quite gauge it. He's slow and methodical with the shaving routine. I realize this is purposeful. I denied him when I walked in the door. It might not have had anything to do with whether I wanted him, but he's taken offense nonetheless. My fiancé is sensitive.

Once he's finished shaving, he moves on to brushing his teeth. Then he rinses with mouthwash and follows up with a Listerine PocketPak strip. It's probably overkill, but he's courteous like that, and the onion breath is the reason we're not currently having sex. When he starts cleaning up after himself, I decide I've had enough of waiting.

I squirt some body wash on my palms and rub them together, then massage it into my chest.

"Alex?" I wait until he looks at me before I press my boobs against the glass. "Are you ready for me?"

His lids lower and the tic below his left eye tells me what I already know: he sure as fuck is.

He drops the shaving cream on the vanity, or at least attempts to, but he misses and it hits the floor with a tinny thump. He doesn't seem to notice as he opens the shower door and steps inside. I don't even get a chance to turn around before he's pressed against me. He runs a palm across my collarbone and along my neck. Turning my head toward him, he kisses the corner of my mouth.

"Don't you have anything to say to me today?" he asks softly.

"I missed you."

"I know that. I missed you, too. Anything else?" He skims my side with his free hand, and I jerk as he brushes past the ticklish spot.

"I love you."

"I know that, too." His fingers travel over my hip and then lower, stopping shy of my very hungry beaver.

He's waiting for something, but I'm not sure what. I filter through our conversations over text today... I acknowledged the beaver, and I'm sure I thanked him for it. Then it dawns on me.

"Happy sexiversary, Alex."

He stills, fingertips digging in. "Anniversary, Violet. It's our anniversary."

"I thought we celebrated that last month. Besides, all the anniversaries we have include sexing, which sounds more fun," I explain.

"Mmm. I see your point. But I think this one is particularly special since you agreed to do more than just let me get inside you." He sounds the tiniest bit hurt.

"Happy anniversary, Alex," I murmur, appeasing him.

I feel his smile on my cheek. Because he's won. I'm okay with that; in the end, we'll both win. He turns my head so he can get to my mouth. It's a soft kiss, warm and wet and minty. I want to turn around so we're front to front, but he still has me pressed against the glass. When I push my ass out, he shifts his hips forward and his erection slides over my wet skin. He cups me with his wide palm, and I groan, anticipating his fingers.

Now don't get me wrong, I jill off like the rest of the female

27

population when our significant other is out of town, but it's not nearly as gratifying as when the person you love does the work for you.

"Happy anniversary, baby. I'm glad I made it home to celebrate with you."

The hand over my beaver moves up instead of down, and I start to protest, but Alex's tongue sweeps out to tangle with mine. I grab his hair and crane my neck, leaning into him, trying to get closer even though there's no space between us. He palms one of my breasts and groans, low and deep. Jesus. We're so fucking horny. This first round is going to be quick and dirty.

Alex releases my chin and takes a step back so I'm no longer pressed against the glass. Now that I have room to move, I try to turn, but he tightens his arm around my waist. With his lips on my shoulder, he drags his forearm down the glass, wiping away the fog.

The bathroom door is open and the fan is on, allowing the steam to escape and preventing the vanity mirror from being obscured. Through the water-spotted glass I have a perfect view of Alex groping my boob with his mouth on my skin. I'm so glad I wore my contacts today.

He's so much bigger than me. The top of my head barely reaches his chin when he's standing straight, and his shoulders are twice as wide as mine. His presence should be intimidating, but I know that under all that fuckhot muscle is the sweetest, most romantic, sensitive man on the planet. Sometimes I can't believe I managed to score such a hottie.

"You want me to take it easy on you?" he asks, sucking on my neck. He's probably going to leave a few marks. Not that it matters; I'll wear my hair down, if that's the case.

"No, thanks. The opposite of that would be good right about now."

He exhales a hard breath. "Fuck, I love you."

Alex holds me against his chest with one hand covering my boob, his fingers separated so my nipple peeks out between them. Once again, this is intentional. He loves my boobs almost as much as he loves the rest of me. It's unlikely he'll let go unless he absolutely has to.

His other hand glides down my stomach, and this time he doesn't stop until he reaches my clit. He begins rubbing circles, gentle but insistent. I hold onto the back of his neck on the not-so-off chance my legs decide to buckle. When I'm panting and moaning, Alex goes lower, easing first one finger inside, then another and another.

This is absolutely essential. It doesn't matter that we've been together for a year or that he sticks his monster cock in me on a regular basis. Alex doesn't have the kind of package I can jump on without any kind of preparation.

It's an aberration. And by aberration, I mean it's huge. Like *Guinness Book of World Records* material. I'm not exaggerating on his behalf, either. Alex and I go through a lot of lube—though mostly for boob sex. But this time we're in the shower, and I'm wet and slippery, so we're good to go.

I think Alex has designs on getting me off before he gets inside me, though. It's been more than a week, so I'm not feeling all that patient. My eyes are glued to our reflection in the mirror. The shower is fogging up again, so I swipe my palm along the slick surface to clear it, then reach behind me for Alex's cock.

We both groan when I slide the head along the crack of my ass, trying not to tense as he passes my backdoor. Alex makes all sorts of jokes about getting up in there, which is impossible. He'd never fit in a million years. Never. I don't think.

"Holy—Violet, what're you—" There's a tremor of excitement in his voice, as if he actually thinks I might offer to let him try. But then I pass my Area 51 and line him up with door number one. He doesn't react other than to curl his fingers one last time, hitting that special spot, before he withdraws.

His lips are soft on my shoulder. His expression turns to ecstasy as he pushes inside. "God, I missed you so much."

"Me, too. I mean, I missed you. Not myself."

The first time we have sex after he's been away is always amazing, but the second time is usually more intense. I'm not sure that's going to be the case this time. I've never been much of a voyeur, but being able to watch what's happening to me, while it's happening, is awesome.

I brace one hand on the glass and widen my stance, giving me an even better view as Alex thrusts and retreats. No wonder guys are either focused on the boobs or the beaver, because this looks fantastic. It also feels amazing, so the two combined make the experience phenomenal.

Alex puts his hand over mine, forcing me to lean forward. It means I can't see as much, but he goes deeper, and I can still see his face, and my boobs are bouncing away, so it gets a thumbs up.

"I'm not going to last like this," Alex warns.

"It's okay," I groan. I'm close anyway. I reach down and rub the beaver button.

"You want to do it again after the shower?" he pants, speeding up.

His eyes meet mine in the mirror, so I nod. His grin is all dimples and primal male satisfaction. He pushes my hand out of the way and takes over the rubbing.

I don't know how he can do this while he's still thrusting away. It takes an incredible amount of coordination. It's like when you're supposed to pat your head and rub your tummy at the same time. They're two very discordant actions, so technically it should be impossible. But Alex is super amazing, so he's able to do both.

The glass keeps fogging up even when I wipe it away, maybe because I'm panting against it, so I look down at Alex's hand moving furiously between my thighs. He's on a mission to make me come, bless his generous soul.

I feel it then, the telling warmth that starts as a tingle and evolves into a burn. It comes fast and hits hard.

Alex is considerate enough to keep his arm around my waist

FOREVER PUCKED

to prevent me from mashing my face into the glass. I claw at it anyway, seeking some kind of traction because sweet Jesus, all I can see are stars and galloping unicorns and hazy rainbows.

"Fuck yeah, baby. You feel so fucking good."

Alex doesn't use excessive profanity. He's actually quite polite most of the time, but he seems to lose that civilized edge when we have sex—more specifically when I come. I like that he's so enthusiastic about it.

His fierce concentration tells me he's getting close. He swipes his arm over the glass to clear the fog.

"I'm not gonna come inside you," he grunts.

"Why not?"

"Because I still wanna eat your pussy."

"Good call." See why I love him? He's such a planner.

He thrusts twice more and pulls out. Fisting his cock, he turns to the right as I spin and sink to my knees. I open my mouth and point to my boobs, giving him options. His eyes bounce between the two, his indecision obvious. I make the choice for him when I lean forward, wrap my lips around the head, and suck.

Alex swears like a trucker as he comes. I swallow, because it's more polite than spitting. When he's done, he drops to his knees and kisses me. He doesn't invite much in the way of tongue, though—not that I blame him since I now have jizz breath.

"It's so good to be home," he says.

I hum in agreement. Alex is the best place in the world to be.

BAD WORDS
MAKE TROUBLE

ALEX

I hate alarms. Especially when I've been up half the night having sex. With my fiancée.

Violet groans from under her pillow and slaps around on the nightstand, searching for her phone so she can turn it off. I roll on top of her, grab the device, and hit snooze. Shoving the pillow out of the way, I burrow through her hair until I get to her neck. Kissing her sleep-warm skin, I say, "Don't go to work today."

"I can't not go to work, Alex."

"I'll make it worth your while." I roll my hips against her ass.

Violet makes a noise, like maybe she appreciates where my cock is, and how hard I am, but she says, "I can't."

"Why not?" I sound whiny. It's not very manly, but I've been without Violet for eight days, and I want time with her. Her working today makes this difficult. I don't like difficult. I like getting what I want.

Violet elbows me in the ribs, so I do a push-up. She flips over. I try to get a knee between her thighs, but she keeps them pressed together. I'm forced to straddle her instead. My dick rests on her stomach, the head poking her navel.

She runs her fingers over my jaw. "I have client meetings today. Buck needs me to look over some stuff for him, and I have a presentation to prepare for."

"Can't you reschedule those and do the rest from home?" I try to sound less petulant, and more like I'm trying to seduce her with the idea.

She exhales through her nose. "No, I can't. Besides, if I stay home, I won't get anything done. Then I'll have to stay late tomorrow, which won't work because you have a game, and I want to go."

I sigh, frustrated. She's not going to give in. I already know it. Violet can be stubborn. I love this about her, but I also hate it, because it means she doesn't cave for me as much as I'd like her to. "You should just quit."

She purses her lips and pushes on my chest. When I don't move she pushes harder. "Get off."

"That's what I'm trying to do, but you won't let me." I nudge her navel with my cock again.

"I'm not kidding, Alex. Get off me."

Shit. She's pissed. Usually my morning advances are welcome—even when we've already had lots of sex, and especially after I've been away for a few days.

"Come on, Violet. You know I'm joking."

That's a lie. I'm not joking at all. She doesn't need to work. Ever. I make more than enough money to provide a very comfortable life for both of us. And our children. When we have them. Eventually.

"Liar! Now let me up. I need to shower. I can't go to work smelling like your jizz."

I give in and roll to the side.

She throws off the covers and pops out of bed. She's naked. So, so naked. Her pert ass looks biteable as she crosses to the bathroom and slams the door. Huh. Maybe she's getting her period or something. She's usually not this testy. Well, if I can't convince her to stay home, I can at least enjoy some shower sex before she goes to work.

I roll off the mattress and head for the bathroom. Turning the knob, I push and get nowhere. I try again, but the handle doesn't budge. "Baby, want to open the door for me?" I call out.

"I'm in the shower," she yells back.

"Uh, yeah. I get that. I was thinking maybe I could join you."

"Sorry. I can't hear you over the water!"

She can hear me fine, obviously. Goddamnit. What the hell did I do wrong? I look down at my hard-on and give it a reassuring pat, even though I have a bad feeling I'm not going to get to use it the way I'd hoped this morning.

When the water turns off a few minutes later—Violet takes quick showers when I'm not in there with her—I lean my forehead against the door and tap on it. Incessantly.

"There are five other bathrooms in this house, Alex. If you need to pee, go use one of them!"

I don't say anything; I just keep knocking.

"For fuck's sake," she grumbles from the other side of the door. I hear the lock turn so I step back. She throws it open. "What?"

She's covered by a towel. But there's cleavage. "Why are you mad at me?" I say to her boobs.

She snaps her fingers in my face. I look up. Her cheeks are red and her eyes on fire, though not with lust, even though my hard-on is pointing at her, waiting for her to use it as a handle.

"Why?" she asks, incredulous.

"Yeah. What did I do?"

She throws her hands up in the air. "What did you do?"

"I don't know what I did to make you this angry, but I'm sorry, whatever it was."

"That you don't even know is a problem." She turns away, but at least she doesn't shut the door on me. I'm taking this as progress.

I review the events since we woke up. Maybe my rolling on top of her was the problem, but I do that all the time. "Is it because my dick was near your ass again? I promise I'm not going to try to get in there."

She huffs, opening the vanity. "It's not about anal, Alex."

I scratch the back of my neck. "Is it because I asked you to stay home with me today?"

"No." She grabs her brush and yanks it roughly through her hair, cringing when it gets caught on a bunch of knots.

Shit. I know what I did wrong. "It's because I said you should quit your job. I wasn't serious, Violet."

I'm lying again, but I don't want her to be angry. And I'm still mostly hard, so if I can get back in her good graces, I might be able to get some action before she leaves for work. I'm really horny.

Violet spins around, her wet hair slapping me in the chest. The head of my cock rubs her hip and pokes her stomach through her towel. She uses the end of her brush to push me back so my excited parts aren't touching her anymore. "You do realize this is the *fifth* time in the past two months you've told me I should quit my job, right?"

I know I've said something about it before, but I didn't realize it was that many times. "You had to work a lot over the holidays."

"I was off the whole week between Christmas and New Year's."

"But my family was here, so I didn't get as much alone time with you as I wanted. And you've been working late a lot since then. We're always playing catch-up after I get back from away games, and then I'm gone again. I don't like it. And you're mad at me."

Violet sighs, her expression softening. "I'm just frustrated. My mom and Sidney put all that money toward my education. I don't want it to go to waste. And I like my job. A lot. I'm good at it."

"What about when we have kids? You won't want to work then, will you?" I cringe at the way I've worded this and the resulting change in Violet's posture. She goes stiff, and not in a good way.

"Whoa. We're not even married yet; why are we talking about kids? And what's with the plural? There's nothing wrong with being an only child."

"We can talk about that later." I can only imagine how big her boobs are going to be when she's pregnant. I'm so fucking excited for that: her boobs, us getting married, her having my babies. I bring her hand to my lips and kiss her knuckles. "It's not a bad thing that I want to be with you as much as I can, is it?"

"Wanting to spend time with me is different than wanting me to quit my job."

"But if you don't have to worry about a job, we'll see more of each other. It's not like I can't afford to take care of you. Besides, you put in all those hours, and for what? Less than a hundred grand a year."

She snatches her hand away, her lips pressing into a thin line. "I get that you make way more money than me, but it doesn't negate my need to have a purpose beyond being your fiancée. If you weren't raking in the millions, my salary would actually be really good. Great even."

"I'm sorry. I didn't mean it that way." I drag a palm over my face. "I just—I'm home for less than a week, and then I'm away again, and you're going to be working for the next four days. It doesn't leave me with much."

Violet adjusts her towel and rests her hand over my heart. "What would I do with all my free time if I quit my job, Alex?"

"Come to the away games."

"On the bus with you and the team? Am I going to fly everywhere? What about practices and training sessions? Will I go to those, too, or am I going to sit in a hotel room? No wait, I'll spend every day at a spa, getting treatments so I look twenty-three forever."

"Some of the other wives—"

"I can't spend my time waiting for you to come back from games or practices. Be reasonable. That's not a life."

She has a point. Violet isn't the kind of woman who would enjoy the endless pampering. She'll do it on occasion, but it's not something I can see her wanting to get used to. She struggles enough with the few grand I put in her account every month.

This conversation isn't going the way I want. I take the brush she's still holding and tuck it under my arm. Then I take her hand and play with her engagement ring. The one I gave her back in August.

We still haven't set a date. Weddings stress Violet out. She's started getting hives whenever we talk about it. Apparently she had a terrible experience with her mom's wedding—she was just a teenager—and she hasn't gotten over it. I've asked about it, but she's vague with her explanation.

"I don't like being away from you," I tell her. "The away games are hard. I miss you."

"I miss you, too, but that doesn't mean I should quit my job any more than you should quit yours." She raises a brow, like she's waiting for me to stick my foot in my mouth again.

The difference between our annual salaries is astronomical, but I keep that to myself since I don't want to shovel my own grave. And I do understand, and appreciate, her need for a purpose, even if I'm being a self-centered dick about it. "I feel like I don't get enough time with you."

"We'll get used to it. It'll be off-season before we know it, and then you'll be home all the time, and I'll be driving you crazy."

"You won't drive me crazy."

"We haven't been living together that long, Alex. Just you wait."

"Maybe when my games are in Chicago you could see about working from home once in a while? Do you think your boss would go for something like that?" I peek up at her.

"I can talk to him," she says after a moment.

"Okay." I run my nose along her shoulder to her neck, then follow with my lips.

"I need to get ready for work," she says softly.

"I'll give you one quick orgasm."

"It's already seven-thirty."

"I'll be superfast." I mash my hard-on against her stomach. "I don't want to wait all day to get rid of this."

"I'm going to be late as it is, Alex."

I kiss her bare shoulder, nipping. "So be a few minutes later."

She stops me before I can tug her towel free. "I have a client meeting first thing this morning. I can't be later."

"They'll wait."

"They shouldn't have to. It's unprofessional." She's snappy again. "Can we wait until I get home tonight? I'm not really in the mood anyway."

"Okay." I back off. "We can wait."

I leave her alone in the bathroom and pull on a pair of jogging pants and a T-shirt. It doesn't take long for my hard-on to fizzle, considering I just got turned down by my fiancée. Violet never turns down sex. Ever. I must have really pushed her buttons this morning.

I try to redeem myself by making a pot of coffee. And I toast a bagel for her, slathering it in lactose-free cream cheese so she doesn't have to leave for work hungry.

This morning is definitely not going as planned.

Violet rushes down the stairs at five after eight. I meet her at the door with her travel mug and bagel.

"What's this?"

"Breakfast. It's that mocha coffee you like and one of those French toast bagels with extra lactose-free cream cheese."

She wraps her arms around me and lays her cheek on my chest. I return the hug as best I can with my hands full.

"Thank you. I'm sorry I got so upset with you this morning. It's just that my job is important to me. You already take care of me on so many levels. I don't even have to do my own laundry anymore. Beyond needing a purpose, I don't want to waste the skill set I've acquired, because God knows I'm seriously lacking in the housekeeping department. Plus we already have someone who comes in and does all that stuff I'm not good at. We don't have any children, and we're not making any anytime soon. I don't think I could spend all day updating my Facebook profile and using entire cans of Aquanet on my hair."

She's referring to my mom with that last part. "I think she uses Aussie."

"Same difference."

"Aussie smells a little better."

Violet releases me, puts her hands on my shoulders and kisses my chin. "I'll give Super MC a big, warm hug when I get home tonight, okay?"

"We can hardly wait." I drop my head so I can give her a real kiss, with some tongue.

Violet grabs my shirt, bending backward as I keep leaning in. "I really have to go," she mumbles around my tongue.

"I'm not stopping you."

She realizes then that I'm right. My hands are full. I'm not keeping our mouths fused, she is. She releases me, and a long breath. I grin, having succeeded in making her not mad at me anymore—and now she's probably thinking about sex. Good. She can't take care of her needs at the office the same way I can at home. All damn day, if I want.

"I'll see you tonight." I pass her the bagel and coffee and open the door leading to the garage.

Violet stops short. "Shit."

Her car isn't in its spot. "Did you leave the car in the drive-way?" Sometimes she does this. Violet isn't the best at parking. She dings the corners or hits the mirrors all the time. I usually do the driving when we're together, mostly so I won't lose my mind.

"It's at work. Charlene drove me home."

"I'll take you in. Gives me more time with you." I kiss her cheek.

"You're so good to me. I love you." She sounds contrite now.

"I want to take care of you as much as you'll let me." I give her a pat on the ass. "You get in the car; I'll throw on shoes."

Violet grabs the keys to the SUV, and I head back inside, waiting until she can't see me before I smile. I'm winning all kinds of points. It's perfect. I'll have dinner ready when she gets home, and then she can be dessert. By that time, my comment about her quitting her job should be all but forgotten.

Violet's in the car scarfing down her bagel as I slide into the driver's seat. She puts her hand up to cover her mouth. "This is so good."

"Extra creamy, the way you like it." I stretch my arm across the seat so I can rub the back of her neck while I pull out of the garage. The maintenance guys have been by again, so the driveway is clear, but the streets aren't in quite the same condition.

"So creamy. I feel like I owe you a blow job or something for denying the Super MC this morning."

"He misses your mouth," I say, like my dick is actually a person.

Violet's named him, she dresses him up on occasion, and she's made a Play-Doh sculpture, so I suppose in some ways he is his own man.

"That's because I give seriously awesome blow jobs." She

takes a bite of her bagel and cream cheese squeezes out of the corner of her mouth, like jizz would if she happened to decide to go down on me in the car.

"This is true." I shift my erection around in my jogging pants so it's sticking up, tenting my sweats. The head rests on the base of the steering wheel, covered by gray fabric.

"Wow, you're really excited about a blow job, eh?"

"Uh, yeah. I'm always excited about your mouth on my cock."

Violet takes another bite of her bagel, oblivious to my hint. Or maybe ignoring it. So I try to be more obvious. I pull down the waistband so my erection pops out, the cool air making my balls tighten.

Violet glances down. "What're you doing?"

"You said you felt bad. I'm making it easier to alleviate your guilty conscience."

"Using more than one fifty-cent word in a sentence isn't going to get you road head."

I stroke the back of her neck. "You've given me road head before."

"Yeah, but that was in the summer, and we were on back roads, not in the middle of the city." She gestures to the traffic around us, which is filling in quickly as we head into the Loop.

"The windows are tinted. No one can see."

"The roads are slick. I don't want your attention divided between me bobbing on your dick and driving. This isn't Canada, Alex. Not everyone here believes in snow tires. I need you focused on our safety, not how warm and wet my mouth is, or how far I can get your dick down my throat."

"Just for a minute?" I'm pretty much begging at this point, but she's so descriptive, I can imagine how good it will feel.

"I can't go into work with blow-job lips." She shoves the last of her bagel in her mouth, pushing it to the side so one of her cheeks puffs out, reminding me exactly what she looks like when she's doing what we're talking about, minus the chewing.

"Blow-job lips?"

She swallows, then swipes the back of her hand across her mouth to get rid of the crumbs. "You know, when they're all swollen and flushed, like I've been licking them too much. Charlene will notice."

"Why would it matter if Charlene notices?" He's still exposed, hanging out, all lonely like, so I grab on to him and give him a stroke, drawing Violet's attention there.

"Jimmy and Dean will notice, too."

Those guys work in Violet's department. The four of them work on a lot of projects together. I'd be more concerned about how much time she spends with them, except Violet once kindly informed me that they're much more attracted to me than they are to her.

"You could touch it instead." I cringe at my pleading tone.

I earn more than eight million dollars a year. I'm team captain and center. I have the second-best scoring stats in the league. My cock is huge. I'm nice to look at, and I'm in great physical condition. I shouldn't have to beg my fiancée to touch my dick; she should want to ride it every minute of every day—in my fantasies anyway. In reality, I know that's not how life works.

"I don't think a handy is a good idea, either. Still too distracting. Besides, we're already here." She gestures to her work, which I almost drive past. Instead I double park and piss off the cars behind me.

"I'll see you tonight." She leans over and kisses me, then lowers her head and plants one on the head of my poor, throbbing cock. "I'll suck you later."

Popping back up without so much as a lick or a stroke, she smiles brightly. "Thanks for driving me in! I better get out before someone goes ballistic behind us." Honking follows, so she opens the door. "I love you!"

A cold gust of wind forces me to tuck my hard-on back in to my sweats. "No problem. See you—"

She slams the door and runs into the building, leaving me and my raging blue balls alone. Another horn blasts behind me, so I take my foot off the brake and move along. I keep one hand on the wheel and the other holding my handle all the way home.

As soon as I'm inside, I rub one out, leaning against the side door. I manage to make it to the laundry room, where I come in the sink. The ache in my balls makes it less enjoyable than it should be. Also, Violet's hands are much softer than mine, which is a huge factor in how good it feels.

After I'm done sorting out my issues, I call Darren to see if he wants to hit the gym early. We have a training session early this afternoon, but my right shoulder's been acting up on and off for the past couple of months, and I want to do some additional exercises to work out the kinks. Also, I need a release for all the energy I'd hoped to burn today with Violet.

Darren's all for it, probably because we're in the same boat today: women at work and us at home. I change into my gym gear, pack my duffle with extra clothes, and pick him up. He tosses his bag in the back and slides in next to me.

"How's it goin'?"

He adjusts his sunglasses and gives me one of his private smiles. "I had a good night, and an even better morning. You?"

Darren isn't a details guy. But then, he doesn't need to be. His relaxed posture and tone say it all.

"Last night was great." It comes out with an edge.

"Your morning didn't go well? You bring up the wedding with Violet again or something?"

Darren is one of the few people I talk openly to about the wedding stuff, or the lack of wedding stuff.

"I haven't mentioned it in weeks."

After the fiasco that was our engagement party, I left the topic alone for a while. Our moms went overboard with the guest list and invited two hundred people to celebrate in my backyard. Violet doesn't like to be the center of attention in a

43

crowd like that. She ended up with a raging case of hives, which took setting a date off the table.

By the holidays, I figured she would've gotten over it, but every time our mothers started in on setting a date, Violet broke out. We've gone through a lot of Benadryl in the past several months.

Now, I get that Violet has had some embarrassing things happen to her over the years. Something about a serious wardrobe malfunction at her mother's wedding is all I know. But I understand her concerns.

Violet says it like it is most of the time, and whatever pops into her head usually comes right out of her mouth. It's cute and funny when it's just us, or our friends, but in highly public situations, it can be mortifying for her—and sometimes other people. I've told her several times that we can keep our wedding small, but she's still reluctant to set a date.

"Not making progress there, huh?" Darren asks.

"Nope." I tap the steering wheel in agitation.

"I'm sorry, man. I know you want this to happen." His phone buzzes in his pocket. "You mind if I take this?"

I wave him off. "No. Go ahead."

"Hey, sexy. What's up?"

It's Charlene. Darren's been seeing her for a long while, now. He's always been a low-profile guy, but since they started dating, he's gotten a lot more media attention. He doesn't really like it, but he seems to like Charlene, so he deals.

"You didn't get enough of me last night or this morning, is that it?" he asks quietly.

I try not to eavesdrop, but he's sitting right beside me and we're in my car, so it's impossible.

"Oh, really?" Darren makes a clicking sound with his tongue. "That sounds like a lot of fun, but I'm on my way to the gym with Alex, so you'll have to put that thought on hold... Uh-huh...Yeah, you can come to my place. That'll work better anyway. Mmm...I think the red one." He shifts around in his seat. "That's entirely up to you."

When I glance at him, he raises his eyebrows. There's a long pause, during which his smile grows even wider.

"You know what I like, Charlene. Okay. I'll see you around six... Looking forward to it." He ends the call and tucks his phone back in his pocket.

"Things getting serious there?" I ask.

He shrugs. "I like her, and we have a good time together."

It's not an answer, but then that's kind of how Darren is.

"So what happened this morning?" he asks.

"Everything was fine until I joked around about Vi quitting her job."

"Why would you do that?" He sounds incredulous.

"I don't know. I just...the away games aren't my favorite. I don't like the long spans of time away from her, and she doesn't have to work. I make more than enough, right?" I'm looking for some kind of affirmation. Darren is probably the wrong person to ask, though, considering his relationship with Charlene isn't anything like my relationship with Violet.

"Does this have anything to do with the Darcy account?" Darren asks.

"What?"

"The Darcy account. Are you worried about that?"

"What are you talking about?"

Darren gives me a look. "Mitch Darcy. You know, our teammate?"

"Did he say something to you? He's got his own damn wife. He needs to stay the fuck away from mine."

"Settle down, Waters. Didn't Violet tell you last night?"

Anxiety makes every muscle in my body tighten. "Tell me what?"

"Jesus, you're edgy today."

"Yeah, well, my fiancée, who won't set a damn wedding date, denied me sex this morning after I'd been away for a week, and now you have information I don't, so there's something she's keeping from me."

"I don't think she's keeping it from you. Apparently Violet drew up a proposal for his account, and she's presenting it next week."

"Oh. That's it?" When Darcy's wife, Bunny, found out Violet manages finances for sports professionals, she got her contact information. I vaguely remember Violet telling me about creating a proposal a few weeks ago. She's had to stay late a bunch of times over the past few months.

"What do you mean, *that's it*? It's a big fucking deal."

"It is? How do you know?"

"Charlene told me. Junior accountants don't present on multimillion-dollar accounts."

"She already manages Miller's accounts."

"Yeah, but this is different. Darcy isn't family, and Bunny specifically requested her. Charlene said this is atypical."

"Oh. I didn't realize that. Well, I guess that explains her reaction this morning. I wish she would've said something."

"I'm surprised she didn't."

"We were kind of busy last night, with other things."

"Apparently."

I like Darcy well enough. He's a good guy, and Bunny's always pleasant. She seems like the one in charge in that relationship. I tap the steering wheel, considering my options and how things could have gone differently had I known this information.

"I should do something nice for her tonight. Plan a dinner or something."

"Good idea. Then maybe you'll get some action and you won't be so bitchy on the ice tomorrow night. We could really use a home win."

"Yeah, don't I know it."

While we managed to win the first two away games—just barely—on this last trip, we lost the second two. It's been like that this season: a lot of up and down, and not a lot of consistency.

My scoring average is also down, and Randy Ballistic, who's new to the team, has been responsible for more goals than I have lately. It's good for him, but not so good for me.

I'm silent for the rest of the trip to the gym. Darren doesn't push for conversation, which is good because I'm mulling. As much as I'm disappointed that I didn't hear this news from Violet, I'm also a little relieved it's Darren who told me. It gives me time to process.

As exciting as this is for Violet, it also means she's going to be busy planning for the presentation this week. Which means we'll have even less time together. I'm happy for her, because she works hard at her job, and she's amazing at it, but this isn't just about this week. The better she gets, the higher she'll climb, and the more time it will take away from us.

As a kid, my mom was always there: taking me to skating or hockey, making breakfast, working on homework with Sunny. I've always kind of imagined it'd be the same for my kids. I want that for my family, and I have the ability to provide it. Maybe Violet isn't ready to look at it that way.

As soon as we get to the gym, I jam in my earbuds so I don't have to talk to anyone and hit the treadmill. Darren leaves me alone. He knows better than anyone that sometimes I need time to think.

Lance Romero, one of my teammates and a good friend of Miller's, steps onto the treadmill beside me and nods. I've gotten to know him a bit better in the last few months. He's a notorious partier, and a while back he had a fling with the team trainer, Tash, which resulted in us getting a new trainer. It sucked for everyone, but since then he seems to have calmed down a bit.

I pull out an earbud. "How's it going, Romero?"

"Yeah, all right."

He looks tired, like maybe he was up late last night, probably with a bunny.

"You gonna be on for tomorrow's game?" I ask.

"Damn right. We're not letting Toronto near the net." A hint of Scot creeps in, telling me he's as fired up as I am about the losses we've been taking lately.

We spend the better part of three hours working out, though it's not all heavy training. An hour of it is stretching for me, working out the kinks in my right shoulder. I need to schedule a massage for later in the week so I can stay on top of things. Not only is this my shooting arm, it's my fingering-Violet hand as well. I can't have anything interfering with my career, or my ability to get her off.

I decide to order takeout from her favorite restaurant, as well as a bottle of champagne, her favorite flowers, and some chocolates. That should cover all the bases and win back some of my lost points from this morning. I also recognize that this opportunity is a big deal for her, and I do want to celebrate her accomplishments. I get that right now this is what she wants, so I'll support her. Her work ethic is honorable, if not always easy for me to handle.

After training I spend a few hours at Darren's watching Toronto games and planning our strategy for tomorrow. I get home around four-thirty, which gives me plenty of time to get things set up for the romantic dinner. First I remove the cardboard effigies of myself from the front hall. The giant stuffed beaver finds a new home in the sitting room, which is where I discover a picnic-like set up in front of the fireplace.

My workout mats, covered with fluffy blankets and pillows, are laid out close to the fireplace—it's gas so there's no worry about burning down the house. Pink paper litters the surrounding area. I crouch and pick one up; it's dick-shaped, with balls and everything. Some have little red capes glued to them in honor of Super MC.

It looks like half the work has already been done for me. Violet had some elaborate plans last night, it seems. I didn't make it past the kitchen yesterday, too focused on getting the cardboard cutouts set up and readying the bedroom for a serious sex-a-thon, with only half an hour to accomplish it all.

Beside the pile of blankets is a box of Fruit Roll-Ups. I'm not sure what those are for, so I leave them where they are and make a trip to the wine cellar. Champagne never lasts long with Violet, so I want to have her favorite wine handy as well.

Once everything is organized, I shower and shave, throw clean sheets on the bed, and wait.

Dinner arrives promptly at six. I put everything in the oven on warm, apart from the salad, which goes in the fridge. It's already full in there. Violet has some sort of fruit platter and a bunch of dips, including chocolate and non-dairy whipped topping. I move things around so everything fits.

By six-fifteen I'm antsy. Usually Violet's home by now, so I send her a message to check her status.

I get one back five minutes later:

> **Leaving work in 10!**

It's accompanied by a kissy face emoticon. That's disappointing. It takes her a good twenty minutes to get home, and that's in good weather. It started snowing again around three. It's just flurries, but it'll slow her down. That means she'll be at least another forty minutes. If not longer. I stay busy by setting the table and lighting candles. I put the bottle of champagne on ice and uncork a Riesling.

At twenty to seven, I get another message from her:

> **Sorry, got tied up! Just walking out the door. Home soon** ♥

This is definitely not going the way I planned. I check on dinner. It's still warm, so that's good, but it's been in the oven for almost an hour. I figure there's nothing I can do but wait, so I flop down on the couch, turn on the TV, and channel surf.

Half an hour passes, and Violet's still not home. I don't want to annoy her, but I'm starting to worry. Just as I'm about to send her another message, the house alarm beeps.

"I'm home!" she calls.

I pick myself up off the couch, straighten my button down, which is now wrinkled, and greet her at the side door. She's leaning against the wall, tugging off her knee-high boots. She shrugs out of her coat and lets it drop, along with her purse. On the floor beside her is a box of files.

She blows her hair out of her face and opens her arms, leaning forward as I step into her. She mashes her face against my chest. "I could fall asleep right here."

My irritation at her lateness wanes. "Long day?"

"So long, and hard. Like your dick."

I chuckle. "Hungry?"

"For your dick?"

I laugh again. "For dinner, but you can have him for dessert, if you want."

She pries herself off me. It seems to take some effort. She really does look like she could pass out standing up. "Jimmy got me takeout from that Thai place down the street a couple hours ago."

Fucking Jimmy. Ruining my date plan. "Oh."

"I'm sorry. I mean, if you want to order takeout I'm sure I could have something small." She fingers the collar of my shirt. "Oh. Were you planning to take me out?"

"No. I, uh, I ordered in for us. Darren told me about the proposal for the Darcy account, and I thought we could have a kind of dual celebration. You know, like celebrate our anniversary and the account at the same time since we didn't get to have dinner last night."

"Oh, Alex, you're the sweetest. I meant to tell you about it, but then we got naked and obviously I forgot. I didn't eat all that much, and it was at, like, five, so I can eat again."

She slips a hand behind my neck and pulls me down for a kiss. It's a quick one, though, with no tongue.

"We can eat in the living room," I offer. "It looks like you'd set up for a picnic or something there last night."

Violet bites her lip and her eyes widen with mischief. "Oh my God! I totally forgot about that! We'll have to save room for my dessert."

"To go with my cock?"

"Mmm." She pats my bulge. "I have special plans for him."

I smile. "I love special plans. Why don't you go hang out in the living room and get comfortable. I'll bring dinner to you."

"You sure you don't want any help?"

"I got this." I kiss from her neck to her cheek, then send her on down the hall.

I guess it would've been a good idea to tell her what I was planning instead of assuming she'd be home by six like usual. I make a detour to the dining room and clean off the table, blowing out the candles and putting away the dishes so she doesn't find them later and feel bad. I bring the champagne and glasses with me to the kitchen. It takes me a while to find the salad bowl. It's in the wrong cupboard.

I take dinner out of the oven. It looks a little dry, but smells fantastic. I give Violet a small portion, in case she feels obligated to eat it all, and transfer the plates to a tray.

Crossing to the living room, I notice she's changed the station from hockey to TLC. I stop short when I find her lying on the makeshift bed by the fireplace.

Her skirt is on the floor, but she's wearing leggings, so she's still mostly dressed. The first three buttons of her shirt are open, with her lacy bra peeking out. She looks like she's ready for some fun. My dick thinks so, too, and immediately stands at attention. Except her eyes are closed and her lips are parted—and not because she's got her hand in her panties.

I set the tray on the coffee table. Her chest rises and falls at regular intervals. Sinking down beside her, I run a finger across her cheek. "Violet? Baby?" She doesn't move at all.

I could wake her, but she's obviously exhausted from last night. And probably stressed about presenting her proposal for the Darcys. I press a kiss to her forehead, cover her with a blanket, and grab the remote. Sitting on the couch on the other side of the room, I change the TV back to hockey and settle in with my dinner.

So much for an awesome night of celebrations and blow jobs.

4

UNBLISS

VIOLET

I wake up at three in the morning. The first thing I notice is that I'm starving. I'm also in bed. With Alex, which makes sense considering the time. Except I have zero recollection of getting here. And I'm wide awake—like, ready to get up and start my day, which is insane, considering it's the middle of the night.

Alex is sleeping on his side, one massive arm tucked under the pillow. He protectively cups my boob with the other hand. He's frowning in his sleep. He has a game tonight, and when he's worried about his competition, sometimes he gets anxious. They're playing Toronto, and Alex has a longstanding hate-on with one of their players.

My stomach rumbles loudly, so I slip out of bed. A midnight

snack will help calm the beast in my belly. I'm wearing a tank top and a pair of my Marvel Comics underpants. I wasn't wearing them when I went to work today, and I don't remember getting changed.

Confused by my lack of recall, I grab my robe from the bathroom, shove my feet into slippers, and pad down the hall. The light from the kitchen illuminates the stairs enough that I don't trip my way down. I head straight for the fridge. Inside are takeout boxes from my favorite restaurant and the fruit platter I prepared two days ago.

I review what happened when I arrived home from work last night. I was tired—that's for sure. After a night of very little sleep and a lot of make-up-for-missed orgasms with Alex, plus our argument before work, I spent the morning in meetings, the afternoon working on Buck's account, and then finally, at the end of the day I made time to review the changes on my PowerPoint for the Darcy account.

It shouldn't have been difficult. All the legwork has already been done, but it's my first presentation, and the account is huge, so I don't want to fuck it up. I stayed at work way later than I'd planned.

Alex told me he had a nice dinner prepared to celebrate our most recent sexiversary and the Darcy account. I went to hang out in the living room to wait. I even freshened up my beaver in the bathroom. And then I laid down…

Oh, shit.

I fell asleep on him.

I owe Alex a blow job. Probably more than one now. And I still haven't had the opportunity to use all the fun treats and items I purchased to celebrate our sexiversary. Not that we didn't do a good job celebrating already, I just had other tasty plans to go with it.

I check the takeout box. Alex ordered me chicken parmesan from the place that uses lactose-free cheese. It's stupidly expensive, but it tastes amazing and doesn't give me the moops. He's so sweet and considerate.

It makes me feel bad for denying him sex yesterday morning, and then taunting him with the prospect of a blowy in the car, but his dismissal of my job is frustrating. My modest salary doesn't mean my career is valueless. I like doing what I do, and it helps people. For one thing, I know I've kept Buck from screwing up his monetary future. Plus, my minimal financial contribution at least allows me to pretend I have some kind of independence.

I'm living in Alex's massive house, driving the car he bought me, wearing the clothes his credit cards pay for, and rocking a huge diamond. I need to hold on to at least a tiny piece of my old self. My damn job is the way I'm managing this. I'm good at it. It gives me something to do with my time. I have friends there. And a few enemies, but they're mostly jealous. Understandably so. I get a lot of perks, and not just because I know how to manage money.

My mom might be a bit of a hippie flake, but she taught me some things—such as never be dependent on someone else to feed you. She never relied on anyone to pay the bills or make life easier. We made our life what it was. The second I was old enough to have a part-time job, I got one. I volunteered, I tutored, and I always had money in my bank account because I put it there.

I don't want to end up being one of those overly pampered women whose entire life revolves around her man. And I'm not referring to the ones with kids, because I can't even imagine what you do with those things *after* they shoot out of your vag. Gold stars to them. I mean the ladies who exist from one lunch date or Botox injection to the next. The fact that I get my nails done every three weeks already feels highly overindulgent.

While I hate it when Alex is away, it's actually good for me. Otherwise I'd likely stop hanging out with my friends and only spend time with him. Quitting my job takes me one step closer to that reality, and I've never been *that girl*.

I mean, eventually I'll take reduced hours, or work from home or something. One day I'll want to have Alex's pretty little hockey babies, but that's years away. First we have to tie the noose. I need to be his ball and chain for a minimum of three years before his super sperm start doing the job nature intended. I figure we can start with one and see how it goes. If it doesn't completely ruin my boobs, we can go for round two.

The microwave beeps, and I take out my reheated meal. The edges of the chicken parm are dried out, and some of the noodles are crunchy, but it's still tasty.

It's four a.m. by the time I finish my snack. I'm still not tired. I consider waking Alex with a surprise BJ, but with the game tonight, that's not a good idea. He needs to be well rested. If he's up before I leave for work, I'll get on my knees and choke on his dick.

He's been stressed since Balls was traded to the team this season. He's a forward, and younger than Alex. He's fast on the ice and showing his worth to the team. It worries Alex, not only because Balls is an excellent player, but because Alex's shoulder has been giving him problems lately, and he thinks it's affecting his game.

Aware that going back to bed is pointless, I put my dishes in the dishwasher and grab my files for the Darcy account. I might as well get some work done if I'm awake.

By six I'm tired again. I trudge upstairs to catch an hour of sleep before my alarm goes off. Alex is starfished on the bed, hugging my pillow. I fit myself into his body, and he immediately pulls me up against him, nuzzling his nose into my hair. He palms my breast, and his dick nestles against the divide in my ass. I tense for a second, but I'm wearing underwear, so it's not like he can attempt an invasion. Plus, he's said he wouldn't.

He grumbles something and settles back into sleep. I close

my eyes and drift, lulled into dreams by the warm comfort of his body.

My alarm goes off at seven-ten. Alex's arm tightens around my waist when I reach for my phone.

"If you want a morning blowy, you need to let me shut off my alarm."

He releases me instantly. I chuckle and cut the music blaring from my phone. When I turn to look at Alex, he's already thrown the sheets off. His erection stands straight up, flag-poling with excitement. His fingers are laced behind his head, thick biceps flexing and the outline of his new tattoo jumping with the movement.

I have to admit, it's pretty damn sexy. It's such a cool design with the Cup and his team logo intertwined. I went with him when he got it done. His tattoo artist is a goddamn wet dream, even if he's super intimidating. All the artists in that shop are drop-dead gorgeous. It's like a hotbed of sexy covered in tattoos and piercings. I'm definitely going when he gets the color done so I can get in another ogle session. It almost makes me want a tattoo, except they hurt, and I don't like pain.

I hold up my finger. "Give me a sec."

"You don't need to brush your teeth. It's cool," Alex's voice trembles with anticipation.

"Seriously. One second." I jump off the bed and run to the bathroom, stripping off my tank as I go. I fill a tiny cup with mouthwash, tip it back, and then refill it while I swish and spit. Running back to bed, careful not to slosh the mouthwash, I hand Alex the cup and climb up to straddle him.

I run my hands over his abs, lightly dragging my nails across his skin on the way down. He shudders, then tips the cup back, swishing a few times before he spits it back in. A little bit dribbles down his chin, but he swipes it away and grins.

"I'm ready."

"I bet you are." I crawl up his body, his erection bumping my stomach as I lean down to kiss him on the lips. "I'm sorry about last night."

He settles his hands on my waist. "I'm sorry about yesterday morning."

"I know you didn't mean it, not the way it came out." I kiss the center of his chest and move lower, stopping at each defined ridge along his stomach. As I get closer to the monster cock, I lift my gaze.

Alex's lids lower, and he groans when my breast bumps the head.

I cup my boobs and squeeze them together. "Maybe you want to slide between these instead?"

"I want it all," he grates.

"Tits, mouth, beave? In that order?"

He nods, his smile dark.

"Mmm… Feeling greedy?"

"You have no idea." He sits up in a rush, then flips me over so he's on top. He yanks my panties off and tosses them over the side of the bed. He fits himself between my legs, his monster erection making contact with the Land of Beave. So of course I moan, because what other sound is there that adequately expresses my love for him and his super-special penis?

Alex kisses me, his tongue warm and minty. Then he grabs the lube from the dresser, squirts a generous amount onto his cock, and starts stroking. I have a feeling I'm going to be walking funny this morning.

I'M NOT WRONG. After sliding his dick between the valley of the boobs and getting his dick lollipopped, Alex fucked three orgasms out of me. Getting dressed isn't easy when my bones are made of pudding.

Work is fine, but word has spread that I'm presenting the

Darcy account, and I'm getting lots of looks from some of the people who've been here slaving away for much longer than I have. Most of the looks aren't very friendly.

Charlene stops by my desk at lunch. "Want to run across the street and get a bite to eat?"

"I can't. I need to work on this." I motion to my computer screen and then my desk. It looks like a paper bomb exploded. The presentation is essentially done now, but I'm so stressed about fucking it up that I can't stop going over the stats, double and triple-checking to make sure everything is accurate for my run-through with Stroker at the end of the week.

"Just take fifteen minutes. We'll get it to go and come back. We can eat in the conference room, and you can tell me about your blow-job lips from this morning."

I give her the bird, but relent. She's right. I need to take a break. I've been at it for almost four hours, and my eyes are starting to cross.

I grab my coat and purse, and we head for the elevators. Dean comes out of the men's bathroom as we pass. He's wearing his coat and a fedora. I thought that hat trend had died, but it seems to work for him.

"You ladies lunching?" he asks, falling into step with us.

"We're grabbing something and coming right back, but you're welcome to join us."

"Thanks."

"Where's Jimmy?" He and Dean are usually together.

Dean stuffs his hands in his pockets. "He's got a meeting with a client in twenty, so I'll bring him something back."

The elevator arrives, and it's packed, but we manage to squeeze in. I face Charlene and stare at her cheek the entire ride down while she stares at Dean's neck. I blow on her hair to be annoying.

"So, I gotta ask, how's Waters feel about you taking on the Darcy account?" Dean asks once we're out of the elevator.

"I'm presenting; that doesn't mean the account will be mine."

I sincerely hope the account will be mine, but there's always the possibility that I'll say something dumb or mess up and screw my chances. Usually with work stuff I keep it together, unlike in real life when my censor button isn't required most of the time.

"Come on, Vi, you know if you rock it they're giving you the account. And with you managing Butterson's finances, and marrying Waters, you've got it in the bag." Dean doesn't sound encouraging, more like he's irritated and jealous.

"I don't manage Alex's money."

"He's got contacts, though, obviously, and you'll be managing his money soon enough. Or is he making you sign a pre-nup?"

"Say what now?" I stumble when I hit a slippery patch on the sidewalk and grab Charlene's arm for balance.

"You can't honestly think he'll marry you without a pre-nup. I mean, he's worth a fortune. His house alone has to be worth two-point-five mil, and all the other property he owns, plus bank?"

I frown. "He's never mentioned a pre-nup."

"They haven't even set a date yet, Dean," Charlene snaps.

"I'm just saying, don't be surprised if he does. He's protecting his assets. You can hardly blame him."

I don't say anything in response. Obviously I have no desire to bleed Alex dry should our relationship not work out the way we intend, but a pre-nup seems a lot like failure is an expectation. This indicates again why I need to keep this job. I can't imagine being left with nothing and no employment prospects. I guess I can see Dean's point, but it would kind of hurt if Alex dropped something like that on me without discussing it first.

Especially since he's constantly throwing money at me. He'll ask me to buy something sexy for one of our date nights and then drop three thousand dollars in my account. What the hell kind of sex wear am I buying? One of these days I'm going to bedazzle my vagina with Swarovski crystals to be a smart ass.

"So anyway, back to my original question…" Dean looks at

me expectantly. When I stare blankly back, he rolls his eyes. "Waters? How does he feel about the Darcy account?"

"He's happy for me, I guess?" Despite his repeated comments about quitting my job, he did want to celebrate me getting to present, so that has to be good.

"Really? Huh." Dean raises his perfectly groomed villain eyebrows and opens the door to the café, ushering Charlene and me in ahead of him.

I accept his chivalry. "What's that supposed to mean?"

Dean blinks innocently. "Nothing."

We get in line, and I look to Charlene, who's doing a terrible job of ignoring me while she reads the menu. She points enthusiastically at the special. "Oh, look! They have mushroom quiche!"

I wrinkle my nose. "Mushrooms are disgusting. They remind me of severed dick heads."

Dean makes a gagging sound. "You need a therapist, Violet."

"People who eat mushrooms need therapists," I shoot back.

"Shh!" Charlene warns.

I roll my eyes; it's a noisy café. "No one cares about my aversion to phallus-shaped fungus."

A tiny old lady in front of us turns to glare. I guess her hearing aids are working fine. I smile at her until she looks away, and then address Charlene. "So I don't get it. What's the deal with the Darcy account? I mean, aside from everyone being pissed that I might get it even though I don't have any real experience dealing with massive amounts of money, other than Buck's."

She and Dean exchange another look.

I throw up my hands. "Seriously, you two, if you're trying to be incognito about this crap you're failing. What's the damn deal?"

Dean tries to smirk, but it looks more like a weird facial tic. "I'm guessing you haven't heard the rumors."

"What rumors?" Sometimes Dean is worse with gossip than a

thirteen-year-old girl. Occasionally his style is also reminiscent of that particular age group.

"They're swingers."

I blink at him. It's loud in here. Maybe I heard him wrong. "Pardon?"

"Swingers." He says it slowly, making it two distinct syllables —like I'm an idiot, which admittedly, sometimes I am. But he's being a jerk, and not in a funny way. More of an intentionally antagonistic way.

"I'm assuming you don't mean they have a trapeze-artist fetish or something."

"Nope."

"So, like, they sleep with other people's significant others?" Who the hell does that in this decade?

"That's the rumor."

"Well, where did the rumor come from? And how do you know it's even true? I mean, let's be logical. People used to think Alex was a manwhore who slept with three chicks in one night, and we all know that's not true."

"We don't really *know*, though, do we? He just told you it didn't happen, and you believe him," Dean points out.

"He refuted the evidence, and the people who were with him that night corroborated it," I reply.

"And all of those people happen to be *his* people. Like his sister." Dean has the villain eyebrow going again. "Of course she's going to defend his position."

"His position?" I snort, even though my stomach is doing horrible somersaulty things. "This isn't a criminal court case. And Sunny can't lie. She's worse than me. Have you ever seen her try to lie? It's ridiculous. Alex did not bone three chicks in one night. End of story."

"If you say so." Dean's smirking again.

"Why are you being like this today?"

"I'm just making a point. Usually there's some truth in rumors. Waters may not have banged loads of bunnies, but he sure stuck his tongue in a lot of their mouths. Who knows if he did it with his dick, too."

"Dean!" Charlene hisses, slapping his arm.

"What?" He looks around.

People are staring, and for once, I'm not the cause of the embarrassment. But I'm sure feeling the effects. I'm sure my face is blotchy. I look at the floor and let my hair shield my face from all the curious eyeballs.

Thankfully it's our turn in line. I step up to the counter and order a BLT and a drink, then move aside. I don't say anything else while we're in the café, and Dean's busy on his phone, doing whatever he does when he's not being an asshole to me, apparently.

Once we have our food, we return to the office. I'm not interested in hearing more about the Darcys' swinger habits, Dean's thoughts on Alex's sexual history, or a potential pre-nup.

"I really need to get back to work. That took a lot longer than I expected." It's not a total lie. Getting food took all of the twenty minutes I'd allotted to lunch.

Charlene seems conflicted. "Come sit with us for five minutes before you go back to work."

"I can't. I have too much to do. It's cool. I'll catch up with you later. We have the game tonight, anyway. If I don't want to bring a file folder full of work, I need to get back to it."

"Oh, that's right, you two get great seats, don't you? Must be nice to have all those connections." Dean takes a break from his texting, or messaging, or snapchatting to join our conversation again.

"Did you forget to take your PMS pills today?" Charlene asks.

Dean's mouth drops open. He twirls around and stomps down the hall.

Charlene waits until he's out of earshot before she says, "Don't take anything he says to heart, Vi. I think he's got some personal stuff going on, and last week he made a bookkeeping mistake and got in trouble for it. He's jealous."

"That doesn't mean he can be a jerk to me."

"I'm not defending him. I'm just telling you what I know."

"Right. Okay. I'm still going to go back to my desk. I don't need to put up with that."

"I could come with you."

"It's okay. I really will be working, so I won't be any fun."

"Okay. I'll see you in a bit."

I grab her arm before she walks away. "Do you think he's right, though?"

"Right about what?"

Just then a few of the women from the senior accounting department round the corner. Their giggling stops when they see us, and they plaster on fake smiles to go with their fake hellos.

"Nothing. Never mind. I'll see you after lunch."

Charlene follows behind the others. Looking over her shoulder, she sticks her tongue in her cheek like she's giving a blow job. I smile and wait for her to disappear around the corner before I let my shoulders droop. I'm definitely beginning to feel the divide between me and them. And I'm not sure how much I like it.

Back at my desk, I flop into my chair and set my sandwich next to my keyboard. Shrugging out of my coat, I turn my monitor on, waiting for my login prompt.

Dean makes a valid point. While he wasn't a manwhore, Alex did make out with a lot of girls prior to dating me. There are literally hundreds of pictures of him with his tongue in various girls' mouths. Now, I don't know how many of those girls ever got their hands down his pants, or got on their knees and tried to get his massive cannon down the hatch, but I'm imagining there were at least a few. Maybe more than a few.

Combine that revelation with the conversation about a pre-nup, and now I'm feeling less secure. Plus, the rumor about the Darcys being swingers is disconcerting, even if it is just a rumor.

I don't want to think about them boning other people while I'm presenting their financial portfolio next week.

I thought swinging was popular in the sixties and seventies, when everyone was doing coke and didn't understand the ramifications of banging all sorts of people. I shudder at the idea of Alex putting his hands, or any other part of his body, on Darcy's wife.

Her name is Bunny. How's that for irony? She also has big boobs. Bigger than mine. Although, I think hers might be the paid-for variety. Not that it matters much. Boobs are boobs. If Alex can grab them and put his dick between them, he's a happy man. What if he wants to slide his dick between her boobs? What if she wants to fondle mine? What if Mitch wants to have sex with me, and Alex wants to watch? Why has my life suddenly become a cheesy porno?

I try to focus on work, but I'm distracted by porntastic scenarios involving Alex and Bunny. I need answers. The internet will have some, but those aren't necessarily reliable, as I've learned over time.

Buck is a good option. I pick up my work phone under the guise of doing my actual job and punch in his number. He answers on the third ring.

"Hey, Vi. How's it going?"

"Okay. Fine. Good. You?"

He goes into immediate brother-protection mode. "What's wrong?"

"Why would you think something's wrong?"

"Seriously?"

"No, really, what tipped you off?"

"You sound like a prepubescent boy."

"I have a throat thing."

"No, you don't."

"Okay. No, I don't." I need to get better at lying. I wonder if there are classes for that kind of thing.

"So what's wrong? You and Waters get into it or something? You want me to break his nose again?"

"No. Please don't do that. He doesn't snore yet, and if you break his pretty face, that might change, and I like sleeping beside his fuckhot body. Especially when he's naked, and I'm naked, and there's nothing but warm skin." I inhale one of those deep breaths and release it so it makes the Darth Vader whooshing sound when I exhale into the receiver.

"Thanks for sharing all of that. Sunny tells me I'm like a cuddly warm blanket when we sleep naked." Buck returns the overshare.

"That's because you are a blanket. A big yeti blanket."

"Ah, there we go. Whatever's wrong can't be that bad. So what's the problem?"

"Are Mitch Darcy and his wife swingers?"

Buck coughs, like maybe I've made him choke on something. "Where'd you hear that?"

"It doesn't matter where I heard it. Is it true?"

"Shit. I don't know, Vi. There are rumors, but then there are always rumors, ya know? Why're you asking? Does Waters want you to go on a double date with them or something? I'll shove my fist up his dick hole."

I make a disgusted sound. "No, Buck, Alex doesn't want to go on a double date with them. And please don't put images of your fist near Alex's dick in my head. That's just awful. I'm supposed to present a proposal for the Darcys' account next week, and Dean told me they're swingers."

"Who's Dean?"

"Another guy who works here."

"Oh." Buck's silent for a few seconds. "So what does them being swingers have to do with you managing their account?"

"I don't know. Nothing, I guess. I mean, I wondered if maybe they want me to manage their account because they have a secret agenda to get me and Alex to partner-swap or something."

"Yeah, I don't know much about swinging, 'cause I want to

be the only one eating Sunny's cookie, but I don't think that's how that whole deal works. If Darcy's into screwing other people's women and his wife wants to ride other guys' dicks, they're not gonna go after his teammates and their partners. That seems like a super-bad idea."

I nod, even though he can't see me. He makes a good point. "Kind of like when you got caught with your coach's niece in the public bathroom?"

"Thanks for bringing that up."

"Sorry. You know I'm not getting on your case; I'm just making a comparison."

"I don't really think screwing around with a chick in a bathroom and wife-swapping are the same thing."

"Right. Lance boning the trainer in the locker room seems like a better comparison."

"Yeah. I guess."

"How's he doing, anyway?" I ask. Now I'm making small talk. Also, I'm still following Tash on Instagram, and she keeps posting depressing inspirational sayings about the mistakes people make that they can't take back, and letting things go, so I might be doing a little fishing.

I hear beeping in the background on Buck's end. "He's his usual self. Well, not quite, but he's okay. Why're you asking about Lance?"

"I don't know. No reason."

"Sunny told me Tash has been messaging her lately, asking about him, so if you want to know what's going on between those two, I don't have an answer. She fucked him around, and he's not over it. That's all I know."

"It doesn't seem like she's over it, either."

"Yeah, well, she's the one who screwed him over, apparently, and Lance is pretty good at holding grudges, so I can't see him jumping back into that, but you never can tell."

"Yeah. Right. Relationships are so complicated."

"Only because we make them that way." He makes a slurping sound. "You need to talk to me about anything else?"

Sometimes Buck is surprisingly deep.

"Not right now."

"Okay. Well, I'm gonna stuff my face with this leftover stew thing Sunny made and then go pick up Balls so we can hit the arena and get ready for the game."

And sometimes he's just Buck.

"Oh, wait. I have one more question."

"Shoot."

"Do you think Alex will ask for a pre-nup before we get married?"

Buck is silent for a few seconds. "I don't know. Maybe? I mean, the guy's worth more than forty million, and he's still got three years left on his contract with Chicago. So that's another twenty-four coming his way, plus endorsements. I guess it's possible, maybe even probable?"

Buck knows a lot about Alex's salary; I suppose it is common knowledge. "Oh."

"It wouldn't be personal if he did, Vi. He has to protect himself even if you two do end up together forever."

"Right."

"Did he bring it up or something?"

"No. Dean mentioned it."

"This is the same guy who told you Darcy was a swinger?"

"Yeah." I pull up images of Darcy and his wife from the internet. She really is gorgeous—curvy, busty, leggy. I bet she lets him put it in her ass. *Whore.*

"This guy sounds like a shit-disturber. You need me to come down there and rip him a new one?"

"That's a sweet offer, but you don't need to tune up my coworkers. I can handle myself."

"I'm almost positive the Darcy stuff is bull, but Alex knows him better than me since they've played together longer. You could ask him." More slurping follows.

"Yeah. Okay. I should get back to work. I'll see you tonight after the game."

"All right, Vi. Try not to worry about the pre-nup stuff, or Darcy."

"Okay."

I try to focus on work after I hang up, but I have the attention span of a toddler on a sugar high. And I'm emotional. I end up hiding in the bathroom so I can silent-cry for a few minutes. I have a horrible feeling, and I don't know what to attribute it to.

The game tonight will be a welcome break from all the other stuff. It's been weeks since I've seen Alex play live. I'm hoping we can have hot, aggressive, post-game sexy times and tomorrow I can be appropriately exhausted for all the right reasons. Not because I can't stop worrying.

5

NO SIREN LOUD ENOUGH

VIOLET

I call Alex around five. The game doesn't start for a few hours, but I won't get to see him until it's over, and he'll turn off his phone by six so he can get into play mode.

He answers the call on the first ring. "Hey, you gonna be home early so I can see you before I leave for the arena?"

"I haven't left yet, so I don't think I'll make it before you have to go." I glance at the pile of papers on my desk and the endless list of things I need to finish. Yeah, there's no way I'll make it home, so the "think" part is just to ease the blow of disappointment. Unfortunately, it doesn't work.

"What about my pre-game good luck kiss? How'm I gonna get that from you if I don't see you before I leave?" His voice is low, the way it gets when he's thinking about sex.

I cross my legs as the fountain of beave turns on. "I gave you loads of good luck kisses this morning. Those aren't going to carry you through?"

His words come out even grittier. "Those were hours ago. They don't count."

He's so cute. "None of them count? Not even the ones I gave Super MC? Or the one my beaver gave him?"

Alex groans. "That visual is burned into my brain for all eternity. You know this means I have to rub one out on my own, right?"

"I promise me and the beave will take care of you and Super MC tonight after the game, okay?"

Alex sighs. "Fine. Come by the locker room on your way to your seat, though. I'll make sure they know you're coming."

"Are you feeling nostalgic? You want to bang me in the locker room again?"

I'm rewarded with another deep sigh. "Yes, but that's not why I want you to stop by. I'm getting my kiss before I hit the ice tonight. We need a win, and I need your lips."

I shiver at his tone. He's been intense in bed lately—like, locker room intense.

"Okay, and after the game you can have them anywhere you want them."

"I like the sound of that."

I peek around the office to make sure no one's listening and lower my voice. "My beaver's already drooly."

"I fucking love how wet you get for me."

"Only for you, Alex."

This is a weenie lie. I mean, no one turns me on like Alex, but it really doesn't take much to make my beaver drool. I've always been this way.

Alex doesn't need to know that though, and any kind of ego stroke, especially after losing the last two games, is good for his pre-game morale.

"That's right. Only for me, baby."

"You and Super MC. I'll see you soon, okay?"

"Uh-huh. I love you, Violet."

He hangs up before I can respond, likely because he's jacking off.

JUST LIKE HE ASKED, I stop by the locker room before settling into my front row seat at center ice, and as he said, the security dudes are expecting me. Of course, they aren't expecting Charlene, Lily, and Sunny to be tagging along. And neither is Alex.

Instead of it being him and me, there are suddenly eight of us: four smelly, horny hockey boys—because no matter how much they wash their jerseys and pads, they always smell like the inside of a hockey bag—and four equally horned-up women.

The potential for a serious mouth fuck is thwarted by the awkwardness of too many witnesses, at least for me, but it doesn't seem to stop Balls and Lily from trying to get each other off with their clothes on. I settle for a less aggressive, mini mouth fuck with promises of more later, when no one is watching or listening—and Lily isn't moaning right beside me.

Buck has to pry Balls off her so he can finish getting ready. He's all pads and no jersey, and it's actually pretty entertaining. Even with Buck attached to his back, he won't leave Lily alone.

"You really are a Horny Nut Sac, aren't you?" I ask.

He grins, possibly at my commentary, but doesn't look my way at all. Instead he rubs Lily's bottom lip with his thumb. "What do you say to no sleep tonight, luscious?"

"Sounds like fun." She bites his thumb.

"Which we all know is code for sex. Okay, let's go, Balls. We have a game to play before you can get her naked." Buck is only successful because Lily steps back and Sunny shuffles Lily behind her, hiding her from view. That seems to break Randy out

72

of his trance, so they're able to corral him back into the locker room.

"Are you two planning to find a bathroom to screw in after the game?" I ask Lily.

I'm only kind of joking. Lily and Randy seem to have a strange affinity for getting it on in bathrooms, even when there are perfectly good bedrooms available.

"Depends on whether Randy can wait until we get back to his place tonight." Lily seems strangely serious.

We make our way through the stadium to our awesome seats. My mom and Sidney, my stepdad, are already there, talking to a couple. Actually, Sidney's doing all the talking while my mom and the other woman stare at him. Sidney always knows someone, being a scout and Buck's dad and all. We settle into our seats and order drinks and snacks.

The games have become a lot more fun now that we're all dating these super-hot hockey players and attend them together. I can't believe I used to read books while they played. Now I can't take my eyes off the action.

"I hope they win tonight," Sunny says from my left, sipping what looks like juice. Along with not eating animals, Sunny doesn't like beer. Not that one is related to the other in any way.

Chicago needs a win to get some morale back. They lost against Buffalo when Lance got a five-minute penalty, leaving them down a player in the final period of the game. Buffalo scored not one, but two goals during that time, and Chicago never recovered the lead. They lost the game before that as well, but there wasn't a penalty to blame it on, just some sloppy playing and chippy behavior.

Alex has been staying out of the penalty box for the most part, but I can see his frustration on the ice when things aren't going the way he'd like. It's tough after taking home the Cup; the expectation of repeating the previous season is unreasonable, but they still want the glory. Making it to the finals last season means they had a shorter off-season and less time to recover, which put them at a disadvantage this season right from the start.

Add to that a change in team trainer—Tash, who had been training the guys for the past two years, was recently replaced by a guy named Evan Smart—and it's been a rough season.

The Chicago crowd goes crazy when the team takes the ice. Women scream the names of the players they want to get naked with. Some girl a few rows back starts bellowing Ballistic's name. Lily, who's managed to convert him from a serial player into a one-vagina man, turns to check out the yodeler. She pales and coughs out an expletive, so I turn around to see what's going on.

There's a blond chick dressed in very little, considering we're in a cold arena surrounded by ice, and she's holding up a home-made sign. It looks like something I might've made in junior high. A selfie of her and Randy, in color, takes up half the poster-board. It's captioned with: I WANT TO GET BALLED BY BALLISTIC AGAIN!

I cup my hands and yell, "Nice sign! Super classy!"

I should probably keep my mouth shut, based on the death stare I get from her, but her reaction fuels my desire to poke her with the proverbial stick—although not the kind she wants to handle.

"You're a little too late! This one over here actually owns Balls' balls now." It sounded funnier in my head.

Lily slouches in her seat. Charlene looks back to see who I'm yelling at and elbows me. "What're you doing?"

"Being an idiot."

The blond hockey hooker gives me the bird and turns her ragey eyes to the back of Lily's head.

"What happens when you have to go pee and she follows you to the bathroom and sprays you in the eyes with her glitter body mist?" Charlene asks calmly.

"You'll be my bodyguard. Or I'll get my mom to come along and she can mortify her into leaving me alone."

The team skates around the rink, and of course, Alex pauses to tap the glass and wink at me. Darren follows and takes a moment to stop in front of Charlene. He pulls at the front of his jersey. Charlene unravels the scarf around her neck and touches the pearl necklace she's wearing.

It's so weird that that's their thing. We've talked about pearl necklaces before, but I thought it was more of a joke. Maybe it's not. Maybe Darren really likes to jizz on her throat. The necklace would suggest that. Actually, it's more of a choker.

I glance at Darren again in time to see him mouth, *Your ass is mine.* At least that's what it looks like he says.

"Oh my God. You let him in your Area 51?" I shriek. Thankfully, it's loud enough in the arena that most people can't hear me.

Darren skates away, and Charlene turns her attention to me. "What?"

"Your Area 51! You let Darren near it?"

Charlene looks confused as she strokes the pearls around her neck. As much as I constantly overshare my sexual exploits with her, she hasn't been sharing all that much with me, aside from the conversations we've had about blowies. Obviously she and Darren have sex. Often. I mean, she says they do, and she has no reason to lie.

"What's that code for?" she finally asks.

"What's what code for?"

I look over to see Buck skate by and blow Sunny a kiss. Several girls behind her start screaming like they're having spontaneous, simultaneous orgasms.

"Calm your tits, ladies!" I yell while pointing at Sunny. "He bones this one on the regular."

Sunny looks at me with what seems to be horror, which is appropriate. I'm unable to control my mouth tonight, and I've only had a sip of my beer. I'm chalking it up to stress.

"Miller and I don't bone. We have sex or make love," Sunny informs me. "Also, your parents are right here."

"Sorry. Make love doesn't sound nearly as badass when we're dealing with the bunnies, though." I thumb over my shoulder at the shrieking whores.

Sunny nods as though this makes sense. "Sometimes, when he's really excited and so am I, we have intense sex. It's my favorite."

I have to wonder what intense means for Sunny. I'm not about to ask. She's such a soft person, so I can't really see her swinging from the rafters. Lily, on the other hand, I can totally see getting freaky, considering her penchant for public love.

"And when it's nice out, Miller loves to have sex outside." Sunny brushes the end of one of her thin braids across her lips.

I have to bite my tongue, literally, to prevent myself from saying something about how yetis are notorious for the outdoor sexing. Luckily for Sunny, I'm distracted by Randy when he comes barreling up to the plexiglas barrier.

He throws himself at it, scaring the people next to Lily and making the blonde behind us go insane. But he's focused only on Lily. He points to her, says something we can't hear, and then humps the boards a couple of times before skating away.

"He's almost as bad as you," Charlene says.

"Right? It's like we're twins of inappropriateness or something." Lily's still slouched in her seat, now with her hood pulled up.

I find her embarrassment ironic considering how often Randy drags her into the closest room with a door whenever he's been away for more than five minutes. That girl's vagina has to be made of leather for all the dicking she takes.

But the attention and the media crap does take some getting used to. Before, when she and Randy just used to bone each other in the privacy of a bathroom or a bedroom, Lily didn't have to deal with the publicity crap. Now they're official, Randy's proving to be an incredible player, and he's getting attention and endorsements, which means he's higher-profile in the hockey world.

Lily's learned quickly that people are always watching, and one heated kiss caught on someone's camera phone is all it takes for their relationship to go viral. She's been getting the bunny hate lately. It's a rite of passage for girlfriends of NHL players.

"So back to your Area 51," I say to Charlene as Toronto take the ice.

"Which is what exactly?"

I lower my voice. "Your bum."

"Bum?"

"Yeah, bum."

"Who even says that?"

"Alex. It's a Canadian thing. Like beavers are vaginas, *bum* is a nicer word for *ass*. Unless you prefer fudge machine."

"Bum it is." Charlene tips her beer back.

"So?"

"So what?"

"Darren has access to your Area 51?" It's cold in the arena, so I can't be sure, because her cheeks are already pink, but she may be blushing. "Charlene?"

"Did Alex say something?"

"Why would Alex know about access to your Area 51?"

The top of her beer is suddenly very interesting. "You know how guys talk."

I sure do. But I have a feeling Charlene and I are way worse than Alex and Darren could ever be. Or at least I am. It takes a few seconds for what she's not saying to really sink in. "Wait a second! That means Darren *does* have Area 51 access?"

"Shh!" Charlene smacks my arm and looks around.

A few people are looking at us, but they don't know what we're talking about. I lower my voice, "How does that even work? I mean, isn't he equipped? How does it even fit?"

"Skin stretches, Violet."

"Not that much." I put my beer between my knees and wrap my fingers around my wrist to demonstrate.

"Darren isn't quite so girthy, but yes, essentially."

77

I gape at her, slack-jawed, because seriously, that's insane.

"Honestly, Vi, it's not that big a deal. I don't know why you're so uptight about it." She snickers and glances around before leaning in and lowering her voice to a whisper, "Hasn't Alex ever tickled your chocolate starfish?"

I'm taking a sip of my beer when she says this, so I spit-spray it all over the plexiglas—and her. Char uses my scarf to wipe her face, and I fake cough to cover up my accident.

"I mean, sure, Alex has snuck a finger in my Access Denied hole. And yeah, it felt okay." I pause and consider this for a moment. He did it once. Back when I lived in my apartment. It was some hot sex. I can feel the heat in my cheeks. "Well, maybe better than okay, but there's a huge, massive difference between the size of his finger and his monster cock. I can't imagine him ever getting that in there."

She shrugs, unwilling to comment, possibly because we're in a very public arena. That's fine. I can carry on this conversation all by myself. Her facial expressions are the only answers I need.

"I don't get the fascination. Why aren't vaginas and mouths enough? Why do guys need to stick their dicks in all the holes, not just the ones they fit in easiest?"

"What are you two talking about?" my mom asks. Sidney's still standing in the aisle, talking to some guy. I have no idea how long she's been eavesdropping.

"Nothing!" Charlene glares at me.

My mom pats her hand and winks. "It's okay, honey. You know, it's totally natural to want to experiment with anal play."

"Mom!"

She smiles and rolls her eyes like I'm a prude for not wanting my ass invaded.

"Now Sidney has a lot of package." My mother gestures to her crotch. "But that doesn't mean it's impossible. It just takes a bit more work to make it happen."

Charlene's absolutely horrified, based on how wide her eyes are. She's not going to forgive me anytime soon for this. I don't think I'm going to forgive myself, either. This is probably the last thing I ever wanted to know about my mom and her sex life with Sidney. And I know a lot. More than any daughter should, that's for sure.

"Thanks for that, Mom."

She doesn't take the hint to drop the conversation, which is likely where my censor-free gene comes from. Instead she keeps on talking, like it's a normal thing to chat about with her adult daughter and my friend. "There are some really great lubricants out there, which help a lot. Not the numbing ones, but the relaxants. Right, Charlene?"

Charlene nods and takes a giant gulp of her beer.

"Wait. There are different kinds of lube? I mean, other than the regular stuff?"

Charlene lowers her beer and shoots hate beams out of her eyes at me.

"What? I know there's stuff that's fruity, and stuff that warms up, and stuff that has silicone, and stuff that's water soluble," I say, defending my lube knowledge.

"We should go sex-toy shopping!" my mom says.

Charlene grins. It's horribly evil. "You're right, Skye. We totally should. And we can bring Sunny and Lily along. It'll be so much fun. We can do that for your bachelorette party, Vi, once you've picked a date for the wedding."

"Oooh! That's a great idea!" My mom claps.

"You've picked a date for the wedding?" Sunny asks, leaning over.

I scratch my nose with my middle finger at Charlene, who's still wearing her evil smile. I turn to Sunny. "Not yet. We're trying to figure out what works best."

This is somewhat true. Alex has thrown out a bunch of dates, all in the off-season and complete with available venues. My issue is that I want to keep it small, and our mothers want the entire world to be there.

Every venue Alex has suggested has capacity for more than

two hundred guests. I'd like it to be our immediate friends and family. That way, if I do something dumb, which is likely, there will be fewer witnesses.

Sunny's face falls. "Oh."

"It has to be off-season, of course. I think maybe next summer would be better instead of this summer. More time to plan, you know?" I say, hoping I don't sound as high-pitched to her as I do to me.

"Yeah. Of course." She gives me a small smile.

"We'll figure it out soon."

It's not that I don't want to marry Alex. I do. I can't imagine my life without him. He's sweet, romantic, alpha at all the right times, intelligent, gorgeous, and so amazing in bed. He's everything I could ever want. So why can't I settle on a date and let this happen? It's anxiety related.

We had an engagement party several months ago, before the hockey season started. I ended up with the worst case of hives ever. I took so much antihistamine I was high for two days.

After that Alex backed off, but our mothers were still all over me about it during the holidays, and I ended up with hives again. Alex has skirted the conversation since then; he's likely giving me a reprieve.

I know he's going to bring it up again soon, though, and I'm going to have to gently argue my case for next summer instead of this summer. When he proposed, he said we could have a long engagement. I don't think two years is unreasonable. It gives us adequate planning time.

Alex can be particular. He's going to want his hand in all the pies. Well, his hand only ever goes in my pie, but he'll be hands-on about this, I know. That's how he was with the engagement party. And he's going to want it to be perfect. Only the best of everything.

I'll be surprised if he doesn't end up riding in on a white horse, wearing a suit of armor like he's straight out of a fairytale. He's that romantic. Sometimes I feel like the guy in this relationship. Like, after sex, he always wants to cuddle for at least fifteen minutes. Sometimes I zonk out on him while he's talking.

The buzzer sounds, drawing my attention to the rink, and the guys take the ice with Alex facing off at center. I love watching him play. My beaver gets so drooly. And we have the best sex after games, win or lose. He's needier when they lose and more aggressive when they win. I like it both ways. I like it all ways, actually.

Alex gains control of the puck and skates toward the goalie. He passes to Darren, who easily avoids the opposition's defense. Alex and Darren have been playing together for years, so they know each other's moves. They should be predictable to their opponents by now, too, but they strategize every week, devising ways to throw off the other team and shake things up.

Darren doesn't pass to Alex right away; he plays the puck, shifting to Lance, who checks a Toronto player into the boards as he shoots the puck back to Alex. I recognize the name on the back of his jersey. It's Cockburn, the guy Alex got into a fight with last year. He was ejected from the game, and we had hot sex in the locker room.

Alex is in front of the net now, but his shot hits the post, and the goalie captures it, taking it out of play.

He gives his head a furious shake when Darren comes around to pat his shoulder. He's disappointed. I'm sure he was hoping for a quick goal to boost team morale.

The game resumes, but the first half of the period remains goal free, with several close misses for Chicago. Then Toronto scores with four minutes left in the period.

Alex isn't happy. He runs an aggressive hand through his hair while he and Darren close-talk. They're shoulder to shoulder, and Darren's calm and level while Alex isn't. My man can get agitated when he feels he's not performing well enough. He hates letting people down.

I'm so busy watching Alex and Darren, I totally miss what's happening on the ice until Lily jumps out of her seat.

She slams her fists against the plexiglas barrier. "Hell yes, babe! That's my man!"

I check out the scene: Randy's grinning widely and getting back pats, and the score's been tied. I clap and cheer, keeping an eye on Alex. He's been struggling lately with Randy's place on the team.

Alex says he's captain material. Alex might be more graceful, but he has to work a lot harder to keep up than he used to. And it's easy to talk about what he wants to do when he's done playing, but the reality is a lot tougher to take. He's getting loads of endorsements, and has a few more years with Chicago, but after that, well, there's never a guarantee they'll renew, or that he'll have many more seasons on the ice.

I think that's part of the reason he's pushing so hard for a wedding. He wants something to look forward to. He wants security and to feel settled because his hockey trajectory is changing. That's the difficult thing about hockey; it's a short career—hard on the body and the ego.

Alex pats Randy on the shoulder when they pass each other. Randy's smile is huge, as is Lily's when she turns to say something to Sunny.

The goal is great for Chicago, helping carry them through until the end of the second period. Unfortunately, Toronto manages another goal while Alex is on the ice at the beginning of the third, tying the game again.

His frustration with himself is obvious as he trades off with Randy. This time Randy doesn't score either. I'm not sure whether this is good or bad. Chicago really needs the win. With three minutes left in the game, Alex returns.

He gains control of the puck right away, flying down the ice with singular focus. He wants this so badly; it's painful to watch. He skates around the players, shifting the puck as he goes. He's so absorbed in getting close to the net, he doesn't see Cockburn coming at him from the right.

The guys were talking about him the other day. He and Lance

are fighting for the top spot in the league for number of penalties and most fights. He makes Alex look like a saint. He's also huge.

Alex sees him as he gets within shooting range, but Toronto defense is on it, blocking his shot. He passes to Darren, and switches course, skating behind the net.

That's when it happens. Cockburn hooks Alex's skate and rams him from behind, sending him head first into the boards.

The crack echoes through the arena. I'm out of my seat before Alex hits the ice. My beer slips from my fingers, and the contents splash over my legs. The roar of the crowd is deafening. Rage expands and consumes the Chicago fans, blanketing the arena in an explosive outcry. And I scream right along with them.

Darren drops his stick and skates to Alex as a ref does the same.

He's not moving.

Alex isn't moving.

And still I scream. Like I'm on fire. Like the world is ending. Like I've gone insane. I jump and grab for the edge of the plexiglas barrier that prevents me from getting to him. I'm too short. It doesn't mean I don't keep trying.

People converge on Alex like metal to a magnet until I can't see him anymore. Then Randy jumps the boards, stickless. He and Buck skate away from Alex. I don't understand why, until I follow their path to mayhem incarnate.

Lance has Cockburn on the ice, and he's beating the living shit out of him. When he brings his fist up, it's a blur of red. Vibrant splatters dot the ice. Buck catches his fist on the next upswing, and Randy grabs Lance around the waist, hauling him off. Cockburn's face is covered in blood. He might spit out teeth as he rolls to his side.

I want to feel something other than vicious gratitude for Lance's aggression, but I can't.

When Lance tries to go for Randy, Randy gets him down on the ice and holds him there with his forearm on the back of his neck. They knock helmets. It reminds me of fighting bulls with horns clashing, except it's helmets and hockey instead. All of this takes no more than a few seconds.

I'm still screaming and trying to scale the barrier when an arm clamps around my waist. "Put me down! He's not moving! I can't see him! I need him!" My words come out in a stream of nonsense through my blubbering.

"Calm down, Violet." Sidney's deep voice is loud in my ear. "Calm down. We need to go, and we can't do that if you're melting down."

"Vi, honey, we need to go now," my mom says gently, but firmly.

I stop fighting and screaming, realizing they're right. I can't get to him this way. We have to go around. I'm too panicked to do anything but take Charlene's and my mom's offered arms.

I need to get to Alex.

My stomach feels like the contents are at risk of reappearing. Sidney leads the way, and I stumble along behind him. I'm not really carrying my own weight. It's my mom and Charlene who are managing.

Sunny's terror-stricken voice comes from behind me, along with Lily's broken soothing. I crane my neck for a glimpse of anything, but I still can't see Alex. Paramedics flood the ice. Most of them go to where Alex is surrounded, but one heads for Cockburn. He's moving, so he's not the primary concern.

Sidney pulls his scout card when we reach security. The closer we get to Alex, the more frantic I am. I push free of my mom and Charlene, but one of the security guards grabs me by the arm before I can get anywhere.

"Let go of me! I'm his fiancée!" I hold up my hand with the monster diamond.

"I can't let you on the ice." His face is hard.

I pull at his hand, but he doesn't loosen his grip. His fingers are like steel. He's not hurting me, but he could, and I could hurt myself if I can't calm down.

But I'm not calm. I'm desperate and terrified. My voice is

hoarse from all the screaming. "I need to know he's okay!" Tears stream down my face, blurring my vision as I gesture toward the ice. The closest I can get is the plexiglas, so I press myself against it and watch while the paramedics stabilize Alex's neck with one of those brace things.

He's too far away. I have too many questions. I'm so scared. "Why are they doing that? Why isn't he moving?" I look to Sidney for answers, but he doesn't have any.

Sunny folds me in an embrace, and I realize she's as scared as I am. He's her brother. He's my life. And we have no idea what his injuries are or how bad it is. They lift him on to the stretcher and wheel him toward us.

"Out of the way!" the paramedic yells.

Sunny and I are pulled aside. I get the briefest glimpse of Alex. Of his ashen face. Of the laceration cutting across the bridge of his nose. The trail of smeared blood across his cheek.

All of those things terrify me, but nothing compares to the crushing fear that swallows me at his complete and utter stillness.

And then we're running. Sidney's practically carrying me as we follow the EMTs. I'm gripping Sunny's hand as we go. I'm so desperate to touch him. Be near him. Feel his chest move and make sure he's breathing. Flashing lights greet us as the doors burst open. They're ready for him, lifting the stretcher into the ambulance, Alex's limp body rocking with the movement.

"Wait!" I try to break free of Sidney's grip, but he holds on even tighter. "I'm coming in that ambulance."

One of the EMTs puts up his hands. "You need to calm down, ma'am."

"I'm his fiancée! I need to go with him!" I can't seem to take a breath, and my words are stilted.

"I'm sorry, ma'am. I can't let you go in your condition. It's not safe." He looks to Sidney, whose arms I'm clawing at, trying to get free so I can be with Alex.

Beneath my hysteria, I know he's right—that I'm likely a distraction and a hazard—but I can't stop the panic.

"I don't want him to be alone." I'm sobbing again, struggling and failing to keep myself together.

Sunny steps forward with her hand raised. "I'm his sister. Can I go?"

The EMT assesses her state. She's so much calmer. "Get in. We need to go. Now."

Sunny looks to me, as if she needs permission. I can't speak any more, so I flail a weak hand toward the ambulance.

One of the EMTs helps her up. They're already hooking Alex up to monitors. Sunny's shoulders curve in; one palm presses against her face, and the other settles on Alex's arm. It should be me in there. I can't breathe. He's my everything.

The doors close with a heavy slam, cutting off my view, and drive away with my life, sirens blaring.

It's what my heart would sound like if it could scream, too.

TOO CLOSE TO THE EDGE

VIOLET

Thankfully the crowd hasn't spilled out of the arena yet to gum up the parking lot and exits. Sidney's driving with my mom in the passenger seat. I'm in the back, sandwiched between Charlene and Lily. The ride to the hospital is painful. I feel like I'm going to barf. My whole body is numb and hyper-alert at the same time.

Buck calls my phone minutes after we pull out of the parking lot. I try to answer, but my hands are shaking too badly for me to hit the button.

"Here. Let me get it." Charlene gently pries the phone from my hands and brings it to her ear. "Hi, Miller... She's right here with me. He's in the ambulance, and we're following. Sunny's with him. Vi's having a hard time. I know... Yes... No."

"I want. To talk. To him." I hiccup through the words and hold out my hand.

"Vi wants to talk to you."

Charlene passes me the phone. I can't get the shaking under control. I think this might be what shock is. I clutch my phone with both hands and bring it close to my ear. "Buck?" It comes out as a horrible-sounding sob.

"Shh. It's okay, Vi. He's gonna be okay." His voice is cracking, though, so I don't know if I should believe him.

"He w-wasn't moving. H-he w-w-wasn't—I c-c-can't." I suck in a gasping breath. I'm losing it again, not that I had anything under control in the first place.

"He took a hit, Vi. It happens. You gotta trust he's gonna be okay. We're gonna meet you at the hospital. We're all gonna be there with you. 'Kay?"

"H-how long will you be?"

"Half an hour tops. We're right behind you."

"Do Daisy and Robbie know?"

"I talked to them. They're on the first flight out. They'll be here by morning."

I try not to think about how many hours that is, and what could happen between now and then. "'K-kay."

"He's gonna be fine, Vi."

"He has to be."

"Put Lily on for a sec."

"'K-kay."

As soon as I pass the phone to Lily, Charlene drapes an arm over my shoulder and pulls me to her side. I'm a snotting, sobbing mess. I can't stop, and it's making breathing difficult. "I'm scared."

"I know. We all are." This is what I love about my best friend. She doesn't tell me it's going to be okay when she doesn't know if that's true. She's just here for me.

I can tell Lily's on the phone with Randy by her tone. I'm crying too hard to listen. It feels like it takes forever to get to the hospital. We lose the ambulance at a red light, so I start panicking again. My mom turns in her seat and holds out her hand. I want to crawl in her lap and make her tell me it's all a bad dream, like I'm a little kid, even though I know it's not.

Sidney stops at the emergency entrance, and we pile out. I stumble-run through the doors. It's busy and bright and loud. Everything is moving too fast and too slow.

"Vi, take a breath, honey." My mom's hand is on my back.

"I just want to see him." I search for Sunny's blond hair, but there are too many people, and I can't seem to focus on any one thing.

My mom guides me to intake, which is where we find Sunny. She's not in much better shape than me.

"Did he wake up?" I ask.

Her bottom lip trembles. "He made a noise when they put in the IV, but that was it. He's had a concussion before, but he's never been out like this…"

She doesn't have to say more. We both start crying again, because we just don't know.

There are no answers, and all the questions keep piling up, burying me until I feel like I'm going to suffocate under the pressure.

With Alex's medical information already passed over, we don't have to go through the process of filling out forms. A very sweet nurse takes us to a private waiting room while Alex is assessed by a team of doctors. He'll have the very best care, but it doesn't provide much in the way of solace when none of us has any idea of how severe the damage is.

My knees feel weak, so I sink in to one of the chairs. "I don't even understand what happened. One minute he was fine and the next…what if…" I don't finish the statement. I can't think about what ifs. My mom sits beside me, and Charlene's on my other side. Sunny and Lily are huddled together across the room.

"So all he did was make a noise? He didn't open his eyes? Not even for a second? Did the ambulance attendants say anything?" I throw too many questions at Sunny, grasping for anything positive to hold on to in this nightmare of a situation.

Sunny rubs her forehead. "It was just the noise. Um, they think maybe he has a broken collarbone and possibly a dislocated shoulder. He could have a compressed spine? They're worried about fractures. And trauma to the brain. They said something about that."

None of what she says makes me feel any better. "But he was wearing a helmet. His brain should be fine. He should be fine. He has to be fine." The words spill out in stilted streams as I try to reassure myself.

"He's had injuries before." That's all Sunny says, because what else can she tell me?

I nod. The words are all stuck, and I can't seem to speak any more. I look down at my hands. They're still shaking. I straighten my engagement ring, my super-ostentatious, giant diamond gleaming in the horrible fluorescent lights. It's exactly the kind of ring I expected from Alex: excessive and beautiful and so much more than I deserve. I won't allow myself to consider what it means if he's not okay.

Twenty-five minutes later, which seems like a million years in hospital waiting time, Buck shows up in our little waiting room followed by Randy, Darren, Lance, and the coach. Their giant frames fill the room, their deep, male voices low as they ask the same questions I have.

Sunny practically falls into Buck's arms, her sobs shaking them both. He folds her into his lap and strokes her hair, all soft and sweet—so different from the stepbrother I knew less than a year ago. Randy goes to Lily, crouching in front of her, skimming her cheeks with his fingertips. Lily's like family. Alex is her brother even though they're not related, so she's almost as upset as Sunny, but she's handling things a lot better than me.

I'm surprised when Darren doesn't automatically go to Charlene. Instead he comes to me. I stand. My mouth is dry, my palms are sweaty, and when he hugs me, I almost fall apart all over again. He isn't the person I need right now, but it's better than watching all the people I love care for each other, reminding me what's at stake.

When he lets me go, Lance steps up beside him. His face is bruised, and his lip is bloody. He has a fly bandage holding a split in his eyebrow together. I glance down to where his thumbs are hooked into the pockets of his jeans. His knuckles are wrapped, but blood seeps through them, red spreading unevenly across the white.

"Have you seen a doctor? You should see a doctor."

His half-smile is distorted by the swelling on the right side of his face. "Aye, I'll be fine. It's just surface wounds."

In this moment I hear clearly the accent that's hidden most of the time.

I raise a trembling hand to his face. His eyes flare, but he doesn't move away when I press my palm to his cheek. "Thank you for fucking up Cockburn."

"It was worth the five-game suspension."

A laugh bubbles up in me, but it breaks free as a hysterical sob. Lance—the hardest of these boys, the one I know the least about, but who's clearly loyal beyond comprehension—pulls me into a hug.

"I don't understand what's going on," I mumble into his hard chest.

"He's tough. He'll make it out of this."

I'm just concerned about the condition he'll be in when he comes out the other side.

It feels like we wait forever for news. Sidney has disappeared twice to check in with a nurse. Ten minutes after he returns with no news, Darren gets up and leaves the room. I look at Charlene.

"He'll get answers," she assures me.

I don't see how he'll be able to make things happen when Sidney hasn't, but the anxiety of nothingness is the worst torture.

A nervous nurse none of us has seen before appears in the doorway with Darren behind her soon after. She looks over her shoulder, and he smiles. Now, Darren is a nice-looking guy. His features are angular, almost severe, but when he smiles, everything softens and he's stunning.

The nurse turns back to us and we wait. "Alex is responding—"

I'm out of my chair before she can finish her sentence. "He's awake? Can I see him? I need to see him."

She puts her hand up, her smile patient and practiced. I want to punch her sweet face.

"He's awake, but the doctors need to finish setting his shoulder. As soon as they're done, someone will be out to see you."

"Is his shoulder broken? Is he okay?"

"The doctor will have the results of his X-rays and his CT scan shortly."

I hate the non-answers almost as much as I hate the waiting. Darren stops her before she can walk away and murmurs something. Instead of heading back toward the emergency entrance, she takes off in the other direction.

"She's getting a doctor now," he says softly. But then that's the only way Darren ever speaks. Softly. He's deliberate with his words. He's usually more of an observer. I don't know why I'm noticing this, or why it matters.

Fifteen minutes later, a doctor comes in holding a clipboard. Alex has what he says is a "moderate to severe" concussion. He was unconscious for more than a few minutes, which is a big concern. He's also experiencing some loss of memory, the doctors call it retrograde amnesia, which is apparently not unusual for this kind of head trauma.

The phrase *head trauma* causes more tears. My mom puts her arm around my shoulder, but I'm numb, so I can't feel anything other than bubbling panic.

The doctor keeps talking. Half of it is medical jargon, but I get the important parts. He sustained no injury to his spinal cord, thank Christ. The thought of Alex having to spend the rest of his life in a wheelchair starts a whole new round of tears. I can't get a handle on myself at all. I should be embarrassed, but I can't find it in me to care that I'm such a mess.

Alex has a dislocated shoulder, a fractured collarbone, and a cracked rib. It could've been so much worse. He's lucid, but on pain medication, and he experienced confusion and some aggression when he initially came around.

"Aggression?" I ask.

"It's not uncommon after a concussion like this one. Is he usually an aggressive person?"

"No," I say.

"Sometimes," Darren says at the same time.

We look at each other.

"Not outside of hockey," I say.

Buck coughs.

"Or when it comes to me, or his sister." I wring my hands as more than one throat clears. "Okay, sometimes he's aggressive. But only when he's really, really upset." God. I sound so defensive. "He's never aggressive with me. Ever."

"Locker room," Buck mutters.

I spin to face him. "That was hot sex! I've never been afraid of him."

The room is silent apart from the doctor tapping his pen on his clipboard.

Buck sighs. "I'm not trying to be a jerk, Vi. I'm just saying, Alex has a history of aggressive behavior, and while it's generally directed at someone other than you, it's important to remember he's been concussed, and sometimes people get weird and act in ways they usually don't after something like that. Right, doc?"

The doctor's eyes shift between me and Buck, and then he nods. "Sometimes the trauma to the brain causes atypical behavior. We'll observe him closely for the next forty-eight hours and decide if we need to monitor him longer. There are additional tests scheduled for the morning."

"What kind of tests?"

"Just standard tests after this kind of injury."

I know what he's saying between those words. He wants to make sure Alex's brain is working properly, that he hasn't sustained lasting brain damage. Beyond being an amazing hockey player, Alex has a gorgeous, intelligent mind. Thinking about that part of him being affected by this is too scary.

The doctor will let us see him, but we're only allowed in two at a time, and the visits must be brief. Sunny and I go first.

"He's no longer aggressive, but he's experiencing some difficulty with memory and some confusion, so be patient with him."

If Alex can't remember me, it'll be like that Adam Sandler movie where they go on their first date over and over.

I take Sunny's hand when the doctor opens the door, because I'm relieved and terrified at the same time. He's okay, but not.

"You have visitors, Alex."

I'm unprepared when he comes into view. The lights are dim, but I can still see the damage, and that's only the obvious stuff. He has black shadows under his eyes and the bridge of his nose is stitched and taped. His arm is braced and his shoulder wrapped. I can see it under the hospital-issue gown. His eyes are tired and glassy, medication making him slow to react.

As big as he is, he looks fragile hooked up to all the monitors and beeping machines. And what's worse, he regards me with curiosity, not familiarity.

I shield my face with my hair so he can't see my fresh tears. I can still see him, though. Confusion is the strongest emotion on his face apart from pain.

"Oh, Alex," Sunny whispers brokenly.

"I look that bad, eh?" He cracks a weak smile.

"You've been prettier," she says. It's a joke, but it comes out with a stuttered sob at the end.

Neither one of us is really good at this whole keeping-it-together thing. I wish I could be stronger.

I let go of Sunny's hand and rush over to him, stopping when I reach the side of his bed, unsure where or if I should touch him. "I was so scared." I wipe away my tears, but they keep falling.

He focuses on my hand, the one with the huge rock. I don't know if he actually knows who I am, or is drawing conclusions based on deduction.

"C'mere, baby." He pats the edge of the mattress.

I sit gingerly beside him and take his hand. There's an IV needle taped to it, and it's cool and clammy. I lift it to my lips and kiss his knuckles, then rub my damp cheek on the back of his fingers.

"I love you," I tell him. "I thought—I didn't know. It was so fast, and you weren't moving, and I didn't kn-kn-know—" I can't take a deep-enough breath to get the words out.

Alex cradles my cheek in his palm. "It looks a lot worse than it is," he whispers hoarsely.

I don't believe him. The pain in his eyes and his voice are obvious.

Sunny comes to stand on the other side of the bed. Alex glances at her without moving his head. She gives him a small smile, then reaches out to brush his hair off his forehead before giving him a tentative one-armed hug. He needs a haircut. He's been putting it off for a while.

"You had us worried," she says quietly.

"I'm gonna be fine."

She nods, but she's crying, too, relief mixed with the fear now. "Mom and Dad'll be here in the morning. They're pretty shaken up."

His brow furrows and then smooths. "They know I'm okay?"

"They know you're conscious," she replies, probably because okay is subjective. Alex is breathing and conscious, but that doesn't mean he's honestly okay.

After another minute, it becomes clear that talking is taking all of Alex's energy. His blinks grow longer as he fights to keep his eyes from staying closed.

Sunny says she'll go get Darren. No one makes me leave. Instead they rotate through in pairs, ignoring the two-people rule while I sit on the bed beside Alex, holding his hand in both of mine. Each time a new person comes in; curiosity and confusion dominate his expression. But he always smiles even though it seems to take him a minute to remember who he's talking to—except for Darren and Lily. He recognizes them both almost immediately. After ten minutes, the doctor comes in to tell us Alex needs to rest.

I don't want to go anywhere, but it sounds like I'm not being given much of a choice. I'm slow to stand.

Alex grips my hand tightly. "No."

I run my fingers through his hair. It's greasy, but I don't care. He's lucid and seems to have all of his faculties. For now. We've been warned that the confusion and memory loss can persist and recur. "You need to rest."

"I'll sleep better if you're here. They'll bring in a cot for you."

I look to the doctor, who doesn't seem to think this is a good idea, based on his pinched expression.

"She's my wife. She stays."

My head whips around. Or maybe he *doesn't* have all his faculties. I'm glad the doctor can't see my face, because I'm sure it's all about the shock. Alex isn't looking at me; he's glaring at the doctor as if he's challenging him to say no to the demand, because it certainly wasn't a request.

"Either my wife stays with me, or I go home."

"I won't sign your release papers."

Alex's smile is tight, and tired. "Then I guess she's staying."

The doctor clears his throat and looks down at his clipboard. It's odd. It's not like Alex can get out of the bed and pummel him or anything. Or maybe he can.

"I'll have a nurse bring a cot and some blankets."

Alex loosens his grip on my hand, and his body relaxes. As soon as the doctor leaves the room, he closes his eyes.

I lean in, kiss him on the forehead, and whisper, "Alex, we're not married."

A small smile makes his right dimple appear briefly. "I know, but we will be, and I got my way, didn't I?"

I laugh a little. "You always get your way. I'm going to say goodbye to everyone. I'll be right back."

"'Kay." He's already half-asleep.

I'm pulled in for hugs, even by the coach. The mood is somber, tempered with cautious relief. He's okay, but *how* okay is the question.

The nurse still hasn't come with the cot by the time I return, and Alex is asleep again. I pull a chair up to the side of the bed and lay my cheek on the sheets by his hand.

I have to believe he's going to be fine. Accidents happen on the ice all the time, but usually it's bruises and aches and pains for a few days. This is so much different. It makes me aware of just how dangerous this game can be. And just how much I never want to lose this man.

I slip my hand under his, and he curls his fingers around mine. I watch his chest rise and fall, taking in the fly bandage across the bridge of his nose. I don't think it's broken again, which is good. He's got a decent bump as it is. Another break would be bad. The bruising under his eyes is getting darker, and there's some swelling.

I want to crawl into the bed with him, but he takes up almost all of it, so I stay in the chair, hold his hand, and wait for a cot. I'm emotionally and physically exhausted. Fear does that to a person. So I close my eyes and listen to the sound of Alex breathing until mine matches his.

7

PAIN
IN THE BRAIN

ALEX

E verything hurts.

My head feels like it's going to explode. My face aches, and my right arm and shoulder are screaming in agony. What the fuck happened?

"All right, I need you to wake up there. Open your eyes."

I don't know that voice.

I don't want to open my eyes. I don't want to do anything. I just want to stop feeling pain. There's so much of it. I make a noise, but that's about all I can manage.

"This'll only take a minute. I need you to open your eyes, Alex."

Alex.

Is that me? That sounds about right. It's familiar anyway.

I pry my lids open. It takes a lot of effort. My vision is blurry. The room is dark, so it must be night, but there's a light somewhere. It stings my eyes. I try to raise my arm to shield them, but there's something heavy on top of it. Heavy and wet.

"There you are. I was getting worried."

I try to turn my head toward the voice, but this makes lights explode behind my eyes. I groan.

"I need to check your heart rate and take your blood pressure."

"Wher'mai?" My mouth is too dry to manage anything else.

"You're in the hospital, dear. Do you remember what happened?"

This feels like a conversation I've had recently. I blink a few more times, clearing my vision. I search my mind for events, things, places, but everything is hazy, indistinct. Thinking makes the ache in my head worse.

A feminine moan vibrates through my hand. I glance down and notice there's a girl—no, a woman—sleeping in a chair with her head on the bed. I'm cradling her cheek in my hand. She looks familiar, unlike the woman checking my heart rate.

"I would've moved your wife to the cot, but I hated to wake her," the nurse says.

Wife?

I scour my foggy, sluggish brain for a wedding. It seems like that should be a monumental event, something I would recall, even as out of it as I am.

My *wife* rubs her face against my palm and moans, "Alex."

I slip my hand out from under her cheek, wipe the sweat on the sheets, and stroke her hair. It's soft. Waves of auburn tumble over her shoulders and across her neck.

Yes. This woman is mine.

My brain might not be online, but my body is. The agony on my right side lessens as I touch her, as if I've been dosed with morphine.

She lifts her head, lids heavy with sleep as she blinks. She swipes her hand across her mouth and licks her lips. "Alex?"

Her voice clears the haze. Memories trickle in, like the beginning of a rain shower.

A pink leopard-print bra.

A first kiss that started a quest to get her to date me; green tea lattes and cake she shouldn't have eaten because it had dairy in it; my air hockey table; me outside her apartment, begging to be let in; a public declaration; a proposal; an engagement party—loving her, being inside her, wanting her, needing her.

I may not know how I got here, or what happened to put me in the hospital, but I know I love this woman more than is probably rational. I also still have zero memory of this apparent wedding.

"Baby? Are you okay? Do you know where you are?"

"Hospital," I croak.

"Do you know how you got here?"

I go to shake my head, but those white lights burst into my vision and steal my thoughts, shattering them. I suck in a breath and groan, struggling to piece together the mosaic of fragmented memories again.

"Alex? What hurts?"

My wife puts a gentle hand on my cheek. It's warm, soft. I lift the hand that doesn't hurt to keep the contact.

"Everything."

"Can we get him something for the pain, please?" she asks the nurse, running the fingers of her free hand through my hair.

"I'll be right back," the nurse says.

"Water?" One word seems to be all I can manage.

"Of course." She disappears into the hallway, leaving us alone.

I look back up as my wife leans down and kisses my forehead. Then she dips lower and brushes her lips over mine. It's brief, but it feels like love.

"Do you remember what happened?" She sits on the edge of the bed.

"No."

"Do you know who you are?"

"Alex." I rest my hand on her thigh.

She's wearing jeans. They're tight. She's small—tiny even—but she's curvy and gorgeous. God, she's just beautiful. Perfect.

"What's your last name?"

It takes me a second to find the information. "Waters."

She threads her fingers through mine and brings them to her lips, exhaling a shuddering breath. "What do you do, Alex Waters?"

"I love you."

She smiles. It makes her even more beautiful. "And you do it very well. But I'm talking about your job. What do you do for a living, other than love me?"

I close my eyes and think. My head throbs. "I play hockey."

She releases another long breath. "That's right. You play professional hockey. You're the team captain."

"For Chicago."

"Exactly." She kisses my knuckles. "Do you know who I am?"

"Mine."

She nods, a soft smile curving her lips again. I return the grin, but it hurts my face, so it's short-lived.

"What's my name, Alex?" Her voice is so soft, I barely hear the question over the beep of the machines.

I keep my eyes on her instead of closing them. I see purple. Flowers. "Violet." A single tear drifts down her cheek. I brush it away with the back of my fingers. "Don't cry, baby. I know all the important things."

"I was scared tonight," she whispers.

"C'mere." I slip my hand behind her neck and urge her closer. She puts her head on my chest, and I hold her with the arm that works. Breathing hurts. Thinking hurts. Everything hurts.

There are still a lot of missing pieces, like what happened to put me in this kind of pain, but I'm too tired to think any more.

The nurse comes back and gives me water, which I sip. I feel sick. Then she hooks another bag up next to the IV, presses a button, and I feel nothing but warm. Violet moves away from me, and I want to protest, but my tongue isn't working.

I WAKE up sometime later confused, disoriented, and in pain. It's still night, and it takes me a good minute or two to remember who I am and where I am. Violet—my fiancée, who I said was my wife, because she will be eventually—has pulled a rolling cot up beside my bed.

Her arm is stretched out, fingers gripping the sleeve of my hospital gown. I check the clock. I don't think I've been asleep very long. The nurse keeps coming in, checking me, shining a damn light in my eyes. Last time I told her I wasn't in pain. I wish I'd lied because I sure am now.

"Violet?" It comes out as a rasp.

Her eyes pop open, and she sits up. "Alex? Are you okay?"

"Can we get the nurse?" The words slur together.

Violet strokes my hair. "You in pain?"

"Yeah."

She presses the button, not to call the nurse, but to release a dose of painkillers. I'd forgotten we don't need the nurse for that.

Violet sits on the edge of the bed, stroking my hair. It feels nice. The medication is starting to work. She presses her warm lips to my forehead. "I love you, Alex." She moves as though to get up.

I grab her wrist. "Lie with me."

She looks at the bed. There's hardly any room for her, but I don't want her away from me.

"I don't know that the nurse will like that," she says.

"Fuck the nurse."

"She's not really my type. I prefer dick, yours specifically."

I smile, even though it ramps up the pain in my face. I tug her wrist, and she swings her feet up, carefully stretching out beside me. She adjusts the covers, easing one leg over mine because there really isn't room for two bodies in this bed. She's right up against the bedrail, but at least she's not out of reach anymore.

She settles her head on my chest, and I suck in a breath as the pressure causes a sharp pain to shoot down my side.

"Are you okay? Am I hurting you? Maybe I should go back to the cot."

"No." I keep my arm around her.

"Alex."

"No."

"You're so stubborn." She eases back down, but puts her head in the crook of my arm and my shoulder, which doesn't cause pain.

I grunt because she's right. I want to tell her I already spend half my nights without her beside me, and I'm not willing to lose more, but the medication is making me groggy again, so I close my eyes instead.

The next time the nurse comes in to check on me, she gives me a look. I'm holding Violet's boob, and her hand is conveniently covering my dick. Whatever. I don't care. I have what I need right beside me.

My sleep is repeatedly broken, and I'm exhausted and in even more pain when the sun starts to come up. Every time I wake, I'm confused again, and I have to wait for some of my memories to return. At least I can remember who I am and who Violet is, but except what people have told me, I still have nothing tying me to why I'm lying in this bed.

I've taken a hit before, but the memories have always come back, even if it took a while. That I still have nothing from this one is scary. I'm aware that too many hits is bad news.

My parents stop by early in the morning. Violet's still half-asleep, curled up along my side, as they enter the room. I'm still holding her boob. I move my hand to her ribs and give a slight squeeze. She nuzzles me, and the hand tucked under her chin unfurls and smooths down my chest. I don't have an extra one available stop her from sliding her fingers under the sheets and grabbing my semi-hard junk. I'm in too much pain for a real hard-on, thankfully.

"Violet, baby, wake up. My parents are here."

Her eyes fly open, and she retracts her hand like she's been bitten by my dick. "Robbie! Daisy! Hi!" Violet pushes up to a sitting position, throwing the covers off. Which would be fine, since she's completely dressed, except that my hospital gown has ridden up during the night, and now my semi is on display.

My mom gasps and turns away.

My dad lifts his eyes to the ceiling while Violet pulls my gown down and the sheets back up, mouthing *Shit. Sorry!* at me. I'm too medicated to care, but she looks embarrassed.

Getting off the bed is more awkward for her than it should be, but she's flustered, so she's even more uncoordinated than usual. She's coordinated as hell in the bedroom, but outside of it... not so much.

"I'm so glad you're here." She hugs my dad, who squeezes her tight.

"I wish it was under less distressing circumstances, but I'm glad we're here, too." He's looking at me, his concern obvious.

My mom stands with her palm covering her mouth, and tears track streaks of black mascara down her cheeks. I must really look like hell.

She hurries over, her hands fluttering in the air around my face. "My baby! Oh, God." She looks like she wants to touch me, but she's afraid to. "That's going to leave a scar. Robbie? Will that leave a scar?" She's motioning to my face.

"I'm sure they had a plastic surgeon do that, honey. You'll hardly know it happened in a couple of years." My dad goes back to whisper-talking to Violet.

"But the wedding! We'll have to cover it."

She's been here less than a minute, and already we're on to the wedding business. I look at Violet to see her reaction, but she doesn't seem to have caught it since she's close-talking with my dad.

"They have Photoshop now, Mom, and we don't even have a date set."

"If you'd gone to the Olympics like you should've, your beautiful face wouldn't look like this."

"Daisy!" my dad snaps.

Oh, shit. The last thing I need is my parents arguing, or Violet having to listen to my mom's projected lost dreams.

Violet disengages from my dad, and her expression reflects a lot of things: concern, stress, anxiety, fear, love. "Daisy, you must be exhausted. Can I get you something from the cafeteria? Maybe you'd like to come with me?" She looks to me. "Alex, do you need anything?"

It's then that I notice her red, lacy bra hanging off the foot of the bed. I check out her chest. Oh yeah, she's braless. Her nipples are extra nipple-y.

I look down, and then back up, and back down until she notices her bra.

She snatches it from the end of the bed, hugging it to her chest. "I need to use the bathroom first!" She zips across the room and slams the door behind her. Which alerts me to the fact that I need to relieve myself. And getting there isn't going to be easy with all the shit I'm hooked up to.

"Is she okay?" my dad asks.

"Yeah. I mean, it shook her up, but she's managing okay." At least I think she is.

"Are you okay?"

"I hurt, but that's to be expected." I'm downplaying it. I have to; otherwise my mom will freak out. "Did you come straight from the airport?"

My mother nods. "We would've been here sooner if we could have." She adjusts my pillow and rearranges the sheets.

Her hair's a mess. Her face is blotchy. I'm sure she's been panicking since she saw me go down on the ice. They always watch my games, and it's usually a pleasant evening in front of the TV. I've scared a lot of people.

"I'm going to be fine, Mom."

She's about to dispute that when Violet bursts out of the bathroom, no longer braless. "Okay, Daisy, let's go get some snacks. Alex, you must be starving."

I'm too hopped up on drugs to think about food, but Violet needs to take care of me, or stay busy, so I tell her whatever she gets me will be good. She links arms with my mom and pats her hand as they leave the room.

My dad waits until they're gone before he starts with his questions. "Do you remember what happened last night?"

"Not yet, but I'm okay, Dad."

He raises an eyebrow. "Have you seen your face?"

"It can't be too much worse than when Buck broke my nose," I joke.

When he stands there, stoic, I know maybe it really is that bad.

"I need to take a leak."

He taps the rail. "You want a bedpan or the bathroom?"

"I'm not pissing in a pan."

"Bathroom it is." He drops the rail that keeps me from falling off the bed—not that I could since I haven't moved in hours—and uses the controls to get me into a mostly sitting position.

I groan as I ease my legs over the edge. I've got bruises all up my shins. There are other ones on my arms, so dark they're almost black. Every damn muscle in my body aches. My head throbs, and my vision blurs.

"You want me to get a chair?"

"I can walk."

"You sure about that, son?"

"I need to walk."

My dad sighs. He's used to my stubbornness. "Let's give it a whirl, then." He moves my IV stand over so I have something to hold.

I grab it and take a deep breath before I push up. It hurts like a motherfucker. There's no limit to the discomfort: my legs, my shoulder, my face, my ribs. Pain radiates out until all I can do is breathe around the white spots in my vision and the sharp stabbing ache that makes it impossible to move.

"Alex?" My dad puts a hand on my shoulder.

"Give me a second."

"I can get you a chair."

"I'm just stiff. I've been lying down for hours." I shuffle forward, and my stomach rolls. I've taken hits before. I've had some bruises and bumps, stitches, a couple of previous concussions—but they were nothing like this—and I've never broken anything, let alone multiple anythings.

I hold the IV tighter and take a few more cautious steps. Not having the use of one arm makes everything harder. My balance is off, and the aches are worse than I expected.

I grit my teeth and keep going. Ten feet seems like ten kilometers. My dad keeps his hand close to my elbow. Though if I drop, he's not going to be able to do a damn thing to stop me. Sweat beads my forehead and drips down my back. A trip to the bathroom has never been this difficult. I finally make it to the toilet and drop onto the seat, breathing hard.

"I'll give you some privacy and bring a chair for the trip back," my dad says.

I don't argue.

He closes the door, and I let my chin fall. Even that small

movement causes my head to swim. I'm freaked out. I've never been injured this badly. I relieve myself, but I don't think I have the energy left to get up and wash my hands. All I want to do is lie down and close my eyes.

A knock at the door reminds me I'm still sitting on the can. "Gimme a minute."

"Do you need any help in there?"

It's Violet. Fuck. "I'm good."

After a pause she says, "Okay. Your dad has a chair out here, so when you're ready I can bring it in for you."

I definitely don't want her to see me like this. "You can send my dad in with it."

"O-okay."

Muffled conversation filters through the fake-wood panel before it opens. My dad backs into the bathroom with the chair. Violet's holding the door for him, so she ends up seeing me anyway, sitting like an asshole on the fucking toilet because getting up is too difficult. She drops her eyes and turns away, her fingers going to her mouth. Then the door closes, and it's just me and my dad.

He's usually an easygoing guy—mellow, doesn't interfere much with my life and my choices—but today he seems far less passive than usual. He's frowning, hovering. There are very few things I hate more than appearing weak, mentally or physically. Right now I feel both.

I make the move to the wheelchair. My dad flushes and pushes me over to the sink, where I finally get to see my face. I look like I've been in a serious fight. With a truck. Both of my eyes are black, and the stitches across the bridge of my nose are dark with blood, making it look worse than I'm sure it is. My face is swollen, not to mention bruised along the left side of my jaw.

"It was a hard hit, Alex. It took your helmet off. We were watching the game. You can stop pretending it's not that bad."

Well, that explains the stitches and bruised jaw. I wash the one hand I can move, focusing on my fingers. "I'm pretty fucking scared."

He rests a palm on my shoulder. "You're worried about your career?"

"Yeah."

"Because of the concussion." It's a statement.

"I've never had one this bad. I keep waking up confused." One serious concussion is manageable, maybe even a couple, but after a certain point, the stakes get higher and the residual impact becomes too risky.

"We don't even know the extent of the damage yet, Alex, or the projected recovery time. Let's focus on accepting that you're not getting back on the ice next week and move forward from there."

He's right. I know this. But hearing it makes it more real than I want it to be. I have to hope for the best, which is quick healing and a fast recovery so I can get back in the game before the end of the season.

When my dad wheels me out of the bathroom, we find Violet and my mom having a whispered conversation. They're both red-eyed. Violet turns when she hears the door open and comes to me, maybe with the intention of helping, but there's nothing she can do since she can't lift me. I manage to get my own ass into bed, but I allow her and my mom to fuss over tucking me in.

I get another dose of drugs, and then I'm back to la-la land.

I SPEND the next three days in the hospital. Violet refuses to leave. Charlene and my mom bring her laptop and some files so she can work, and a change of clothes—something more comfortable than jeans.

I try to tell her she can go to work—I know she's got that

proposal to prepare—but she tells me I'm more important than work, which makes me feel good and bad at the same time.

After more than seventy-two hours of observation, the doctor gives me his verdict on Sunday morning before I'm released. Violet, my dad, and my coach are with me when he gives me the rundown. The stitches in my face are the least of my worries. The dislocated shoulder is further complicated by my fractured collarbone and broken rib. I have at least four weeks before I can start any kind of rehab on my shoulder, which was already bugging me before the hit. My rib will have to stay taped for the next three weeks.

The worst part of the discussion revolves around my concussion. I still have no recall of the events leading up to the hit, or anything that happened afterward.

The first memories that have really stayed with me since the injury are when I woke up with Violet in the hospital bed with me, and even that's hazy. They want to monitor my brain activity closely over the next several weeks, testing for residual impact, I guess. It makes me nervous.

Even if I end up progressing quickly with rehab, which is beginning to sound unlikely, I'm still looking at a good month of sitting on my ass before I can start real training. After that, it'll be another four to six weeks before I can get back on the ice. It's already mid-March. Unless we can maintain a solid winning streak, we don't have much of a chance at the playoffs this year.

Which means I'm out for the rest of the season.

With only three years left on my contract, this kind of injury could change a lot. And not in a good way.

I turned twenty-six recently. While hockey careers are short, I never imagined mine being over already. I figured I'd have at least another five years before I have to make decisions on what's next. I've been planning, but nothing immediate. I assumed Violet and I would have started a family by the time my hockey-playing days were over. We'd have a couple babies, maybe with more on the way.

I'm happy to hang out and be a dad for a few years, take some down time—by then Violet might be working from home, if at all, so we can travel and just enjoy life. Then I'll get into coaching, if that's something that feels right. Why did I make millions of dollars to keep working my ass off if I don't have to?

But that's all supposed to be later, years from now. I'm not ready to slow down yet.

I'm quiet as I listen to the doctor talk, nodding and agreeing when he sets up what will be a period of rest, followed by a fairly rigorous rehabilitative regime beginning several weeks from now. But my mind is racing, and all I can think about is how hard I worked to get here, and how one hit could take it all away.

Violet grips my hand, her throat bobbing as she swallows thickly. I squeeze back, and she looks at me. Her smile is weak and tears hang heavy on her lashes. Her fear is my own.

I hope this season is the only thing I'm going to lose.

FULL HOUSE

VIOLET

Once we know Alex is out of the proverbial woods, he gets to come home on Sunday. Robbie goes to the airport once Alex is released so he can make his meetings Monday morning. I'm not sure what those meetings entail other than talking about weed, since his job is to research and perfect medical strains of marijuana, but it seems necessary for him to be there.

Daisy stays, settling in a guest bedroom. She loves to cook, and she loves to dote on Alex, so she's totally in her element. I'm not used to Alex needing to be taken care of.

He's typically self-sufficient. If anything, it's me who gets doted on most of the time. Alex wakes up early some mornings to make me breakfast and coffee. He's the one who makes sure groceries are added to the list when we're running low. With him out of commission, that's going to fall on me. Am I a little indulged? Yup. But Alex likes it that way. And honestly, I like it, too, probably more than I should. I've never been with someone who takes care of me the way he does.

But that's not to say I can't do it when I have to. Growing up without a dad for all those years meant me and my mom had to manage on our own. We were fine. She had a good job, and I never really longed for anything. I mean, obviously I didn't get the pet pony, but if there were ever financial issues I didn't know about them. She and I worked together and got things done.

Then Sidney came along in my late teens, and our lifestyle changed significantly. We moved into a bigger house. I inherited an annoying stepbrother. Buck was only around for about six months before he was drafted, and even before then, he was always at hockey practice, "studying" in his bedroom with one of his tutors, or out with his hockey friends.

I spent my time taking extra classes and studying with my nerdy friends, or working a part-time job at an accounting firm, because even in high school I liked working with numbers.

I'm a long way from my self-reliant roots at this point, so having Daisy here as an observer to my lackluster housekeeping skills is concerning. Our relationship started out tumultuously, and while things are much better than they were, Alex will always be her baby, and I'll always be the woman who took him away from her.

Add to that the presentation for the Darcy account, and I'm pretty sure I'm going to have some kind of breakdown soon. Mr. Stroker is obviously giving me some leniency, and we're postponing the meeting until the end of the week. I hope by then Alex is settled and things are less insane.

Anyway, the presentation is good to go. I uploaded it to the shared account at work so Charlene could review it, and I sent it to Stroker, who gave it the thumbs up, apart from minor tweaks. However, despite being ready, I'm still in no state to present a multimillion-dollar portfolio. As important as this job might be, I need to be home with Alex. And I need sleep and a seriously long shower.

Once we're in the house, Daisy decides we need groceries, which is true. I haven't been home at all since the game four days ago, so our leftovers are less than fresh, and the vegetables are wilty according to Daisy's standards. She helps herself to the keys to my car, and off she goes.

I'll take private time with Alex since I haven't had any for the past few days. A nurse or doctor seemed to be constantly popping by the room to check on him, which made for more than one almost-embarrassing moments.

The hit Alex took scares me more than I let on—or at least more than I've let on since my initial freakout when it happened. I'm afraid not just because he got hurt, but because there's no guarantee that was the last time. If he gets injured that badly again, his career is done, and I don't know how well Alex will handle that.

More than that, I can't stop worrying about how different things could be if his injuries were more severe—and they're already pretty damn bad. He might have amazing medical coverage and lots of money, but life can change in an instant with a head injury. What if Alex wasn't Alex anymore after this? I try not to think about it as I climb the stairs to our bedroom. I want to cheer him up, be a comfort not a burden.

I haven't been alone with him since the morning of the game. I worry that our disagreement over my continued commitment to my job may indirectly contribute to his on-ice stress.

Guilt is my biggest enemy right now. And it's making me want to eat a lot of dairy, which is a seriously bad idea. I hope being at home will make Alex feel more normal. And me. He's been quiet ever since he got the news that he's out for the rest of the season. I'm nervous about how he's going to manage that information once it sinks in fully.

For all these reasons, and probably a few more, I'm not expecting anything beave-tastic when I get to the bedroom. Alex tires easily, and he's still in pain, partly because they're weaning him off the super-awesome pain meds. He still has the extra potent Tylenol and a prescription anti-inflammatory, but it's got nothing on what they were shooting into him while he was hooked up to the machines.

When I enter the room, Alex is lying sideways on the bed, staring at the ceiling.

"Can I run you a bath?"

His eyes flip to mine. "You gonna join me?"

"If you want me to."

His gaze drifts down my body and back up. "That'd be nice. My mom usually takes a long time when she gets groceries."

"Oh, really?"

"Really."

"I'll set up the tub, then?"

"Sounds good."

I try, again, to tell my beaver to calm down. Alex is in no condition for a monster cock ride, but the drooling has already commenced. She's like Pavlov's dog; any potential MC contact gets her all excited.

I run the water, throwing in some Epsom salts to help manage the aches. When the tub is half full, I strip out of my clothes and return to the bedroom to get Alex.

His eyes are closed. At first I think he's just resting, but then I note his chest rising and falling evenly. The physical and mental toll this is taking on him is unfathomable. I return to the bathroom and turn the water off so the tub doesn't overflow. Then I pad across the floor, shivering as I climb into bed with him. I pull the covers over me and snuggle up to his side.

Neither of us slept particularly well in the hospital, and I'm happy to be back in our king bed with our nice sheets and my favorite pillow. I don't close my eyes; I just watch him, grateful that he's okay enough to be lying next to me.

It's in this moment that I realize the only future I want is one with him in it. My fears about doing something stupid at our wedding can be managed. This job I cling to isn't nearly as important as he is. Nothing is. And that's a scary thing to come to terms with, because all of this could have gone so much differently.

I could've lost him.

I decide that the next time the wedding is mentioned, we'll pick a date. And we can start to plan. I don't want my fear getting in the way of my future.

EVENTUALLY I MUST STOP STARING at Alex's profile and fall asleep, because I have nightmares about the trip to the hospital. I'm running, but I can never seem to get close enough to touch him, and all my screams are silent.

I'm woken by gentle shaking. "Violet, honey?"

I pry my eyes open. Light pours in through a slight gap in the curtains. Alex is lying beside me, lines creasing his forehead, jaw clenched. His tension never leaves him, even in sleep.

I roll over to find Daisy smiling sadly at me. "I think you were having a bad dream."

My face feels damp. I lift a hand and skim my cheek. It's wet.

"Would you like me to let you go back to sleep?" She sweeps wet hairs away from my face. "I know you must be exhausted."

I check the clock. It's four in the afternoon. Even though I'm not going to work tomorrow, if I keep sleeping, I'll be up all night.

I shake my head and crawl out from under the covers. Daisy's eyes go wide. Which is when I remember I got into bed naked. I scramble to pull the covers back over me.

"I'll meet you downstairs." Poor Daisy's cheeks are red as she scurries out of the room, closing the door behind her.

Shit. I flashed my mother-in-law. She saw my naked beaver. I'm embarrassed, but it's not really all that huge a surprise, considering my propensity for self-humiliation. I'm careful not to jostle Alex as I get up again, creep over to my dresser, and throw on some leggings, a sports bra, and a sweatshirt.

When I get downstairs, Daisy's in the kitchen, busy chopping fresh vegetables. She's found the only apron I own, which features a picture of Alex's hot body in a pair of boxers. I wonder if she knows she's wearing her son's torso.

She looks up from the head of broccoli she's started on and gives me a bright smile, like I didn't flash her my beaver moments ago. "We'll let Alex sleep until dinner?"

"Sure." I stand in the middle of Alex's kitchen, which is also my kitchen, at a loss. "Can I help?"

"I bought a few bottles of wine. The whites are in the fridge. Why don't you pick one and pour us each a glass?"

"Okay." I open the fridge and find Daisy's stocked us with serious groceries. It's loaded with fresh fruit and vegetables and the wholegrain bread Alex likes—the stuff with all the seeds and nuts in it, like someone dumped in a box of granola and messed up perfectly good food. Daisy's also picked up a loaf of enriched white Wonder bread and a brick of lactose-free cheese. For me. Three bottles of white wine line the middle shelf, all my favorites.

I'm overwhelmed with emotion. Which has kind of been the way of things for the past few days. Daisy always tries to be helpful. And she also likes to be heavily involved in her children's lives, which sometimes means she gets a little meddle-y. But that doesn't seem to be her intent.

Her ability to keep it together makes me worry about exactly how fail I'll probably be as a wife. I can't cook—at least not good food. Sure, I can manage Kraft mac 'n' cheese or putting a pizza in the oven, but other than opening a can or heating something from the freezer, I'm fairly unskilled.

I couldn't even hack Christmas dinner, and that's just turkey and potatoes and some veggies. Or at least that's what I thought. Turns out it's a huge production. Daisy was here to help me manage that. In actuality, she usurped my kitchen, and I was mostly a bystander, taking orders.

I don't even have to clean this house. Not that I'd want to clean four thousand square feet of living space, but I can leave my underwear in a pile in the middle of our bedroom, and they'll disappear once a week and reappear, clean, in my drawer every Friday.

But I can give a mean blow job. And I have a great rack. So there's that.

I can't decide whether I feel grateful or useless. I decide it's probably a combination of the two. Stupid tears fall as I take the Niagara Riesling out of the fridge and retrieve two glasses. I choke back an annoying sob.

Daisy sets down her chopping knife. "Violet? Are you okay?"

I wave the bottle and the glasses around in the air and nearly hit myself in the face. "I'm fine." It comes out all high-pitched and unconvincing.

She takes the bottle and the glasses, likely so I don't maim one of us with them, and places them gently on the counter. Then she pulls me into a hug. I turn my head in time to avoid her helmet of hair and rest my cheek on her shoulder pad.

She pats my back while I cry. I'm such a mess. "I don't know what's wrong with me," I sniffle.

"It's been a difficult few days."

I nod into her shoulder. It makes a crinkly sound. It feels like it's filled with foam.

"He's going to be okay now, though. He's a strong man. He'll get through this. And you'll be here to help him."

"It's going to be so hard for him." I pull back and wipe my nose on my sleeve, leaving behind a disgusting snail trail. "Not playing for the rest of the season? I don't know how he's going to deal with it. Hockey is his world."

"Alex has always been an intense person." She smooths her hands over my hair. "When he's passionate about something, he puts all of his energy into it—and that's not limited to his career.

He's a very driven man, and sometimes he has difficulty with moderation. When he's in, he's all in; he'll bury himself in something so he can be the best. It's what he's been doing for the past six years with hockey, and before that he was just as involved in school and figure skating."

"I can see that."

"And now that's how he is with you as well." Her voice is soft, and so is her expression.

"He loves hard." And for once I don't mean it in a pervy way.

"He does everything hard." I'm almost certain Daisy doesn't mean that in a pervy way either.

I also don't think Alex will be doing *anything* hard right now. I'm not even sure he can get hard. Well, okay, he can get hard. I saw him sporting a semi a few times in the hospital, but I don't know that he has the energy to do anything with it.

"Sitting around isn't going to be easy for him. He gets pent-up a lot."

Daisy seems to miss my accidental inappropriate reference.

"He'll find a way to manage himself, I'm sure," she says.

I doubt he'll achieve that by whacking off constantly, but that's where my mind goes, maybe because I haven't had an orgasm in days, and now that we're home I can. Not now, but later. When everyone else is sleeping, I can get out Buddy and give myself a little beaver bang. I stifle a laugh through the sniffles, so it sounds snort-cryish.

"I can stay as long as you need me, of course."

"Thanks, Daisy. I know how much Alex loves your cooking."

"I could teach you how to make some of Alex's favorites while I'm here, if you want," she offers.

"You'd do that?"

Her electric pink lips spread until her dimples appear. "Of course! He loves breakfast for dinner, so I thought we could make omelets tonight."

So that's what we do. When dinner's almost ready, I go

upstairs and wake Alex. It takes some coaxing to get him out of bed. He's sore and grumpy, but when I tell him what we're having for dinner, he gets up. Getting down the stairs is slow.

Daisy serves him like he's the king of the world, and he shovels in food, groaning his pleasure. The sound is reminiscent of his orgasm moan. Or maybe I'm horny.

Except then I look at him, and all the buzzing in my beaver stops. Alex is eating like a pig. His mouth is two inches from his plate, and he keeps jamming more food in before he even has a chance to swallow. He's also eating with his left hand instead of his right, so bits of egg have fallen off his plate and onto the table.

"This is so much better than hospital crap. Thanks, Mom," he says around a mouthful of omelet.

"Violet helped." Daisy sits primly at the table with her napkin in her lap. She has amazing manners. My legs are crossed like I'm sitting on a yoga mat. I rearrange them so I'm sitting nicely, even though they're visible to no one.

Alex stops with his fork halfway to his mouth. "Really?"

I focus on my plate. I shouldn't be hurt by his surprise. Usually I take something out of the freezer and follow the directions Alex's personal chef has left us. He shows up every Monday to make a week's worth of meals when Alex isn't on the road.

Daisy pats my hand. "She did a great job. She even made her own omelet."

Alex looks at my mangled, misshapen omelet, and then back at what's left of his own perfect one, which his mother made. "That's awesome."

"Thanks," I say. I need to stop being so sensitive. Daisy's just here to help, not show Alex I'm poor wife material.

When the guys are on the road, Charlene and I do takeout half the time. The other half we eat ramen noodles like we did in college, or Kraft mac 'n' cheese, and occasionally, when Charlene is feeling particularly ambitious, she makes shepherd's pie—but with those fake potatoes, because mashing real ones takes work. Hopefully Daisy can teach me how to make something even better than that.

Eating takes all of Alex's energy. So as soon as dinner is over, he goes back upstairs. I plan to help Daisy with dishes. She insists on washing most of them even though we have a dishwasher, which I usually load to capacity and often forget to run. The housekeeper takes care of it when I don't. Daisy seems more than happy to wash them by hand.

I reach for a dish towel to dry, but she puts her hand on my arm.

"I can take care of this. I'll be fine for the rest of the evening. Why don't you go up and see if Alex needs you."

"Are you sure?"

"Of course, sweetheart."

"Thanks, Daisy." I kiss her on the cheek, because it feels right.

Her smile pops a dimple. She pats my cheek and turns back to the dishes, humming as she pulls on a pair of yellow gloves and dunks her hands in the soapy water.

Alex is struggling with his hoodie when I get upstairs, swearing under his breath. I close the door with a quiet click and turn the lock.

"Need some help?"

"I should be able to undress my damn self." He's managed to get one arm out, but he can't get it over his head.

I walk to the bed and pat the mattress. "Come sit, baby."

He huffs, but does as I ask. I tap his knees, and he parts them so I can get in between. I unsnap his sling and ease the collar over his head, careful of the stitches and bruises on his face. The bruising on his injured arm is mottled and so purple it's almost black in some areas.

I skim the side of his neck. "Do you want that bath now?"

Alex looks up, his gaze stopping briefly at my chest before meeting my eyes. "That'd be nice."

"Do you want me to join you?"

"Please."

"Okay, let me warm the water."

"'Kay. I won't fall asleep this time."

I lean down and kiss him softly. "I'll be right back."

I run to the bathroom and check the water temperature. It's barely tepid. I drain the tub and start over, dumping in new Epsom salts and lavender, since it's calming.

I strip out of my clothes, toss them in the hamper, freshen up my beaver real quick, and peek around the jamb.

Alex is lying down again. But his entire body isn't on the bed, which is a good sign. I hope. His feet are still planted on the floor, the upper half of his body prone on the mattress. When I approach, his eyes open, and he slowly turns his head.

He groans. It sounds like a word, but I can't be sure.

"Do you need some Tylenol? Or an anti-inflammatory?"

"No. Not the kind of anti-inflammatory you get in a pill, anyway."

I round the bed and realize my anxiety is unnecessary. Alex's sweats are tented at the waist. I smile, glad my boobs have their desired effect. "Lift your bum," I order.

Alex cocks a brow, but does what I ask. I hook my fingers on either side and pull the waistband down. Super MC pops out. He's massive. And his purple head peeks out of the turtleneck. "Looks like someone needs some attention."

He nods somberly.

Alex has an intense sex drive. It's been several days since he's had any relief. I skim the slit with my fingertip; it comes away wet.

He moans. I'd go ahead and lick my finger, because I'm sure it'd drive him crazy, but he hasn't had a bath or a shower since he went into the hospital other than me sponging him down. I'm not all that interested in knowing what his dirty dick pre-cum tastes like.

Later, after it's been soaped up, I'm all for loving on it with whatever he wants me to. I'm not sure sex will be on the table, considering all his broken parts, but a beaver can dream.

"Come on, let's get you cleaned up so I can do naughty things to your dick."

I don't have to ask twice. Alex sits up with a wince. He has to take a few shallow breaths before he can do anything else. I gently run my hands over his thick shoulders, careful to avoid the bruises on the right one. Alex is built. I've never really been into the alpha guy. Before him, I always dated guys who focused more on intellectual pursuits than physical fitness. Being with Alex means I get both.

My boobs are right in his face, which was the whole point of getting in close. He only has the use of one hand, and his face is beat up, so he turns his head and presses his cheek against one boob while he kisses the swell of the other. He closes his eyes and sighs. I let him do the nuzzle thing for another minute, until his breathing is as regular as it's going to get. He's also started kneading my ass.

"I'm ready to be your naked nurse, if you're ready for bath time."

9

SPONGE BATHS

ALEX

I don't care how much my shoulder aches, my balls ache more. I could probably take care of the situation on my own, but I don't want to. I want Violet to take care of things for me. And she's so naked. So perfectly, gorgeously naked.

She holds out a hand, and I take it. It still hurts to move, but I shuffle along behind her, watching her ass jiggle. Except it's not quite as jiggly as it used to be. I let go of her hand and grab her ass. It's definitely firmed up in the past few months.

She squeals and holds her bum. "What are you doing?"

"You been working out?"

"Sunny's been making me do yoga when you guys are away. It's a lot harder than I thought it would be. It's not all humming and saying *Namaste* and pretending to be a tree."

"Is that right?" My sister's a yoga instructor, among other things. "Well, your ass is looking good."

"Don't get any ideas about my ass."

"I was just noticing it looked good. That doesn't mean I want to violate it."

"Liar." She holds her bum cheeks.

She's right. I'm lying. I've never cared about ass sex until I started dating Violet and she made it clear it would be off-limits forever. She calls her ass Area 51. So now I've taken to joking about getting in there, except I'm not always joking anymore. I'm sure she can sense my infatuation.

But it's not like she has anything to worry about. I barely have the energy to get my ass to the bathroom, let alone try anything on hers. Especially anything like that.

I sit down on the edge of the tub and lift one leg over, then the other. Not having use of one arm makes it tough to stay balanced, and I'm banged up enough as it is. I don't need additional broken parts.

Violet waits until I'm settled in the tub. It's deep, so only the tip of my erection floats above the water. She sits on the edge, facing me, and lifts one leg over. I get an awesome view of her pussy. It's too far away for me to touch, which is completely unacceptable.

I'm so fucking mopey, I'm annoying myself.

She dips a toe in, testing to see if it's too hot. Violet has sensitive skin when it comes to hot things, and sometimes my jizz. We've decided suicide wings could be the culprit. She lowers a leg in.

I crook a finger. "Come closer."

She scooches forward until I can reach her ankle. "Is this good?"

I run my hand up the back of her leg to her knee. "Almost."

Her skin makes that wet, rubbery sound when she slides up a little more. I leave a wet trail as I ease my hand along the inside of her thigh.

She watches my fingers move higher. "What're you doing, Alex?"

I lick my lips, focused on the place I haven't been in several days. "What does it look like I'm doing?"

She covers herself with a palm. "I'm supposed to be taking care of you, not the other way around."

"Have you had an orgasm in the past three days?"

"No."

"So I should give you one."

"Or I could do it," she suggests shyly.

When Violet and I are getting it on, I'm usually the one taking care of things for her. I like being the one to give her orgasms, and she doesn't seem to have a problem with me taking control in that department. She's rather vocal about how much she enjoys what I can do for and to her. It's great for my ego.

But when it comes to touching herself, she gets stage fright. It's cute. And sexy. Until she's in the moment, she's a little reserved about the whole thing, especially if I'm watching. We're working on it. Well, I'm working on it.

I figure I'm in a good bargaining position. I've had a shitty few days. So has she. I'm not sure I can manage actual sex. I'd like to, but every part of my body hurts. So I'm going to use all my leverage to help Violet get more comfortable with me watching her, and then I'm hoping she'll want to give me a hand in making at least one ache go away.

"Why don't I get you started?" I offer, walking my fingers up the inside of her thigh.

She scoots closer, like maybe she's on board with that idea. When I get close to her pussy, she moves her hand aside. I would love to bury my face in there, but my jaw is killing me, so that's out.

I brush my fingers back and forth over her soft, smooth skin. Her clit is already peeking out, so she whimpers at the contact.

"Does that feel good, baby?" I keep up the tender touch. It drives her crazy, and makes her insanely wet.

"So good," she whispers.

"You miss me?"

Her eyes lift from where I'm touching her. "So much."

There's more in the weight of those words than need. There's fear.

I get it. I share it. But as far as Violet should be concerned, I'm on the road to recovery. My fears go deeper. There's a lot more at stake now than bruises and a cracked rib.

I push those thoughts aside, because they take me out of this moment, which I need more than anything else. This I can control: Violet's response to me, what I do to her, how I make her feel. I circle her clit with a knuckle, slow, teasing. She doesn't push me to go faster, just holds on to the edge of the tub to keep steady and spreads her legs farther apart.

When she starts to shift her hips, I go lower and ease a single finger inside. Violet moans my name, and it echoes off the tile. She clamps a hand over her mouth to stifle the sound.

It makes me feel like a teenager again. Except as a teenager I didn't have to make girls be quiet, because I didn't actually get much of an opportunity to date.

"Did you lock the bedroom door?" I brush the pad of my thumb over her clit.

She sucks in a breath. "I think so."

"Want me to stop so you can check?" I'm about to withdraw my fingers, but Violet covers my hand with hers.

"Your mom's washing dishes; she'll be a while, right?"

"Yeah, probably."

"I can be quiet." Violet's eyes roll up when I curl my finger, and her teeth press into her lip so hard she turns the skin white.

"You sure about that?"

She grips the edge of the tub and reaches out with her foot, her toe catching the door. It closes with a quiet click.

"Okay, we should be good." She skims my wrist with tentative fingertips, and moans softly when I add a second finger on the next slow thrust.

I'm so hard. The head of my cock is visible, water lapping at it. If I had a free hand I'd stroke it. But that one isn't working too well, so it'll have to wait.

The next finger flutter makes Violet cry out. I'm still rubbing her clit with my thumb, and it's not the easiest thing to do.

"You can help me out if you want." My voice is all gravel.

Violet's eyes roll back down, and she gives me a demure smile. "I love helping you out."

The hand that's been resting on the base of her throat starts the descent. She pauses at her right boob. Biting her lip, she glances at me, and then down at her perky nipple. It's hard, because she's excited. She circles it with a manicured nail. It's painted red, with a tiny little team logo, and my number is on the next one. A few chips mar the edges, she hasn't had time to get them redone, because of me being in the hospital.

She gives her boob a squeeze and pinches her nipple, glancing up at me and then away just as quickly. She continues over her stomach until she reaches the crest of her pelvis. Then she slides two fingers between her wet, swollen lips, capturing her clit. Watching Violet touch herself is the only thing I like better than doing it myself.

She's tentative at first, as expected, but as she gets more comfortable, she makes tight, aggressive circles, rubbing faster and harder than I do. I add a third finger, in case there's a possibility I can provide another kind of relief after she comes. The hot water is easing some of my aches, as is getting Violet off on my fingers and hers.

Her moans get louder and more frequent. Then the chanting starts; this time it's a low *fuck me* on repeat. "Oh, shit, Alex." Her mouth drops open as ecstasy crosses her perfectly stunning face. She comes all over my hand.

I wait until her shoulders sag before I ease out. Then I lick my finger.

"Oh, God."

"It's as close as I'm getting to eating you until my jaw heals, so at least I get a taste."

"When you're ready, I'm happy to sit on your face."

"I'll be taking you up on that offer really damn soon." Violet shivers, and I extend a hand. "Get in with me."

She glances at the head of my cock, bobbing under the water, and back up at me. "Where should I go?"

"I'll move over. You can straddle me."

"Your legs don't hurt? You've got some bad bruises." She runs her thumb back and forth over my knuckles.

"Just be gentle with me." I wink, even though I'm kind of serious.

Violet holds on to the towel bar and sets her foot beside my hip. The slip guard isn't in the tub, though, so she doesn't have traction. I put my good hand out, afraid she's going to topple over, but she manages to stay steady. We both breathe a sigh of relief. She's extra careful as she settles her weight on my thighs. It doesn't feel too bad, probably because she's sitting close to my cock, and I know I'm going to be touched by some part of her soon.

She leans forward, bracing a hand on either side of my head and kisses me. "Thank you for taking care of me. Can I take care of you now?"

I cup her cheek and trace her bottom lip. "Please."

"Such good Canadian manners." She kisses me again, slipping her tongue inside my mouth as she rubs up against my cock. Maybe I can deal with sex. I want it. Her. I want *in* her.

She moans, and I know she can taste herself. Eventually she breaks the kiss and sits back. She doesn't rest much of her weight on my legs, which is good, because she's right, there are a shit-load of bruises.

Violet grips the base of my cock and runs her fingertip across the slit at the tip, over and over, around and around. I groan. The touch is too soft. My cock kicks in her palm. I wrap my good hand around hers and tighten her grip, guiding her strokes.

"You need to come so bad, don't you?" she whispers in the voice that makes me want to take her back to the locker room and repeat that entire event, minus us getting caught at the end.

"I really fucking do."

"Do you want me to use my hand, or do you think it would be okay…" She trails off, uncertain.

"If you take it easy, we can def—" I don't even get to finish the sentence before she rises. She rubs my cock over her clit and goes lower until the head disappears inside her.

"Oh, fuck."

"Don't worry, I don't expect you to last long."

I grip her thigh and close my eyes as she sinks down, hot water replaced by even hotter skin. "That's good, because I won't."

As soon as I'm inside her, I want to start thrusting, but that's not a great plan, unless I want to hurt worse than I already do. Violet holds the edge of the tub with one hand and the towel bar with the other as she starts to roll her hips. It feels fucking amazing. I reach up and fondle her boob.

She does all the work, because I really can't help out much other than holding her tit. She doesn't seem to mind. She keeps moving over me, slow and easy. Eventually she leans in and braces her weight behind me. Her nipples graze my chest.

"I really needed you like this." Her lips touch mine.

"Me too, baby."

"I was afraid I was going to lose you," she says softly, her voice cracking.

I run my fingers through the hair at the nape of her neck, smoothing my thumb along the ridges of her spine. "I'm right here."

"Don't scare me like that again." She kisses me, not letting me answer, which is good, because that's not a promise I can make or likely keep.

Her kisses are as soft and slow as the way she's loving me. I'm so close. I don't think it's even been three minutes. "Violet…"

"I love you." Her nose brushes mine.

I tighten my grip on the back of her neck, kissing her as I groan her name. I try not to tense up, but it's impossible with the way the orgasm punches me in the spine. It actually feels like it's punching me in my cracked rib, but I block out the pain so I can focus, as least for a few seconds, on the pleasure.

Violet doesn't come again, which I don't like, but I also don't have the ability to control that right now. She doesn't move when I'm done. Instead she smooths her fingers through my hair and kisses me with the same languor we made love with. Or that she made love to me with, because I sure didn't do a whole hell of a lot. Still, even that exertion has wiped me out. I don't particularly like that either.

"I should probably wash you, eh?" she asks after a while.

"I can do that myself." I stroke up and down her side, intentionally grazing her boob with each pass.

"Where's the fun in that?" She doesn't get off me. Instead she grabs her body poof, squirts my body wash on it, and starts at my neck, working her way down my arms and chest. While it sucks to feel like shit, and I'm not a fan of being incompetent, it's nice to have her take care of me like this.

When she's done with my upper body, she lifts off. I've gone soft, but I'm still disappointed. Usually I'd be able to get hard again by now and go for round two, but my dick is slower to recover than usual, like the rest of me. At least the water is still warm, so there's no cold shock.

"Give me a sec." She gets out of the tub and towels off. Grabbing the red robe with my number on the back from the hook, she puts it on and ties it loosely at the waist. Violet owns a lot of red clothes now. And she looks amazing in them.

She kneels on the mat beside the tub. Her nose wrinkles, and then she smiles. "You do realize you're bathing in your own jizz, right?"

I laugh and then cough-groan at the sharp jab in my side. "Thanks for pointing that out."

"Apparently it's a great moisturizer." Violet takes care of the bottom half of my body, paying lots of attention to my dick, which eventually makes me hard all over again. It's a relief that I haven't lost the ability to do that, too. She takes care of it with her hands this time. When I warn her I'm about to come, she doesn't grab the washcloth. Instead she covers the head with her mouth and swallows.

I love her so fucking much. For so many reasons.

10

CONTENTS UNDER PRESSURE

VIOLET

The week following Alex's accident is comprised mostly of doctor's appointments, learning how to cook new things with Daisy, periodic short visits from friends, frequent appearances by Sunny, lots of fruit baskets and get well cards, and sadly infrequent and very gentle sex.

I don't go in to work, doing what I can from home when Alex is napping. Which is often. In the year we've been together, I've never seen him so drained of energy and motivation. Not being able to do anything isn't good for his psychological wellbeing.

Surprisingly, Daisy's presence in the house isn't a total nightmare. Apart from the overwhelming smell of hairspray, she's mostly pleasant to have around. Sure, it's a challenge to have another woman encroaching on my territory, especially one who's so good at the domesticated shit, but I've learned a few new things, so that's a plus.

My mom has never really been all that awesome at that part. She was always fun, but we ate a lot of fast food when I was young. It wasn't until Sidney came into the picture that my mom took an active interest in eating things that didn't come from the frozen section of the grocery store.

As Alex starts to feel better, Daisy takes the opportunity to go out for lunch and manicures with my mom. Those two get along disturbingly well. What blows my mind entirely is the fact that neither of them has mentioned anything about the wedding, or lack-thereof.

I'm just waiting for the right time to bring it up with Alex. I've almost mentioned it more than once, but I held off because I don't want him to think it's because of the accident. Because it isn't. Not directly, anyway.

At the end of the week, after a long conversation with Alex in which I express my guilt and he assures me he's more than okay enough for me to leave him for a few hours, I decide to go to work on Friday. It's been a week and a half since the accident. We rescheduled the Darcy presentation, and they offered to postpone it again, but I don't want it hanging over my head, dividing my attention, which should be on Alex.

Plus I need to get out of the house and Daisy can be overwhelming with how much fussing she does over Alex. He's a grown-ass man, not a baby.

I stop to get Charlene on the way. With her picking up my slack at work, me managing Alex, and Daisy being here, we haven't had a lot of time to talk. We've mostly been reduced to brief conversations and texts in which I tell her I'm fine, even though I'm not.

Charlene hops in and gives me a side-hug. "How are you? Can I tell you how much less exciting work has been without you there?"

"Jimmy and Dean not keeping you entertained?" I pull away from the curb.

"Jimmy and Dean are obnoxious and bored without you."

"That's because you don't do and say half the stupid shit I do."

"I miss our ridiculousness," Charlene says.

"Me, too." Charlene is the one person I miss seeing every day at work.

The closer we get to Stroker and Cobb, the more anxious I become. Working from home has been nice—nicer than I expected. I'm highly conflicted over going in today, and not just because of the guilt.

Alex is actually doing surprisingly well physically. Mentally and emotionally, it's a different story. He's been obsessively watching the games he's missing, replaying every goal, most of which are being scored by Randy. The team won the past two games, which should be good, but it worries me, because it probably worries Alex. Being away from him worries me.

"Are you okay?" Charlene asks.

"I'm fine." I avoid looking directly at her. I have makeup on today, including mascara, which I'm not sure is waterproof, and the buildup of emotions threatens to overwhelm me. Maybe I need to get a part-time job at Hot Topic so I can immerse myself in the emo that's become my life.

"Violet? How are you, really? I know this hasn't been easy on you. You can talk to me. "

"Can we do the serious stuff later? After the Darcy presentation is done and I don't feel like I'm going to hurl?"

"Okay. Sure. How are you feeling about that? Other than barfy?"

"Good, I guess. I mean, I'm as prepared as I'm going to get. Can you open the glove compartment?"

She hits the button and a bag of Swedish Fish falls into her lap.

"Thank God!" I nab the bag and tear it open with my teeth.

"You're going to eat those now?"

"I need something to calm my stomach."

"So you're going with sugar and caffeine?" she asks as I pull into the Starbucks drive-thru.

"And gelatin. Don't forget the gelatin." I tip my head back and dump a few fish into my mouth, savoring the artificial fruit flavor. Of course, this is the exact moment the car in front of me moves forward and I'm due at the speaker. "Whaddya want?" I ask through a mouthful of candy.

Charlene orders a latte and some healthy egg-white crap while I chew furiously. I swallow in time to secure my own caffeine fix, adding one of those fudge squares and a cake pop.

"Wow. You're really aiming for gut rot today," Charlene says. "We're going out for lunch, the two of us, and we're going to talk about how you're managing. We haven't had any girl time in almost two weeks."

"It's been busy what with Alex being broken."

Charlene purses her lips, but doesn't say anything as I stuff another handful of fish into my mouth.

I'm slick about hiding candy from Alex. Otherwise he eats it and feels guilty. The man burns five thousand calories a day, but during the season he has the most boring diet in the world. He's ultra-healthy. Healthier than Sunny even, and that's saying something since she doesn't eat anything animal-related. I'd be so sad if I had to give up cow and pig.

My secondary candy stash is in my "office" in the house. Alex had one of the six bedrooms converted after I moved in. I don't do much in the way of work in there—until the last week anyway. Before that it was where I keep all the stuff I don't know what to do with, and my sewing supplies so I can make costumes for Alex's Super MC.

Once we have our coffees, Charlene's normal breakfast, and my sugar fest, we get back on the road.

"Other than Jimmy and Dean being pains in the ass, has work been okay?" I ask.

"It's been the usual."

"What about Darren? You see much of him?" I feel like such a bad friend, although I think I've probably had a solid reason to not be as engaged with the rest of my life recently.

Charlene slips her fingers under the scarf thing she's taken to wearing and finds the pearls underneath. "We saw each other right before the away games, and I'll see him tonight. He's missing Alex. The whole team is."

"Yeah. It bugs Alex that he can't be with them."

The team's been on the West Coast most of the week. They came back late last night. Alex and Darren text each other and talk on the phone when they can, but they haven't seen each other since he got out of the hospital since the team has been away.

"Brunch tomorrow should be good for their bromance."

"Yup. Daisy has the most elaborate menu set up. She's been to the grocery store every day this week. It's crazy."

"I don't know how she has time with all the hair styling she has to do," Charlene jokes.

"Seriously. It's so big. So hard. And not in a well-endowed-dick kind of way. I thought maybe when she and my mom went to the spa she might've come back with a new hairstyle, but no such luck."

"That's too bad."

"Yeah. She goes through an insane amount of hairspray. I've found three aerosol cans in the garbage. I think either she should buy stock or we should stage an intervention."

"That's an awesome idea."

"Buying hairspray stock?" I scoop up another handful of fish.

"No, the intervention. You should get rid of her hairspray."

"She'll go buy more."

"Not if you do it in the middle of the night. Then you can save the day by offering to style her hair for her."

I pause with a handful of fish halfway to my mouth. "Oh my

God. That's brilliant. I can't believe I haven't thought of it before."

"You don't want her to have that hair for your wedding pictures—you know, for whenever you decide to set a date." Her eyes are wide, like she's afraid she's said the wrong thing.

"Yeah. We definitely need to get that helmet under control before then." I don't say anything else about weddings and dates. That's a conversation for later.

But I do know I want to tie the knot this summer. And I also know the longer I wait to say anything, the less chance there is that we'll be able to secure an excessively large venue.

I pull into the underground lot and park in an empty spot between some expensive sporty car and a Land Rover. Files and coffee in hand, we make our way to the elevator. I'm still nervous. And angsty.

I shut down thoughts of potential wedding plans and stop wondering how Alex is doing so I can focus on what's important, which is the presentation. Of course, that makes me think about how getting this account could make things really different at work, and I'm already experiencing a lot of change as it is.

I'm realizing that ultimately, my job—the one I'm good at but is causing me conflict and stress—is really the last normal thing I have, the last part of my life that's the same as it was before Alex. I think the reason I've been holding on to the nine-to-five grind—resisting even the flexibility of working from home—is because it's normal, and nothing else about my life is anymore.

Sometimes I wonder how my life got so complicated, and then I remember I'm engaged to a professional hockey player who's currently broken. As the elevator rises, I realize every single person in this office knows how broken he is. It's been all over the news—as has the massive suspension slapped on Cockburn.

Charlene puts a hand on my shoulder. "Hey? Are you sure you're okay?"

"What?" I'm eating my fingernails so I drop my hand. "Oh, yeah. Just bracing myself for all the fake sympathy."

"It's not fake, Vi. People are really concerned about you."

"No, they're not. They're worried about whether Alex is going to play the end of the season and how much this is going to hurt Chicago's shot at the playoffs."

She opens her mouth to respond, but the elevator dings.

I'm not braced enough as the doors open and we step into the office. It's like being smacked in the face with an empathy dick. All these people come out of their cubicles— half of them I don't even know by name—to hug me and tell me how I'm such a trooper and blah fucking blah.

It takes seventeen minutes to get to my cubicle. I'm frazzled and on the verge of tears by the time I make it. I need to get it together. Jimmy pops his head in before Charlene can even leave. He's holding a box of cinnamon buns. My favorite kind. My stomach is all sorts of upset over the crap I've already put in it.

"Hey, girl, how you doin'?" He grimaces, indicating I may look like yesterday's garbage. "Ohh, rough start?" He opens the bun box. "Want one?"

"No thanks." My smile feels constipated.

My professional and personal relationship with Jimmy hasn't been the same since Alex and I got engaged. I don't know if it's because he secretly hoped the rumors about Alex being gay from years ago were true, or because I've been fortunate enough to get some sweet opportunities, like managing Buck's money and now the Darcy account, if I don't screw it up. It's a lot of personal attention from Stroker, which he's usually stingy with. If I had to guess, I'd say it's a combination of the two. Jimmy's always had a crush on Alex.

"It's so great that you're here! Are you just coming in to get some stuff? I thought Stroker was letting you work from home for a while." He checks behind him before he makes his customary jerk-off gesture.

139

"Thanks. He was; he is—"

"Who's dealing with the Darcy account? Are you still presenting? I checked out the PowerPoint. I hope you don't mind."

Charlene puts a hand up in front of his face. "Calm your balls, Jimmy."

He drops a hand to his crotch. "What? I haven't seen Vi in, like, a week. I'm being a good friend."

"You didn't even ask her about Alex."

"How *is* Alex? I've been watching all the news and stuff, but some of that is probably skewed, right? He's not really out for the rest of the season." His voice rises instead of lowers at the last question.

I should've known I would get this, but it still throws me. Alex hasn't done any interviews yet. He wants to wait until his face isn't quite so banged up.

I don't get to answer because Mr. Stroker's bald head appears at the top of my cubicle wall. "Violet, can I see you in my office?"

"Of course, Mr. Stroker." Charlene and Jimmy get out of the way so I can follow him to his huge, comfy office at the far end of the hall.

He gestures to one of the plush chairs, where I sit. Instead of sitting behind his desk, he takes the one across from me and steeples his hands. "I'm not going to ask you how you are, because I'm pretty sure I already know the answer."

"I appreciate that." I'm not thinking it requires more of a response.

"Are you sure you want to present to the Darcys today?"

"I'm sure."

"You know it's just a formality at this point. They're very much set on having you manage the accounts."

"Well, that's good to know, but I think it's best for me to present. It's an experience I don't have yet."

"You have lots of experience presenting, Violet. You do it every week at our meetings."

"This is different." I tap the arm of the chair with my nails. They need to be redone in the worst way. I had to touch up all the chips last night before I went to bed so I didn't have cheap-hooker hands today.

Mr. Stroker regards me for what seems like forever, but is most likely only about ten seconds. Still, it's a long time since I'm trying not to fidget, or get emotional. And my stomach is not happy.

He slaps his hand on the arm of the chair, startling me. "Okay then, meet me in the conference room in five minutes, and we'll have a quick brief before they show up. Sound good?"

"Sounds great." This is what I need. Business as usual. A reminder of why I want to be here, doing this job I don't actually need.

I head back to my cubicle with purpose, a smile plastered over my cheeks. Gathering up my notes, I check my face in the little mirror beside my computer. I look tired but otherwise okay, and go directly to the conference room to set up.

I've got my PowerPoint ready by the time Mr. Stroker arrives. It's already twenty to ten. The Darcys will be here soon. Stroker and I have been over the whole proposal already—not face-to-face, but through email—so I'm feeling okay about it.

This isn't a social visit, so I'm less nervous than I would be at, say, a work function, or my own engagement party. Which the Darcys attended and witnessed my hives outbreak. It hasn't deterred them so far, so I guess it couldn't have been as bad as I'm remembering it.

I click through the slides and give Mr. Stroker a brief over-view. I have three left to go when we get the call letting us know they're here.

"It's game time," Mr. Stroker says.

I meet the Darcys in the waiting room. Bunny folds me into a tight hug. Her boobs are hard and unyielding. I'm now certain they're not real. Or her bra is made of steel. I can feel her nose against my neck. When she pulls back, she gives me one of those sympathy smiles. It's not really a smile, but it's not really a frown. It's more like a frile, or a smown. She's definitely had some surgery on her face, as her eyebrows don't move at all when her expression changes. It's a little unnerving.

"How are you? How's Alex?"

"He's okay. The doctors have him resting, and you know how that is." God, I sound like a wife. A hockey wife.

Bunny gives me a knowing smile and winks, but her eye only closes halfway. "These boys are so hard to keep down, aren't they?"

"They sure are."

I left him tenting the sheets this morning in his sleep. But I don't think that's what she means, or maybe it is.

I expect Mitch to shake my hand, but he comes in for a solid hug. "He'll be fine; don't you worry."

I've heard that line enough times to make me want to dick-punch someone. Or multiple someones. I know it's meant to be encouraging, but honestly, this isn't a bounce-right-back kind of injury, so the *fine* part seems like it's going to take a long-ass time to get to.

I redirect the conversation away from Alex, because talking about him makes me feel guilty for not being home.

The proposal is seamless until I get to the second-to-last slide. When I click to it, the screen fills with a picture of me and Alex from the night we met. We're mouth-fucking—like, hardcore. The letters D-T-F spin onto the screen below my tongue sliding into his mouth. Mitch clears his throat. Bunny giggles.

"Oh my God. I'm so sorry. That isn't part of my proposal. I mean, obviously watching me and Alex mouth-fuck has nothing to do with managing your financial portfolio. I don't—" I choke on the words as I move to the next slide, hoping to get rid of the horribly inappropriate image. But another slide of Alex and me making out pops up. I hit the back button, revisiting the previous mouth-fuck before I finally get to one that isn't embarrassing.

"I apologize," Mr. Stroker says.

I can feel the tears. They're so close to spilling over. I don't want to look at him, because I can hear how angry he is. I've blown it. I don't know how those pictures ended up in my proposal, but I've lost the account for sure now, and possibly my job. This is the worst week ever.

"Violet has some colleagues who like to play practical jokes. Unfortunately, their timing on this one is poor." He hits the button on the phone beside him. Edna, his personal secretary, answers in a chipper voice. "What can I do for you, Mr. Stroker?"

"Have Jimmy and Dean from accounting come to conference room B, please."

"Of course."

"What're you doing?" I whisper—not like it matters, the Darcys can still hear me.

"They need to apologize."

"It's okay. I mean, it's not. But it's not like everyone hasn't already seen those pictures. They were everywhere for a while. And Alex and I have been caught doing worse." I wish I could stop my mouth from opening and spewing out words.

"Like in the locker room." Bunny winks at me. "Mitch told me all about that!"

Jesus. Could this get any more embarrassing?

Stroker's eyebrows rise, wrinkling his forehead. I try not to react, but I can feel the heat in my face.

"We don't need to see anything else, Violet," Mitch says. "Bunny has done her research on you, and we know you'll do an excellent job handling us."

My mind is stuck somewhere in the gutter thanks to the mouth-fuck pictures because when Mitch says "handling us" I think he means his junk, not his financial portfolio. Thankfully, a knock on the door prevents me from saying something even more embarrassing.

Jimmy pops his head in the room. Dean's right behind him,

shoving him forward so he can get in, too. "Hey, Mr. St—" Jimmy stops when he sees the Darcys, and his perfectly shaped eyebrows shoot up toward his artfully styled hair.

"Oooohhhh…" Dean lifts his hand to his mouth.

I'm fairly certain we're matching in our horror.

"I assume you know why you're here." Mr. Stroker has put on his angry face. It's super convincing, maybe because he really is upset.

"I think so," Jimmy says slowly.

In case there was any question, Mr. Stroker cues up the PowerPoint and goes to the incriminating slides. I close my eyes to block out the view of my tongue in Alex's mouth.

"I'm so sorry. I put the mouth-fucking slides in a while ago and forgot to take them out." Jimmy cringes when Dean elbows him in the side. "I mean the kissing slides. Violet calls it mouth-fucking, which we think is funny—"

"Shut up," Dean hisses.

"It's okay," I mutter. "Can you just—"

"It's not okay, Violet. This is unprofessional behavior. What if the Darcys weren't so understanding?" Mr. Stroker gestures to the massive image on the screen. My tongue is the size of my actual head.

I sink down in my chair, wishing Stroker would take the hint and change the slide. I steal a peek at the Darcys. Mitch's eyes are darting between my tongue in Alex's mouth, Jimmy and Dean, and then back to Bunny.

My humiliation knows no end.

I raise my hand. "Mr. Stroker."

"Yes, Violet."

"Can we change the slide to something that isn't me with my tongue in Alex's mouth, please?"

He glances over. "Oh. Right. I was making a point."

"I think it's made."

"You two, go to my office and wait there. I'll deal with you when we're done in here." Stroker waves them out.

Jimmy and Dean trip over each other to escape. I have no idea what the damn point of that was.

"Well, this has to be the most entertaining financial meeting I've ever attended." Bunny flips her hair over her shoulder and gives me what should be a smile, but her lips hardly move. I wonder what it's like getting a blow job from her.

We spend the next half hour talking informally, and not about mouth-fucking. As excited as I am, this is a huge responsibility. It also comes with a significant incentive. Big accounts mean more money. I get one percent of whatever I make for the Darcys, and when I'm handling more than thirty million dollars, that adds up. Nothing like what Alex makes, but it's way more than I'm making now.

Bunny hugs me again on their way out. "When Alex is feeling up to it, let us know and we'll do dinner. And if you want to get together and have some girl time—you know, facials, Botox, bra shopping, stuff like that—just call!"

"Of course. Thanks so much." I try not to read anything into it. I'm sure she just wants to be friends. And even if the rumors aren't a load of BS, Buck said he doubted the Darcys would stick their noodles in the team pool anyway.

"We hockey wives have to stick together." Bunny winks at me again. Maybe it's a tic.

She called me a hockey wife. It's starting to sink in what that really means. It's more than changing my name from Hall, which makes me sound like the location of a low-budget horror movie, to Waters, which turns it into a sweet romance.

It's going to mean moving around if Alex changes teams, and possibly more than once when he eventually changes his entire career. He's already twenty-six. I know the stats on hockey careers and their longevity. It's my job to know that information so I can help these guys plan for their futures. It's surreal to think he's approaching the end of his first career when I've barely started mine.

Stroker pats my shoulder once the elevator doors close

behind the Darcys. "You did a great job, Violet, even with the tongue pictures."

"Thanks."

"You should get some lunch, or maybe go home for the rest of the day. You're probably exhausted."

"Are you sure?" I'm totally done. I didn't realize how much energy this whole office experience was going to take.

"Positive. I know this thing with Alex has been tough on you. That you even came in to do this today is commendable." He stuffs his hands in his pockets and jingles his keys, regarding me carefully. "You know some of our senior team do a lot of their work from home, and based on what you've managed to accomplish while you've been out of the office—and dealing with everything else—I think that could work for you, if it's something you're interested in."

"Uhh…" This is exactly what Alex has been asking for, which makes me suspicious. "Did Alex call you or something?"

Stroker purses his lips. It makes him look like he's sucking on a lemon. "Why would Alex call me?"

"I don't know. No reason."

"Anyway, you think about it, and we can talk later. I'm going to go deal with Dumb and Dumber."

"Oh, God, I forgot they were waiting in your office! What are you going to do to them?" I ask.

"Make them review all the files from the Phillips account."

"There's a whole room of boxes dedicated to that account."

Stroker smiles. It's very Joker-scary. "Exactly."

"That'll take weeks."

"Yup. And they'll be too busy to play any more juvenile pranks."

"Good point."

His creepo smile fades. "All right. You go find Charlene and tell her she can take an extended lunch break with you." He turns to walk away again.

I suddenly feel like I'm getting special treatment I don't deserve. "Mr. Stroker?"

"Hmm?" He glances over his shoulder.

"Why are you giving me all these extra privileges?"

He laughs. "You don't know?"

"Because I'm engaged to Alex and you don't want to lose his account?"

"You really just say it like it is, don't you?"

"Unfortunately, yeah." I can feel the giraffe spots appearing on my neck.

He pulls his keys out of his pocket and twirls them around on his finger. "It's not Alex's account I need. It's *you*."

"I don't—what?"

"I've been dealing with professional athletes for a long time, Violet. Don't forget my dad was pro. Being married to one of these guys is a full-time job. You're brilliant with numbers. I haven't seen you make a bad decision yet when it comes to managing Miller's account, or any of the other ones I've handed you, so if being flexible buys me more time with you as a member of my team, that's how I'm going to play it."

I don't even know what to say. I mean, I know I'm good at what I do, but coming from Stroker—who is definitely not an *ego* stroker—this means an awful lot. I open my mouth to speak, but all I make is a sound that's kind of like a whine. I start to tear up.

He waves a hand in my direction. "Okay, you're gonna get emotional, and that's not my area. Go find Charlene and have some lunch. We'll talk next week."

"Okay," I choke out as he rushes down the hall, away from my teary reaction to his niceness.

I dab at my eyes with the back of my sleeve and text Charlene, asking her to meet me in the foyer with my coat and purse so I don't have to deal with anyone else. Less than two minutes later, she comes speedwalking around the corner and almost slams into me.

"How'd it go? Are you crying? What happened?" She jabs

the down button on the elevator frantically.

"I got the account."

"Are these tears of happiness then?" She rummages around in her purse and pulls out a shredded tissue. Then she tries to blot my face with it.

"What're you doing? Did you blow your nose with that?" I shield my face with my hands.

"No!" She inspects the tissue. "At least I don't think so. But seriously, why are you crying?"

"I'll explain when we're eating." The elevator doors open. There are people inside, so we smile politely and don't say anything until we're on the street.

"So you got the account, but what? Did something happen with Alex? Is he okay?"

"Alex is fine. At least I think he is." I stop in the middle of the sidewalk and check my phone, to make sure.

I have six new messages from him. There are lots of kissy faces and emoticons with heart eyes. He's also discovered how to make a jizzing penis out of the alternate symbols, as well as boobs.

"Alex is fine." I show her my phone.

"Are those boobs?"

"Yeah."

"What's between them?"

"A dick, I think."

"Right. Okay. He must be feeling better then."

"Yeah." I pocket my phone. I want to tell him in person that I got the account.

"So if Alex is okay and you got the account, why the tears? Are you PMSing? Wait. Oh my God, are you *pregnant*?"

"Seriously, Charlene?"

"Sorry. Jimmy's been watching a lot of bad reality TV and then giving me a play-by-play of the episodes at lunch. I really miss you." She side-hugs me. "So you're definitely not pregnant?"

"No."

"Okay, great, because I think we need drinks."

We're seated immediately. The host knows me, not just because we eat here at least once a week, but also because of Alex. We order drinks and then haul ass to the buffet.

Once we're back at our table, Charlene returns to asking questions. "So you got the account, and you're happy about that, right?"

I shove a dumpling in my mouth and nod while I chew. "Definitely happy. Nervous because it's a big deal, but happy." I give her the rundown, including the shitshow with the DTF mouth-fucking slides.

A forkful of noodles unravels on to the table. "Oh my God."

"Yeah."

"How did the Darcys react?"

"Well, Mitch has seen me mostly naked and heard me come, so, you know, it could've been worse."

"What about Bunny?"

"She didn't seem too concerned about my tongue in Alex's mouth."

"Well, that's good, right?"

"Yeah. Definitely. She was really nice, offering to do lunch and Botox, or whatever."

"I love that lunch and botulism are a thing." Charlene pulls a face.

"Right? But she seems nice, despite that. I'm having a hard time getting past the swinger rumor, though. I keep examining her motives."

"I honestly think Jimmy was being an asshole, but I can find out for you." She picks up her phone and types away.

"What're you doing?"

"Asking Darren." Her phone rings, so she answers it. "I'm having lunch with Violet right now, so that's not possible... I can't excuse myself for a minute... Mmm-hmm. I understand that, and I'm okay with it." She starts playing with the pearl necklace under her infinity scarf. "Yes, Darren. Which pink one? But I thought—of course. Right. I definitely want to be ready for that." She touches the back of her hand to her cheek. "My question? Oh. I thought so. Thanks, sexy."

She ends the call and sets her phone on the table, staring into space.

"Char?" I wave a hand in front of her face.

She snaps out of whatever trance she's in. "Huh?"

"To swing or not to swing?"

"Oh, right. Darren says no; he doesn't think it's true."

"But he doesn't know for sure?"

"You can never be a hundred percent on anything, but he's been playing with the guy for a long time, so he's pretty confident."

"Okay. That's good. I'm still not sure I want to go to the spa with Bunny. I kind of like that my face moves."

"Good point. Anyway, Alex is doing better?"

"Physically for sure. He's still uncomfortable, but the bruises are healing, and he's not walking like he belongs in an old folks' home, so that's a plus. He doesn't really like needing to be taken care of, though. He gets frustrated."

"He's not really one to sit around and veg—none of those boys are. I know Darren's missing his workout partner."

"Yeah, so am I."

"I didn't know you worked out with Alex."

"That's not the kind of workout I'm talking about."

Understanding dawns in her eyes. She looks around and lowers her voice when she asks, "Are things not good in beaverland? Is Daisy making that a challenge?"

"Daisy's not really the problem." I push the food around on my plate.

"Oh my God, did he pull a groin muscle or something? I know it was a hard hit. Why didn't you say anything before now?"

"He didn't pull a groin muscle. Super MC still works fine. It has more to do with Alex's level of frustration than anything. He's used to having a lot of stamina, and at the moment, well, he doesn't, so I have to do all the work. Anyway, it's good that I've been doing all that yoga with Sunny, 'cause my legs are getting a serious workout. Sex makes my abs hurt."

"Right?" Charlene exclaims. "Some days it feels like I've done a P90X workout after a night with Darren."

"Especially after away games. Sunny should come up with some kind of pre-sex yoga ritual so I don't walk like a robot for three days afterward." I'm joking about it, because otherwise I'm at risk of crying. I'm all over the place today with the emotions.

"Agreed."

We're silent for a minute—Charlene probably because she's thinking about all the sex she's been having and will be having tonight, and me because I'm thinking about all the sex I'm missing. Well, it's not that the sex is missing, it's that Alex isn't in the right condition to bang on the beaver the way he usually does.

While I enjoy how sweet he can be, and how considerate he is during sex, I miss some of the intensity and aggression. But I know it will return.

"Honestly, Char, I can deal with the temporary lack of hot sexing. Mostly I'm glad he's okay. It could've been so much worse."

"But we know he'll be fine."

"That's what the doctors are saying anyway." The retrograde amnesia persists, with the hours surrounding the accident still missing, but otherwise he seems okay. I push my plate away. I'm so overwhelmed. Because fine is relative. Goddamnit. The tears start leaking out.

"Vi? Are you okay?"

I take a few deep breaths, trying to get myself under control. "I'm okay."

"No, you're not."

"It's been a rough couple of weeks. I just...I don't know. I mean, now I have this account, and that's awesome, but it's going to be a lot of work, and right now all I can think about is being with Alex—and how much worse the accident could've been. He's getting better, but he's still a long ways from being totally fine. What if he'd had a serious brain injury? What if—" I can't finish the sentence.

Charlene puts her hand over mine. "But he didn't, and he's okay. He's going to be fine. You have to believe the doctors. It just takes time."

"I know. But that's this time. There's no guarantee it won't happen again."

"Try not to think that way, Vi."

I stare at my plate. "But it's the reality of this profession. Bad things can happen."

Char squeezes my hand tightly. "So what does that mean?"

"All I can really think about is how I don't ever want to lose him." I feel the wave building inside me. I've been holding it together decently since Alex came home from the hospital, but today it seems I'm due for a breakdown. A tear drops onto my sticky rice. "I love this job, but I'm starting to realize the nine-to-five isn't something I'm going to be able to keep up over the long term. And I don't think I'll want to. So I need to figure out what's realistic and adjust my plans."

Charlene sits back, contemplating. "You've been thinking about this a lot."

"I have."

"I also think you should consider how stressed out you've been. Alex's accident, the Darcy account, it's a lot for anyone to handle."

I set my fork down, my appetite gone—which is sad, because the food here is awesome. "I know, but it's made me reevaluate what's important."

"Which is what?"

"I want to set a date for the wedding."

"Seriously?"

"Yeah. If I've learned anything from this, it's that life is too unpredictable to let my propensity for self-humiliation stop me from getting hitched. I want to spend the rest of my life with this man, and postponing the start of that because I'm going to embarrass myself is silly. That's just the way I am. Waiting isn't going to change it."

AFTER LUNCH I pack a box of files and head home, feeling lighter. I won over the Darcys, I'm going to work from home for a while, and as soon as the time is right, I'm going to tell Alex we should set a date.

I find him in the living room, lying on the couch with the remote control pointed at the TV. He rewinds and then presses play, turning up the volume. He doesn't notice me watching him. I glance at the screen and realize too late it's the footage from his injury. The crack when he hits the boards is amplified by the surround sound. Then the screaming fans drown out everything else.

The camera angle changes, giving me a different view of the events than I had at the game. While I was panicking, his team-mates were checking for a response. The whole thing comes flooding back in a rush of fresh fear. I put my hand over my mouth to silence my sob, but I'm not quick enough.

Alex suddenly realizes I'm here. He stops the video and pats the cushion beside him. "C'mere."

He's wearing his current uniform of a hoodie and sweats, and I'm still in my dress pants and blouse. He moves over so I can get my ass on the sliver of cushion.

"Why are you watching that?" I ask with a sniffle.

"To see if it'll jog my memory. It sure as hell explains why I look the way I do." He cracks a smile.

I try to return it, but I can't. "I'm glad Cockburn got a twenty-game suspension."

"He deserved it." He caresses my cheek. "You must have been so scared."

I nod, working through the lump in my throat. We haven't really talked about this, mostly because Alex doesn't have any memory of the hit.

"When you didn't get up, and then they wheeled you by me on that stretcher and you weren't moving...I thought I was going to lose you. I couldn't keep it together enough to be able to get in the ambulance with you. Sunny had to go, and all I could think was that I was never going to..." I don't continue. The words are unnecessary.

"But I'm going to be okay now."

I take a deep breath, trying to calm myself. I've purposely avoided the footage up to this point. "There was an hour or so when I didn't know if I was ever going to be okay again. It was awful."

"I'm sorry I scared you, baby."

He doesn't promise not to do it again, and I know it's because he doesn't want to lie to me. Which scares me even more. He reaches over, bringing my mouth to his. It's a soft kiss, and there isn't any tongue, but he finishes with a lip nibble. When he's done, I back up a few inches so his eyes don't merge into one.

"Let's talk about something nice." He glances at the clock. "You're home earlier than I expected. Did the presentation go okay?"

"I got the account."

"That's awesome." He means it; I can tell by the dimple that appears in his left cheek.

I kiss the divot. "I have a question about the Darcys."

"Oh? What's that?" He twirls a lock of my hair around his finger.

"There's a rumor out there—"

"There's always a rumor. What is it this time? The one about them being swingers?"

"How'd you know?"

Alex rolls his eyes. "People are assholes. They were invited to participate in an event at a hotel a couple of years ago. There were two parties going on the same night in the same venue. One was a fundraiser, and the other was for swingers. They accidently went to the wrong one for, like, a minute, but Darcy's been fighting the rumor ever since."

"Wow. People really are assholes."

"Who told you that?"

"Dean."

"I really don't like that guy."

"He was just being a jerk." I trace the line of his eyebrow. "I have some more good news."

"Oh? What's that?"

"I talked to Stroker about working more from home."

Alex blinks his surprise. "Really?"

"Really. And he said yes."

"And you're okay with that?" He skims my bottom lip with his thumb.

"I'm more than okay with it."

This time when he smiles, I get both dimples.

I drop another kiss on his lips. I'm rewarded with a little tongue action. "Where's your mom?"

"She went out to pick up more food. I might need to buy another fridge if she doesn't stop soon." We're kiss-talking now, and Alex's hand has started wandering lower, over my shoulder to my boob.

"The entire freezer is full of meals for the next three months. How long ago did she leave?"

"Maybe twenty minutes?"

"So she won't be back for a while?" I finger one of the buttons on my blouse until it pops open, revealing cleavage.

"Probably not."

"Wanna go upstairs so I can hug Super MC with my beaver?"

Alex pushes to a sitting position and nuzzles my boobs. "That sounds like the best fucking idea in the universe."

11

TRICKY TRICKSTER FOR THE WIN

VIOLET

My post-sex hair is damp, and I'm tucked into Alex's side. He brushes the hair away from my forehead. "I'll be a lot happier when I can give you more than one orgasm at a time."

"There are a lot of women in the world who have to fake every single orgasm they have, so I don't think you should feel too bad about doling them out one at a time for a few weeks."

Alex makes a disgusted sound. "What does that even say about the guys those women are with?"

"You can't really fault them when the women are pretending to get off."

"I don't know. You'd think it'd be obvious when a woman is faking it."

"Not if she fakes it from the beginning," I argue.

Alex shifts so he can look me in the eye. He's particularly intense. "You've never faked it with me, have you?"

"Is that a serious question?"

"Yes."

"No, Alex, at no point have I had to do Kegels to cover a lack of orgasm."

"You're sure?" His insecurity is endearing.

"You make me come every time. Super MC is my beaver's soulmate."

He laughs. "I love you, Violet Hall." For some reason he sounds sad.

"I love you, too, Alex Waters."

We lie there for a few minutes, and I start thinking about the conversation I had with Charlene today. I could tell Alex now that I want to set a wedding date. I probably should.

I lift my head. His eyes are closed, and his breathing is even. "Alex?"

I don't get a response.

"Baby?"

Still nothing. He's out cold. The man can fall asleep faster than Sleeping Beauty.

I blow out a breath, annoyed at myself that I've missed a perfectly good opportunity to make him happy. I press my lips to his temple and whisper, "I can't wait to be Violet Waters."

When it's clear Alex is in serious nap mode and my mind is too busy spinning for me to join him, I get out of bed and put on clothes.

While Alex naps, and Daisy's out adding to the bomb shelter's worth of food in the pantry and cold cellar, I sneak into her bathroom, open the window, and empty her aerosol cans of hairspray. There are three on the counter. I leave a tiny bit in one and then hide the one can I have in the back of my closet.

I finish Mission: Dehelmetify Daisy's Hair as the house alarm beeps, signaling she's back. I don't let the guilt eat at me too much, because I'm doing this for a woman whose hairdresser clearly doesn't know what decade it is. Someone has to step in.

THE NEXT MORNING Daisy comes knocking on our bedroom door at an ungodly hour. I roll out of bed and grab my robe. I'm wearing shorts and a tank, but still. The tank is white, and Daisy's already seen more than enough of me while she's been here. She knocks, but often doesn't wait until she gets the go-ahead to come in.

Shrugging on the robe, I tiptoe to the door before the knocking wakes Alex. He's been having performance anxiety dreams, so his sleep has been broken, and so has mine. He's also used to sleeping on his right side most of the time—so he can spoon me and nestle his dick in the cleft of my ass—and he can't currently do this because of his shoulder. To compensate, he holds on to some part of me, whatever is closest—my arm, my hair, my boob. The latter is the most common.

I check to make sure I don't have any dried drool on my cheek before I slip out into the hall, closing the door behind me. "Is everything okay, Daisy?"

"I'm so sorry I woke you, but it's an emergency." Her eyes are frantic. Her hair is flat and wet.

"What's wrong?"

She touches her hair. "Well, I have to pick up Robbie from the airport at nine, and I don't have any hairspray left."

"Oh." I have to suppress my smile of victory.

"I was wondering if you had a can? I could make do with the pump-spray bottles if that's all you've got."

"I can check for you."

She releases a tense breath. "That'd be great."

I steal back into the room. Glancing at the clock, I'm horrified to see it's only six-fifteen in the morning. It must take a considerable amount of time and hairspray to coif her 'do into rock-hard helmet mode.

Padding to the bathroom, I give it a good minute or two of fake searching before I grab an alternate hair product. As I step out into the hall, I put on my sad face. "I'm so sorry, Daisy. I don't have any hairspray, but I have gel." I hold up the bottle. I know it's not even remotely the same, but I'm pretending to be helpful.

"That really won't work. Do you think you have any in the spare rooms?"

"We can check." I know for a fact we don't, because I've taken care of removing all traces of hairspray from the house. Phase one of my mission is complete; now we're on to phase two: Fix the Helmet.

It might be a disgusting time to be awake on a Saturday morning, but I'll bite the bullet and manage if it means I can finally hug Daisy without getting a mouthful of crunchy, over-sprayed hair.

I go through the motions while Daisy hovers behind me, growing more and more distressed. When I come back empty-handed, she starts to tear up.

"I don't have time to go to a store and get more hairspray. What am I going to do? I can't pick Robbie up looking like this." She motions to her head.

It's the most normal her hair has ever looked in the time Alex and I have been together. Daisy is actually gorgeous under that over-teased mop. She and Sunny look almost identical, apart from the fact that Sunny is blond and Daisy is more auburn. I hope I age as gracefully as Daisy. I pat her shoulder. "Come on. I'll see what I can do."

Daisy glances at my hair, her apprehension clear. And under-standable. It can't be good, but then she's woken me up, and I'm an active sleeper. It probably looks like something decided to nest in there. I leave the bathroom and she follows, as there really isn't another option. I send her back to her room and sneak into mine to get my hair supplies.

Once I'm armed with my arsenal, I knock on her door and wait, because I definitely don't want to see the parts of Daisy that she's seen of me. I have no idea if she's sporting a seriously overgrown beaver bush to match the one on her head, and I have no desire to ever have the answer to that mystery of life.

Daisy appears, her eyes red, and I experience some serious remorse. This has been hard on her. She's been watching her only son, who pursued a career she wasn't fully supportive of—for a variety of reasons, unable to take care of himself because of an injury that rocked us all. And now her hair is unsprayed.

But my torment has a purpose. One day I'm going to have wedding pictures. Probably soonish. Daisy will be in them. I would selfishly like her to have normal hair on that day, so I think it's reasonable to make her cry if it means I don't have to face this battle later. Besides, she's three decades behind. It's time to move past the glory days of college.

I make her sit on the toilet seat, partly so she can't see herself, and also because I'm short and she's tall. I use a rounded brush for volume, aware that we're going to have to move away from her terrible hair in stages. First we need to all but eliminate the need for hairspray; then we'll work on toning down more of the hugeness. In reality, without spray, her hair will look big for the first ten minutes, and then it'll settle nicely.

Now I'm no aesthetician. I have the makeup basics down, and I know how to use a flat iron on my hair. But I'm pretty damn confident I can make Daisy look decent until we can visit a hairstylist she doesn't need a time warp to get to.

I spend the next twenty minutes working my magic. When I'm finished, Daisy's long hair curls softly around her pretty, delicate features. I know she's probably going to ruin it with her eighties-style makeup, but it's a one-step-at-a-time kind of thing.

I set down the hairdryer and brush, finger-comb a few

wayward strands into submission, and gesture to the mirror. "Check it out."

Daisy hesitantly stands, smoothing her hands over the dress that no longer matches her hair. I need to get my mom to take her shopping. Anything is better than the shoulder pads. Well, except maybe my mom's miniskirts, but mostly her taste is decent. She turns and faces her reflection. Her eyes go wide—I'm not sure if it's horror or surprise. They kind of look the same on Daisy. She reaches up to touch her hair, then stops.

"You can run your fingers through it." I demonstrate by pulling mine through the underside, helping to give it more volume, so she doesn't miss the helmet-y type look.

She exhales a long, unsteady breath and pats her hair. She fingers one of the curls. "It's so soft."

I grin, because seriously, what other reaction is there? I feel like I'm a host on that TLC show where they humiliate a person by putting them on national TV, then give them five grand to buy a new wardrobe and stop dressing like a bum, or a cartoon character. For once, I'm not the one who's under the microscope. I'm also doing a good deed—more for myself than Daisy—but we both win if she likes this look.

"Do you like it?" I ask.

"I-I think I do." She pats her hair again and gives me a wavering smile. I can't tell if she's just trying to be nice until she spins around and pulls me into a rib-cracking hug. "Thank you, Violet. I don't know what I would've done if you hadn't been here to help me."

It takes me a few seconds to react. This is full-on momma love. I might get emotional about it. Which is the norm these days.

When we break apart, we're both doing the eye-wipe thing. Daisy hasn't put makeup on, so there's no risk of smearing it all over her face yet. It's the kind of bonding moment we've needed —one that isn't related to the accident or Alex. As helpful as she's been, it's been hard not to feel like she's taking over my place, particularly with how much she dotes on Alex and how much he seems to like it.

I tiptoe back to my room and get my camera so I can record this moment in history before Daisy puts on her carnival makeup. With her toned-down hair, her resemblance to Sunny is uncanny.

I offer to go to the airport with her, but she tells me to get some more sleep and apologizes for waking me up so early. I'm almost disappointed I won't get to witness Robbie's reaction when he sees her new hair. I sneak back to bed; Alex is still sleeping.

Unfortunately, I don't seem to be able to fall back asleep. My mom and Sidney, and Miller and Sunny are coming over for brunch, along with the rest of our close friends, and I fully expect someone to mention the wedding and the lack of a set date. As I lay there, staring at Alex's profile and the five o'clock shadow covering his cheeks and chin, I realize something important: Even with all the uncertainty, not once did I consider myself unable to handle this situation. Hell, I even took on a bonus mission with his mom's hair. I know I'm ready for this—to be in this life with him—no matter the challenges it brings.

Today is the perfect time to set a date. All the important people involved will be here, so there's no reason not to. Besides, with Alex out for the rest of the season, he needs something to occupy his time. Planning a wedding seems like the perfect distraction.

And then I don't have to do it, and we all win.

12

MOTHERS
UNITED

ALEX

I wake up to warm, wet suction. I'm slow to open my eyes, sifting through the aches in my body until it's just pleasure. I look down to find Violet kneeling beside me, her hair pulled up in a ponytail. It's swept over her shoulder and out of the way so it doesn't impede my view. And that's awesome, because her lips are currently wrapped around my cock.

I groan her name and reach out with the hand that works to stroke her cheek. She does that thing where she slides the head across the inside of her cheek before it pops out of her mouth.

"Good morning." She grins, then goes back to bobbing.

"It sure is." Sitting up is still more of a chore than I'm up for at the moment, so I settle for rearranging my pillow to get a better view. Then I go back to stroking her cheek and her shoul-

163

der, hoping she'll take the hint and move closer so I can hold her boob while she blows me.

Violet, being the intuitive woman she is, shifts on the bed and settles her boob in my palm while continuing the suck-stroking. I would really love to get her on her back and slide my dick between her tits, then have mind-blowing sex, but my fuck speed is still set at geriatric. It's pathetic. I know it's not going to be like this forever, but it pisses me off.

I try to bring my focus back to what Violet's doing, but now that I'm thinking about what I can't give her, it's hard to concentrate on anything else. My hard-on starts deflating. While it's in her mouth.

That's never happened before. *Never.* I glance down at the boob I'm kneading and roll the nipple between my fingers. Usually that helps. I need to get back to maximum hardness quickly, but things seem to be going in the opposite direction.

Violet pops off again, frowning as she strokes me. "Alex?"

"Mmm?" She's noticed. I can tell. *Fuck.*

"Is everything okay?" She loosens her grip.

"It's good; that feels good." The crack in my voice doesn't help things at all.

"But you're..." She trails off. "Are you in pain? Should I get you something? Maybe this isn't..."

"I'm fine." I'm not even close to fine.

I stop fondling her and cover her hand with mine. Lacing my fingers with hers, I squeeze tightly and start stroking, hard and fast.

Violet sits back on her knees, her other hand high on my thigh. But I need more than her hand or her mouth. I need to be in her. I miss a lot of things, but being able to love her, and sometimes just fuck her, is high on the list.

"Get on me," I grind out.

Violet's eyes flare. "Are you sure?"

"I want in you." I almost sound angry, probably because I

am. I want to take care of her, and part of that is showing her how much I want her, the effect she has on me.

She exhales a quick breath, but she doesn't ask any more questions. Instead she carefully straddles me, trying to stay clear of the healing bruises on my legs. She looks uncertain. I can understand why.

I'm typically a considerate lover, and I make sure I take care of Violet the way she needs. I'm not usually pushy or aggressive unless I'm pissed off—like I was that one time in the locker room. Yet even then I made sure Violet came long before I did, and more than once. But my ability to do even that is limited.

I soften my tone as I make a suggestion. "Why don't you get yourself ready for me, baby."

She eases the hand that's not on my cock between her thighs and rubs her clit, slow at first and then faster. I keep up the mutual stroking, easing up when I'm back to a reasonable level of hardness.

"Finger yourself, Violet." Again it comes out sounding more like a directive than a polite request.

"Yes, sir, Mr. Waters, sir." She even salutes me.

She means for it to be snarky; regardless, it definitely helps with the inflation—especially when she pushes the first finger inside and moans my name.

"Careful. The walls aren't soundproof," I warn. I don't need my mom to overhear us.

"Your mom's on her way to the airport to get your dad."

I forgot it's the weekend. "We're alone?"

She nods and eases in a second finger, whimpering.

"In that case, be as enthusiastic as you want."

She smiles, and it's as sweet as it is coy. "Okay."

She pumps a few times, then circles her clit before sliding a third finger in with the first two. Her hands are much smaller than mine, though, so her three fingers is a lot different than my three fingers.

"Want me to hug the Super MC now?" she asks, a little breathlessly.

"You should use one more finger first."

She arches a brow. "I'm not sticking my whole hand up there."

I snort. "I'm not asking you to fist yourself, Violet."

"Fist myself?" She sounds appalled, even disturbed. "I can handle your endless jokes about getting into my Area 51, because apparently it's the in thing to do these days, but if you start with other weird requests, I will totally revoke the boob sex."

I try not to smile too wide. "Weirder than you dressing up my dick?"

"That's cute, not weird," Violet says.

She's still got her fingers where I'm going to be soon and her other hand wrapped around my cock. I squeeze my erection to draw her attention there. "Look at the size of your hands compared to mine."

She glances at our fingers. "Oh, huh... I guess that makes sense."

I stroke up, sliding my thumb over the head. Violet follows with her own, and I groan. "You know what, you should take over here, and I'll take you over."

"Okay." She eases her fingers out and links them with her other hand, so both surround my cock. Then she shifts around so I have the access I need. It's a great visual, and it feels fucking awesome with how slick her hand is.

I circle her clit with a knuckle, savoring her quiet whimper, before I push inside.

"Oh, God, Alex. I love your fingers."

"Does that feel good?" I already know it does, but I also like hearing it, and I need the ego feed.

"So good." Her grip on me tightens when I add another finger, and she moans. Loudly.

"It's a little different than your three fingers, isn't it?"

"Uh-huh."

Her chest is blotchy—the way it gets when the dirty talk turns her on.

"You want me to make you come?"

"Please."

I curl my fingers and rub her clit with my thumb. It's awkward since it's my left hand instead of my right, but I use more pressure and rub faster, like she did, to see if it works better than my usual method.

She looks down to where my fingers disappear inside her. "Alex, I'm—oh, holy orgasm!"

Violet bows forward as she groans my name. She's forced to let go of me when she almost topples over on my chest. She braces a hand on either side of my head, shifting her hips as she fucks my hand. Her face is inches from mine. I can feel each hot pant across my lips as she whispers how good I make her feel and how much she loves my hands and wants my cock.

It's really hot, and for the first time since this stupid fucking accident, I feel legitimately good. I can still take care of my fiancée like I'm supposed to.

She shudders and sucks my bottom lip softly.

"Was that good?"

She makes a sound that's probably a word, but her tongue is in my mouth so it's unintelligible.

"What was that?"

She stops kissing me long enough to say, "I wanna fuck you."

"Well, you should probably get on my cock, then, shouldn't you?"

"I should. Definitely get on your cock."

I wait until Violet pushes up and sits on my thighs before I withdraw my fingers. She shimmies up, then rises and grabs hold. She doesn't sit right down, though. Now that she's had an orgasm, Violet goes into tease mode. Her head drops, her eyes focused on where she's rubbing the head of my cock over her clit.

"Hello, Super MC. Are you excited for beaver hugs?" she whispers.

Some of the intensity dissipates. It's not uncommon for Violet to talk to my dick like it's going to answer her.

I flex so it kicks in her hand. She jumps and giggles. "Ohh! He's really excited, isn't he?"

"It would appear that way. Maybe you should stop with the teasing and give him what he's looking for." That I also refer to my dick as a person is probably something most people would suggest therapy for.

Violet takes my comment seriously and shifts her hips forward, lining us up. I tense when she lowers herself, taking in the head, and all the aches in my body flare until I relax again.

"You know…" She stays like that for a few seconds. "If Super MC could breathe, sex would kind of be like breath play, right?"

"What?" I have no idea what she's talking about.

"You know, those people who like their air supply cut off during sex."

"I think you need to take a break from some of those smut books you're reading."

"It's Charlene's fault. She's the one who keeps recommending them."

"Can we not talk about Charlene when we're about to have sex, please?"

"Right. Sorry." She drops down until her ass rests on my thighs.

I groan and ball my hands into fists—which makes my right shoulder sing with pain—and wait for her to move. I can't decide whether I like being at her mercy or not. Violet circles her hips, and her soft moans keep me in the present instead of hanging out in my head, feeling sorry for myself. I feel badly that she has to do all the work, but it's pretty fucking hot watching her.

"Is it good? Does it feel good?" she asks.

"So good."

She keeps moving over me. I know she's taking it easy, unsure exactly what makes me feel good or bad. While I appreciate the view, I'd like her closer. Besides, she's more likely to come again if she's rubbing up on my pelvis, and she can't really do all the work and rub herself at the same time.

"C'mere." I crook a finger.

She leans forward and puts a palm on either side of my head again. Her nipples brush my chest, but she holds her own weight. "It's a good thing Sunny's been forcing me to do all this yoga, eh?"

She's sweaty, and her cheeks are flushed. She looks gorgeous and sexy. "Definitely a good thing."

She does some more hip shifting and moaning. "This takes a lot of coordination."

"You're doing awesome, baby." I clasp the back of her neck and bring her lips to mine.

She has a hard time keeping her rhythm and kissing at the same time, so I let her go after a minute. She stays nice and close, though, boobs bumping my chest as she rides me. I decide I don't mind it all that much. I do what I can, but I'm limited in the thrusting department for the time being.

I know she's getting close when the cock-love chanting starts. Which is good, because I'm right there with her. Her arms are shaking; she's struggling to hold herself up. Normally I'd take over now and give her another orgasm, if not two. "You almost there?" I ask.

She nods frantically. "I can't—I'm gonna—" Her muscles lock. "Oh, God. Your cock is amazing."

That's the sign we're good to go. I let the orgasm slam into me while Violet continues to moan. When she's done, her arms give out, and she flops onto my chest. I grunt, but grit my teeth against the spike of pain in my ribs. Most of the time, after sex, we cuddle for a bit. Violet likes to keep hugging my dick until it's mostly soft. We go through a lot of sheets that way, but I don't mind since I'm not the one who washes them.

I stroke her back and kiss the top of her head, enjoying the weight of her, even if it's making my ribs ache.

"Oh, shit!" She quickly flips over to her right. It's definitely one of her more graceful moves. "Sorry! I forgot about how broken you are!"

"I'm not broken."

"But your ribs." She skims the tape binding me together. "And I was lying on you." She grabs her pillow and pushes it next to mine, then snuggles into my good side.

"I'm not made of glass."

"I know." She puts her hand on my chest, over my heart, and sighs. "That was a lot of work. I'm so sweaty."

"I like you sweaty."

"It's gross; I need to shower, and these sheets will have to go. Plus now I'm leaking you and me all over them." Violet circles my nipple with a fingernail. "You make it seem effortless, but obviously it's not."

"I'm an athlete, Vi. Sex isn't a difficult workout; it's a fun one."

"I have a new appreciation for your level of endurance when we have sex."

"Making you come isn't work. I like taking care of you. I want to make you feel good. This—" I motion to my messed-up shoulder. "I don't like not being able to give you what you need."

"You just did."

"No, you got you off, not me."

Violet pushes up so she can look directly at me. "*You* got me off the first time. *We* got me off the second time. Super MC is a huge part of that equation. This is only temporary, Alex. You'll be fucking me into oblivion again soon enough."

"I'm looking forward to that."

Violet gets a warm washcloth and cleans me up. That part I'm good with. Her having a shower without me is another thing I'm perpetually bummed about these days. I could get in there with her, but washing myself is awkward, and then she'll want to do it for me. It's one thing when she's playing around and does it, but actually having to be my nurse is different. She's got enough extra work to do right now.

I watch her from the bed. She rubs her boobs all over the glass and then turns around and does the same thing with her ass. Any other time I'd get out of bed to do something about all the teasing, but sex has worn me out, so I stay where I am and admire the view.

My phone dings with a text from my dad as she gets out of the shower. We've had daily conversations, and there've been a lot of messages back and forth about how I'm feeling and the progress—or lack of—I'm making. This time he's letting me know he and my mom will be at the house in about fifteen minutes. I put on a clean pair of sweats and find a zip-up hoodie so I don't have to mess around with my shoulder too much.

"So, I did something, and I don't want you to be upset with me," Violet says.

I stop fighting the zipper and look at her.

She's wearing a red bra and matching panties. They're satiny. And distracting. This feels like a set-up.

"You can't use that as a conversation starter without making someone edgy, Violet."

"I'm making it sound worse than it is." She crosses over and adjusts my zipper, pulling it up for me. "So I figured your mom needed some help in the hair department."

"What did you do?" I sound snappy, because if there's one thing no one should ever mess with, it's my mom's hair. It might be two or three decades past it's prime, but it's how she wears it and no one, not even my dad, has ever been able to get her to change. It doesn't help that her longtime hairdresser supports the excessive use of hair products and teasing.

"Last night I emptied out all the cans of hairspray she brought with her, and then made sure we didn't have any more in the house."

"What the hell were you thinking?"

"That your mom is living in a time warp, and I'd like to be able to hug her without worrying about chemical poisoning or being ensnared in her web of hairspray! She's fine. I managed the situation." Violet adjusts her bra, pushing her boobs together.

"Managed it how?" Her cleavage is amazing, so it's impossible not to stare. I hope by the end of next week I'm not so stiff. Then maybe we could do boob sex. I miss it.

"I did her hair for her this morning."

"You what?" I'm getting hard again, which is a good sign.

"You can hold one if that'll help you pay better attention to this conversation." She takes my hand and puts it on her left boob. Then she puts a finger under my chin and gently encourages me to look her in the eye. "I styled her hair for her. If you could mention how nice it looks, it would be helpful. Hopefully your dad likes it, and we can convince her not to go back to her eighties time warp."

"You styled her hair? When?"

"Six-thirty this morning. She came knocking when she couldn't find hairspray."

"That was nice of you."

Violet shrugs. "I had selfish intent. I don't want her to have helmet hair for our wedding photos. Besides, it's time she dove hair-first into the twenty-first century. Next we'll have to take her clothes shopping. I'm going to get my mom in on that."

I stare at Violet and continue to hold her boob. First of all, I don't know why no one else has ever thought to do something like this to cure my mom of her eighties-hair-band-reject 'do. Second, Violet mentioned the wedding without making a face like she'd eaten something rotten and without any external prompting from me.

She drops my hand and leaves me standing in the middle of the room while she picks an outfit. She chooses a pair of jeans, which I had tailored specifically so they hug her ass, and a sexy red shirt that shows a tiny hint of cleavage.

"Aren't you going to put on pants?" She motions to my bottom half. "You can't hide a hard-on in those."

I glance down. She's right; I have an obvious semi. I haven't worn anything but sweats since coming home from the hospital. Zippers and buttons are a challenge. Violet disappears into the closet and returns with a pair of jeans. Then she helps me out of my sweats and into my pants. It puts her at eye level with my dick. She doesn't do anything but give it a pat and rearrange it so it's sitting at a nice angle.

I'm still slow on the stairs, but it's better than when I first came home. We're in the kitchen when my parents come in.

"Just act natural," Violet says.

"Okay." I can't imagine a change in hairstyle is going to make that much of a difference when my mom still dresses like it's 1986. I guess I'm so used to it that it's become normal for me.

We wait for them to appear, but all I hear are giggles from my mom and then nothing. Violet and I look at each other and head for the foyer. Now I'm seriously curious as to what's going on.

We catch them on the stairs. My dad looks like he's trying to hump her from behind.

"Hey, where are you guys going?"

My mom startles and moves to the next step, away from my dad. "Oh, Alex! I didn't expect you two to be awake! We were taking your dad's bag to the room."

I glance at the front door where my dad's suitcase sits. "Kinda helps if you take it with you."

"Oh! Oops! Well, that's okay. We can do it later."

My dad doesn't seem all that excited about doing it later. He looks more annoyed than anything, but he comes back down the stairs, turning on a smile for Violet.

"Hi, sweetheart. How's your week been? Alex is a mopey shit when he's not feeling well. I hope he hasn't been driving you insane." He pulls her into a hug and shoots a glare at me over her shoulder.

"He's been good, keeping the moping to a minimum for the most part."

My mother clears her throat like she's choking on something. I haven't been that bad. I don't think.

He whispers something to Violet, and she chuckles.

I turn my attention back to my mom, who's come down the stairs to join us. She's touching her hair, twirling it around her finger like Sunny often does when she's nervous or thinking. She looks ten years younger.

"Wow, Mom, you look great."

"Doesn't she?" My dad checks out my mom the way I do Violet after I've been at a series of away games—like I want to get her naked and do dirty things to her. It's a little weird. They must've been on their way upstairs to get their freak on before we stopped them.

My dad hugs me and grumbles something about me being a cockblocker, then slaps me on the back, making me groan. He eases up. "Still pretty sore?"

"It's getting better."

He nods and doesn't push me to say anything else, which is good, because talking about how long it's going to take to recover from this injury puts me in a bad mood. After the first couple of days I was sure I'd be fine by the end of the month. But considering the slow progression this week, and the reading I've done, I'm starting to come to terms with the fact that I'll be on the bench quite a while. I can't even start rehab for at least two more weeks, and that'll be limited to the recumbent bike and lower body only. Dislocated shoulders are almost as bad as broken bones, and concussions as serious as mine mean a significant recovery period. Next season has never seemed so far away.

My dad and I sit at the island and eat the fruit platter Violet's preparing while my mom puts fresh bread in the oven to bake. My dad eats the fruit almost as quickly as Violet cuts it up.

Everyone should be here soon. Along with Violet's parents, my sister and Miller, Charlene, Darren, Lily, and Randy are all coming over. Lance might even stop by. I have a newfound respect for him since he was benched for five games after beating the shit out of Cockburn.

On the other hand, I'm feeling ambivalent about Randy's recent string of goals. The team has won the last two away games, thanks to his superior skills. As good as that is, it's not so good for my position when I return to the ice. I'll be at tomorrow's home game, even though it means warming the bench and watching Ballistic get all my ice time.

Skye and Sidney are the first to arrive, and Skye freaks out about my mom's hair. It's weird to see two grown women get that excited about anything, let alone hair, but the attention seems to make my mom happy.

Sid gives me a light back pat while Violet hugs her mom and they talk about how awesome my mom's hair is.

I'm nervous about our moms being together today, because it's unlikely they'll be able to stop themselves from asking Violet about the wedding. She may have mentioned it of her own accord this morning, but I don't want anyone to push it. Not if I'm finally making headway.

I've already asked my mom not to bring it up, because we've got enough going on, but that doesn't mean Skye won't say something.

"I brought some things!" Skye sets a bag of groceries on the counter. It's not actually a bag of groceries. It's orange juice and several bottles of champagne.

"Mimosas!" my mom says, clapping excitedly.

I'm not so sure Skye is the best influence on my mother. Skye likes to drink, and she can hold her liquor. My mom, on the other hand, tries to keep up but gets sloppy a lot faster. This should be an interesting meal.

Violet chops up a pineapple while her mom gets out champagne glasses and starts mixing drinks. Violet almost chops off one of my dad's fingers because he can't seem to wait until she puts the fruit on the plate.

"Robbie! Be careful! You need those fingers," my mom admonishes.

Skye whispers something in my mom's ear, and the two of them giggle like teenage girls.

Violet rolls her eyes and keeps chopping. She stabs a chunk with a toothpick and reaches across the island. Instead of taking it, I bite it off the toothpick.

"Looks like the Waters men are interested in getting some action later. You should get on that, too, Sidney." Skye winks at him.

"Mom, please."

"What?" Skye takes a sip of her drink, testing it out. "Too much orange juice."

"Can we please have one family get-together without me needing therapy afterward?" Violet mutters.

"I didn't say anything."

"Mom..."

"Well, you know what they say about pineapple," Skye whispers.

My mom cocks her head to the side and twirls her hair around her finger.

Violet speaks before Skye can. "Seriously. Please do not tell Daisy that pineapple makes jizz taste better. It doesn't. That's a lie some man made up so that women will willingly swallow a load of splooge."

Sidney slaps the counter. "I think we should go sit down in the living room and let the girls do their thing."

My dad grabs the fruit tray and follows him. Violet shoots me a look that tells me she's not going to be all that excited if I leave, but I shrug and push away from the island. There's no way I'm staying for a conversation about the taste of jizz.

CONVERSATIONS WE SHOULD NEVER HAVE

VIOLET

Alex backs out of the kitchen, leaving me to deal with my mom and Daisy and conversations about pineapple-flavored jizz, as there's no one else here yet to act as a buffer. After all my efforts and sweating this morning, I'm less than impressed with Alex's choice to escape. Thankfully Charlene and Darren show up shortly thereafter.

They stop in the kitchen to say hello, but Darren soon disappears into the living room with the rest of the men. On the way out he spears a piece of pineapple from the cutting board and shoves it into his mouth. My mom and Daisy start giggling again, of course. The two of them have already polished off half a pitcher of mimosas. I haven't even touched mine. If I'm going to set a wedding date today—or at least commit to setting one

—I'm damn well going to be sober. That way no one can talk me into doing something I don't want to. Like having it televised.

"Charlene, maybe you can help us out," my mom announces. "Violet thinks pineapple doesn't change the taste of…" She gestures to her crotch meaningfully. "But Daisy and I disagree."

"You don't have to answer that," I jump in. "In fact, it's probably better if you don't encourage these two." I narrow my eyes at the moms.

My mom *tsk*s me. "Since when have you become such a prude, Violet?"

"Prude? Seriously? Are there no boundaries here? Since when is it appropriate to talk about the flavor of jizz with my mom and my fiancé's mother?"

"I think it's a perfectly normal discussion. Don't you, Daisy?" My mom looks to Alex's mom for confirmation.

"I think it's great that you and Violet have such an open relationship, Skye," Charlene says with an evil smile. "I wish I could talk to my mom about this kind of stuff, but she's kind of reserved."

I kick Charlene, so she pinches my side. Her mom isn't reserved at all.

My mom puts her hand on Charlene's shoulder. "You know you can always talk to me about these kinds of things, sweetie. I had a lot of fun before I settled down with Sidney, if you know what I mean."

"Robbie's the only man I've ever been with." Daisy's doing that twirling thing again with her hair.

My mom is definitely on the road to drunk, based on how touchy she's become. She pulls Daisy into a side-hug. "Since I already know the apple doesn't fall far from the tree in the package department, I can see why you would've claimed Robbie as soon as you could!"

"It was a little scary the first time."

"For the love of—" The doorbell rings. "I'll get that!" I yell, already on the move. Right about now I'd accept a stitchable laceration to get out of this dick discussion.

"I'll come with you!" Charlene follows me down the hall to the front door.

"Thanks for encouraging that. My therapy bills are going to be through the roof after today." I elbow her in the side.

"Those two are crazy."

"Do you think we'll be like that when we're their age?"

"I sure as hell hope so."

I open the front door to find Buck and Sunny, Balls and Lily, and Lance standing on the doorstep. Lance's massive lime green Hummer is parked in the driveway behind them. It's like a tank, but way more conspicuous. Kind of like Lance.

"Come on in, guys. Lily, Sunny, you're just in time to be emotionally scarred by hearing my mom and Daisy talk about jizz."

"So the usual?" Lily comes in for a hug.

"Do you girls talk about anything other than sex?" Randy helps Lily out of her coat and adjusts the strap of her dress, bending to kiss her shoulder. Those two radiate hormones.

"Not really," Charlene replies.

"I'm more than willing to hang out and talk about sex with you girls," Lance says.

"Over my dead fucking body, Romance," Randy says.

"So territorial." Lily rolls her eyes, but she's grinning.

Lance winks and squeezes my shoulder. "How's the captain doing?"

"He's getting better. It's slow going, but he looks a lot less like he's a victim of a mugging."

"Good to hear. He's missed on the ice."

"You should tell him that. I think his ego is almost as broken as his body."

I like Lance a lot more since he kicked the shit out of Cockburn. Not because of the reciprocated violence, but because of the retribution. He also dropped by the hospital more than once.

I still think he's the biggest manwhore in the entire league, but he's a good guy, even with the serious commitment and anger-management issues. He's a softie under that mountain of muscle and rage. He's messaged me every day and called to check on me and Alex. It's sweet.

Buck and Sunny are standing off to the side, whispering. Buck's cradling her cheek in his palm, forehead creased, and Sunny seems pale.

"Everything okay with those two?" I ask Lily, since they don't seem to be paying attention to anyone outside their bubble.

"We were playing charades until late." Lily says. "And drinking too much wine."

"Charades, huh?"

"The boys refused to play strip poker." Lily shrugs.

"Only I see you naked," Randy growls.

I'm missing all the action. With Alex being injured and Daisy here, company hasn't been an option, and I haven't felt right about going out to have fun while Alex suffers alone.

Buck and Sunny finally break apart. It's normal for him to fawn over her, but this seems excessive. "Sweets, I think you should sit down," he tells her.

"Honestly, I'm fine, Miller." She pats his hand and smiles, but she looks tired, and her eyes are red and puffy when she turns to me. "How's everything? Is my mom driving you nuts? What about Alex?"

"I haven't had to make a meal since she got here, and Alex is doing well, considering."

"She really does love to cook."

"I think we have meals covered for the next month."

"You need help with that, let me know; I'm always available for dinners on off-game days." Lance pats his insane shirt-covered six-pack.

"So are we." Randy slips his arm around Lily's waist and pulls her against him. Probably so he can rub his dick on her.

"I can cook just fine." Lily looks legitimately offended.

"You sure can, luscious, but I'm just offering our exceptional company in case Vi and Alex need it. Plus, I like their bathrooms."

I point a finger at Lily, because she's as bad as Randy with the sneaking off to have sex. "You two aren't allowed to disappear upstairs. Daisy's sleeping in the room you two like to get your fuck on in."

"There are plenty of rooms in this house, and beds are totally overrated." Randy rubs his beard on Lily's neck and she shivers.

It's like beard porn. I don't know how she stands it. I can't manage Alex with a scruffy face in the winter. My skin gets all red, and then it chafes and peels. Not sexy.

"You should ignore those two," Sunny motions to Lily and Randy. "It's like mating season."

"Really? You're going to talk to me about mating?" Lily shoots back.

Sunny's eyes flash, and Lily makes a face like she crapped her pants.

"Where's Alex?" Buck asks.

"They're all in the living room. They left when our moms started with the flavored-jizz talk."

Sunny either pretends I didn't say that or misses it completely. "Alex has been okay, though? He can be difficult when he's not feeling well."

"Oh, God! Remember when Alex got the flu, and he hurled in the middle of the hallway after eating a Big Mac combo? That was the worst idea ever." Lily makes a gagging sound.

Sunny puts her hand to her mouth. I think she might legitimately be gagging. "I need the bathroom." She hurries down the hall and slams the door.

"Guess we won't be using that bathroom later," Randy says to Lily.

"Is she okay?" I ask.

"Just feeling under the weather, that's all. She'll be fine," Lily reassures me.

Buck rubs the back of his neck. "You guys go ahead. I'll make sure Sunny's okay."

"I can stay with her if you want," Lily offers.

"It's cool. I got this."

Lily pats him on the shoulder, and we leave Buck in the hallway, tapping on the bathroom door.

"Must've been one hell of a night." I'm not sure if I'm disappointed I've been missing out on the fun, or worried about Sunny getting so drunk she's sick the next day.

When we get to the kitchen, my mom and Daisy are holding bananas and close-talking. I don't even want to know what's going on there.

My mom drops the banana on the counter and wipes her hands on her ass. "Randall! It's so good to see you! I can't remember the last time I chatted with you. How've you been? How's your family?"

My mom's excitement over Randy's arrival is unexpected. Her voice takes on that high-pitched, girly tone that makes everyone around her cringe, except Daisy.

"I remember when you and Buck used to have pimples, and you smelled more like goats than boys. You've really grown up, haven't you? Hasn't he?" She turns to me like she's looking for some kind of confirmation.

"How would I know? I only met Balls this year, when he and Miller were getting in trouble for all the stupid bunny business."

My mom ignores the bunny comment. "Oh, of course. You were too busy tutoring and being part of the Mathgeeks to be bothered with coming to games when Randall and Buck played rep."

"Mathletes, Mom, not Mathgeeks." It's already obvious I'm a math nerd. I don't need my mom outing my geek status from high school.

"You were a Mathlete?" Lance asks.

"I needed an extracurricular for college applications, and sports were out," I mumble.

Lance looks me over, but not in a typical pervy Lance way—more like he's assessing my level of physical fitness. "You look athletic to me."

"Dude." Randy punches him in the shoulder.

"What? It's an observation." Lance rolls his eyes. "Anyway, I was a Mathlete in high school, too."

"Really?" I don't know why I'm surprised. At this point I'm well aware that a lot of these guys are not just incredibly physically competent, but have brains to match.

"We won the all-state championship my senior year. I still have the trophy."

"I still have mine, too! I think it's packed away in a box in my office somewhere."

While Lance and I revel in our nerdiness, my mom rounds the island and approaches Randy. He and Buck have been friends for a long time, and obviously while I was out being a supernerd in high school, my mom was busy being a good stepmom to Buck.

She hugs Randy, which is a normal thing to do, but I should know better than to expect her to be appropriate, particularly since she and Daisy have already plowed through a bottle of champagne. My mom puts her hands on either side of Randy's face and pats his beard. Then she runs her fingers through it. "This is really impressive."

"Mom, what're you doing?" I'll be honest, I've actually considered doing that on more than one occasion. It really is an amazing beard.

Lily snickers. "It's soft, isn't it?"

"So soft!" My mom nods in agreement. "Daisy, you need to feel this. I never realized a beard could be so soft."

"He conditions it a lot." Lily's smirky face probably has a lot to do with the number of times those two have ended up in a bathroom with Randy on his knees.

"Really?" Daisy asks.

"Not as often as you probably condition your hair to keep it this soft," Randy fingers the end of Daisy's no-longer-solid hair, and she looks like she might combust. Balls has that effect on women.

Randy shoves his hands in his pockets while the moms stroke all over his beard. His smirk matches Lily's. "But I shampoo it like I do my hair."

I can see my mom's wheels turning, and I know for a fact that the next question out of her mouth is going to be embarrassing. I clap my hands to distract them. "Okay, well, I think that's enough beard fondling for today! The boys are in the living room, probably watching sports and drinking expensive scotch, so you guys can all go do that, too."

The moms stop with the beard love, and the guys disperse.

"Didn't Sunny and Miller come with you?" Daisy asks.

"They're here. Sunny's not feeling well this morning," Lily says.

"Oh?"

"She's in the bathroom. I think she's hurling," I offer.

Daisy and my mom exchange a glance, which they then share with Lily.

"I'll be right back." Daisy tosses her dishtowel on the island and takes off in the direction of the main floor powder room.

"Is there something going on?" I ask.

"You know how us moms worry," mine says.

I distinctly remember my mom's reaction to hangovers when I used to live in the pool house. She'd bring me a bottle of Gatorade, and that was about it.

Five minutes later, as we're putting brunch on the table, Sunny appears with Daisy. I swear they could pass for sisters now. Buck trails behind them. He looks stressed.

I want to corner him and find out what's going on, but everyone is gathering in the dining room to eat, so I don't have an opportunity.

My mom ends up sitting across the table from Randy. She puts her hand on Sidney's arm. "Sid, do you think you could grow a beard like that?"

"Like what?"

She gestures to his beard. "Like Randall's."

"Probably. Why?"

"I think you should."

"Beards are the best." Lily leans her head against his shoulder while she peers up at him with half-lidded eyes.

I point a finger at Lily. "No disappearing into the laundry room."

Randy grins as Lily's eyes go wide. "I have a laundry room in my own house, so I don't need yours anymore."

"Oh my God." Lily elbows him in the side and ducks her head, her hair barely covering her flushed cheeks.

"Was your washing machine broken?" my mom asks.

"In a manner of speaking."

"Let's eat!" I yell, much louder than I intended, because it's either that or I further degrade our level of conversation and embarrass Lily even more by explaining how she came on my washing machine during a dry-humping session with Balls. After we wiped it down with antiseptic, Alex and I tried it out—except we were naked and the machine was on.

Moments later, everyone's chatting and eating, except for Sunny, who's pushing food around on her plate. Buck keeps whispering in her ear and rubbing her shoulder. Lily does the same thing every once in a while from the other side. There's definitely something going on.

Daisy and my mom are seated beside each other, and I hear the word *wedding* get dropped. Alex tenses. I can feel his eyes on me. He hasn't said anything about setting a date for a long time. He's been so understanding about this. Maybe too understanding.

"Oh! That's a great idea. Violet, your mother is full of wonderful ideas." Daisy's hands flutter in the air.

"What's that?" I put my hand on Alex's thigh and give it a light squeeze.

"You and Alex could get married in an arena!"

"Mom, I thought we talked—" Alex begins.

Daisy cuts him off. "Isn't that fantastic? It's where you first met!" She flips her non-rock-solid hair over her shoulder.

I wanted to be the one to bring this up today, not the moms, and I want to decide, with Alex, where and when it's going to be.

"Aren't we looking at a wedding in the off-season?" I point out. "Why would we get married in a freezing arena? Isn't the point of a summer wedding that it's warm? Isn't that the same thing as taking an Alaskan cruise in the middle of the winter?"

"We could have the reception outside," my mom says.

"I don't think now—" Alex tries to cut in again, but I'm already on a tangent.

"I think we're all forgetting that I'm about as coordinated as a weeble-wobble. I'd probably fall on my face and knock my own damn teeth out if I had to be on skates. Or worse, I'd murder someone. And then I'll be in jail." I look to Balls. "Remember when we had that talk? About me going to prison for skate murder?"

Randy nods slowly. His eyes keep jumping from me to Alex, like he's unsure whether he's allowed to respond.

"I can totally give you lessons," Lily offers. "You made so much progress when we practiced before."

"What if you're my murder victim? What will Balls do with his balls then?" I shudder in my seat, holding back a thrust.

Randy chokes on his drink.

Buck clears his throat. "Uh, Vi—"

"Besides, Alex and I first met in the hotel bar when I accidentally flashed everyone my bra."

Alex coughs. As embarrassing as it is, it's true.

"That's a technicality," my mom says. "Don't you remember when Alex smashed into the plexiglas in front of us at the game?

You were all involved in reading something, not paying a bit of attention to what was happening on the ice, and then there he was! It was love at first sight."

"I'm pretty sure it was lust at first sight. And I spilled my beer all over myself." I'm still nursing my original mimosa, so I can't blame my mouth on anything but sudden nerves.

"I think it's perfectly romantic," my mom says.

Alex cuts in again, as if he's trying to save me from this conversation. "Now probably isn't the best time for this, Mom."

I can't keep putting him in this position where he feels the need to protect me from what should be an exciting time. I recognize that we belong together. Looking back, I can see clearly what I didn't before.

I remember every detail of the night Alex and I met. From Alex throwing a snit in the penalty box, to him smashing into the plexiglas and scaring the living crap out of me. I remember how pretty his eyes were and how I got caught there. I remember the immediate drooling in my panties and how it amplified when he got into the fight. I remember him sitting next to me in the bar, his rock-hard arm brushing mine. I tried so hard not to look directly at him, because his chiseled jaw and his sexy, beat-up face were hotter than I wanted them to be. His face is in a similar state right now.

I also remember my mortification over flashing the entire team my ridiculous bra, and eye-toking my cigarette when I ran away from him and indulged in my fake habit. And later I remember my shock and awe over the unveiling of the Super MC, my accidental cock-love chanting, and how sweet Alex was —and how even though I ran away from him again, he kept pursuing me. Because he knew then what it took me months to figure out: We belong together.

And now here we are, engaged since August while he's been patiently waiting for me to be ready to set a date. I'm such an idiot—and incredibly fortunate that Alex is secure enough not to take it personally. I hope, anyway. I think I may owe him an unconscionable number of sexual favors.

Before I can say what I need to, which is that I'm ready to put a ring on it, Sunny pushes away from the table, her chair making an awful grating sound on the hardwood, pulling the attention away from me and Alex.

Sunny's disturbingly pale as she stands up and says two words I totally don't expect to hear:

"I'm pregnant!"

14

WELL, THAT WAS UNEXPECTED

VIOLET

The entire table goes silent. Buck stands beside Sunny, his face ashen. Which tells me Sunny isn't blurting lies as an attempt at a kind distraction. Also, she's an abysmal liar.

"Uh, sweets…" Buck puts his hand on her lower back.

"Oh." She clamps a palm over her mouth, eyes tearful as she surveys the table. I'm sure my shock is mirrored around the room. Alex's thigh tenses under my hand. I'd squeeze more, but he has a lot of bruises.

Sunny turns to Buck. "Sorry. It slipped out."

Alex pushes back his chair like he's about to get up and throw down with Buck. "You're shitting me, right?"

"Alex, language," Daisy says.

He looks incredulous. "Seriously? Sunny tells us she's pregnant, and you're worried about my language?"

"We didn't mean for it to happen." Sunny does the hair-twirl thing.

I'm not sure what to say. I mean, I guess it should be congratulations, but if I got pregnant, I don't think I'd be all that excited. Alex and I are just getting started. I'm not very mature. I'm highly aware of my inability to manage more than Pop-Tarts most days, let alone being responsible for all of someone else's needs.

Daisy's being here has made it apparent that I have a lot of work to do before I can be considered an accomplished housewife. I should be able to do better than the four dinner items I've mastered thus far.

Sunny and Buck have only been together officially for a few months, though they've been dating for the better part of a year. They aren't even living together. This is going to change their entire lives. Or it already has. A lot like Alex's accident has inadvertently changed ours.

I press my boobs against Alex's arm, hoping they'll calm him down. He's clenching his fist, not seeming happy at all that Sunny is preggers.

"I should—" Alex takes a deep breath.

"What're you gonna do, Waters? Kick my ass? Pretty sure you're not gonna win the fight this time around."

Of course this is like throwing lighter fluid on a burning firecracker. Alex pushes up out of his chair. Since I'm holding onto his good arm, I come up with him. I'm ashamed to say my beaver gets a little drooly over it.

"Buck," I warn.

"What? It's not like we planned this," he snaps.

"Heard of birth control, asshole?" Alex fires back.

Robbie throws his napkin down. "Alex, you're making your sister upset. Sit down."

For whatever reason, Robbie doesn't look surprised about

this. Maybe he's not. Actually, as I survey the room, I can see that Charlene, Darren, me, and Alex are the only ones who seem the least bit shocked by this shocking news. Lily looks anxious, and Randy's uncomfortable, maybe because Alex is being his usual overprotective self and he's Buck's bestie.

"You should apologize to Miller," Sunny pipes up. "He's not an a-hole. He loves me, and I love him, and I know you don't use condoms either, Alex. Sometimes things happen that are outside of our control." She gestures to his slowly healing face. "You should know this."

"Congratulations?" My voice is excessively loud, and it comes out a question instead of like I'm happy for them.

Sunny gives me a small, watery, "Thanks, Violet."

"You need to hug your sister," I hiss at Alex as I round the table to do just that.

There's a flurry of feminine chatter as we all gather around Sunny and hug her like she's won the lottery, not like she's going to spend the next nine months getting fat and uncomfortable. And the next twenty years dealing with a lot of responsibility.

Sunny has just become legal in the US. And now she's going to be a mom. She's in the middle of finishing school. She teaches yoga, which can't be easy with a basketball hanging off the front of your body. It's more than I can fathom.

And Buck, well, Sunny's the first girl he's ever been serious with. I mean, he's really serious, but babies are a lot of work. More than house plants, that's for sure. I can't imagine he's ready for that kind of full-on, endless responsibility. Why the fuck do people have babies? I can barely manage my own life, and taking care of Alex while he's recovering from his hockey accident is like being punched in the tit by reality. And I haven't even had to do it on my own yet.

Life isn't all roses and unicorn farts made of glitter and Chanel No. 5. There are as many downs as there are ups. I need to learn how to manage them.

No one mentions the wedding again during brunch. The

entire focus has shifted to the impending birth of Sunny and Buck's accidental insemination.

One positive is that neither one of them mentions getting hitched before the baby pops. If Sunny and Buck jump on the wedding wagon, it'll make things more difficult for Alex and me. Not that I wouldn't understand. But I know Alex would have something to say about them tying the knot first, because Sunny is younger, and Alex likes to be number one, in all senses of the word—except the selfish context. I always come first.

By three in the afternoon, it's obvious the number of people in the house has taken its toll on Alex. His sister being pregnant and suddenly planning a baby shower probably hasn't been helpful, either. So it's not much of a surprise when he starts nodding off on the couch while people are chatting.

He's only been home a week. He's still recovering.

So everyone leaves, except his parents, of course. There's a conversation brewing. I know this. But Alex isn't in any state to have it. I rouse him, gently, and get him to amble his way up to the bedroom.

He won't let me go when he lies down; his one good arm is strong enough to keep me from getting away—not that I would want to do that anyway.

I let him pull me to him. I fully expect him to fall asleep again, but that's not what happens. He lies there with his arm around me, breathing steadily, but I can tell he's not out.

"Are you okay?" I ask, opening the door to angry town.

"I don't know."

"Because Sunny's pregnant," I say it more than ask.

"Yeah. No. I don't know." He sighs, and his grip on my waist tightens.

"What don't you know about?"

His chest rises and falls a few times. "I just...she's not ready."

"I don't think anyone's ever ready."

"Miller's less ready."

I think about that. About how good Buck is with kids. How patient, how caring. I also consider his dyslexia, which he manages fine, and how that will factor in with a kid, and how likely he is to pass it on. I don't know the statistics on this kind of thing, but I know it's something he'll worry about.

Knowing Buck the way I do, I feel like this is something he'll be super stressed about. He struggled so much with school and expectations. It'll kill him if he has to watch his own kid go through the same thing. But his experience will make him able to manage it better. At least I hope it will. I'm sure it will. He's a beautiful person. Hairy as a motherpucker, but a great human.

"He'll ask for help if he needs it. He always does. He'll be an awesome dad."

Alex is quiet for a while—so long I'm not sure if he disagrees or maybe he's fallen asleep. "Do you think I'll be an awesome dad?"

There's no hesitation in my response. "Of course." He'll be doting, wonderful, and probably a whole lot overprotective. Lord help us if we have a girl somewhere down the line. "You know, as much of a shock as it is and how the timing could be better, it could be way worse."

"How so?" Alex asks.

"Well, first of all, at least it's not her ex-boyfriend's baby."

"You mean Kale?"

"Yeah. That guy's a dick."

Alex nods. "He really is. Miller's a good guy; I know that. I just feel like all this has happened really fast for the two of them, and Sunny has always wanted a career. This is going to put that on hold."

I repeat Sunny's words. "Things happen that are beyond our control all the time, Alex."

He sighs. "I figured we'd have kids before they did."

I consider that as he strokes the nape of my neck with his thumb. It's softer than usual, possibly because he hasn't been on the ice, wearing those gloves, or lifting weights.

As juvenile as it might be, Alex is very much a competitive person. He's used to being the center of attention all the time, and Sunny has never been one to steal the limelight. Until now. I think I was right. This really is bugging him. "Is this about being first? Or because Sunny's stealing your spotlight?"

"What?"

I lift my head off his chest so I can look at him. "Is this because Sunny's younger and doing it first?"

Alex regards me for a long time while he chews on the inside of his lip. "Having kids young isn't the worst thing in the world."

I don't fail to notice he hasn't answered the question. When all I do is stare, Alex takes the opportunity to explain.

"Think about it, Violet, that kid is going to be out of the house before those two are fifty."

"And? What does that matter?"

"They'll have all this time after they retire to do whatever they want. By the time they're in their forties, the kid will basically be doing his own thing—or her own thing. Think about all that time together. Alone. With no real responsibilities other than making sure the kids don't fuck up their post-secondary education."

"Buck dropped out after the first semester of college and Sunny's going to get a diploma she might never use," I point out.

"She can focus on a career later, if she wants one," Alex argues.

"*If* she wants a career? You think she won't?"

He lifts his good shoulder in response.

"She could've moved here, dropped out of college, and sponged off you, but she doesn't. She pays rent, and she actually thinks it's going toward the mortgage."

"Putting money into stocks for her is a good financial investment."

"I'm not saying it isn't. But she very easily could've shacked up with Buck and not paid rent at all. She chose not to. Just like I chose to live in that shitty apartment for a while with my stinky, metal-loving stalker neighbor. Just like I want to keep my job in some capacity, at least for a few more years until I get used to all of this." I gesture to the room and the massive bed we're lying on.

"I don't want to take away the things that make you you, Violet." Alex seems distressed, maybe by the parallels I've drawn between me and Sunny. "That's never been my intention. I want to build us a life that's going to allow you to do all the things you want and more."

I touch his pretty, beat-up face. "I know that. It's just… It can be scary being engaged to a man who can give me everything, because this is all I have." I gesture to my rack, trying to lift the weight of this conversation.

Alex doesn't take the bait. "Baby, you underestimate how incredible you are. Even though it's a challenge and sometimes seriously inconvenient for me, I love that you assert your independence, that you have your own mind."

His acknowledgement makes me feel all warm and gooey, liked melted caramels. "So you get that Sunny needs to be her own person. She doesn't want to be defined by who she's with, either. It's kind of the reason she was hesitant to date Buck in the first place."

"She was hesitant about Miller because he fucked anything with a pulse."

"Okay, fine. That was part of it. But she wants to take care of herself, not have everyone else do it for her. And she didn't want to end up being like your mom."

"There's nothing wrong with the way my mom did things."

"Maybe the way your mom did things was right for her, but

that doesn't mean it's right for everyone. Isn't it for Sunny to decide what's right for her?"

"Of course it is. But babies change things, Violet. Priorities change."

He has a point. "Okay. I can see that. Maybe she'll decide to forgo the career and have enough children to start a hockey team." I shudder at the possibility of shooting multiple kids out of my vagina.

"You say that like it's a bad thing."

"Do you have any idea what happens to a vagina when a litter of babies are pushed out of it? I don't want to end up with a baggy beaver."

"You won't end up with a baggy beaver from having a few kids."

"A few?" He's said something similar before. I want to know what constitutes *a few*. "As in more than two?"

"I kind of like the idea of a big family." Alex skims the side of my boob with his fingertips.

I prop myself up on an arm so I can look him directly in the eye. "When you say *big*, what do you mean, exactly?"

Alex looks unsure of himself. "I don't know. Four kids seems reasonable, maybe more."

"Four?" If I sound incredulous, it's because I am.

"You think that's too many?"

"Uh, I'll definitely have a baggy beaver if I push four kids out."

"Things go back to normal."

"No, they don't."

"Come on, Violet. It can't really be that bad."

"Is that you hypothesizing, since you can't actually push a hockey puck out of your dick hole?"

Alex cringes, which I can understand. The image I've created is rather unappealing.

"You're still tight like you were the first time we had sex, and we've been together for more than a year. You'd think if I was going to stretch things out, it would've happened already."

He's got a half-smug, half-horny smirk on his half-healed face.

"Yeah, but you're comparing a beer can to a watermelon. It's not the same thing. I can see after pushing one watermelon out, things might go back to mostly normal, and maybe you wouldn't notice much beaver bagginess. But after three or four, things aren't going to be the same."

He gives me this look, like he thinks I'm being dramatic.

"Haven't you seen that documentary with that female porn star who had all that anal sex? She had a nice, normal Area 51 until it wasn't nice and normal anymore. Now it's all loose and baggy, just like my beaver would be if I happened to pop out a hockey team's worth of babies."

"So you don't want a big family?"

"I'm an only child, Alex. I think I turned out almost okay even though I never had a sibling until I was in my teens. I figure if I have two kids, they'll drive each other nuts, and they won't be lonely or have to deal with either one of us without backup when we're old and crotchety."

"What about compromising at three?"

"Odd numbers don't work for me. I don't like them. If your team number was odd, I think I might not have found you all that attractive."

"My number is odd."

"Not when you add it together."

I'm being an asshole, but seriously. Alex is talking about what seems like a minimum of four kids. I'll low-ball it to something more reasonable, like two, and if he gets more than that it'll seem like a win for him.

Honestly, though, I can't imagine the damage three babies will do to my body. I like my boobs. Alex loves my boobs. Three babies will turn them into empty sacks, according to all the horrible conversations I've overheard from women I work with.

And babies interfere with sex. I don't want to deal with that yet either.

"I don't know why we're talking babies when we don't even have our wedding planned."

Alex's jaw tightens, and he retracts his arm from around me. Oh, shit. I've hurt his feelings. He seems like he's about to get up and possibly leave the room.

"Which I think we should talk about," I add.

He's halfway into a sitting position. He drops back down on the pillow and eyes me warily. He looks uncertain. Afraid, even.

I sit up and face him, crossing my legs. "You're going to have some time on your hands while you're waiting for your shoulder to heal."

He still looks unhappy.

"So I figure it's probably a good idea to plan something for the summer, before you have to start hardcore pre-season training."

He stares blankly at me.

"Unless you think you're going to be too busy with physical therapy. I mean, then maybe we should just wait until the following off-season…" I poke at the hole in my sock until my middle toe peeks out.

"You want to get married this summer?" Alex sounds like he's having a hard time believing it could be possible.

"You'll have the time to help me plan it. I know I'm organized with numbers, but that's really about the only thing. There won't likely be another year where the timing will be on our side. We can make the best out of an unfortunate situation." I peek up at him. He's still frowning. "I thought you'd be excited about setting a date."

"I would be if it didn't feel like you were only doing this to make me feel better about being out for the season." He's sulking. He's so cute. And sensitive.

"It has nothing to do with that!" I say. Then I consider my

reasons and decide I should rephrase. "Okay, so it has everything to do with you being out for the season."

Alex pushes back up into a sitting position. I grab his good arm before he can try to run away from me. Not that he would be very fast, but I don't want him to hurt himself. "You're misunderstanding me. This accident opened my eyes to a lot of things, the most pivotal being how important you are to me."

That stops him. He shifts so he can look at me. He's still stiff, but he's sensitive, so I assume he's trying to reconcile his fragile ego.

"I know how hard this is on you. I know it's killing you to see Randy doing so well. That's not why I want to marry you this summer. This—" I gesture to his body, because there are a lot of parts that are still injured. "—made me very aware of how we only get one shot at life."

"I don't want this decision to be fear-based," Alex says.

"It's not." I take his hand in mine and play with his fingers. His nails are longer than usual. Probably because he can't cut them on his own. "Look, my mom's wedding wasn't fun for me. And you know how I am when I get into a group of people. I always make an ass out of myself. But I'm willing to deal with that kind of potential humiliation if it means I get to spend the rest of my life with you."

He regards me for a long moment. "You really want to get married this summer?"

I nod.

"And it's not because you feel bad for me?"

"I wouldn't marry you just to make you feel better about yourself, Alex. Usually your ego is plenty big without my help, anyway."

He wears a small, cocky grin. "So you want to marry me to stake a claim on my dick?"

"Super MC deserves a wedding all his own. We'll have a private Super MC and beaver ceremony." I've thought about this a lot. I've even researched the costumes. Not that Alex needs to know this. A beaver only gets promised to her Super MC once in a lifetime.

"That sounds like fun." His grin widens.

"It will be if my beaver has anything to do with planning it."

Building him up is the best thing I can do for both of us. Also, it's true. Alex is a lot of things—confident in the bedroom, amazing on the ice—but he also needs a lot of positive reinforcement. I used to think his asking if I was enjoying myself when we had sex was about courtesy.

Partly it is. He likes to know he's making me feel good. It's also because he wants affirmation that he's getting me off. He loves that I chant my love of his cock when I come. It's the biggest ego stroke in the world for him. I've realized he's like that with everything. The more praise he gets, the better he feels about himself.

That's not to say he's egotistical. He thrives on reinforcement. And I'm not above giving it to him to make things easier for everyone. My man can be a delicate flower. It's a sexy contradiction to the badass hockey player I get to watch on the ice.

Except not for the rest of this season, hence the need to fill the void. And what better way to fill it than with a wedding?

I have lots of thoughts on weddings. Mainly, I feel like they're an archaic, patriarchal method of staking a claim on a beaver. Which might have been necessary in the dark ages, but isn't so much now.

Beyond that, I'm kind of excited to dress up like a princess for an afternoon, as long as I can wear flip flops under the dress, because heels suck.

"So you're sure about this summer?"

"Positive."

"I can check out venues this week," he offers.

"That'd be awesome." Score one for Violet. Just like I planned, I won't have to do all the legwork, and Alex will have something to occupy his time while he's recovering.

However, I'm not a wedding savant. I have absolutely no

idea how much time and effort goes into planning one, or how challenging it's going to be to rein in Daisy and my mom once we tell them it's happening.

I also have no idea how gung ho Alex is going to be about the wedding. And I should. Because I know how he is about everything else in his life.

He's two-hundred percent about being the best hockey player.

He's two-thousand percent about being the best orgasm distributor.

He's two-million percent about being the best fiancé.

So of course he's going to up his game when planning a wedding. I should know this, but all I can think about is how I'm making my life easier while I stroke his ego.

I really should know better by now.

15

DON'T TAKE THE EASY WAY OUT

VIOLET

My phone buzzes for the eighty-millionth time. It's a group message that includes my mom and Daisy. This whole feed started this morning. At six a.m. On a Saturday. It's been endless since Daisy left three weeks ago, and it only seems to be picking up momentum.

"You should turn that off," Charlene says. "The whole point of this afternoon is to relax, and your phone buzzing constantly is the opposite of relaxing."

"I'm sure it's just some pictures." I shove a biscotti into my mouth so I'm unable to answer questions.

I follow it up with a sip of my lactose-free latte. My dairy cravings have gone through the roof. It's directly related to Daisy and my mom's incessant texting.

Daisy and Robbie are coming for a visit next weekend. I'm not sure why since I talk to her every single day.

About the wedding.

The motherpucking wedding.

And of course Sunny's pregnancy figures in heavily. Weddings and babies are Daisy Waters' crack fix. And my mom's. I had no idea she was such a baby freak until Sunny got herself impregnated with Buck's yeti spawn.

Despite the incessant texts and emails, I'm not having regrets about agreeing to the wedding this summer. Not real regrets. Not the kind where I'm all, *shit, let's hypothesize what it will be like if someone gets murdered before this is over and I have to have a prison relationship with Alex where they put me in a facility that doesn't allow for conjugal visits. I'll have to smuggle cucumbers in my vagina so I can get myself off.*

Nope. I'm not worried about murder.

It's not like that at all. Mostly. Sort of.

Cucumbers must be in high demand in women's prisons.

I give in when my phone registers eleven new messages and check them.

There are ten pictures, all potential locations for our wedding. Which Alex has been working on finding since I gave him the all clear to start planning.

"I don't get why Daisy can't find a venue that houses less than two hundred people. Actually I don't get why she's finding venues at all. I need this thing to be small."

"That's because my mom thinks two hundred people is small," Sunny says. She turns the nail polish over and reads the fine print on the back. "Should I be worried about the chemicals in this? Are the oils they use here natural?" She pats her tummy —her still mostly flat tummy. She's not really showing yet. She looks mostly like she ate a large meal and hasn't quite digested it.

"I researched everything before we scheduled the appointments," Lily reassures her. She gives her best friend's mini-bump a rub. "Everything is baby-safe."

The four of us have been spending a lot of time together. While Alex is busy planning our wedding—with the unneeded interference of our mothers (I don't know why they don't just text him)—I'm helping Lily plan a baby shower for Sunny. Baby stuff is way more fun than I expected; it's all cute and tiny.

"Yeah, well, my idea of small is more around the forty-people mark. We could have it in the backyard and be done with it."

"You had two hundred people at the engagement party in the backyard," Lily points out.

"I'm surprised you remember that since you spent half the night locked in a spare bedroom getting boned by Horny Nut Sac."

"You sound jealous, Vi." Lily has adopted Randy's snarky tone and his smirky smirk. It's almost as cute as it is annoying.

Normally I wouldn't be jealous, but Alex's physical state has continued to put a damper on the beaver lovin'. He's much better than he was when he first came home from the hospital, and the Super MC hugs are increasing in frequency, but he's not at his pre-accident level of stamina. It's driving him insane. My legs look great, though, so that's a plus.

Still, Lily's sex life is something to be envious of. If anyone should be pregnant in this room, it's her. I think she gets more dick than any of us. Possibly combined. Those two are fuck-crazy.

Instead of owning my jealousy, I return the snark. "Jealous of your sex life? Hardly. My sex life makes your sex life look like a cheap prostitute."

"A cheap prostitute?" Lily scoffs. "If anything, my sex life is the most well-paid prostitute out there."

The lady working on my toenails coughs.

Charlene gives Lily a high five and laughs. "Uh, from all the bitching you've been doing lately, I'm gonna call beaver bullshit on you."

"I'm getting monster cock injections," I snap.

"Not enough, based on how cranky you are and how many times you've watched the final scene of *Magic Mike XXL*."

I shoot Charlene a glare. "He's a great dancer."

"Right. And that's why you're watching that scene all the time and then disappearing to the bathroom."

"That's a total lie! I only did that once." I'm much too loud. Thankfully, it's only the four of us and the ladies who work in the spa, plus some ancient, overly plastic-surgeoned lady getting a pedicure on her terrifying feet. But I assume she's too old to eavesdrop, or understand the content of our conversation.

"I know of at least three occasions when you've referenced that movie and marble rolling," Charlene counters.

Damn it and damn her for throwing me under the bus.

"I don't think about anyone but Miller when we're having sex," Sunny says.

"Randy makes it impossible to focus on anything but him. That man's tongue. God." Lily sort of sigh-moans.

"I'm fully engaged in boning with Alex, but there's less of it lately than I'm used to, and unlike Lily White Balls over here, Alex and I don't send each other masturbation videos every five minutes."

Lily gasps, and she pokes Sunny in the arm. "That's supposed to be a secret!"

I come to Sunny's immediate defense. She isn't the reason I know about the amateur porn. "She didn't tell me. Miller let it slip. Apparently Randy inadvertently sent him one of the videos he meant to send to you."

Lily grabs her phone, but I snatch it from her before she can do something stupid, like call Randy and get pissed.

"It was a video of his frank and beans." I cringe, because my wiener reference could be mistaken for insensitivity. "Sorry, I don't mean that the way it sounds."

Lily waves me off, apparently relieved that Buck didn't get a shot of her beaver. Her titanium, magic beaver.

"I'm sure Miller has seen Randy's junk plenty of times. As

long as it's not my parts he got to see, I think we're good," she says.

"Before I moved to Chicago, Miller and I used to have Skype sex. And we still do when he's at away games, obviously," Sunny says and sighs. "I'm not sure I'll feel like doing that when I'm busting out a baby belly, though."

"You never know. Maybe he'll be one of those guys who's all about pregnancy porn. I can definitely see Buck getting into that." I'm trying to be supportive, not sound like a creep, but based on the looks from the women who work at the spa, I'm unsuccessful.

"I just mean he's down with you being pregnant," I add to clarify.

"He's actually really excited. And now that I'm only a few weeks from graduation, I am, too." Sunny gives her non-existent belly an affectionate pat.

"You're going to be the most amazing mom, Sunny." Lily's smile is one-hundred-percent genuine.

"You really are," I agree. I've seen her with her dogs. It has to translate. This might've been a surprise, but she's rolling with it. I have to say, I'm kind of envious of how easily she manages life-altering changes.

Not to mention, Buck seems to have embraced impending daddyhood now that the shock has worn off. I think he was mostly apprehensive about the family reaction.

Skye can't wait to be a grammy, and Sidney, well, I think he's relieved Buck's in an actual committed relationship.

Robbie didn't threaten to murder Buck for knocking Sunny up—that's Alex's role apparently. And even that didn't last long. Daisy's been hinting that maybe Alex and I want to jump on the baby bandwagon so Sunny and I can deal with the little barnacles of bliss together.

Alex, who has already expressed his desire to produce a hockey team's worth of offspring, doesn't seem to have any problem putting a bun in my oven now that he's past the whole anger and rage phase—which was a lot shorter than I expected it to be, with a twenty-four-hour residual irritation hangover.

While I'm excited for Sunny and Buck, I'm not on the same page as Alex when it comes to creating spawn. I'm not even reading a book in the same damn series.

No babies. Yet. First we get married and have lots of married sex.

I scratch my arm and immediately check for stress hives, which usually only appear during wedding-related discussions. They start in the same place every time: about two inches below a small mole on my right wrist. If I catch it fast enough, I can stop them from spreading up my arm and covering my chest. If I don't, I'll be covered head to toe within an hour or so. Thankfully they've been infrequent these last few weeks. I'm attributing it to the amount of yoga I've been doing to get all Zen.

I root around in my purse for my antihistamines, to ward off a potential problem. The hives upset Alex because he thinks they mean I have reservations about the wedding, which I don't. It's the mom interference that's my issue. I pop one, washing it down with my sparkling lemon water.

I honestly don't give a flying fuck where we get married. It could be in our damn bathroom.

Okay. Not true. Our bathroom is kind of gross most of the time, even though someone comes to clean it regularly.

But beyond that, the location is simply a means to an end. All I want is to be Violet Waters and look pretty for a day. Then I want to dress up Alex's dick in a tiny tux, or maybe a superhero cape, and make him marry my beaver.

"Vi?"

I look up from my phone. "Yeah?"

"Did you hear anything I said?" Charlene asks.

"Oh yeah, of course." I nod in affirmation.

She regards me dubiously. "Really? So you think it's a great idea for me to blow Darren during your wedding ceremony?"

"Uh, I think we've already established that you blowing Darren in a public place is not appropriate. However, if I say or do something dumb during the ceremony and you decide you want to pull that stunt to save me from personal humiliation, by all means, go right ahead."

"You gave Darren public fellatio?" Sunny looks more intrigued than disturbed.

Lily's biting her nails with this little smile tugging at the corner of her mouth.

Charlene scoffs. "It's called road head, girls."

Lily's grin gets bigger.

"You've totally given Horny Nut Sac road head!" I point an accusing finger at her.

"Of course! It's the best way to make sure he's going to last the first time we have sex after away games," she says.

"This!" I throw my hands up and almost kick the girl working on my toes in the face. "Shit. Sorry." She pats my ankle. I see her once every three weeks because Alex likes it when my toes and fingers are pretty, so she's used to my antics. "This is what I'm talking about. That's smart thinking, girl. Although, based on your condom usage, I'm not so sure you need to do that prior to getting balled by Balls."

Lily shrugs. "He went a lot of years without the joys of blowies. He deserves every last one of them."

"Sometimes I give Alex the lollipop treatment so he isn't as hard on the beaver," I add.

I get murmurs of agreement, except for Charlene. She's quiet on this one. Maybe because she lets Darren Area 51 her.

"At least you have boob sex as an option," Lily points out.

I glance down at my rack and give the girls an affectionate squeeze, then poke Lily's much smaller, but still nice, boob. "I'm sorry you don't have mountains to slide between."

Lily shrugs. "I make do with what I've got, and Randy loves them just fine."

My phone buzzes with several new messages, all from Daisy

and my mom. I give in and check them. Apparently there's some urgency to booking one of these places, as they have five people interested in the same weekend in August that Alex and I suggested. This particular venue accommodates four hundred people.

It's excessive and unnecessary.

I keep saying I want to keep it small, and Alex agrees. I've sent the moms messages indicating this, as has Alex, but then his mom sends me stuff like this, and I wonder if we're going to be able to get away with having the wedding we want. Or more that I want. Alex doesn't have a thing against big weddings. He just wants me to be happy and to be his wife. But I'm not sure even he has enough power to keep the moms in check. Although in his defense, I haven't told him about the recent insurgence of interference. I think they're having trouble understanding that he's taking the reins on this one.

We spend the rest of the afternoon being pampered and eating those tiny tea sandwiches with the crusts cut off. It's luxurious and ridiculous, but I feel like I deserve it with the accident, the pregnancy, and now the wedding plans.

When we're finished, Charlene drops Lily and Sunny off at their house first. I think the plan is for Buck to move in there as soon as he can.

I check my phone again and sigh. Twenty-three new messages from my mom and Daisy have appeared between leaving the spa and now. Two more are from Alex. Those are the ones I check. He wants an ETA so he can get dinner started. He also says he has an idea for the perfect wedding venue. I really hope so.

I message back to let him know I'm on my way.

He follows up by telling me he has some great news, and he can't wait until I'm home so he can tell me. I wonder if it's wedding-related—and then congratulate myself on the budding maturity that allows me to see something wedding-related as potentially good news.

"Alex is totally into the whole wedding thing?" Charlene says.

"*So* into it. I figured he'd be excited since he doesn't have a whole lot to keep him occupied these days. He's taken most of the details out of my hands, which is a good thing because I am not an event planner, as evidenced by the engagement party and the way our moms took over."

"So he's not driving you insane?"

"Surprisingly no. He's been really good about it. It's our moms who are the issue. They keep texting me."

"You need to put a stop to that."

"I'm sure once we figure out the venue it'll be fine." All the nice places Alex likes are booked out all the way until next summer. Now I get why people plan weddings way in advance.

"I hope so, for the sake of your sanity. How's rehab going for Alex?"

"Slower than he'd like." He's only been able to start light workouts in the past week, but it's been limited to lower body and he wants to do more than he should.

"Darren says he's pushing himself hard."

"He's used to minor injuries. Logically he knows he won't play again this season, but it's really eating at him that he's not going to be on the ice during playoffs."

Charlene nods. "It's been a hard season for the team."

"It really has. He's also been worried about what next season is going to look like. It'll take the entire summer for him to recondition his shoulder." I bite my nail, but stop before I ruin my manicure. "He thinks Randy's going to take his position as primary center."

"I don't know about that."

"Randy's really stepped it up since Alex has been out." I feel like a traitor saying it out loud.

"That doesn't mean they're going to hand him Alex's spot."

"I know, but he's concerned about it. If he isn't planning our wedding, he's watching the games on repeat. He makes notes on

Randy's moves, but if I ask he plays it off like he's just staying on top of things."

"He's so competitive."

"He really is. And he's hyper-aware that he's getting older. There aren't a whole lot of players who make it much past thirty. Alex is afraid this injury could speed up his retirement." I scratch my wrist. I've already taken an antihistamine. I can't go home with hives.

"He has a plan for what he wants to do after his hockey career is over, though, right?"

"Oh, he sure does. He wants to get me pregnant so I can birth his next hockey team."

Charlene barks out a laugh. "You and Alex will have pretty hockey babies. Let's hope they have his coordination; otherwise they'll be well-read accountants."

"Amen to that. It'd be nice to have kids whose GPAs aren't thrown off by crappy marks in phys ed. You know, if they had a class in like, Tai Chi or something, I might've had a hope in hell of getting a legitimate, solid B."

"Instead your boobs got it for you."

"Gotta love the perks of perky boobs. I'll be sad when mine start sagging."

"Shh!" Charlene cups one of hers. "Don't talk about things like that. Besides, you'll be able to afford to have the girls lifted if you're desperate to defy gravity."

"So true. But this whole marrying a hockey player thing is way more complicated than I ever imagined."

"At least you've found the love of your life. You'll work through all the hard parts."

"He really is amazing. I can deal with the complications if it means spending the rest of my life with him."

Speaking of hard parts, I'm looking forward to jumping on Alex's when I get home. My nails aren't the only thing I had decorated this afternoon.

EXTRA-LOUD MUSIC GREETS me when I open the door, as does the smell of bacon and pancakes. I've discovered Alex likes to cook, and he's good at it. Being out for the rest of the season means he's less restrictive about his diet, too, so it's not all whole-grain this and high-fiber that.

I find him in the kitchen, standing in front of the stove making pancakes. In his boxer briefs. His Super MC boxer briefs. On the back it says Violet's ASS. On the front is a Superman-style logo with MC in the middle instead of an S.

His hair is wet. It's still longer than usual these days, curling around his ears. I observe him for a minute, since he's still unaware that I'm home thanks to the music blasting through the speakers. This isn't Alex's usual music choice. I listen to the lyrics as I stare at his ass—his super-tight ass, enveloped in red cotton.

I realize I know this song. It's from my favorite movie, and it's about Oreos. Actually it's about beaver licking, and it's super dirty. Alex busts out when the chorus comes on and shakes his ass a little. It's awesome. And cute, and kind of sexy.

It isn't until he flips the pancakes that I realize his arm isn't in a sling, and his ribs aren't taped. The bruises are gone, apart from a few yellowish spots on his shoulder and legs.

"What's going on here?"

Alex startles and looks over his shoulder. "Oh, hey. I didn't hear you come in." He grabs the remote from the counter and turns the volume down.

"You're not wearing your sling."

I drop my purse on the counter and come up behind him. Snaking an arm around his waist, I press my boobs against his back. His skin is warm, and he smells like my favorite body wash.

"That's what I wanted to tell you! Doc gave me the all clear. No more sling."

It's been over a month since the accident, but the doctors projected at least six weeks before he'd be out of a sling. "Really?"

Alex moves the pan off the burner and turns around so my boobs are pressed against his abs instead of his back. And now his snuffie is pressed against my stomach.

He tucks my hair behind my ear with the hand attached to the injured arm and shoulder. "Really. And it looks like there isn't any negative residual impact from the concussion either."

I hug him tightly, relieved. More than the broken body parts and obvious physical wounds, this was the part we were most anxious about. "That's awesome news. Doesn't this mean you're ahead of what the doctors projected?"

"Yeah, by almost two weeks. The doctor said I can start a modified workout schedule to rehabilitate my arm."

"That's so good, Alex."

"I think so, too. I'm looking forward to having my stamina back." He shifts his hips so I can feel him growing.

"I love your stamina."

He skims my arms with his fingertips, unhooking my hands from around his waist so he can see my fingernails. "You have a good time with the girls?" It's a French manicure except for my index fingers. Those are painted white with the Super MC logo nail stickers I had made for shits and giggles.

"We had fun like we always do."

He kisses the back of my hand. "I like these."

"I thought you might."

Alex has a weird fixation with nice nails. He's definitely mostly hard now.

"You get anything else done today?" He kisses the tip of every finger.

"My toes."

"Oh yeah? Is that all? You were gone most of the day." Alex bites my pinkie.

"Nope."

"What else did you have done?"

I shrug. "Just the usual."

"The usual?"

"You know, waxing, plucking, that kind of thing."

"Does that mean you're too sensitive?"

"Too sensitive for what?" I pretend like I don't know what he's talking about; obviously he means his dick, because it's hard.

"What do you think?" Alex runs his hands down my sides, then reaches around and palms my ass, pulling me tighter against him.

"What about the pancakes?"

"They'll stay warm in the oven."

"Wanna go upstairs?"

"Not really." Alex pulls my shirt over my head. He doesn't bother to do any pre-bra-removal nuzzling; he flicks the clasp and bites his lip as the straps fall and my nipples appear.

He sighs and cups my boobs.

"You know what I've really missed?" Alex walks me backward until my butt hits the island. Then he lifts me by the waist and sets me on the counter.

"What's that?"

"Being able to use both hands on you at the same time."

He cups my boobs again and bows his head, pushing his face into my cleavage. "And my mouth."

The stitches across the bridge of his nose came out two weeks ago, and the scar isn't as bad as I expected it to be, thanks to the plastic surgeon. The scar fits in with the slight bump from his nose being broken more than once.

I run my hands through his hair and over his shoulders. The muscles in his back flex with my touch, and his deep groan vibrates through my body.

Ever since the accident, Alex has been understandably frustrated by the restrictions and limitations. His inability to take control of things has been a source of angst and irritation. I tried to do what I could to make it easier for him, but I don't think I realized how much it impacted his sex drive until now. Because when he lifts his head, the look on his face is eerily similar to the one he wore when he fucked me against the lockers at the arena.

Or the time he fucked me against the wall when I lived, however briefly, in that apartment building. My beaver perks right up, getting nice and drooly in preparation for what I'm thinking is going to be a seriously kickass sex session on our kitchen island.

Alex threads his fingers through my hair and kisses along my throat and over my chin. He backs up enough so I can look him in the eyes, though he's still holding my hair. His eyes roam my face. God, he looks intense. And totally in control. Oh, Christ, I think my man is back.

"Do you know what I want to do right now, baby?"

"Make sweet love to me?" I breathe, hoping the answer is no.

His lip curls up. It's more a lecherous sneer than his cute, dimple-popping smile. He shakes his head.

"You don't want to have sex?" I'm playing dumb again. My beaver is so excited. If she had legit teeth she'd be gnashing through my panties to get to his wood.

The head of his cock is poking out of the convenience flap of his boxer briefs. The lights above us highlight the fact that the tip is glistening.

"I wanna have sex." He bites my chin. "Just not the sweet kind." His lips touch mine again, soft and tender, so contrary to his tone and his words.

I pull out my phone sex operator voice and run my socked foot up the outside of his leg. "What kind of sex do you want to have, Alex?"

He trails kisses along the edge of my jaw to my ear and whispers, "The dirty kind."

I shiver.

And then, because no matter what, Alex is still a polite Canadian man—even when he wants to have hot, dirty sex—he adds, "But only if that's okay with you."

I drag my nails down his chest and over the ridges of his abs. "Maybe you should tell me what kind of dirty things you want to do to me before I decide."

Having been with Alex for a year, I can say with absolute certainty that sex with him is never boring or predictable. Sometimes he's a gentle, sweet lover, and other times, like now, he's good for an intense, hard fuck.

He kisses his way back up to my mouth and slips his tongue inside, stroking softly. At the same time, his grip on my hair tightens. He's in quite the mood this afternoon. We haven't had beaver-banging sex since before the accident. I'm looking forward to walking like I've been riding a horse.

Before I can deepen the kiss, Alex pulls back. Actually, he uses my hair to pull me back. "First, I'm gonna get you naked right here. You on board with that?"

"Totally on board."

"Excellent." He kisses me again, but this time there's no tongue. When he breaks the connection, I moan, and he smiles. It's so sinister. And hot. *Jesus.* I can't wait to get sexed. "And then I'm gonna finger-fuck you until you come all over my hand. Sound good?"

I make another noise. It's similar to gears grinding. "That sounds fucking fabulous, Alex." I pop the button on my jeans and yank the zipper down.

He's still standing between my thighs and holding my hair, so I can't do much more without some help.

He loosens his grip. "Lie back for me, please, baby."

I do as I'm asked, because—hot damn!—after more than a month of me riding him and feeling compelled to be careful, we're going to get our fuck on. But as a bonus, my ass has never been tighter.

I shiver when my back hits the cold granite, and flinch when I bang my head in my zeal to obey.

Alex pauses with his thumbs hooked in my belt loops. "You okay? Is it too cold? Should I take you upstairs?"

And there he is, my sweet, awesome fiancé, being his considerate self even when he's hornier than hell and ready to bang me until I see stars and the Milky Way comes shooting out of my vagina.

"No, I don't want to go upstairs. I want to get naked, and I want you to do what you said you were going to do." I push my jeans and panties over my hips and pull my knees up so I can get them off.

Alex gets with the program and helps out. Except I'm in such a rush to get my pants off I don't bother to lose the socks first, which complicates things. As much as skinny jeans look good on, they can be a pain in the ass to get off. We finally manage to wrestle me free of them. I shimmy back up on the island until my hair hangs over one end, and I can plant my feet at the other.

If I turned ninety degrees, I'd have a lot more room, but Alex's hands are already smoothing up my shins, and I'm not about to stop him.

I spread my legs nice and wide so he's got lots of room to work. He stops at my knees, frowning as he stares at my naked beaver. "Uh...Violet?"

I look down to see what has him so concerned. Which is when I remember I had my beaver decorated.

"Oh! Um...surprise!" I throw my hands up in the air and wave them around.

Alex sweeps his fingers over the awesomeness that covers my bare beaver mound. "How did you get these on here?"

"With glue. Like it?"

"Uh..."

"You don't like it?"

"No, no, I like it," he says quickly. He traces the outline of the letters that spell *Waters'* in red Swarovski crystals. Below that is a tiny beaver crafted out of more crystals. "Do I have to be careful? Like, do I need to worry about friction? Will I rub them off?"

"Uh, no? They're stuck on pretty good. I think." My waxer/beaver beautifier promised they'd stay on for at least a week if I covered them with Saran Wrap before I shower. I imagine they'll stay put with friction, too, but I didn't ask that question specifically. However, I'm not about to lose out on hot sex to preserve my vagazzling.

"This must have taken a while." He settles both hands on my inner thighs.

"About an hour."

"I'm gonna ask you an important question, 'kay, Violet?" His hands glide lower, thumbs skimming my beaver lips. Back and forth, up and down. He's about half an inch shy of my clit on either side. I spread my legs wider, hoping to encourage a little clit rubbing while we converse about my bedazzled girl parts.

I moan instead of using words, because all I want is for him to touch me, damn it, and he's not.

"What's the person's name who did this for you?"

That's a weird question. "Jamie."

Alex's eyes lift to mine. The right side of his jaw tics. Oh, shit-balls. I've seen that look before a few times.

"What does Jamie look like?" he asks.

I roll my eyes when I realize what he wants to know. "Jamie's a girl, Alex. There aren't any boy vagazzlers."

"Right. Of course not."

I'm not about to tell him Jamie has a girlfriend, though. I'm not her type, anyway, and I like penis way too much, especially his. Which I'm definitely getting a dose of soon, if he can stop asking about the blinged-out beave.

I might be less tolerant of his insecurity if I didn't know he was struggling with not having been his full-on alpha, protective self for the past month. But because I realize how challenging it's been, I'm much more patient. Also, his fingers are close to my vag.

And then I get what I've been waiting for: Alex grazes my beaver button.

I whore-moan nice and loud. I also lift my pelvis to encourage more contact.

Alex mutters a low *fuck* and starts circling, slow and soft. It's killing me, but I'll take it. The torture is definitely going to be worth it. We have more than four weeks of pent-up hot-sex-on-hold to release, and this is likely going to be round one of many as Alex recovers his stamina.

I'll need to make sure I have Epsom salts handy.

"Know what I love?" Alex's voice is all sexy rasp. His attention is fixed on his fingers, still circling.

I have a feeling I already know the answer to this question, but Alex wants to tell me, because sometimes he likes to say dirty things. "What do you love, Alex?" I mostly moan his name.

His eyes flip up to mine. Mother of all things orgasmic, the expression on his face alone is almost enough to send me hurtling through Come-topia.

He slides one of his amazing fingers inside me. My eyes roll, taking away my fucktastic view for a second. He waits until they roll back down before he answers. "How wet you always are for me."

Alex often comments on the rainforest-like state of my vag when he's all up in there making me feel good. It's as if my wetness is a litmus test for his sexiness.

"I can't help it," I tell him. "You're just so good at making me hot."

He adds another finger, fluttering faster. "Do I make you feel good?"

"So good." I grip the edge of the counter behind my head and start rolling my hips to help him reach the goal. I have a feeling I'm going to be the recipient of a lot of orgasms.

The first one is like being punched in the clit with a gift bag of awesome. I moan Alex's name extra loud.

"That's it, Violet. I can't wait to fuck you with my tongue."

"Oh my God, yes, please."

I'm not even done coming yet when he covers my still-throbbing clit with his mouth and starts sucking. I shriek and try to get away from his tongue, but he splays his hand out over my boob and holds me in place.

Releasing my death grip on the edge of the counter, I grab his hair and pull, hard. Alex groans and sucks even harder. My entire field of vision clouds with a starburst of white, a black haze crowding the edging. I can't stop coming; it's insane. I'm chanting something incoherent—words interspersed with moans.

I clamp his head with my thighs, and when my vision finally returns to normal, I look down my body, past where he's holding onto my boob, over my stomach and bedazzled vagina mound to where his nose is pressed right below the crystal beaver.

His dark gaze is locked on my face. My mouth drops open when he stops with the rough sucking and starts the tongue swirls. He's going to kill me with orgasms. I pull in a gasping breath when he leaves my poor, overstimulated beaver button, replaces his fingers with his tongue inside me, and makes good on his dirty promise to fuck me that way.

It's like he's trying to eat me alive, but not in a horror movie kind of way, in a love-the-fuck-out-of-me kind of way. Maybe I should vagazzle more often.

I think he's going for an orgasms record. I don't even know if I've stopped coming since I started. I throw my head back, but I don't connect with granite. Instead my head hangs over the edge of the counter. The living room is upside down behind me.

Across the room I can see it's dark out now. And the windows offer a mirror-like reflection of Alex's massive, broad shoulders and his head between my legs. Wow, do we ever look hot. This is some seriously intense foreplay we've got going on. I glance to the right, where the sliding glass doors provide another version of the view, so of course the orgasm that hasn't stopped revs right back up. I'm shuddering and moaning and fisting Alex's hair while I grind all over his face.

He lifts his head and swipes across his mouth with the back of his hand. His chest is heaving, abs tight, expression fierce as he drags me down the counter toward him.

I try words, but all I get are some sounds and maybe part of his name.

His right dimple pops. "What was that?"

I push up on my elbows. It's not that easy since my body seems to be made of wet noodles. "So many orgasms."

"You want more?" He slides his hand into his Super MC boxer briefs and pushes the cotton down until his cock pops out. It's one of my favorite parts of his body.

He really doesn't need to ask. I think it's pretty damn obvious with all my scream-coming that I'm more than happy to be on the receiving end of his orgasm gifts. But Alex would like to hear me say it, so I'm going to go ahead and give him what he wants, so he'll give me what we both want, which is his magical dick inside me.

"Please."

He's stroking himself. I can't decide where I want to look—at his gorgeous face or at his wide palm wrapped around his enormous cock.

"Please what?" He circles the head a few times with his thumb before he reverses the motion.

"I want more orgasms." I scoot forward. The counter is slippery under my ass, possibly from my excessive coming, possibly from Alex's sloppy eating.

Alex takes a step closer so his thighs rest against the counter. He taps my clit with the tip of Super MC.

I moan, because really, he's so hot, and I'm so ready to be fucked.

"You want my cock, baby?"

I shudder and nod. "So bad."

He keeps his eyes on me while he rubs the head up and down my slit. "You want me to fuck your pussy?"

Jesus. He's really into the dirty talking today. Not that I'm opposed. I'm not. He just hasn't been like this in a long time, and I'm surprised at how much I've missed this side of him.

"Yes, please."

Alex palms the back of my neck with the hand that isn't gripping the Super MC and encourages me to sit up. We both look down as he lines himself up and the head disappears.

He doesn't give me any more. Instead he pulls out and glides the head back up to circle my clit. I lean in and kiss his chin. His whole face smells like me. We're both going to need a shower after this, and the island is going to need a hose down.

He lifts his head until his lips touch mine. I cup his face in my hands—they're shaking, my whole body trembling with anticipation and residual orgasm aftershocks.

"I need you," I whisper against his vagina-flavored lips.

On the next pass down he goes in a little farther. "How much of me?"

"All of you." I'm not actually just referring to his Super MC, though I'd be more than happy to hug all of him. I'm referring to the entire package of gorgeous, sexy, NHL-playing, sometimes insecure, sensitive, alpha, polite, and thoughtful man.

Alex must sense this, because his eyes stay on mine as he eases inside, inch by mind-numbingly amazing inch. We both whore-moan. It feels so good to be full of him.

"I love you." He strokes along the side of my neck.

"I love you back." I nibble on his bottom lip.

He kisses me. It's soft and warm, full of all the things I need: love, tenderness, and desire.

Neither of us does any hip shifting. I sit with my legs spread wide, topped up with Super MC, while we make out. Eventually Alex breaks the connection between the lips on our faces.

His nose brushes my cheek, and he breathes me in. "I'm gonna fuck you now, is that okay?"

"So okay." I flex the beave, hugging his dick tightly.

He chuckles, then grabs my ass with his free hand. We both look down to watch as he eases out. The recessed lights overhead make his cock glisten. I get a glimpse of the ridge, and then he pushes back in.

At first I think maybe he's lost the desire for the hard fuck, but then I realize he's just warming me up. After four more slow strokes, Alex releases the back of my neck and puts a hand on the center of my chest, right between my boobs. I lie back on the counter again.

He runs both hands up my sides and palms my breasts. "I can't believe I've ignored these." He leans over me and kisses each nipple, sucking one and then the other. I run my fingers through his hair and try not to grip too tight as he starts up a hard grind. I'm slammed with another orgasm.

Alex straightens, grabs my hips, and then he rams me. It's the fuck of the ages. He goes from slow to vigorous in an instant, pumping hard. When he can't get the leverage he wants, he grabs both of my ankles and rests them on his left shoulder, pulling me right to the edge and fucking me like we're making a porno.

God, he's hot. His muscles strain, his biceps and forearms flexing. When that's not enough for him—or maybe he's not feeling like he can get deep enough, or he's not close enough, who knows—he shifts my legs to the right, changing the angle. Then he puts his knee up on the counter and covers my body with his.

It's a weird position, particularly since we're on the island and both of us can't really fit up here. Not that I'm going to complain. I'm on orgasm number sixty-five million, so it can be as awkward as Alex is comfortable with. I'm definitely going to have a few sore spots tomorrow, though. Which is also okay.

Alex keeps pounding away, and we migrate up the counter until my head is hanging over the edge again. Alex, being the considerate man he is, even in the middle of our fuck-a-thon, cradles the back of my head so I don't have to hold it up.

"Look at the window," I manage to rasp between moans.

"What?"

"The window, it's like a mirror." I let go of one of his shoulders so I can point behind us.

Alex lifts his head, and his rhythm falters for half a second. He breathes out a *fuck*, and suddenly I'm rearranged so one of my legs rests on his shoulder and the other is wrapped around his waist. And then he's back to pounding, his attention divided between our reflection in the window and me. It's a good thing it's treated glass, otherwise those living nearby would be getting a whole lot more neighborly love than they anticipated.

The sex seems to go on forever. Alex must have jacked off while I was out.

When he comes, it's on a guttural groan that includes my name. He collapses on top of me, his lips on my neck, his back expanding with each hard pant. I can feel his heart beating furiously against my boob.

We're disgustingly sweaty. My hair is wet around my temples, and my forehead is damp. I'm pretty sure I just felt sweat drip in my ass crack.

It's awesome.

16

NOW I GET WHY
THE EVASION

ALEX

Violet smells like lavender and sweat. And I feel like I've been on a breakaway that lasted an hour. It really doesn't take me long to lose endurance anymore. But now that I have the green light from my doctor, I'm going to work on getting that back as often and as quickly as possible.

I'm still inside Violet. I'm also lying on top of her, and I'm not doing much to prevent her from bearing the full brunt of my weight. Every breath she takes is accompanied by a moan and a small clenching of her pussy around my cock, which is part of the reason I'm not moving yet.

Her right ankle is beside my ear. Her other foot drops to the counter with a low thud. I pretty much have her pretzeled in half. On a slab of granite. Christ, I'm an asshole.

225

Favoring my left arm, I push up to survey the damage I've done to my fiancée. Her lips are red and puffy, her bangs are sticking to her forehead, and her mascara is smudged under her eyes.

I caress her cheek, furtively rubbing away a black smear. I really did a number on her. "Are you okay?"

Her eyes roll down. She looks drunk. "Am I okay?" She sounds drunk, too.

I puff out a breath. "That was...I shouldn't have. I was just..." I don't know what I'm trying to say. I think I feel bad because it was so good to finally be the one in control again.

Violet puts her hand over my mouth. "Do *not* apologize for loving me hard, Alex."

"That was okay?" I ask from behind her palm.

"I came like a bazillion times. It was more than okay."

"I was worried I got carried away." I ease off the counter so I'm not on top of her anymore. Unfortunately that means I'm also not inside her.

"Carried away? Honestly, Alex, I needed another round of gentle lovemaking like I need your dick to be any bigger than it already is."

I look down at my cock. He's at half-mast and slow to deflate. I also have a bunch of those crystal things stuck to my abs.

"Beyond all the coming, my cock-love chanting should tell you I enjoyed myself. A lot. Anytime you feel the need to drill me like a porn star, I'm game."

"God, I love you."

Violet smiles, and it's gorgeous. "I love you, too." She slides off the counter and makes a face, looks over her shoulder, then gags. "I think I just slid through a puddle of jizz."

"We should go have a shower. Then we can come back down and have pancakes."

"I forgot all about the pancakes!" Violet looks down and touches the mess of crystals smeared across her abdomen, the letters no longer readable. "Hmm. I guess hot sex and vagaz-zling don't go together."

"Maybe not."

"Oh well. It was worth the time if you're going to sex me like that."

We have what's supposed to be a quick shower, but turns into a long one because I get hard again. This time I'm much more careful with my fiancée. Afterward we return to the kitchen to appease the appetite we've worked up.

Violet sanitizes the island three times before we eat. The pancakes are dry, but she doesn't seem to mind. She slathers them in butter and dumps maple syrup over her entire plate, including the bacon.

A faint buzzing sound comes from her purse, which ended up on the floor—no surprise—during sex.

I pick it up and set it on the island as the buzzing continues. Violet glances at her purse, but goes back to eating. And still the buzzing goes on.

"Do you think maybe you should check your messages?"

"I will. When I'm finished eating." She picks up a strip of bacon, dripping with syrup, tips her head back, and lowers it into her mouth while looking at me out of the corner of her eye. She gets all but one inch in before she bites it off. It's phallic. And then she moans her maple pleasure.

We only have the real kind of syrup. When Violet and I started dating, she ate the cheap crap that's mostly corn syrup and food coloring. Then I introduced her to real maple syrup. Now she won't eat anything else, and we have a pantry full of maple products.

"You know, I have something I think you might like dipped in maple syrup," I offer.

"That's one way to get a blow job out of me."

"Can't get enough of my dick, eh?"

Violet snorts.

Her phone chimes again, four more times in succession. I shove my hand in her purse and root around for it.

Violet drops her fork and grabs my wrist. "Don't do that!"

I retract, surprised. "Whoa! What's the deal?"

She clutches her purse to her chest, her eyes wide, panicked almost. It's an odd reaction over me sticking my hand in her purse. What's in there she doesn't want me to see?

"I, uh…" Her eyes dart around the room. "I have…girl things in here."

I raise a brow. "Girl things?"

Her phone keeps buzzing. "Uh…yeah…like tampons. And stuff."

"Violet, I've bought tampons for you before." Darren was with me. I'd never ventured down that aisle on purpose before. There are an awful lot of options.

She's still clutching her purse to her chest. Something's going on. She looks way too terrified for this to be about "girl things."

"What's going on? What are you hiding from me?"

"Nothing!" The high pitch to her voice tells me without a doubt she's lying.

"Who's texting you?"

"No one." She purses her lips, seeming aware that I know she's bullshitting.

I cross my arms over my chest, ignoring the twinge of discomfort in my right shoulder. I probably overdid it with the finger-fucking and hard sex, but making Violet come that many times makes me feel awesome. "Really? So no one has texted you fifty times in the last ten minutes?"

"It's probably Sunny, or Lily, or Charlene. We're on a group chat, and everyone's guessing the sex of the baby."

I might buy that if they hadn't spent the entire day together and Violet's face wasn't an unnatural shade of red.

"I think you're lying."

As soon as she loosens her grip on her purse, I grab it and turn it upside down. The contents spill out all over the counter, including her phone. There are a lot of receipts and tissues in there. And pens. A ridiculous number of pens. I don't see one tampon, though.

I snatch up her phone before she can.

"Alex!"

When she grabs for it, I stand up and hold it over my head. I'm just playing. I won't actually invade her privacy, even though I know she's hiding something. She'll tell me. She's not very good at keeping secrets.

She puts a hand on my left shoulder and tries to jump up and grab it from me. Violet's close to a foot shorter than I am, and she has almost no vertical, so she can't even get close to her phone. But her boobs are rubbing on my chest, so I'm not all that inclined to stop being a dick.

Her phone buzzes again, so I glance up at the screen. The name *Daisy* comes up with the number eighty-seven beside it in brackets. It's followed by another text from *Mom* with the number eighty-two bracketed beside it.

"Why do you have over a hundred and sixty texts from our moms?"

Violet stops jumping and rests her forehead against my chest. Actually, she bangs her head three times and sighs. "They're discussing wedding venues."

"Why? I'm taking care of that."

"Because they're excited that we're getting married, and they want to plan everything—just like they did with the engagement party."

"And that warrants more than a hundred messages? Why aren't they messaging me? How long has this been going on?"

"That's since I got home. They've been going back and forth all day."

I pass her the phone. "Can I see, please?"

She pulls up the messages as three more come in and hands me the device. I scroll through them, trying to get to the beginning. It's not just about the venue; it's about bridesmaid's

229

HELENA HUNTING

dresses, Violet's dress, my tux, what we should eat, where we should go for our honeymoon. The list is endless.

"You weren't going to tell me about this?"

"I was. I would have."

"When? After they booked a place on our behalf?"

"I wanted to enjoy the afterglow of awesome, dirty sex for a while first because I knew you'd be upset about this."

"Of course I'm upset, Violet. I don't want our moms to railroad you into thinking we have to invite the entire world to our wedding. I know that's not what you want."

She fists my shirt and looks up at me. "What about what you want?"

I cradle her cheek in my palm and kiss her. "Don't you get it? I don't care where we get married. We can do it on a raft in the middle of the ocean and have the service presided over by a damn Wiccan for all I care."

"I don't think it would technically be a legal marriage then."

"You're missing the point. *You* are what I want."

Her bottom lip trembles, along with her chin.

"What's wrong, baby?"

"I love you."

"So you're crying?"

"I'm crying because I'm relieved and because you're amazing."

I wrap her up in a hug. "I have a really great idea for the wedding location."

Violet sniffs. "Where's that?"

"The Chicago cottage."

"There's a lot of room for chairs and people there."

"That doesn't mean we have to fill the space with bodies. We can keep it as small as you want, Violet. Like I said, it's not about the wedding, it's about you being my wife."

"Your mom isn't going to like this."

"The question is, do you like this?"

"I love this."

"Then that's what we'll do. I've already made a few calls; it shouldn't be hard to get it all organized, especially if we're keeping it close friends and immediate family."

Violet runs her hands up my chest and links them behind my neck. "Why are you so good to me?"

"I just want you to be happy."

Violet's phone buzzes again with more messages from our mothers.

"Should I message them back?"

"I'll deal with it. I'll bring out the big guns if that's what it takes to make my mother see reason."

"Okay."

Her smile makes the shit conversation I'm facing worth it. My mom will deal. She has her own daughter; she can plan something for Sunny. I'm sure Miller will propose sooner or later —hopefully sooner, but not before Violet and I get married.

Violet kisses the bottom of my chin. "Want to go upstairs and play hide and seek with the Super MC and my beaver?"

"That sounds like a lot of fun."

Violet takes my hand, and I follow her upstairs. This time I don't love her hard; I love her softly and slowly and sweetly.

"ALEX? ARE YOU AWAKE?"

I pry open one eye. Violet's long hair tickles my cheek. She's kneeling beside me.

"Yeah?" My voice is sleep-graveled. I clear my throat and glance at the clock on the night table. It's the middle of the night. "Is everything okay?"

"I can't sleep."

"Do you wanna have sex?" My brain might be slow to fire up, but my dick is already getting excited about the idea.

"Not right now. Maybe. It depends." She wrings her hands

like she's nervous. I don't know what could be wrong. We had all that awesome sex, and we decided where we're going to hold the wedding. After that we had more awesome sex, followed by another shower, and then bed. All in all, it was a great night, so her sudden middle-of-the-night anxiety puts me on high alert.

I turn on the bedside lamp and blink against the brightness. Her eyes are bloodshot. "Baby, what's wrong? Have you slept at all?"

She shakes her head and focuses on her hands. "I have a question."

"It must be an important question if you needed to wake me up to ask at three in the morning." I'm hoping to get a smile out of her, but she brings her fingers to her mouth, like she's about to chew her nails. I take her hand in mine. "Talk to me, Violet. What's going on in that head of yours?"

"I've been thinking about how you're going to want a pre-nup—"

"Whoa! Wait, what?" If I was still half-asleep a moment ago, I'm definitely not now.

She lifts her eyes slowly. She's biting her lip. "It makes sense, doesn't it? You want to protect yourself." She gestures to the room. "This."

Three o'clock in the morning is a super shitty time to have this discussion, but clearly it's something she's been thinking about for a while. "I'm not going to make you sign a pre-nup."

"You're not?"

Her surprise is almost offensive.

"But you've worked so hard for everything you have, and I make less than one percent of what you make a year. Logically you should want one."

"Did my mom say something to you?" I'll be seriously pissed if she did.

"No."

"But someone must've."

She drops her chin again. I sit up, because I can't stand it when I can't see her face. I urge her chin up with a finger. "Baby, look at me. Who said I wanted a pre-nup?"

"Dean might've mentioned something—"

"That dick knob you work with?"

"He has a point, Alex. At first the idea kind of hurt, but I would understand if you wanted one. You have a lot of money, and you've worked hard for it. I just..."

I sit back against the headboard and pull her with me so she's straddling my lap, facing me. "Listen to me, Violet. You and me, we're meant for each other. Do you agree?"

"Well, yeah, of course. The Super MC and my beave are soulmates, so logically that means the rest of our bodies are soulmates, too."

I laugh, because this is one of the many reasons I love her. There is no one else in the world who compares to Violet. "And soulmates are forever, right?"

She nods.

"So that means I'm yours, and you're mine. I don't need a pre-nup to make you question my faith in us. I'm going to spend the rest of my life loving you, Violet Hall."

She smiles. "And my boobs—don't forget them."

"They were already included in the package deal."

"I'm sorry I woke you up in the middle of the night to ask you a stupid question." She presses her lips to mine.

"It wasn't a stupid question."

"It was a stupid time to ask it. I could make it up to you?"

There isn't anything to make up, but if she's interested in sex again, I have a semi brewing that could easily turn into a full hard-on with the right amount of coaxing. "What do you have in mind?"

Violet pulls the night shirt over her head. "I'd like to go for a Super MC ride, if you're interested."

DESPITE THIS AUSPICIOUS start to our planning, the weeks that follow are challenging, though not because of the wedding stuff and Violet. Well, mostly not because of those things. My mom is still an issue. While she seemed fine with our chosen location for the wedding, she hasn't given up on alternate location options. She's also struggling with the concept of small.

It doesn't seem that difficult to understand a number less than a hundred, but she keeps arguing that all these people came to the engagement party, so they should attend the wedding as well.

I keep reminding her how that whole event turned out, but apparently downplaying the severity of Violet's hives to a tiny allergic reaction is her go-to defense.

Yesterday she texted me three alternate locations, none of them available on the date we've chosen. It's driving me mental.

Violet's been going to the office more often now that I'm back to training with the team. I like that she has that flexibility, and that I can count on morning blow jobs or sex on the days she stays home. She's a lot more relaxed about the work situation. It's progress.

Today is one of her office days, and I'm off to the gym to train with Darren, so I'm not too disappointed. I plan to keep her up late tonight since she's not going in tomorrow.

Darren picks me up. It's good to be seeing him on the regular again. Me being off the ice and out of the training routine has cut into guy time. We've been tight for the past six years, so it's another thing I'm glad to have back to normal.

Training with the team is good and bad, because I can see how much ground I've lost being out the past six weeks.

Coach wants me to have realistic expectations, as does my team of doctors and the physical therapist. My right shoulder is weak, and reconditioning is going to be slow. But I didn't get where I am by taking things easy, and I definitely don't plan to start now. At least there's no figure skating required for rehab.

Next week I'm allowed back on the ice for practice, but on

game days I'll continue to sit my ass on the bench and watch everyone else doing what I should be.

The team dynamic has shifted; Ballistic seems to be a new favorite. He's getting lots of ice time and scoring goals almost every game. He's an excellent player, and the team is solid. Play-offs are on the horizon, and it looks like we might make it. And that would be primarily because of him.

I really want to hate him. Part of me does because he threatens my position, but the other part of me is glad he's meshing with the team and we're not lagging behind as bad as we were in the middle of the season. We're still not in a great place, though, so who knows what will happen. If we make it far enough, I might have a chance to play at least a couple of games. Maybe. If I'm lucky.

"You all right, man?" Darren asks.

"Eh?" I realize I'm staring out the window.

"You're awfully distracted. You okay?"

"Yeah. Fine. Just thinking."

He raises an eyebrow. "I don't buy that for a second, but nice try. What's the problem?"

I shrug.

"You worried about rehab?" He's going to push me until I talk. That's why we're tight.

"Yeah."

"Wanna give me more than that, Waters?" He stops at a light, watching me carefully.

"It's the same concerns. Nothing new."

He taps the steering wheel. "I think you need to stop focusing on what you're not accomplishing and start looking at what you are."

"I know I'm lucky it's not worse than it is. I get that, but Ballistic is running the game out there, and I'm on the sidelines watching it happen."

He nods, and the silence extends, which isn't unusual with Darren. He weighs his words before he uses them. "You also need to consider that all this time watching is giving you a different perspective on the team. When you're back on the ice, you're going to know what to expect and how to plan for it. Randy's not going to usurp you because he's had one good season."

He's right, but it still sucks. I run a frustrated hand through my hair. Soon I'll be able to make one of those man bun things like Ballistic if I don't get it cut.

At my silence, he continues. "Just take it slow, Alex. You don't want to push too hard too fast and end up setting yourself back."

"I just want to be with my team."

He pats my shoulder. "I know, man, and you will. It's just not gonna happen as fast as you'd like."

Everything he says is true, but it doesn't make me feel better.

I prepare myself for the back pats I know are coming when I join the team in the training room. It doesn't matter that I've been at it for a while now; every training session is hard. Especially since I'm unable to keep up with the rest of the team.

Miller drops down beside me on the bench while I do forearm curls with weights Violet could probably use.

"How's it goin'?"

"All right." My prior hockey injuries have been minor compared to this, with rehab being limited to weeks, not months before I was back in the game.

"This isn't easy, huh?" He gestures to the weight I'm holding.

"It'll get easier." I change the subject to avoid discussing how long recovery is going to take and what I'm going to miss out on because of it. I'm lucky this isn't ending my career, I remind myself. "How's my sister doing this morning?" I haven't had a chance to check in with her today, though that's become a habit.

"Good. Great." He moves to the edge of the bench and gets into position for triceps dips. "The morning sickness phase has finally passed. I don't know why they call it that. I mean, the barfing isn't limited to the morning. It was, like, all day, every day for a while. Anyway, she's not hurling anymore, so I'm glad about that. Apparently Skye barfed every day with Vi, so it could be worse, right?"

This really isn't a conversation I ever expected to have with Miller. At least not this soon. "I'm glad that part is over."

"She's feeling great these days. Lots of energy. Horny as he —" He cringes. "Sorry."

"Violet says a lot worse."

He nods. "Dude, I heard all about the kitchen incident."

"What? She told you about that?" I need to talk to her about what she shares with Miller. There has to be a limit.

"She was talking with the girls when she was over the other day. I was unfortunate enough to overhear. I guess it's good you're keeping her happy, right?"

"Uh, yeah. I try my best. It's a lot easier now that I have the use of both arms again."

We both blow out a breath. This is a very Violet-overshare kind of conversation.

"Anyway. So, uh, the wedding stuff is going okay? Vi seems a lot calmer these days."

This is a much better topic. Safer. We're less likely to want to punch each other over it. "Yeah. She hasn't broken out in hives recently. I just need to get my mom off my back about the guest list, and we'll be fine."

Miller rubs the back of his neck again. "Yeah. Sunny's kinda worried she's gonna pull the same shit when we get married."

I'm pretty sure my eyebrows almost shoot off my forehead. I shouldn't be surprised. This was bound to happen. "Is that happening soon?"

"I'mma propose to her soon. I just need to find the right ring. I've already talked to your dad. We considered maybe getting married before the baby comes, but she's starting to show, and, well, I don't care about that, but I think maybe she does. Anyway, I'm cool with whatever she wants, before or after.

Either way. If you ask me, I think she doesn't want to steal your thunder."

"That sounds like Sunny."

"Yeah. She knows you've been waiting for this for a while."

I hate to admit it, but I'd really like to get married before my sister. I know it's not a competition, but I want to be first for this. Which sounds assholey. Because it kind of is. But Violet was right. I've spent most of my life being the center of attention, so I shouldn't be put out that Sunny is going to be a mom before I get to be a dad. I figured I'd go first and be able to guide her through like I always do. But this time she's first, so I won't have any advice to give. I don't know what I'll say.

"Alex?" Miller asks.

"Huh?" I've zoned out. I need to stop being so self-centered. The world doesn't actually revolve around me.

"So you'll stand in the wedding party? I mean, it's gonna be a small thing—I think, anyway. Close friends and family probably, the same as what Violet wants."

"Yeah, of course," I say absently, then finally clue in to what he's said. "Wait, you want me to stand in the wedding party?"

"Well, yeah. You're Vi's fiancé—husband by then. And of course Sunny's gonna ask Vi, but if she's not cool with it, that's fine. Vi's got some wedding hang-ups, as I'm sure you're aware."

"That's great. I mean, not the hang-ups part, but about Sunny asking Violet. I'm sure she'll want to be part of things."

"Maybe. We'll see." Miller doesn't look quite so convinced.

"Was it really that bad?" I hate to have to ask, but I have a feeling Violet's given me the abridged version of the events.

Miller regards me dubiously. "You mean she still hasn't told you?"

"She's told me. But I think I have the watered-down version."

"For fuck's sake." Miller shakes his head. "What did she say?"

"That she ruined the cake and messed up her speech, and

that there was an issue with her dress. But she was a teenager, so I can't imagine it was that bad. Maybe if I have the full story, I can explain better to my mom why Violet doesn't want the entire world at our wedding."

"Maybe if she saw my dad and Skye's wedding video she'd get it." Miller snorts.

"There's a video?" I drop my weight on the mat with a low thud.

Miller pauses in the middle of a dip. "Fuck. You didn't know about the video?"

"Violet never said anything about video."

Miller sits back down beside me. "That's probably because she doesn't want you to see. We had the whole wardrobe malfunction bit edited out, but I have an original copy. It's pretty fucking epic."

"Epic how?"

"Like, she'd probably win that home video show if we submitted it. Which I would never do," he tacks on at the end.

"Does Violet have a copy?"

"Maybe? If she does I'm sure it's locked away somewhere."

"Can I see the one you have?"

Miller chews on the inside of his cheek. "I probably shouldn't. Vi'll be super pissed at me if she finds out."

"I won't tell her."

He rubs his head a few times and heaves a heavy sigh. "Come to the condo after we're done here."

"Thanks, man."

Normally I wouldn't go behind Vi's back on something like this, but if it helps get my mom to calm the fuck down, I guess I can do it this once.

Miller stands. "I gotta do suicides. I'll see you in a bit."

I spend the next hour with my physical therapist, working on strengthening the muscles around my healing shoulder.

I hit the hot tub afterward and then the sauna before I shower.

Back outside, I toss my bag in Darren's trunk and drop into the passenger seat. "We gotta stop at Miller's before we go home."

"Everything okay?" Darren asks.

"Yeah. He's got a copy of Sidney and Skye's wedding video."

"Marriage is a complicated beast," Darren says.

"Seems that way. Violet's who I want, though, so I need to figure out how to make this easier for her."

"Yeah. You two are good for each other. Sometimes people get tied to the wrong person, and then they can't figure out how to get free again."

"Is that why you and Charlene aren't getting more serious?"

I know they see each other a lot, but Darren keeps most people at a distance. I've met his parents once in all the time I've known him. Icy is a good way to describe them.

"My parents have been married for thirty years, and they hate each other. They have bedrooms on different floors of the house. I don't see the point in changing things when it's working fine. Plus, Charlene has her own stuff, so we're good the way we are."

He pulls up to Miller's condo building and lets the valet park the car. Neither of us says anything more about it. The guy at the front desk buzzes us in, and we take the elevator to Miller's.

Boxes line the wall in neat rows with Sunny's flowery printing on them, indicating the contents. On the coffee table are several magazines, most are hockey, but there are new ones with babies on the front as well. And there's a parenting book with little Post-it notes hanging out like tiny pink tongues.

"Sorry about the mess. You know how it is. You guys want a beer or something?"

"Sure, thanks."

Miller grabs beers, and we join Lance and Randy in the living room. Lance is setting up the Xbox, and Randy is sending texts while smirking. I'll bet my left nut it's Lily getting the messages.

"You two gonna play?" Lance works on untangling the controllers.

Darren checks his phone. "Nah. We're not staying long."

"We're just having a quick game. Then I gotta go home and get ready for a date," Lance says.

"A date?" Randy sounds as shocked as the rest of us look.

Lance doesn't look up from the controllers he's still messing with. "Why is that such a surprise?"

"Uh, maybe because you don't date."

"I set up a Tinder profile so I don't have to go to the bars since all you assholes have your dicks nailed down."

Randy chokes on his beer and puts a protective hand over his balls. "Dude, not a nice image."

"Shit. Sorry, man. Bad choice of words."

"I'm going to point out that Tinder isn't a dating site. It's a hook-up site," Miller says as he roots through the cabinet in the entertainment center.

Lance shrugs. "This way I'm guaranteed no bullshit. I'm gonna get naked and come, hopefully more than once, and in as many holes as I can."

Darren coughs. "You're a classy bastard, Romero."

Lance smiles, but it's stiff. "The classiest." He turns to me. "Anyway, it looks like you're really going through with this whole wedding thing, aye?"

"The date's set. We're just finalizing details and ironing out the guest list." I glance around the room. "Obviously you guys are all invited."

Lance goes back to messing with the controller. "You uh... invitin' Tash to your shindig?"

I figured the Tinder hook-ups meant he was over that, but maybe not. "Violet still talks to her, so she might extend the invitation. You gonna be okay with that?"

"For sure. We're long over." The tips of his ears go red, and he chugs the rest of his beer in three long swallows. I have a feeling there was a lot more going on between them than Lance ever owns up to.

"Found it!" Miller holds up a CD case.

On the cover is a picture of Sidney and Skye in their wedding outfits. Skye's dress is…very Skye. It's off-white, short, and tight. Violet gets her body from her mom. They're both petite with big boobs. Skye wasn't doing much to rein hers in for this picture.

"What's that?" Randy asks.

"My dad and Skye's wedding video." Miller passes it to me. "Just put it on."

"Uhh…are you sure you want me to do that?"

"It's fine. You were teenagers, right? It can't be that bad."

"If you say so." Miller slides the CD into the slot, and we wait for the video to cue up. He fast-forwards through most of it until we get to the speeches.

"Nice tux, Butterson," Lance says. "Where are you, Balls? Didn't you two hang out in high school?"

"I was already in Toronto then. I got drafted to the farm team out there in my last year."

Miller pauses the video on a grainy image of a much-younger Violet. "You sure you want to watch this with everyone here?"

"It's fine." I should know from Miller's repeated questions that it's not fine. But I keep telling myself it can't be that bad, and they're blowing it out of proportion. Violet can be dramatic at times.

"All right. Don't say I didn't warn you." He hits play again.

The camera pans in on Violet. Her face is softer, rounder. Her long hair is pulled up into an intricate ponytail, and curled tendrils frame her face. I totally would have wanted to date her in high school. I bet all the guys had boners over her. I'm conflicted by the reaction in my pants, because she's way underage in this video. She's wearing glasses. They're purple with little rhinestone decorations on the side.

"Holy shit? Is that Vi?" Lance asks.

"Yeah."

"Wow. I gotta say, Butterson, I'm surprised you didn't try to hit that. I mean, convenience factor aside, she was a hot nerd! And look at her boobs. Is it just me or are they bigger there?" Everyone turns to stare at him. "Uh, let's pretend I didn't say any of that."

"Good call."

"But I'm still surprised Butterson didn't try to bone her. Or you." He points at Randy.

"Do you have a death wish, Romero?" Darren asks.

"I didn't meet Violet until this year," Randy says.

"Violet was too busy being a Mathlete to hang out with me when our parents got married, and Randy was already in the minors getting his bunny on," Miller says. "I was gonna set you up with her when she and Alex were on the outs back in May."

I throw my hands up. "What the fuck, Miller?"

He shrugs. "You were being a dick and listening to your stupid agent. Violet was fucking miserable, moping around, eating dairy. I thought she might need a distraction."

"So you thought hooking her up with Ballistic was a reasonable option?"

"Hey, I'm a good guy," Randy says in his own defense.

"Calm your tits, Waters. She never went out with him, or anyone else, while you were on your break. She couldn't even manage saying Randy's name without thrusting."

I have to say, I'm damn glad Violet never went out with Ballistic. He is a good guy, but from the stories Violet tells me, he and Lily have more sex than feral rabbits. I'd like to think my bedroom skills are better than his, but I'm very glad Violet has no firsthand knowledge as to whether or not that's true.

"Oh! This is it." Miller turns up the volume.

There's a whispered conversation in which it sounds like Violet is arguing with her mom. She huffs and takes off her glasses, folding them neatly on the table before she pushes back her chair. She adjusts her dress—there's a lot of cleavage—and stands.

"Jesus. How old is Violet here?" Lance asks.

"I think she was turning seventeen or something," Miller replies.

"Man, I wish the chicks in my Mathletes club had looked like that."

"Shut the fuck up, Romance, before Alex breaks your nose."

"Right. Sorry."

I grunt but say nothing because he's right. I would've given my left nut to sit next to her in math class and pretend I didn't know what the fuck was going on so I could look down her shirt while she explained things. Violet's the kind of girl who would've been helpful like that in high school.

She's wearing one of those super formfitting dresses, and it's short—like, way too short for a bridesmaid's dress, hitting her high on her thigh. It must be a guy on the camera because he zooms out so he can get her entire, smokin' hot, highly illegal body to fit in the shot. There's a long lace train thing hanging off the back of the dress that drags on the floor.

Violet's wearing silver platform heels. She's obviously unaccustomed to them. She teeters unsteadily and holds onto the back of the chair. Signature red blotches break out across her chest—her very ample, not-covered-enough chest. She brushes a fallen tendril out of her face and squints, because she can't see very well without her glasses.

She takes a couple of shuffling steps before she squares her shoulders, jutting out her chest. The dress seems to be slipping down. She hikes it up again and stutter-steps across the stage. Those heels are way too high.

Miller is standing at the bottom of the steps to the left of the podium. His hands are shoved in his pockets as he waits for Violet to come down. On the second one, her heel catches the lace train, and she careens forward, head-butting Miller in the junk. He, in turn, stumbles back. He might've been able to recover if Violet hadn't grabbed his tuxedo jacket and rammed her shoulder into his knee.

"Wow, she's not very graceful, is she?" Randy mumbles.

Miller bumps into the table holding the three-tiered wedding cake. It rocks forward and then topples off the back.

As if this isn't bad enough, Violet scrambles to right herself, but her heel is still caught in the back of her dress. It pulls the whole thing down. And there they are: her boobs.

Miller hits pause instead of stop, so the video freezes on a shot of Violet's exposed chest.

"Shit! Sorry! I meant to hit stop before that happened!"

The young Miller on the screen is wide eyed and horrified, just like the one currently in three dimensions. He steps in front of the TV to block the view. Thankfully everyone is looking either at the ceiling or their hands.

"So, um, I guess this kind of explains Violet's aversion to weddings, huh?" Randy asks.

That she's agreed to any kind of actual ceremony with people in attendance is a true miracle.

I clear my throat. "I think it goes without saying that this stays under the cone."

There's murmured agreement and some uncomfortable shifting around.

I definitely need to get my mom to back off. I wait until Darren and I are in his car before I call my mom and gently, but firmly, tell her to stop looking for alternate venues, because the Chicago cottage is where Violet and I are getting married.

She might be disappointed, but she agrees to cease with the texting torture. At least that's one issue resolved.

THE NEXT FEW weeks are full of PT, training, and planning the wedding. I gain a lot of ground, though I still don't get to be on the ice with the rest of the team for games. And we don't make it past the first round of playoffs. It's a challenge to watch my teammates beat themselves up over the loss, especially when we were on such a high last year.

Ultimately, I don't think it's necessarily a bad thing. We'll have a longer off-season, with more time to recuperate and train. I'm trying to see the positive in the situation.

My ongoing issue once again has to do with my mom and her wedding interference. She's switched tactics from alternate venues to expanding the guest list, two "very important friends" at a time. Every other day she sends me another message asking if so and so can be added to the list.

I shut her down, and then Violet feels bad for making me be the bad guy and ends up texting her back to say yes. On the up side, I've gotten a lot of blow jobs in the past few weeks. However, I have guilt over them, so I always return the favor with some kind of orgasm.

Today I get a text from my mom with yet *another* guest-addition request as I'm walking in the door after a particularly intense physical therapy session.

I don't know if I should even bother to say anything to Violet about it as I text my mom back with a no. I find Violet on the couch with her Mac in her lap. At first I assume she's doing something work-related, although usually she does that in her office. Maybe she needed a change of scenery.

She must be engrossed in her research, because she bursts into a fit of laughter, punctuated by a snort.

"Whatcha doin'?"

She looks up from the screen. "You need to see this!"

I sit beside her, ready to be entertained by whatever's on the screen. It's not what I expect.

"Uh...why am I looking at someone's dick? And why does it have a face on it?"

Violet rolls her eyes. "Seriously? You watch internet porn all the time."

"No, I don't." I watch it occasionally, especially when I'm away from home and don't have access to Violet—usually in the bathroom with headphones on while I'm pretending to take an extra-long shower.

"Lies. I see your browser history. You need to stop with the Area 51 porn. It's never going to happen."

It's my turn with the wide eyes. I always clear my browser history.

Violet shakes her head. "So transparent. Anyway, check this out! I was looking for costume designs for the Super MC, and I found this." She points to the smiley-faced dick. "This guy draws a face on his dick—and arms and stuff—and puts it in scenarios. And now he's started dressing him up! People make his dick clothes, just like I made yours a cape!"

"And a Christmas costume; don't forget that."

"That was so much fun. Don't worry, I have something special planned for the wedding night."

"I'm sure that part will be awesome." I drape my arm over the back of the couch and slip my hand under her hair.

"Oh, it will. No accidental suffocation. Anyway, this guy has all sorts of chicks sending him stuff, and look at how tiny his doodle is!" Violet points to the screen.

"I don't think it's fair to call it tiny."

"He's hard."

"I think maybe your perspective is skewed because of my dick."

She shrugs. "You may have a point. I hope he's good with his tongue. Anyway, check this out." She scrolls through page after page of some guy's dick doing ridiculous things.

"Why are you showing me this?"

"We should do it with Super MC! Imagine how much more exciting it would be with your huge dick."

"I'm not posting dressed-up dick pics on the internet, Violet."

"Well, can I at least make a photo album?"

"Of my dick?"

"It'll be fun."

"You're crazy."

"That's why you love me." She closes the laptop and moves it to the coffee table, then straddles my lap. I take her glasses off, set them on the arm of the couch, and pull the tie from her hair, setting it free. It tumbles over her shoulders in loose waves.

"We could start now." She searches my pocket for my phone. "Did you know Balls and Lily make videos?"

"Pardon?"

"Randy and Lily. They make videos so he has something to jack off to when he's gone for away games."

"What kind of videos?"

Violet arches a brow. "What kind do you think?"

"How do you know that?" I seriously hope she hasn't seen one.

"She told me. And she showed me one."

"She showed you a sex video?"

"We might overshare a lot of information, but not that much, Alex. He made a video that time he came to Guelph to see her. She'd fallen asleep on him, and I guess part of the deal was no sleeping, so he videoed her."

"He made a video of Lily while she was sleeping?"

"Don't say it like that. It's not creepy. It was sweet and kinda hot." Violet gets this faraway look in her eye before she shakes her head. "Anyway, he made a video of him waking her up."

"I don't understand why that's hot or what it has to do with sex videos."

"Well, he was waking her up to have sex again. And it ends on a kiss." She flutters a hand in front of her face. "Anyway, we should make some videos like that."

"I don't think we should use your phone if we do, since you've lost two in the past year."

"We could use your phone since you don't lose yours."

"We could." I'm totally down with making sex videos with Violet. I'll have to watch them wearing headphones since she's exuberant in bed, but I can live with that. I would love to make a video of me sliding my dick between her tits.

Just as I'm about to suggest this, my phone lights up in her hand.

Based on the way her face falls, I'm betting it's another text from my mom. "Let me guess, two more guests?" I skim her sides until I reach the hem of her shirt. "I already told her no."

"What are we up to now?"

"Sixty-eight."

"Might as well make it an even seventy."

I slip one hand under her shirt and grab the phone before she can key in the code and respond. "We're not going to deal with that right now."

"She'll start texting me soon, and you know it."

"So let her text." I push Violet's shirt up until a boob pops out. She's wearing black lace. She doesn't own a lot of black lingerie, so when she wears it I get super excited. I don't know why. It does something to me—just like when she wears her Marvel Comics underwear.

My phone beeps again. I press my face into her cleavage and sigh.

She runs her hands through my hair, and I feel her chin on top of my head. "Just message her back, Alex." Her resignation fuels my determination.

"Fuck that." I flick the clasp on her bra and lay her out on the couch. "She can wait."

Violet grins. "Okay."

Kneeling between her thighs, I pull down her leggings and panties. "Leggings are the best."

"Totally the best," Violet agrees.

Then I lower my head and lick her until she comes. And then I make her come one more time with my fingers and my tongue just because I can, and I want to. Couch sex isn't as easy as bed sex, but it's fun, and we clearly both need it. We also totally forget to get it on video.

"It's a good thing this couch is leather," Violet says into my neck. I'm still lying on top of her, because moving means making a mess.

"It's also a good thing the cleaning lady is coming tomorrow. I'll leave out the leather conditioner for her."

"I bet she knows we have the sex on here. I wonder if she fantasizes about it."

"She's in her fifties."

"All the more reason to fantasize about what it must be like to get boned by a superhot, giant-dicked hockey player."

I snort and then groan when my phone beeps again. "Why won't she stop?"

"She can't help herself, Alex. It's frustrating, but I get it. You're her Stanley Cup. She wants everyone to be there when she gives you away."

"That's a weird but accurate analogy." I push up on my elbows so I can see her face. "You know what we need to do?"

"Have sex on Saran Wrap so there's less mess to clean up?"

"Too much preparation, takes the spontaneity out of it."

"You know, once we have babies we'll have to plan sex like all the other real adults in the world. It's another reason to postpone that as long as possible—also daily vomiting and struggling to walk are real negatives for me."

"You know all I hear when you say that is the plural in *babies*, right? The rest I can deal with."

"*You* can deal with? I'm the one who'll be puking and uncomfortable. Let's see how Sunny and Buck deal with being parents before we make my vagina baggy with your offspring."

"That's fine. I can wait." I'm still inside her, and this discussion starts the process of re-inflating. "But we can practice a lot until you're ready, right?"

"It's my favorite thing to do." She nibbles on my chin.

"We should go somewhere. For a vacation. Get away for a few days. Go have some fun. It's been a rough few months. I think we need a break."

"Charlene's been talking about a trip to Vegas for a while.

She wants it to be my bachelorette weekend or something. Maybe we could combine it with your bachelor party, and we can all go!"

I was thinking more of a trip with just the two of us, but having friends there could be fun, and she seems excited by the prospect. Besides, we'll have a honeymoon, and that will definitely just be the two of us. "Have you ever been to Vegas?"

"No. The mathematician in me doesn't like the odds of gambling."

"It's not all gambling, though. There's tons of other stuff to do there."

"You mean like watch girls get naked?"

"The only girl I want to watch get naked is you."

"And the ones who give it up for anal on the internet."

"Not true."

"Totally true. But that's okay. You're allowed to dream. Oh my God, Alex. There are tons of sex stores there, right? I can get all kinds of fun toys, and we can try them out!"

"We sure can."

"I need to call Charlene! She's going to be so excited!"

"First we should have sex again, though." I shift my hips so she can feel what's happening.

Violet moans. "Oh, hey there. Wow. You must be really excited for the sex toys. Charlene can definitely wait."

17

VEGAS, BABY!

VIOLET

J ust over two weeks later, we're all standing in a hotel lobby, ready to get our party on in Vegas.

"We'll see you guys in a couple hours." Balls shoves his room key in his back pocket, grabs Lily's hand and their suitcases, and starts booking it toward the elevators.

"There's a bathroom right over there if you can't wait!" I call after them.

Lily flashes a cheeky grin over her shoulder as she runs to keep up with his long strides. He punches the button a number of times, then dips his head to whisper something in her ear. Oh, wait—he's not whispering; he's kissing her neck. And I think he might be humping her leg.

"Jesus. Watching the two of them is legit like foreplay. How

the hell do you and Buck stand being around them all the time?"
I ask Sunny. "I feel like I'm going to spontaneously break into
orgasm." We're waiting for the boys to sort out the room
situation.

"I bet they're the reason I'm pregnant. We don't ever finish an
entire movie with them. They disappear about halfway through,
and then all the plants start shaking on the windowsills, so..."
Sunny pats her baby bump. It's still tiny, but more prominent
than it was a few weeks ago. "Plus, now I'm all hormonal with
the pregnancy. Sometimes I have to wake Miller up in the
middle of the night so we can give me an orgasm." Sunny looks
over at Buck and smiles.

I love that it's a *we* kind of thing with them, not just a *he*.

Sunny fans her face. "I think we might need some time to
ourselves, too. You don't mind, do you?"

"Pretty sure we're all going to get our serious fuck on as soon
as we get to the suite," I say.

Lily and Randy opted to get their own room, instead of
sharing the four-bedroom suite with us. They said it was so
Lance didn't have to stay on his own, but I have a feeling it's so
they can screw in the bathroom. And everywhere, really.

I kind of feel bad for Lance. Since he's the only one without a
girlfriend, he's like the ninth wheel. But he seemed happy to
have been invited, and I'm sure he's not going to have a problem
finding a random to hook up with. We've already been swarmed
twice by hockey fanatics.

As suspected, once we've got keys, Lance decides to check
out the casino instead of coming directly to the room with us.
He's smart enough to know he'll be listening to a bunch of
banging headboards.

When we get upstairs, no one even pretends they want to
hang out right away.

Buck yawns and stretches. "I think I wanna take a nap before
we check things out."

Charlene *pffts*. "If *nap* is a euphemism for *have sex*, enjoy

253

yourselves. Come on, Darren. Let's go have a nice, long, hard nap." She wheels her suitcase across the massive suite to one of the doors.

Darren smiles and follows her. "I'm in. I like hard naps."

"Nap time!" I yell and sprint to another unoccupied bedroom. As soon as the door closes, Alex is on me. "Let's get naked in the shower."

"I love naked showers." I pull his shirt over his head and work on unbuckling his belt while I walk backward toward the bathroom.

Two hours later I've had four orgasms, I'm clean, and I've had a twenty-minute power nap. I'm standing over my suitcase in a pair of underwear and no bra, searching for something cute to wear.

Alex is standing behind me, holding my boobs. He's getting hard again, despite coming twice already. I have a feeling my beaver is going to get a serious workout this weekend.

"What the hell is this doing here?" Alex picks up my beaver vibrator and shakes it in his fist.

I've used it so much that the tightie whities the beaver is wearing have almost worn off. "I wanted to be prepared."

"Prepared? I'm here. There's no possible reason—short of my dick falling off—for you to have this with you."

Wow. He's fired up about my vibrator. I decide to play with him. "Why are you so angry about Buddy?"

"It's a vibrator, Violet. It doesn't deserve a name."

"But that is his name. It's right on the box he came in. He's Buddy the Beaver, and he takes care of me when you're at away games—you know, 'cause he's my beaver buddy. You should be grateful I have him."

"I fucking hate this thing!" Alex whisper-shouts.

God, he's so riled up. I really don't understand his absolute disdain for my vibrator. I think I must have packed it out of habit. I don't really need it now that Alex has recovered from the accident and isn't traveling.

I'm used to multiple orgasms now that I have him and his magical dick in my life. One seems cheap. So after he fell asleep in those first days after the accident, I'd sneak down the hall into one of the unused guest bedrooms and give myself a few extras with Buddy's help.

I gently take him out of Alex's shaking fist. With my free hand, I drag my nails down Alex's chest, over his fabulous abs that clench under my touch, and slip my fingertips into the waistband of his boxer briefs. He's rocking a sweet, raging hard-on. I grab hold of the amazing girth and drop to my knees. He immediately looks less angry.

"What're you doing?"

"I'm showing you why you shouldn't hate my vibrator." I hold the plastic beaver beside Alex's massive cock. The vibe is pathetic in comparison. "Look at you." I give his cock a squeeze. Then I kiss the tip. He exhales through his nose. "And look at this." I put them side by side so Buddy touches the Super MC. Alex tenses. Buddy has to be at least three inches shorter than Alex, probably a little more than that, and less than half his girth.

I lick along the slit, and Alex makes that low, guttural sound I love to hear. His fists clench at his sides when I open my jaw enough to get the head of his cock in my mouth and apply some gentle suction. Then I pop off. "See how wide I have to open to get you inside?" I brush my lips across the head.

He slides his fingers into my hair. "Fuck, Violet. I see."

"That doesn't look at all like this, does it?" I turn my head and wrap my lips around Buddy's head—he's well sanitized. I use a special cleaning product between uses. He tastes like plastic though, not freshly washed cock. But the look on Alex's face is priceless. He seems like he wants to be angry, but he's definitely turned on. I take in a little more of Buddy until the plastic taste is too much to handle. He's covered in spit when I pull him out.

Then I go ahead and demonstrate on Alex, again, how much wider I need to open and how at best, I can get slightly more than half of him in my mouth before he hits the back of my throat.

I decide now is also a good time to establish the benefits of Buddy's presence. While I'm sucking Alex's monster cock, I part my legs and ease Buddy inside. Then I turn it on and moan. Sometimes I try to rub my beaver button when I'm lollipopping the Super MC, but it's hard to keep the rhythm going. Once Buddy's in, all I have to do is adjust my heel placement and do a little rocking to achieve friction. Then I'm free to suck away.

"Violet?" Alex's voice is rough.

"Mmm?" I mumble since his dick is taking up all the room in my mouth.

"Are you getting off with that damn vibrator?"

"Mm-hmm." I nod, in case he can't understand my response, and then moan again.

He cups my face in both hands and pulls me off his cock. I make a loud, wet, slurping sound and drool on myself.

"*I* make you come," he says.

"Always." It's more moan than word. I'm so turned on and so damn close.

He shakes his head and pulls me up off my knees. "No, I mean this weekend. Every orgasm you have I'm going to be responsible for."

He makes me let go of Buddy and pulls it out, tossing it across the room. It's still vibrating, so it makes a buzzing sound as it bumps around on the floor, like it's searching for a home, which was my vagina a few seconds ago.

"Alex! I was right there!"

"And you'll be right there again." He shoves my suitcase on the floor and lifts me by the waist, tossing me onto the bed.

Holy shit. I have no idea what he's going to do, but I have a feeling it's going to be a whole lot better than anything I would have achieved with Buddy.

Alex follows me onto the bed, tilts my head back, and kisses me, hard. I groan. When he breaks the kiss he skims my cheek with his nose. "Who loves you, baby?"

"You do," I breathe.

"And who do you love?"

"You."

"That's right. You love me."

"And the Super MC."

Alex grins. "He loves you back. Who takes care of you?"

"You do."

His lips barely touch mine. "And who do you take care of?"

I run my hands down his chest. "You. I take care of you."

"Yes, and you do it well. So you're gonna let me take care of you now, aren't you?"

I said something similar to him after the accident, but it sounds way sexier now. I nod as much as I can with the way he's holding the back of my head.

"And you can take care of me."

Alex turns me around so my back is to his chest. Spreading my knees, he leans back and straddles me over his chest. I'm not sure what his plan is until he readjusts my position so my beaver is right over his face.

Oh my God. We're about to sixty-nine. On the plus side, I'm going to have a dick in my mouth to muffle all my moans. Alex bites the back of my thighs and then my ass before he works his way closer to my beaver.

I take his cock in my hand and start stroking, licking around the head at the same time as his tongue circles my clit. And then he's rubbing my beaver button with his fingers and fucking me with his tongue while I suck and moan and try not to make too much noise when I come all over his face.

My mouth is suddenly empty of cock, and I find myself on all fours.

"Do you want this, baby?" Alex rubs the head of his cock over my clit and back toward my entrance.

"Please." Sweet Christ, I need his dick again.

He eases inside, one slow inch at a time. I bury my face in the sheets to stop the sound from carrying. I'm not so sure I'm successful. Alex palms my ass and starts thrusting, slow and torturous. And then I feel his thumb. It's right there, pressing against the base of his cock, close to my Area 51.

"Alex," I warn. But I'd be lying if I said it didn't feel kind of good.

"I'm not going to go anywhere you don't want me to," he reassures me.

He moves his thumb up a little, and there's pressure, like he's right there, covering the Area 51 zone, but he's not breaching it. I reach down and rub the beaver button. My whole body is shaking with the beginnings of an orgasm.

I'm definitely not quiet when I moan his name, and of course, I tell him I love his cock.

When my arms give out, Alex lies on top of me and keeps going. This time he kisses me when I come so I can't profess my cock love loudly, for everyone to hear.

About thirty seconds after Alex comes there's a knock on the door.

"Hey, Violet." It's Charlene. "When you're finished loving Alex's cock, get dressed. We're going to the bar."

I guess I was right about not being quiet. Maybe Lily and Randy were smart to get their own room.

THE BEST-LAID PLANS

ALEX

Everyone stops what they're doing as we come out of the bedroom fifteen minutes later. Fully dressed. Lance must've come up to the suite while Violet and I were getting busy for the third time, because the guys are playing pool, and the girls are sitting on the couch channel surfing. Even Lily and Randy are here.

Charlene stands and slow claps. Lily joins her. Soon everyone is clapping. Except Miller—he looks pissed. I can't say I blame him. If I heard Sunny loudly professing her appreciation the way Violet does, I don't think I'd be all that impressed. Sunny doesn't seem to care, though. She's smiling and clapping along with the rest of the girls.

Violet takes a step back, as if maybe she's thinking to hide in the bedroom, but she collides with my chest.

"Good work, Alex!" Charlene cheers.

I chuckle into Violet's hair when she elbows me in the ribs. "You've could've told me I was being too loud."

I move her hair out of the way and kiss her cheek. "It seemed like a reasonable volume to me."

She looks over her shoulder and gives me what's supposed to be her angry face, but she's embarrassed, and I'm feeling good about my performance, so she looks cute instead. She pokes me in the nipple. "Jerk. I'm going to have silent sex for the rest of the weekend."

"Good luck with that."

This time she pinches me. I fold her in my arms and tuck her head under my chin. "I love you, baby. Never change. Especially not your sex volume."

She mumbles what's probably an insult, but it's muffled by my shirt.

"It's not like we haven't heard you come before," Lance says.

I'm about to thank him for the reminder by flipping him off, but Randy cuts in. "I hadn't, but, uh, yeah, Waters. Whatever you're doing, keep it up."

"Maybe you two should compare notes," Lily suggests with a sly grin.

He strokes his beard and narrows his eyes at Lily. "I'm not giving you what you need, luscious?"

Violet wriggles out of my hold. "Pretty sure Horny Nut Sac doesn't need any help in the orgasm-doling department based on the voodoo magic in my laundry room."

"Definitely not!" Charlene agrees. "But feel free to share your best techniques with Darren. He's always looking for new ways to make me scream."

Darren doesn't say anything, just smirks and lets out one of his dark little laughs.

Sunny raises her hand. "I have quiet orgasms. Lots of them."

"Okay." Miller slaps the pool table. "We should hit the casino."

We all put on shoes and head for the door. Violet seems relieved, and I honestly have no interest in hearing about Sunny's orgasms, particularly since they've resulted in her being pregnant. We find a buffet, because sex makes us all hungry, and then we hit the streets. Sunny turned twenty-one last month, so she's legal to get into all the places; not that it matters since she can't drink in her condition.

"Wow, this is like Niagara Falls on steroids!" she says, chin tilted up as she takes in the tall buildings and excessive people.

"It's wild here," Violet says as we pass girls dressed in very little, dancing in the middle of the street. People hand us cards with boobs on them, but the nipples are covered with black or red dots. Violet hands a bunch to Lance. "There's a number on there. Maybe she wants to go on a date with you."

He shakes his head. "I don't have to pay to get a date, Vi. Besides, some chick in the casino gave me her keycard for later."

"She gave you her keycard?"

"Yeah. Happens all the time."

He's not lying. Girls are constantly looking to hook up with him. While Ballistic had a reputation for living up to his last name, Lance has a different kind of rep with the bunnies.

He doesn't seem to have any issue with multiple partners, according to the rumors anyway. But who the hell knows what's true and what isn't. That shit about the Darcys is proof that not everything you hear is true—just like the rumor about me and the hat trick. Lance is proving to be one of the good guys, maybe a little hotheaded on the ice—and off it—but then so am I.

"But she doesn't even know you. You could be a mass murderer. You could be like that guy from *American Psycho* who throws a chainsaw down a stairwell after he has a threesome." Violet shudders and turns to Charlene. "I should never have watched that movie."

"It wasn't that bad."

"Not that bad? I didn't sleep for three weeks."

Violet's exaggerating, but she did have a few rough nights.

Lance winks at Violet. "Don't worry, I'm not a mass murderer."

"But how does she know that?"

"I'm a public figure in the hockey world. Everyone knows my business in the bedroom, or at least they think they do."

Violet links her arm with mine. "Do girls give you their keycards?"

I tuck her into my side. "Not anymore."

"But they used to?"

"Not all that often."

"What constitutes *often*? And what the hell is wrong with these women? That seems dangerous."

"You didn't know Alex, and you went back to his room the first night you met him," Charlene points out.

"That's different."

"Not really," Lily says.

"Like you're any better? You sucked Randy's face after he busted in on you in a bathroom! And then he locked himself in a bathroom with you after you defaced all his underwear!"

Lily blushes. "The underwear defacing was a misunderstanding."

"Whatever. I'm making a point. Alex played on the same team as Buck. I was introduced as his sister. He couldn't murder me without everyone knowing it was him, so it's totally not the same as handing over a keycard to a perfect stranger."

"That's true," Sunny agrees.

Lance points to an ABC store, maybe because he's not interested in continuing the conversation. "I'm gonna stop and grab something. Anyone need anything?"

"We can drink in the streets here, can't we?" Violet jumps up and down, her boobs bouncing with the movement.

"Want me to get you a water, or maybe some juice, sweets?"

Miller asks Sunny. "You need a snack? I'll get you a bunch of stuff, 'kay?"

She adjusts the brim of her oversized hat so she can tilt her head up for a kiss. "That'd be great."

I stay outside with Sunny while the rest of them go into the store. I put an arm around her shoulder. "You doing okay?"

She takes off her hat and leans her head on my chest. "I'm so good, Alex. I know you worry, but me and Miller, we're made for each other, just like you and Violet."

I nod. I see how he is with my sister. "You know you don't have to wait for me and Violet to get married before you do, right?"

Sunny laughs; the sound matches her name. She puts a hand on my cheek. "Please don't take offense to this, but I'm not waiting for my wedding because I'm worried about stealing your spotlight."

"That's not what I meant." Shit, I feel like an asshole.

"You can't help it, Alex. You're used to being the center of attention. It's what you know, and that's never been an issue for me. It's where you belong. I get what it's like to be the center of someone's universe. I'm that for Miller. And he's that for me. And now that's what this baby is for both of us."

"I don't think people realize how strong you really are," I admit. "I don't know that I'd be handling this situation as well as you."

"It's as hard to be the shadow as it is to be the light, Alex."

There's some real insight in that. "When did you grow up?"

She laughs again and hugs my arm. "While you were off playing hockey and getting famous."

"I mean it, though. Don't feel like you have to work around mine and Violet's plans."

"Miller and I want to wait. We've talked about it, and I want to do all the planning and fun stuff, and I want Mom to be part of that. I think it'll be good for her and me to have that experience together. There's just too much happening in all of our lives for me to be able to enjoy the process. I don't want to be stressed about it like Violet's been. And I don't want to rush it. This baby was unexpected, but he's not unwanted, and while we might be doing things out of order, we're going to wait until after he's born, so we can plan things properly."

"Wait. Did you say he?"

Sunny clamps a hand over her mouth. "Oh, poop. I wasn't supposed to say anything. It's ninety-percent probably a boy, but we have to wait for the next ultrasound. You can't tell Miller I told you."

"I won't."

"And you can't tell Violet."

"Okay." It'll be a challenge to keep this news to myself. "Who knows?"

"No one. Just you."

"Not even Lily?"

She drops her lying face. "Okay, Lily knows."

"Which means Randy knows."

"But that's it. If you tell Violet, she'll tell Charlene, and Charlene will tell Darren, and then the circle of knowledge will expand, and everyone will know."

I run a hand through my hair. "When's the next ultrasound?"

"Not for another three weeks. You're going to tell Violet aren't you?"

I'm going to be an uncle. I get to spoil some kid and do all the awesome things without dealing with the fallout afterward. Of course I want to tell Violet. Then I kind of want to get her pregnant so we can do it, too.

"Have you told Mom?"

"I wanted to wait until she comes to Chicago in a couple of weeks."

I sigh. "I'll keep my mouth shut." If Violet finds out I knew and didn't tell her, she'll be hurt. All I can do is hope someone doesn't slip before Sunny has a chance to disseminate the information.

The conversation ends when everyone comes out of the store, stocked with beverages. Violet has an entire bag. "Look!" She opens it to show me the contents. "They have shooters! Let's all do one! Except you, Sunny." She bends and kisses Sunny's stomach through her dress. "We don't want to get the yeti baby drunk."

"She had a few while she was in there," Lily informs us.

Violet passes out the shooters and makes us all toast to vacations and cock love. Thankfully, in Vegas our behavior doesn't seem out of the ordinary. We stroll the Strip, sipping on drinks and baking in the hot sun, stopping in at the occasional casino to cool off and gamble. At first Violet will only play the nickel slots, but then I coerce her into sitting down at a blackjack table, and she wins two thousand dollars.

On the way back, Sunny has to pee, and the closest place is a twenty-four-hour wedding chapel. All the girls decide to go with her, as always seems to be the way.

I check my phone while we're waiting. I've been avoiding the buzzing in my pocket all day because I want to enjoy this time away. It's been a long time since I've done anything like this. And it's a lot different with my fiancée and my friends than it was when I was a rookie.

"Shit." I have twenty new messages from my mom.

"What's going on?" Darren asks.

"It's the never-ending guest list additions."

"Someone needs to cut those women off," Miller says.

"What women?" Lance perks up.

I gesture between Miller and me. "Our mothers. This whole wedding would be a lot simpler if they would stop interfering."

"You could solve the whole problem right now if you wanted." Randy motions to the flashing Twenty-Four-Hour Wedding sign above our heads.

I laugh, because obviously it's a joke.

"I actually thought that might've been the reason you wanted us all to come along." Miller stuffs his hands in his pockets. "They're gonna do the same thing with Sunny. We already know that. It's another reason to wait until after the baby."

The girls come tripping out of the chapel. Well, Violet's tripping, the rest of them are giggling. "The cutest couple in the world is getting married by Elvis." She falls into my arms. "We should get married by Elvis. Actually, I think there's a choice between Elvis and Marilyn Monroe, or maybe it's Gwen Stefani."

For a few seconds I think she's serious, and I'm actually considering it.

Then she burps wine cooler in my face.

"I'm hungry. Is anyone else hungry? Can we go eat?"

We find a restaurant close by, and I load Violet up on carbs and water so she's not a sloppy mess.

At some point before the food comes, Randy excuses himself to the bathroom, and Lily follows right after. They come back fifteen minutes later, together. Lily's cheeks are flushed, and her eyes have that glazed look about them.

Violet points at Randy's face. "You've got vagina in your beard, Balls."

Randy strokes his beard self-consciously.

"Not possible," Lily says. "He wasn't eating at the Vagina Emporium; I was having a snack at the Moody Dick Café."

The girls burst into a fit of giggles. Randy smirks.

"Is that a euphemism for a blow job?" Lance asks.

"Ding, ding, ding! Give Romance a prize!" Charlene shouts. She needs more water, too.

"I'mma order some cookies for dessert when we get back to our room," Miller says to Sunny.

There's more ridiculous giggling.

We get a limo back to the hotel when dinner is over. Lance doesn't bother coming up to the suite. I almost feel bad, because the rest of us are likely to shower and have sex. I have my doubts Sunny will be doing anything after that aside from sleeping. She looks ready to pass out. I'm sure the rest of us will find a second or third wind.

After a long shower, which includes more sex, Violet and I lie down on the bed, possibly to go to sleep, possibly for another round. She snuggles in and puts her head on my chest.

"I'm so glad you suggested a vacation," she says.

"You were *so* hard to convince."

I draw circles on her shoulder, working my way down her side. She jerks when I hit the sensitive spot by her ribs. Then she sighs as I go lower, to her hip. My phone buzzes in my pants somewhere on the floor. I should've turned it off.

"Your mom messaged me again." I can hear her anxiety.

"Well, we are in Vegas; maybe we should elope."

Violet lifts her head. "You're kidding, right?"

I tuck strands of wet hair behind her ear and trace the line of her jaw. "I don't have to be."

"I don't have a dress."

I follow the contour of her bottom lip with my thumb. Jesus, I love this woman. "We can buy you one."

"You're serious?"

I kiss her softly, not inviting any tongue even though she parts her lips. "Marry me."

"I already said yes to that."

"This weekend. Tomorrow. Be my wife. Be Violet Waters. Be mine."

"I'm already yours, Alex. I've been yours since the moment you slammed into the plexiglas and made me spill my beer on my boobs."

"So let's do it. We're here. There are a million places we can go. We can even find somewhere nice, classy—it doesn't have to be done by Elvis."

"I thought you wanted a wedding, with people, and a party."

"You're the part that matters. I just want you, Violet. Our closest friends are all here."

She leans back, her lips pursed. She's considering it.

"We can do this if we want to. There's nothing to stop us. I want to. I want you."

"What about all the money you've put down for the wedding?"

"It doesn't matter."

"What about our moms?"

"They'll get over it." But even as I say this, I'm not so sure it's true.

Violet sighs. "You have no idea how much I want to say yes to this, Alex. But I can't do that to my mom. I'm her only child. It was the two of us for almost my entire life. I was at her wedding; she has to be at mine. I can't get married without her. And your mom would be devastated."

She's right. "What if I can get them here?"

"How are you going to do that?"

"With a few phone calls and my credit card."

She bites her lip. "What time is it in Canada?"

"My dad will still be awake. Are you in?"

Her smile is a resounding yes.

I call my dad who, as expected, is still up. His first reaction is concern, because we have pregnant Sunny with us, so he thinks something has happened to her. His secondary reaction is confusion, until I explain why I'm calling. As this is going on, Violet is on the phone with my travel agent, booking their flight and transportation to the airport. We can get them here before lunch tomorrow.

Of course, then my mom has to get on the phone and argue her case.

"Mom, we're getting married this weekend, and we'd really like you to be here."

"But what about the cottage in August? I have invitation samples; people are expecting a wedding. Violet doesn't even have her dress. It'll have to be something off the rack. Do they even have nice places to buy wedding dresses in Vegas? I don't know about this—"

"I'm not asking permission; I'm telling you. This is happening. I've taken care of your flight, transportation, and accommodations. I know this isn't what you would've planned for us, but it's what we want, and we want you here with us."

The silence following this statement is long. Violet sits beside me, her bottom lip caught between her teeth. I mouth *It'll be fine.*

She sighs. "Okay. I'll get a bag packed. But can you not get married tomorrow? Can you please wait until the next day because we'll have pictures, and I don't want to have bags under my eyes, and I'm not sure I'm going to get much sleep tonight. And I need a dress. We'll have to go shopping, and tomorrow should be a girl's day. Violet needs a proper bachelorette party."

"We can swing that." I give Violet the thumbs up, and she shakes her boobs like they're maracas.

The call to her mom is much easier. Violet straddles my lap while she waits for Skye to answer. She explains the plan and has to hold the phone away from her ear at her mom's shrieking. Of course Skye is down for a Vegas wedding.

We hang up and book flights for Skye and Sidney as well; they'll arrive around the same time as my parents.

Violet claps her hands. The movement makes her rock over my erection. "Oh my God, we're getting married. In Vegas!"

I hold on to her hips. "We are."

"Why the hell didn't we think of this earlier?"

"Because we wrongly assumed our mothers wouldn't interfere, and we were trying to please the wrong people."

"So true." She puts her hands on my chest. "We need to celebrate!"

"I was thinking the exact same thing." Her half-exposed boobs graze my chest.

"I need to tell Charlene! And Sunny! And Lily if we can get her and Randy to stop fucking for five minutes. Oh my God! Let's order champagne and that fake champagne for Sunny so she doesn't feel left out!" Violet rolls off the bed and pulls the lapels of her robe together, covering her boobs. "Come on!"

She stops when I don't move right away and glances down to where my hard-on strains the cotton of my boxer briefs. There's a big wet spot where Violet was sitting on me.

"I thought maybe you'd want to celebrate in here first, before we celebrate with our friends."

"You're so smart." Violet drops her robe on the floor and drags a red-tipped nail from my ankle all the way up my thigh.

She climbs on the bed and straddles my legs. Hooking her fingers into the waistband, she pulls my boxer briefs down, and my erection springs free. "But I think we should probably scale back on the sex after this round."

"What? Why?"

"I don't want a sore beaver for my wedding night."

"Right, good call. But there's always boob sex."

"And blow jobs, don't forget those."

We have let's-see-how-quiet-we-can-be sex, and then we order champagne, tell our friends, and celebrate the best damn decision we've made about the wedding since we got engaged.

19

SERIOUSLY, THESE MOMS

VIOLET

We are moderately hungover the next morning when our parents arrive. Daisy and my mom have spent the entire thirty-minute drive to the hotel calling all sorts of people: setting up hair appointments for tomorrow and a spa/shopping day today. We have literally half an hour to get our asses in gear, which is asking a lot based on my current state.

Robbie and Sidney are way more laidback. They make themselves comfortable on the couch in our suite's living room while they watch sports highlights.

I want to have an outtie instead of an innie today so I can relax like the boys.

Alex gives me some kind of orange fizzy drink he says will make me feel better, along with Tylenol. Then he dresses me—I

271

don't get to appreciate his fondling because his mom and my mom keep knocking on the door, asking if I'm ready to go—and sends me off with the girls.

By the time we get to the spa, I'm feeling much better. Lily looks worn out, though; she nodded off three times during the drive.

I elbow her in the side and whisper, "Lily, Lily, Lily."

She grabs my hand and puts it on her thigh—high up on her thigh. "Just another ten minutes, Randy. Then I'll open the Vagina Emporium again."

Charlene barks out a laugh, and Lily sits up, blinking rapidly.

"Oh. We're here already? I must've nodded off." She touches her face and smoothes her skirt, which has ridden up.

"What's a Vagina Emporium? Is it a sex shop?" my mom asks.

More laughter follows, along with Lily's embarrassed groan.

"No, Mom, that's what Lily calls her vagina since she lets Balls put whatever he wants in there."

Lily slaps my arm. "Is no topic off limits with you?"

"Why just the other day, Sunny and I talked about sex during pregnancy. Didn't we, Sunny?" Daisy says, as if she's trying to make Lily feel better.

"We sure did!" Sunny smiles, but it's the kind of smile she wears when Miller's eating wings and tries to kiss her.

My mom climbs over Daisy so she can get out of the car instead of waiting since Daisy's fussing with her hair again. She's really owning the new style. In fact, it's been flat-ironed recently, so I think she's checking to make sure it's not frizzy, which isn't going to happen in Vegas like it does in Chicago.

We can't all get manicures at the same time, so they split us up. I get pampered with a massage and some kind of wrap-scrub thing, during which I fall asleep. I feel incredibly refreshed when I pad out to the massager chairs and plunk down next to Lily, who's sleeping while a lady gives her a pedicure.

Three hours of beautifying later, we're prettied up with

matching nails—red, of course—and ready for dress shopping. All I currently have with me are some slutty ones that show lots of cleavage because, well, we're in Vegas.

We discover quickly that classy and wedding is a difficult combination to find in Vegas. There are a lot of dresses that make me look like a seriously well-paid hooker, or a showgirl. After three stores I'm starting to lose hope, and steam.

With the fourth one, we hit the jackpot. Daisy discovers a rack of dresses by a designer whose last name is another word for dick. Apparently she's amazing and coming across something like this is unheard of. The dresses are gorgeous. The first one I try on is super poofy and makes it look like I'm wearing a vagina with really big, floppy lips from the waist down.

I try on a few that are super princessy, and I twirl around like an idiot, partly because it's fun, and partly because Lily bought traveler wine and I've been sipping it since we left the spa. The next one I try on is this lovely flowy thing that's gauzy with a pale purple sheen instead of being off-white.

My mom is in the dressing room with me. She takes a sip from the mini bottle of wine and passes it to me. It's white, so it's safe.

"This is it. This is the dress, Violet."

"You think so?" I turn and check out the back. It's mostly sheer, almost to my ass crack. But it's not slutty. Not by Vegas standards anyway.

She tears up and takes my face in her palms. They're kind of sweaty. "Look at you. You're so beautiful. I did a pretty decent job on you, didn't I?"

"I think so."

"And you're marrying this incredible man, and it has nothing to do with the fact that his dick is as big as his bank account, because he's just so sweet."

Leave it to my mom to turn a special moment into an inappropriate one. At least I know what my future is going to look like after Alex knocks me up.

273

"I love you, Mom."

"I love you, Violet. Let's show the girls the dress you're going to get married in."

Everyone *oohs* and *ahhs* and agrees it's the perfect dress. We find something pretty for the girls to wear so we all match for pictures, and of course Daisy and my mom need dresses, too. I'm amazed Daisy chooses one without shoulder pads.

In fact, I finally notice she's wearing jeans from the current era, with rhinestones on her ass, and her top is definitely new. She looks fantastic. I was too hungover this morning to pay attention to those details.

Loaded with dresses, all bought on Alex's credit card, we stop for lunch and then hit the street again. Sunny is holding up incredibly well; she seems to have an unlimited amount of energy.

"Oooh! We should go in there!" Charlene points to a sex shop.

"Let's get Violet some fun toys for the honeymoon!" my mom shouts.

I glare at Charlene. I can handle a day of mani-pedis and dress shopping with my mom and Alex's mom, but I do not want to go into a porn store with them to look at new lingerie. And maybe a new dildo or some edible underwear and a bra made out of candy.

My mom hooks her arm through Daisy's, who looks shocked. I'm not sure she's a big porn store frequenter. Usually I'm more of a Victoria's Secret and online vibrator site shopper. I'm always at risk of saying something I shouldn't when I'm physically in one of these stores. Which shouldn't be surprising to anyone.

Sunny and Lily follow my mom and Daisy into the store, so I have no real option but to indulge Charlene and do the same. The bell over our heads tinkles, alerting the porn dealers to our pervery. It's a classy shop as far as porn warehouses go.

Skinny mannequins with tiny boobs and long legs model skimpy lingerie—some are pretty and lacy, others boast black leather and chains. I'll take a pass on those. I don't need anything on my body that might accidentally cause damage to myself or Alex. I imagine a little outfit for the Super MC with chains on it and decide it's the worst idea ever. I love his snuffie. I would never put it at risk. Again.

Charlene stops at the mannequin with the leather crotch strap and runs her fingers across the pearl necklace she's taken to wearing all the time. She checks the price tag hanging out the side, then taps her lip, like she's actually considering buying this craziness.

I mean, Alex and I have lots of sex, but it's normal, apart from my cock-love chanting. I think, anyway. We don't use a lot of toys, but then, we don't need them. Alex really likes to be responsible for my orgasms, and he's very good at making them happen.

Lily and Sunny are over at the racks of negligees, and my mom, sweet lord almighty, has dragged Daisy over to the plastic penis area. They're each holding a fake dick, deep in discussion. I do *not* want to know what they're talking about.

"Okay, so what do you need?" Charlene asks.

I shrug. "I don't know. I already have Buddy, and I have plenty of lingerie."

"It's all vanilla lingerie, though. You need some fun stuff."

"I have some fun stuff, like all my Chicago-inspired stuff, and my Waters' ass panties."

Charlene rolls her eyes. "That's not the kind of fun I'm talking about. Violet, you're going to be riding the same disco stick for the rest of your life. You need to keep it interesting."

"For our honeymoon I'm making a cape out of a Fruit Roll-Up and then sucking it off Alex's Super MC. I think I'm good at keeping things interesting."

"I'm not talking about playing dress-up with Alex's dick, Vi. I'm talking about stepping it up a notch."

I eye her warily. "Stepping it up how?"

Charlene glances around the store. Lily and Sunny are still

over by the lacy things, pulling hangers over their heads and modeling nighties for each other while giggling.

"Alex has had a hard year. Not being able to play has been difficult for him, right?"

"Well, yeah." I still don't see what this has to do with sex.

"And I know Randy getting all the center-ice attention has been even more difficult for him," Charlene continues.

Lily's out of earshot. "He's had a rough time with that. Obviously he likes Randy, but watching someone else play his position was painful."

It's kind of like his hate for Buddy. He doesn't want to be replaced by a piece of plastic that looks like a beaver.

"Exactly. You need to give him lots of opportunities to be the dominant, alpha man that he is."

I stare at Charlene. "Have you been reading paranormal romances again? Or BDSM porn?"

"Seriously, Violet. Get out of your comfort zone. You're in your twenties and marrying a professional athlete. These men like to fuck. A lot."

This I know. On a slow week, Alex and I have sex almost daily. I don't know why I have to step it up beyond that, but I'm willing to get some new, fun stuff if it helps repair my man's sometimes fragile ego.

"Okay. I'm open to suggestions."

"Great." She slaps my ass, and I jump. "Let's get you some new outfits to play in!"

Charlene is way too excited for this.

I follow her through the store while she pulls things off racks. She chooses a number of those leather-and-chain getups. I keep my mouth shut, because I can try them on, but that doesn't mean I have to buy them.

I'm not sure where my mom and Daisy are, but we find Sunny and Lily standing in front of a wall of toys and lube.

"We should get you a new vibrator or two while we're here," Charlene suggests.

276

"There's nothing wrong with Buddy." Other than the fact that Alex hates him.

Sunny and Lily stop staring at the wall of dicks and other things to give their attention to me.

Sunny twirls her hair. "Buddy?"

"It's her vibrator," Charlene explains.

"It's a beaver," I add.

"Your vibrator is a beaver?" Lily asks.

"Yup. It's a beaver wearing tightie-whities. I love it."

"And Alex hates it," Charlene says.

"Why?" Lily asks.

"Maybe because it has a name? He got all sorts of riled up when I told him I was in bed with Buddy during away games. I think it bothers him when I have to give myself orgasms."

"That's kind of sweet, isn't it?" Lily says.

"I think so."

"Anyway, you need a new one. Buddy's face has almost worn off, you use it so much." Charlene picks up two packaged vibrators and starts reading the backs, comparing models.

"The face has worn off?" Lily looks disturbed.

"It gets a lot of use during away games, and after Alex's accident, he needed some recovery time, so Buddy had to help out."

"Your vibrator has a face?"

"Oh, yeah. It's, like, literally a beaver with buck teeth and everything."

"You and Alex are perfect for each other," Lily mutters.

I nod my agreement, then turn my attention to the wall of dicks. There's a giant purple one with two heads—one at either end. It's out of the package and lying on the shelf. Maybe it's a tester. I pick it up, and it flops around. I smack Charlene on the ass with it. "What the hell's the point of this? Is this for people who have two vaginas?"

Charlene ignores me. I make lightsaber sounds and then pretend it's a pair of nunchucks. I accidently smack her in the tit. She grabs it and starts beating me.

Sunny and Lily burst out laughing, and I run down the aisle to get away. I end up in the anal section. Of course. On display are tubes of lube and a dildo thing that looks like a bunch of beads, which I actually have in the back of a drawer, along with other things that will never go near my Area 51. My butt clenches in defiance.

Butt plugs in a horrifying array of shapes and sizes taunt me. I pick one up that's the size of my head and turn around. "Seriously? This is a gag gift, right?" I check the price tag. It's more than a hundred dollars. For a giant rubber plug. That people apparently put in their Area 51. "The only ass this would fit in is an elephant's."

Sunny and Lily are staring slack-jawed at the huge hunk of rubber, or whatever the hell it's made of. I pick up one of the tiny ones, which are packaged. I hold them up beside each other.

"Okay." I wave the small one around. "I can maybe understand this. Like, it's about the same size as Alex's finger, but this?" I heft it up so they have a better view. Not that they need one. It's massive in a terrifying way. It's also heavy and awkward, so I lose my grip. It drops to the floor with a thud.

Charlene shakes her head. "Violet, unless you're planning a new career as an anal porn star, I'm confident you'll never have a need for this." She picks up the giant plug and sets it back on the shelf. It has dust on it now, and someone's gum is stuck to it. I hope whatever insane person buys it gives it a heavy-duty sanitizing before they do whatever they're planning to do with it—maybe use it as a door stopper or a paper weight.

Charlene throws more things in the basket she's commandeered. It's mostly full of slutty bedroom wear. She grabs the small butt plug and tosses it in.

"Nope. No way. The finger is enough." I grab for it, but Charlene pulls the basket out of my reach.

"But it's the same size as a finger," she argues.

"Yeah, but if I let him put things besides his finger in there, he's going to think it's okay to put other, bigger things in there, too. It's like a gateway plug to his monster cock!" I'm starting to freak out. It's irrational, but not. I know for a fact that Alex would like to get his giant dick in my ass. He was close with his fingers last night.

"It's not a gateway, Violet. He doesn't even have to know you have it." Charlene keeps a protective hold on the basket.

"What's the point of getting it if he doesn't know I have it?"

"Good question." Sunny has twirled the ends of her hair around her fingers and is rubbing them across her lips. She's staring at the wall of butt-invasion products. Her cheeks are pink. Lily's standing beside her, biting her lip.

Charlene releases a frustrated sigh. "You use it on your own and decide whether you want to share it or not. It's really not that big a thing."

"That one's not, but there are so many sizes." I gesture to the wall of anal implements.

Charlene grabs me by the arm. "Come on!"

"Where are you taking me?"

"The change room."

"I'm not trying that thing out here!"

Charlene bursts out laughing. "Of course you're not. You need to try these on." She jingles the basket of fetish wear.

"Oh. Okay." Suddenly trying on things with chains and buckles is a far less terrifying option. I let her corral me into one of the black-doored dressing rooms.

She tosses all the leathery, chained outfits on one chair and the other ones—the prettier, lacier jobs—on another. "We want to see them all."

Then she closes the door.

I stare at the piles of slutwear. Eventually I'm going to get Charlene drunk enough that she tells me what kind of kinkery she gets up to.

I spend five minutes trying to get my boobs and the rest of my parts into one of the fetish getups, but I can't seem to figure it out. There's no way I'm buying something I can't get into on my own.

After a while there's a knock on my dressing room door. "Everything okay in there?" Sunny asks.

"This thing is like a straightjacket."

"Want some help?"

I debate whether I do. My nipples are poking out and my red Waters' ass underpants are bunched between the leather and chains. I've clearly done something wrong putting this on.

"Gimme a sec." I try to reverse the process, but I'm now stuck. "Yeah. Okay. You can come in." I unlock the door and peek out.

No sign of my mom or Daisy anywhere, thank God. I open the door enough that Sunny can squeeze through.

Her cheeks puff out, and she looks me up and down. "Oh, wow, that's uh…"

"Yeah."

"I don't think you have it on right."

I look down at my chest. One boob is close to my neck, and the other is low. "Me either."

"Let me see what I can do." Sunny turns me around and starts fiddling with the crap that holds it together in the back. It gets tighter around my chest instead of looser. "I don't think I'm doing this right either," she says. "Maybe I should get Charlene."

"Maybe."

Sunny opens the door. Lily's out there now. "Where's Charlene?"

"I have no idea. I lost her a few minutes ago. Your mom and Skye are in the pocket pussy aisle, so I figured this was the safest place to hang out."

Sunny checks behind her, then pulls Lily in and locks the door. "Can you help us figure this out?"

"Uh…this is…is Alex into this kind of thing?" Lily's expression would be priceless if I wasn't stuck in a fetish getup that's cutting off the circulation in my right boob.

"I seriously hope not. Can you get me out of this?" I'm starting to get sweaty and panicky. I don't want to be stuck in this forever.

"I can try." She turns me around and confers with Sunny about all the strappy things. "I think maybe we should start at the front." I turn to face her, and Lily's eyes drop to my boobs. "That looks really uncomfortable."

"It is."

"I think maybe this isn't designed for boobs like yours."

"What does that mean?" I'm snappy, because I'm strung up.

"I don't mean it in a bad way. I just think my boobs would fit a lot better in there than yours. You need something that can house all that you have to offer." Lily loosens a strap and the boob at my neck falls, providing some relief.

She struggles for another minute. A knock at the door startles us. "So? How's it going?" It's Charlene.

Sunny opens the door, and Charlene joins us in the now crowded dressing room.

"What the hell is going on in here?"

"I can't figure this thing out!" I gesture wildly. "None of us can."

"Let me fix this." Charlene swoops in and starts fiddling with buckles, manipulating my boobs into a much less painful position. After less than a minute, all my parts are in the right place and my nipple no longer has tingles from lack of circulation. "Check it out."

The three of them move out of the way and give me access to the mirror. "Holy shit."

"Right? You look hot."

"I don't know if Alex will like this, though."

Charlene crosses her arms over her chest and smirks. "Oh, he'll like it. You should check out your ass."

"She's right. Your ass looks great," Sunny agrees.

"And your boobs, but they always look great," Lily sighs.

"I can't even get myself in and out of this. I'm not buying something I could get trapped in!"

I have to admit, I do look pretty damn hot. I just don't know if this is something I'll be able to manage alone.

"Just try the rest of the stuff on, and we'll decide at the end." Charlene motions to the piles on the chairs.

The girls file out of the dressing room, and I spend the next half hour modeling lingerie. I have to show them every outfit, and then they have a vote. By the time I'm done, I have a larger keep pile than no pile. Half the stuff I'm not convinced I'll actually wear for Alex, but I'm beyond arguing. We've been in this store for two hours. I'm hungry, and we've run out of traveler wine.

Usually my max time in a dressing room is twenty minutes. I try stuff on, pick some things I like, and get out. I'm tired from all the snaps and buttons and hooks and buckles. My fingertips hurt.

Before we hit the cash, Charlene stops by the Area 51 section and picks up a bunch of the small butt plugs.

"What are those for, party favors?" I can't see why anyone would have a use for more than one, unless they were setting up a festive anal toy display.

Charlene ignores me, but jumps ahead of me in line. She dumps her basket of porn paraphernalia on the counter. It's smut heaven. The cashier rings it up, and they have a serious conversation about the benefits of relaxation lube versus numbing lube.

When it's my turn, I try to hide the Area 51 toy under the pile of equally embarrassing chainmail lingerie. The cashier is dressed like a pinup girl. Her boobs are pushed way up in a corset, and she has pin-curls. Her lips are the color of Alex's hockey jersey—and my underwear.

"Oooh, looks like you're going to have some fun," she says.

"We'll see." I wish she'd move faster and put all the whips-

and-chains stuff away before my mom and Daisy find us. I have no idea where they've gone.

"This one is so sexy." Her white teeth sparkle as she holds up the outfit with the most buckles and chains. It also has these cuffs that apparently attach to the hips. Yeah. Like I want my hands restrained when Alex is coming at me with the monster cock.

"On second thought, maybe I won't—"

"You girls find everything you were looking for?" My mom throws her arm around my shoulder.

I close my eyes. Of course. I hear Daisy's choked cough behind me. Fuckballs.

"We sure did!" Charlene says. "I'm super excited to try this on at home." She fingers the lingerie armor, and it clinks ominously. I'm so grateful. I don't think I'd ever be able to look Daisy in the eye again if she knew it was for me.

"I didn't know you were into the kink!" my mother practically shouts.

"We all have our secrets, Skye." Charlene winks.

Daisy pushes between them to get a better look. "Oh...that's, um, interesting, Charlene."

"That's how I like to keep things, Daisy." Her grin is devious.

"And that's what this does?" Daisy gestures to the outfit the cashier is wrapping in pink tissue paper. "Keeps things interesting?"

"Sure does."

Daisy twirls a lock of hair—since it's no longer held in place with six cans of hairspray—as she considers this. "I can see that."

I think she and my mother may have gone for drinks, because they're both glassy-eyed. Or Daisy's been feeding my mom Robbie's scooby snacks. Both are realistic possibilities.

When the cashier gets to the end of the whips-and-chains outfits, Charlene says, "The rest of that stuff is hers. That's what we get for using the same basket." She tosses a credit card on the counter, but not the one she used to pay for the other stuff. The total is more than two thousand dollars. Which seems insane.

"I'll give you the money as soon as we're home."

"It's fine," she whispers dismissively.

"It's way expensive. You're not paying for that."

"I have a special card from Darren."

"What?"

"He has expensive taste. In some things."

"That's cryptic."

She lifts a shoulder and smiles.

"I'm hungry," Sunny says.

"We should get dinner! And then we should go see some male strippers!" my mom shouts.

Jesus. Will this day of embarrassment never end?

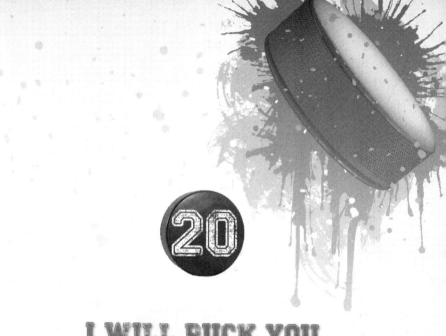

I WILL PUCK YOU FOREVER

ALEX

My dad is a mellow guy, but I guess that's what you get when you test medical maryjane for a living. Not much riles him, and most of the time I really appreciate that. When I decided to hang up the figure skates and pursue a career in professional hockey, my dad was the one who took the brunt of my mother's disappointment.

When I screwed things up with Violet by stupidly denying our relationship in a very public way over endorsement opportunities, he was there to tell me to stop being a fucking idiot, only not in those words.

When I had the accident this year, I was mopey and bitchy

and taking it out on the people around me. My dad told me I should probably start eating weed brownies and appreciate the fact that my injuries weren't more serious and I'd still have a career when I recovered. Weed brownies aside, he was right, as he often is.

When I was struggling to get Violet to agree to a wedding date and moaning over how much she worked, my dad gently suggested I reevaluate my life goals and what was important to me. Money might buy me comfort, but it sure as hell wasn't going to buy me another Violet if I drove her insane with the wedding crap or made her feel like her career wasn't important. Again, he was right.

And when my sister surprised us all with the pregnancy, my dad was the one to point out that of all the people in our family, Sunny was the most equipped to deal with babies, because she'd grown up in a house with two of them—me and him—and two dogs. And he was right, even though I hated to admit it.

But all that aside, right now I'm annoyed with him. He's not sensing the urgency. We have suits sorted out, and we have rings. I'm having custom ones made when we get home, but the simple ones we got will work for now—I just want to put a ring on Violet. So she's mine. Forever. And not in a possessive, club-her-over-the-head kind of way. Okay, maybe a bit like that, but mostly not.

Mostly I'm excited that she's finally going to be my wife, and once we're married I can start arguing my case for a large family.

So the rings are bought and I've even managed to set up a nice dinner for all of us after the ceremony. I've also called her boss to clear an extended vacation. Tomorrow night we're flying to Hawaii for two weeks. My plan is to have an absurd amount of sex with my wife. And to relax. And to love her.

But we have two outstanding problems: the venue and my vows. I've always planned to write my own, not use the stock crap you repeat after the officiant. I'm not too worried about that, even though I've had three beers, and Darren has ordered me another. I know exactly how I feel about Violet, so writing it down shouldn't be difficult.

That leaves me with the venue. I've looked at every twenty-four-hour chapel in a thirty-mile radius of the Strip. It's not that there's anything wrong with them, per se. I would just like someone other than an Elvis impersonator to marry us.

My dad doesn't seem to share my focus on the matter, despite the fact that I'm getting married in less than twenty-four hours.

"I can do it." Lance takes another sip of his beer and leans back in his chair until it's resting on two legs.

Everyone stares at him.

"You can do what?"

"I can officiate the wedding, if you want to see about having it in a real church. I mean, it's short notice, and I don't even know if you'll be able to find a place...or maybe one of these chapels will let me stand in."

I continue staring at him, unsure if he's joking or not. I don't think he is.

"Or not. It was just a thought." He drains half his beer in a big gulp.

Darren looks up from his phone, which he's been involved in most of the day. Apparently Charlene has been sending him pictures. "You're ordained?"

Lance nods, like that's all the explanation required.

"You're shitting me, right?" Randy asks the question I don't.

"Nope." He shifts around, clearly uncomfortable with the way we're all gawking at him.

I don't know what he expected when he dropped that kind of bomb. Lance is the most notorious playboy in the NHL. He has a reputation for taking multiple women to bed. At the same time. Together. All at once. And now he's telling us he's an ordained minister?

"So...does that mean you wanted to be a man of the cloth?" I ask.

"A man of the loin cloth!" Miller smacks his thigh.

No one else laughs.

Lance rolls the bottle between his palms. "A friend needed a favor a while back. I got internet certified. But it's legit." The phrase comes out sounding distinctly Scottish. "Anyway, the offer is there. Whatever you decide."

"That would awesome. If we can find a place that will let you do it, and as long as it's legal and binding."

"Don't want yer girl gettin' away?" Lance laughs.

"Nope."

We spend the next hour combing the area for churches. It's not much of a surprise that getting access to one isn't easy on such short notice, but a sizable donation is always a great incentive to let people have what they want.

We take a trip out to visit the location and make sure what we're seeing on the internet matches the actual interior. It's a beautiful church—much nicer than the chapels on the Strip, particularly the ones that have an annulment center next door.

I send the information to Violet, who seems excited by the prospect of a real church, and is as surprised as I was that Lance is ordained.

I get a text from her later informing me that the girls are going to watch beefcakes get naked, and it was her mother's idea. I'm not surprised. Skye's a bit of a wild one.

We don't end up at a strip club, which would've been awkward with Sidney and Miller. I'd feel weird looking at naked women with my fiancée's dad and brother around, step or not. Instead we hit the casino, where girls dance half-naked on little stages anyway, so it's almost the same thing.

Around midnight we head back to the room. I'm buzzed and looking forward to some easy loving: boob sex and a couple soft orgasms with my tongue for Violet. Except my room is empty of Violet and almost all of her things. For a few harrowing moments I panic, thinking she's changed her mind. Then I see the note on the bed.

Apparently I'm not going to see her until we get to the church tomorrow.

IN THE MIDDLE of the night I'm woken by the sound of my door opening. I haven't been able to sleep all that well—too excited and nervous, I guess.

"Alex?"

"Baby?" I can make out her shadowy form, but it's dark in the room. "What are you doing in here? I thought I wasn't going to see you until the wedding."

She feels her way closer, her hand coming to rest on my sheet-covered ankle. "I couldn't sleep." A low thud follows, and Violet hisses.

I sit up and reach for her, pulling her closer. She's wearing a robe—satin, not terry. She drops down on the edge of the bed, and I bring her hand to my lips, kissing her knuckles. "Are you nervous?"

"No. Maybe a little. I wrote my vows. I think I'll have to hold cue cards."

I smile in the darkness. "No one will care."

"You'll have yours memorized."

"I can hold a piece of paper if it'll make you feel better."

She runs her hand over my chest, pushing the covers down. "Okay."

"You want to lie down with me for a while?"

I see her head move in the darkness, but instead of answering she climbs over my body and pushes her way through the sheets to lie next to me. "I know it's silly, but I didn't want to sleep without you tonight."

I slide my arm under her head and hold her close. "You're going to be my wife in less than twelve hours."

She presses her nose against my neck and kisses my collarbone. "I know. I can't wait."

"Should I set an alarm?" I'm already settling into her warmth.

"I'll just stay here for a few minutes."

"Okay."

She puts her hand on my chest, over my heart. I lace my fingers through hers and close my eyes again.

THE DOOR to the room bursts open, shocking me awake. "I can't find—" Skye's shoulders drop. "Oh, thank God."

Violet lifts her head and blinks groggily. She's been drooling on my chest, and her face and hair are damp from falling asleep on me.

"'S goin' on?" She swipes her hand across her mouth.

"Do you have any idea how much you scared all of us?" Skye asks in an overly loud voice. "We thought you'd been kidnapped!"

"What? Why would you think that?" Violet's voice is raspy with sleep. It has an inconvenient effect in present company.

Charlene peeks her head in. "See? I told you she'd be in here."

"I woke up and you were gone! Do you know how worried I was? And you." Skye points a finger at me. "You're not supposed to encourage this. You were supposed to have a last night apart to make the anticipation more anticipatory for tonight."

"What year is this? Nineteen-twenty? Do I even have the right to vote?" Violet's awake enough for snark, but apparently not quite with it enough to realize I'm sporting a solid case of morning wood. She throws back the covers before I have a chance to react. I'm wearing boxer briefs. They're white. They cover the issue, but they don't in any way hide what's happening.

"Holy Jesus fuck." Charlene slaps a hand over Skye's eyes.

"Was that an optical illusion?" Skye pries at Charlene's fingers while Violet clues in and yanks the covers back up.

"Okay. Now I get your issue with Area 51." Charlene coughs.

When I'm covered again, Charlene drops her hand and Violet climbs over me, holding the edges of her robe together. I don't even know what she's wearing under there. She drops a kiss on my lips, no tongue. She pulls back and smiles. "I'm going to go get pretty so I can marry you!"

I fold my arm behind my head and return the grin. "I'd marry you right this second; you're gorgeous just the way you are."

Skye makes an *aww* sound, and Charlene pretends to gag. Neither of them seems to be able to look me in the eye as they mumble goodbye and usher Violet out of the room. I'm about to take care of my hard-on when my dad busts in, eating a muffin.

"All right, son, let's get you ready to walk your ass down the aisle."

My phone gets confiscated, so I'm not able to contact Violet for the rest of the morning. We have breakfast, and then a stylist —apparently hired by my mom—comes up to the suite to do our hair and make sure our nails look nice.

Lance bites his, so they don't have anything to work with. Darren has lovely cuticles, according to the manicure girl, and Randy refuses to let the chick near his beard. He's really attached to it. A photographer, magically hired by my mom, comes in to snap a bunch of pictures, then disappears—probably back to where the girls are.

At one-thirty, we get into a limo and head to the church. And then we wait for the girls to show up. Darren passes along a message that they'll be here soon, and suddenly I'm nervous. I wipe my hands on my pants and make Darren check his breast pocket for the rings for the millionth time.

"You got this." He gives my shoulder a squeeze.

Ten minutes later, he gets another message letting us know they're here. We don't have to wait for anyone else to show up, or for people to get seated. Lance stands at the front of the church with a Bible tucked under his arm. It's surreal, to be honest.

The organist, who showed up five minutes ago, starts playing wedding music. It's go time. My dad comes down the aisle with my mom on one arm and Skye on the other. Skye's dress is low-cut for a wedding, but that's Skye. My mom is beautiful.

Next Charlene and Darren come down the aisle, followed by Miller and Sunny, and Lily and Randy.

The entire world seems to stop when Violet appears in the church doors, her arm hooked through Sidney's. They pause in the doorway. It's like a damn postcard. She tilts her head up to look at him as he says something to her, and she nods.

She stands straighter, but on the first step she stumbles a little.

Lance puts a hand on my shoulder before I can make a move.

"He's got her. Be patient. She'll come to you."

It's true. I chased her from the beginning, and in the end I've realized it's always about me letting her find her way when she's ready. And she is now. I can see it in her excited smile, and the way she tries to make Sidney walk faster to get to me.

When she's a few feet away, they stop. Sidney whispers something, and she hugs him hard and then, because she's Violet, she pulls a tissue out from between her boobs and dabs under her eyes. Stuffing it back in, she turns to me and smiles.

I extend a hand, and she takes it. "You're the most gorgeous woman on the face of the earth."

Her hair frames her face in soft ringlets. Her dress is perfect, highlighting her insane curves. If I wasn't as nervous as I am, I'd have a serious hard-on.

"You look superhot."

I wink. "Ready, baby?"

"So ready." She leans in to whisper, "And I don't mean that in a pervy way, yet."

Lance coughs.

She cringes, and we both look to him to start the ceremony. I try to pay attention, but I find myself staring at Violet. And then all of a sudden it's my turn to say my vows.

"I, Alex Robert Waters, take you, Violet Marie Hall, to be my wife." I pause to smile, because I love the way that sounds. "I promise to love you with the same depth and intensity as the moment I first fell for you, to treasure you and every moment we share, whether it's full of laughter or tears, or both. I promise to take care of you and to let you take care of me." I pause to wink at her wide eyes and stifled snort. "I promise to be the man you need and not just the man you want."

I run my thumb over her shaking hand and reach up to wipe away the tear slipping down her cheek.

"I will always love you, Violet. I won't ever be perfect, and I'll make mistakes, and I'll definitely say things that will make you angry, but I promise to tell you every day, not just with words, but with actions, that you are the center of my universe. You're the sun in my sky and the breath in my lungs. I promise to be yours for every second of this existence, and to cherish every moment of that love with you."

Violet takes a deep, unsteady breath and sticks her finger in her cleavage. When she looks up, she's panicked.

"I have them!" Charlene rushes over and hands Violet cue cards.

Violet puts her hand to her heart and heaves a sigh of relief. She looks down at them, then back up at me. "Maybe I should've gone first. Mine aren't as nice as yours," she whispers.

I skim her cheek with gentle fingers and follow a trail down to her chest where I rest my hand. "They'll be perfect because they're from here."

"From my boob?"

I laugh. "From your heart, Violet."

"Oh! Duh." She rolls her eyes. "I'm so nervous." After several more deep breaths, she nods. "Okay. I'm ready." She glances down at the cards and then back up at me. "I, Violet Marie Hall, take you, Alex Robert Waters, to be my husband." She looks up and bites her lip, like she likes the way that sounds as much as I do. "To have as the most important person in my life, to hold whenever we're sleeping." She pauses and looks up at me. "At least until you turn into a radioactive furnace, and then I have to take a break, but you always end up wrapped around me later, so..." She looks around, like she realizes she's started rambling and consults her cue cards again. "I promise to love you, all of you, your best parts, and the other ones, too."

Red blotches form on her chest and start spreading up her neck. I'm worried for her. Maybe we should've gone with the traditional vows.

She mutters, "Screw it," and drops the cards on the floor. This could go really well or really badly. Thankfully it's just our closest friends and family here, and Randy can edit the video he's making if he needs to.

"I love you, Alex Waters. I think I started loving you when you sent me that silly stuffed beaver, or maybe even before that. Maybe it was the moment you smashed into the plexiglas and scared the crap out of me. But after that moment, you were always with me. And then we had... Well, anyway, after the night I met you, you stayed in my head, and then you started stalking my emails and my text messages. You tried so hard.

"I love so many things about you. But your perseverance and your tenacity, that's how you won your way into my heart. I promise I'll keep you there forever.

"I want all the things with you, Alex. I want the tears and the laughter, but more laughter than tears. I want the downs so I can appreciate the ups even more. I will try to be the best version of me, so I deserve the best version of you for the rest of my life."

After a brief pause she finishes with, "The end."

Everyone chuckles, and Violet's face turns red.

We exchange rings. Violet drops mine and almost head-butts me in the dick trying to pick it up off the floor. Lance manages to get it for her, and she slips it on to my finger.

I can't take my eyes off her as Lance rambles on with the rest of the ceremony, and then he pronounces us husband and wife.

Violet throws her arms around me, and I lift her off her feet to kiss her.

"I love you."

"Forever," she whispers.

AFTER THE CEREMONY, we go out to eat. I keep a close eye on the time, because we have a flight to catch. I can't wait to surprise Violet with our honeymoon. It's the one thing I've kept secret.

We've been drinking champagne most of the afternoon. Violet has such a low tolerance that we have to start switching out her drinks for non-alcoholic versions.

After our meal, we have exactly enough time to get back to the room, throw all our things into our bags, rush through good-byes, and catch our limo to the airport.

"Where're you taking me?" Violet's changed into a pair of leggings and one of those long shirts that's too short to be a dress because it barely skims the bottom of her ass.

"You'll see when we get to the airport."

"Are we gonna join the mile-high club?"

"No."

She pouts.

"Do you really want the first time we have sex after we're married to be in a bathroom on an airplane?"

VIOLET'S BEEN in the bathroom—and not the airplane bathroom —for a long time. I assume she's getting ready for me, because it's the first place she went as soon as we arrived at our villa in Hawaii. I don't know what could possibly be taking so long. I've had my face between her legs recently, and I'm highly aware of how nice and smooth things are down there, so I'm concerned about what's happening behind that closed door.

After another ten minutes, I start to get impatient. She went in there with an entire bag of things. We've been married for almost twenty-four hours, and we have yet to consummate.

I roll off the bed and pad to the bathroom. Salty ocean air fills my lungs, and a warm breeze blows through the open curtains. I'm not worried about anyone hearing Violet when we finally get to having sex. Our little villa is nicely buffered from the ones surrounding it. The view from our deck is stunning. White sand turns into blue water and in the distance are green mountains rising from the ocean. Later, once we've had time to enjoy each other, we can go for a swim, and then come back and enjoy each other some more.

I put my ear against the door. I can't hear anything but water running and Violet mumbling.

"You coming out soon?" I tap with a knuckle.

"One more minute. I'm almost ready!"

I don't go back to the bed. Instead, I put a hand on either side of the jamb and wait.

It's another two minutes before the door swings open. Violet jumps and screams. "Jesus, Alex! You ruined my entrance! Go lie down and let me do this again."

She shoves on my chest and tries to close the door, but I'm not inclined to move. Violet looks like the bridal version of Little Red Riding Hood.

She's wearing her veil. But that's not all. A white lace bra cups her boobs, and my gaze gets stuck there before I can check out the rest of her as she slams the door in my face.

"Baby, come on out." I try the handle, but she's locked it. Smart woman.

"Not until you lie down."

"Okay." I'm not about to argue with her. Obviously she has a plan. If allowing her to execute it will get me inside her sooner, I'll do whatever she wants.

I lie back down on the massive bed with its gauzy curtains. The setting is perfectly romantic. I'm spending an obscene amount for us to be here, but I only get one honeymoon with Violet, so it's worth the expense.

A minute later the door opens an inch, and Violet's eye appears in the crack. When she sees me lying on the bed in my boxers that say "Just Married" across the front, she opens it wider.

Now I have a fantastic view of the entire package. Sweet fucking Christ, my wife is hot. In addition to the veil and bra, she's wearing garters, and I think a lacy pair of panties. She's clutching what seems to be a picnic basket. And she's wearing red heels. Not super-high ones, but heels nonetheless.

My dick is punching at the release hatch of my boxers with urgency. Violet carefully saunters over.

"Gimme a little spin, please." I twirl my finger in the air. "I wanna see what that looks like from the back."

She does as I ask, her heels clicking on the floor as she gives me her backside. The ribbon edging the veil skims the curve of her ass. Which appears to be bare. I don't think she's wearing panties after all.

"You look incredible, wife."

She turns around again, her smile as shy as it is coy. "Thanks, husband. I thought you might like the virginal slutty look."

"I love the virginal slutty look." She knows me so well.

Violet places the basket, which I hope is full of fun, on the end of the bed. When I sit up and reach for it, she smacks my hand away. "Nuh-uh." She wags her perfectly manicured finger.

"You have to wait for that. I have some special surprises planned."

I raise my hands in supplication and lie back again, watching as she crawls over to me on her knees. Her bra is covered in crystals, and it shimmers in the light. I take in the rest of her, appreciating the dip in her waist and the lace band of the garters as they draw my eye down.

"Uh, Violet?"

She sets the basket down beside her as she settles back on her heels. "Yes, Alex?"

"What's going on here?" I smooth my hand up her thigh, but before I can get anywhere good, she rises up on her knees.

"I made my beaver a veil!" She thrusts her hips forward so I can get a better look. It's a mini replica of the one she's wearing on her head.

"So you did." I laugh, because of course Violet made a veil for her beaver. "How is that even on there?"

"I used double-sided tape." She flicks at it with her fingertip, making the material flutter.

Under the white gauzy fabric are letters. I lift it to find the words Beave + MC stamped with black block letters.

I palm her ass, laughing. "C'mere. I wanna show the beave how much I love her."

"Wait! We have to have a ceremony first!"

"What?"

"The beave and Super MC—I have a ceremony planned. Don't worry, I'll be quick. Then they can hug it out."

I lie back, because honestly, she wouldn't be the woman I love if she didn't do things like this.

She opens the basket and peers inside. Then she plucks something out and puts it behind her back. "Close your eyes."

"You're not going to tie anything to my dick, are you?"

"Nope. No tying."

I do as I'm asked. Violet gives my erection, which is at full mast, a long, slow stroke. I peek through a slit in one lid when I feel the light brush of her veil—the one on her head—on my abs. It's followed by her humid breath on the head of my cock, and the soft press of her lips. I groan when she takes me in her mouth, but just up to the ridge.

"Violet, baby, if you're going to give me a blow job while you're wearing all this, I'd really like to watch." I'm still peeking —because fuck missing this—but it mostly looks like my eyes are closed.

She shifts so I'm looking at her veil and her hair, like she knows I'm not really following directions. "Don't worry, Alex. You'll get to watch me blow you soon enough."

She sucks on the head again, and I groan. I can't shove my hands in her hair because she's wearing the veil. A strange ticklish sensation follows. And then her mouth is on me again. Her warm, wet tongue strokes the length of my entire cock, all the way around. Something smooth and cool is wrapped around me; it's unfamiliar. Violet sits back on her heels again. She's smiling.

I look down at my dick. He currently has eyes, but this time they look like the candy ones, and again there's a mustache. And he's blue.

"Uh…"

"It's his superhero suit!" Violet pulls something else out of the basket. "And here's his cape!"

"Is that a Fruit Roll-Up?"

"Yup! Smart, right? No snuffie suffocation this time, and it's edible!" She licks the edge of the cape and attaches it to the suit.

"You're crazy."

"You love me anyway."

"This is true."

She grabs her camera phone, and I don't stop her when she snaps a few shots of my artificial fruit flavor-wrapped dick. She gets a few more with her veil-covered beaver in the shot as she performs a "ceremony."

I take the last shot, which is of her hovering over my cock so the tip kisses her clit. It's ridiculous, and I'm about ready to get inside her.

"You done with your photoshoot? We've been married almost twenty-four hours, and I haven't made love to my wife yet."

"I really love it when you call me wife, husband."

I toss the phone aside and rearrange her legs so she's straddling me. I sit up so I can kiss her. At the same time, I reach around behind her and flick the clasp on her bra.

I kiss my way from her shoulder up her neck to her mouth. "How about Mrs. Violet Waters? You like that, too?"

"I really like that." Violet moans and rubs up against me. Unfortunately, all the Fruit Roll-Up action is muting the sensation.

"We need to get rid of the costume."

"I was planning to eat it off." Violet pushes on my chest so I lie back again. Her nose wrinkles at the way the cape is now stuck to the suit. "Hmm, maybe not the part that's all wet now."

She starts peeling it away; some comes off easily, but other stuff is stuck pretty good to my shaft. I'm not going to complain as she sucks the little candies off the head and then goes about licking and sucking the bits of blue off. As bizarre as it is, it feels amazing.

There are stains left behind, and her tongue is blue when she's done, along with her lips. She reaches into her basket of tricks and pulls out a washcloth so she can clean me up.

"Looks like you thought of everything. What else you got in there?" I grab the basket and check out the contents. It's full of sex toys and lube and all sorts of amazing things. One item in particular catches my eye. It's still in the package. "What's going on here?"

"Shit. I didn't mean for that to be in there." She tries to grab it out of my hand, but I hold it out of reach.

"When did you get it?"

"Charlene bought it for me. We're not Area 51-ing the first

time we have married sex." She goes for it again, so I pull her down to my chest, then I roll over on top of her. Parts of me still feel sticky as I fit myself between her legs.

I toss the package to the floor. "We'll pretend I didn't see that. Okay?"

"Okay?" It's more question than anything.

"The only thing I want to do is love you right now."

She runs her fingers through my hair and hooks her legs around my waist. "I like the sound of that."

We kiss until we're breathless and my desire to be inside her is too strong to deny.

The crash of the ocean against the rocks, the soft lilt of birds, the whisper of leaves brushing against each other in the breeze fade away as Violet's sweet sighs turn into moans.

I can't wait to love this woman forever.

EPILOGUE

ALL THE LOVES

VIOLET

TWO SUMMERS LATER

It's a gorgeous day at the Chicago cottage. Training camp starts in less than a month, so we're getting in all the relaxation time we can. Alex's contract runs out at the end of this coming season, but there are lots of interested teams, so he's not worried.

I'm about to head to the dock when Alex comes down the stairs. I stop arranging fruit for a second to watch him because he's shirtless and always so damn hot.

The paring knife in my hand clatters to the table. "What the—"

"Ready to go swimming?" He pauses on the bottom stair and

strikes a pose.

"You can't be serious."

"About swimming? It's eight million degrees out, Violet. What else would we do on a perfect day like this?"

"I mean you can't be serious with that." I gesture to his bathing attire.

His hands go to his hips, Superman style. "I don't see anything wrong with my suit. It's aerodynamic."

It's aerodynamic all right. Alex is wearing a red Speedo. Through the tight fabric I can see the entire outline of Super MC, including the ridge at the head. We're not alone. No one can ever be adequately prepared for the Super MC in all his ridge-outlined glory.

"There's too much penis going on, Alex. You'll scare people with that." There's so much business. I have no idea how he's managing to keep himself in there. There will be some kind of wardrobe malfunction before the end of the day.

Buck appears at the top of the stairs, along with a weebling Logan. His mop of white blond hair and dimpled smile draw my attention away from Alex's ridiculous spandex atrocity.

Logan puts his arms out. "Up! Up! Dada!"

Buck hoists him up and ambles down the stairs. Logan is a tank. He's definitely going to be a hockey boy, just like his dad.

"Oh my God. What the hell is that?" I point at Buck's junk and then look away.

"Like it, Vi?"

I thought Alex's Speedo action was bad, but it's got nothing on the thing Buck has containing his man unit. *Containing* is not really the right word. It's like he tied a pouch around his parts and is calling it a bathing suit.

"Can the two of you please, for the love of penis, go put on regular bathing suits? We have people coming over who aren't exposed to your crazy on a regular basis."

Sunny comes out of the bathroom with a sigh. She's pregnant again, and it's the vomiting stage. She has several more months before the baby wreaks havoc on her vagina, but in the mean-time he or she is testing her ability to hold down food.

"Mama!" Logan pushes away from Buck and waddle-runs over to her on his chubby, unsteady legs. He has two speeds, run and bolt. He attaches himself to Sunny's leg.

"Is this some kind of competition?" she asks when she takes in the horror of our husbands.

"I think they want to know who can embarrass themselves the most in one weekend."

"Didn't you invite those people from across the lake to come over? They won't want to be our friends if you're dressed like that." Sunny motions to their crotches.

Lily appears at the top of the stairs next, with Randy behind her. She's all smirky and satisfied looking. Damn her. But then she takes a few steps down, and I'm greeted with the sight of yet another well-endowed man wearing a horribly inappropriate bathing suit.

Sunny rolls her eyes. "What is this? A penis parade?"

I start laughing, and then groaning as I hold my tummy. Alex rushes over and puts his hand on my stomach. "Are you okay? Is everything okay?"

"Other than the fact that I'm probably going to pee myself, I'm fine."

He sinks to his knees in front of me and rests his cheek against my tummy. He slides his hands under my bathing suit cover up and lifts it over my belly. "Alex!"

"I just wanna say hi." He drops the fabric so he's hidden under the material. It would look perverse, except for the fact that he's cooing at my tummy. Or rather, he's cooing at what's brewing in my tummy.

"Hey there, little buddy. I'll see you in a few months, okay? You be good in there."

He pops back out, oblivious to any weird discomfort he's caused for anyone.

Phones start chiming with messages from Darren and Charlene. Unfortunately, Lance can't make it this time.

Commotion follows as food and towels are gathered. Buck has to run after Logan and wrestle him into his little tiny lifejacket before he gets too close to the beach. Sunny follows behind them, and Randy throws Lily over his shoulder, his hand on her ass as he runs across the beach and down the dock, jumping into the water.

Alex drops a kiss on my shoulder. "You feeling okay today, baby?"

"I feel great." I turn and let him lift me onto the counter. He steps between my legs, his flat stomach bumping my rounded one.

The first trimester I felt like an exhausted bag of shit. I was never so grateful to be working from home almost all the time now. But sixteen weeks in, I'm starting to show, and I feel fantastic. And my hair looks amazing.

I'm so happy.

I'm so in love with this man. And lucky me, he's equally as in love with me. I feel it in every touch, every glance, every whispered—and groaned—declaration.

It's amazing how a poorly thought-out one-night stand can turn into a forever kind of love.

Because that's exactly what Alex is: my forever.

BONUS SCENE

THE PERFECT PLACE FOR BUDDY

ALEX

"Maybe we should just elope." I'm not sure if it sounds like I'm kidding or not.

Violet lifts her head, her eyes wide. "You're kidding, right?"

I tuck strands of wet hair behind her ear and trace the line of her jaw. "I don't have to be."

"I don't have a dress."

I follow the contour of her bottom lip with my thumb. Jesus, I love this woman. "We can buy you one."

"You're serious?"

"As serious as you are about keeping me out of your Area 51."

Violet sits up. She's wearing a hotel robe. It gapes in the front and most of her right boob falls out. "I'm only mostly serious about that."

"What? You mean you'd let me in there?" I sit up, too, and stick my hand in the gap in her robe, palming a breast, ready to make all of my fantasies come true.

"Hold on there, trigger." Violet puts a hand on my face and pushes me back down. "I don't mean with the Super MC. He's huge. And there's special lube and stuff for that, which we don't have. I mean maybe we can use some more fingers, or, like, a toy —eventually."

"That'd be a great place to put Buddy..." That's exactly where I'd like to see that fucking dildo go. I would derive so much satisfaction, in so many ways, from watching that stupid beaver face disappear inside her ass.

"Wow. You're totally serious about that. I honestly don't understand the fascination with trying to get something that big into a hole that small." She pokes my hard-on.

"That *is* the fascination, Violet."

"You know, I've done some reading recently about this."

"Oh, really?" I lean against the headboard. "And what did you discover?"

"You're the one with the prostate gland, not me. So if anyone should be putting things where the sun don't shine, it should me giving you a dose of Buddy, not the other way around." She crosses her arms over her chest and cocks a brow.

"Uh, yeah, that's not going to happen. Ever, Violet."

She shrugs. "That's fine. But if you won't let me try it on you, then you don't get to try it on me."

"Okay."

"That's it? Okay? You're not going to argue over this?"

"Baby, c'mere." I pat my lap.

Violet doesn't straddle me, but she sits on my hard-on, so that's okay. I tilt her chin up. "Do you remember what I said to you the first night we met?"

"Am I looking at her beaver?"

307

I smile. "Later. When we were in my suite, and we ended up in the bedroom."

"It isn't that big—which is lie, because it really is *that* big." She shifts so her ass rubs against my still-growing dick.

"No. I mean just before that."

She bites her lip and thinks for a few seconds, playing with the hair at the nape of my neck. "Oh!" Her smile is soft, shy almost. "That we didn't have to do anything I didn't want to. But you had to know at that point I was going to give it up for you."

"Well, I hoped, but it was never an expectation. I mean, fuck —I really wanted to get you naked and get all up in there, but I would've been perfectly fine with some slip 'n' slide or the blow job. The sex was—" I close my eyes, remembering exactly how being inside Violet for the first time felt. So tight, so hot, so… "—much more than I probably deserved at the time."

"I was pretty nervous."

"I was, too. I'm not really a one-night-stand guy."

Her smile is warm. "You got attached to my beaver rather quickly."

"Mmm." I sweep her hair over her shoulders and push the robe down with it. "And the rest of you."

I slip an around her waist and pull her closer so I can kiss her. "What I'm trying to say, Violet, amidst all these distractions, is that I will only take from you what you offer me willingly, and only if it's going to make you feel good. And that goes for everything."

"I love you. But all your sweet-talking still isn't going to get the Super MC Area 51 access."

ABOUT THE AUTHOR

NYT and USA Today bestselling author, Helena Hunting lives on the outskirts of Toronto with her amazing family and her two awesome cats, who think the best place to sleep is her keyboard. Helena writes everything from emotional contemporary romance to romantic comedies that will have you laughing until you cry. If you're looking for a tearjerker, you can find her angsty side under H. Hunting.

Scan this code to stay connected with Helena

OTHER TITLES BY HELENA HUNTING

Pucked Series

Pucked (Pucked #1)

Pucked Up (Pucked #2)

Pucked Over (Pucked #3)

Forever Pucked (Pucked #4)

Pucked Under (Pucked #5)

Pucked Off (Pucked #6)

Pucked Love (Pucked #7)

AREA 51: Deleted Scenes & Outtakes

Get Inked

Pucks & Penalties

All In Series

A Lie for a Lie

A Favor for a Favor

A Secret for a Secret

A Kiss for a Kiss

Lies, Hearts & Truths Series

Little Lies

Bitter Sweet Heart

Shattered Truths

Shacking Up Series

Shacking Up

Getting Down (Novella)

Hooking Up

I Flipping Love You

Making Up

Handle with Care

Spark Sisters Series

When Sparks Fly

Starry-Eyed Love

Make A Wish

Lakeside Series

Love Next Door

Love on the Lake

The Clipped Wings Series

Cupcakes and Ink

Clipped Wings

Between the Cracks

Inked Armor

Cracks in the Armor

Fractures in Ink

Standalone Novels

The Librarian Principle

Felony Ever After

Before You Ghost (with Debra Anastasia)

Forever Romance Standalones

The Good Luck Charm

Meet Cute

Kiss my Cupcake

Made in the USA
Las Vegas, NV
19 January 2023

65904734R00181